Sherlock Holmes and the Sixty Steps

A Sherlock Holmes Novel

by Séamas Duffy

Paperback ISBN 978-1-80424-017-5
ePub ISBN 978-1-80424-018-2
PDF ISBN 978-1-80424-019-9

Published by MX Publishing
335 Princess Park Manor, Royal Drive,
London, N11 3GX
www.mxpublishing.com

Cover design by Brian Belanger

For Declan D, Éireann, Cavan, and Níamh McGrory.

Sixty Steps Preservation Trust

The author is donating all the royalties from the sale of this book to the Greek Thomson Sixty Steps Preservation Trust Limited, Glasgow, Scotland (company No. SC277072).

https://www.sixtysteps.org.uk/

This is a charitable organisation dedicated to restoring the Sixty Steps, built by Alexander Thomson in 1872, to their original Victorian glory.

The year 2022 is the 150th anniversary of the construction of the Steps.

Four new adventures in
"Sherlock Holmes and the Sixty Steps".

Séamas Duffy's fourth novel, "Sherlock Holmes and the Sixty Steps" follows a similar format to his previously published Holmes collections: a novella together with some shorter stories. The four stories are: "The Tragedy of Langhorne Wyke" (1890); "The Mystery of the Thirteen Bells" (1895); "The Adventure of the Sixty Steps" (1897); "The Problem of the Coptic Patriarchs" (1898).

"The Tragedy of Langhorne Wyke" sees the detective and his chronicler travel to Yorkshire's North Riding to solve the double murder of a well-heeled but mysterious honeymoon couple. Holmes and Watson are immediately confronted with the sudden, and ominous, disappearance of the two witnesses to the murder – an elderly widow and her travelling companion. The trail eventually leads back to London and to crimes committed, but unavenged, from Holmes's past.

In "The Mystery of the Thirteen Bells", Holmes and Watson, along with Inspector Lestrade, are involved in a grisly treasure hunt of a murder. In a London mired in thick November fog, their footsteps are dogged by a silent unseen adversary as they follow a series of cryptograms which they must decipher. These macabre clues lead them to some of Victorian London's queerest places, and to one of its most bizarre institutions (which Holmes describes as "a citadel of the mad and the dead").

In "The Adventure of the Sixty Steps", Holmes and Watson travel to Glasgow in an attempt to save a man – who has been wrongly convicted of the brutal murder of a rich, elderly spinster

– from the gallows. Their peregrinations take them into some of the lowest quarters of the city, peopled by shady underworld characters such as "The Moudie," "Cauld Kale," and "The Acrobat." In uncovering a web of police corruption and malpractice, they are perplexed by the enigmatic genealogy of the victim and encounter more than one miscarriage of justice.

"The Problem of the Coptic Patriarchs" (a reference to one of Holmes's unrecorded cases from the canonical "The Adventure of the Retired Colourman". Inspector Lestrade of the Yard arrives at Baker Street to inform Holmes that the rare and priceless 9th century Alexandrian Scroll has been stolen and Father Philoxenus of the London Coptic Patriarchate has been kidnapped and ransomed. Holmes and Watson travel to the sleepy Thameside village of Bourne End to unravel the mystery of how the burglar-cum-kidnapper managed to escape from the scene of the crime in the middle of a blizzard without leaving a single trace in the snow.

About the author:

Séamas Duffy lives and works in Glasgow and is a member of the Sherlock Holmes Society of Scotland.

By the same author:

Fiction

"Sherlock Holmes and the Four Corners of Hell," Robert Hale, June 2015.

Foreword to "The Aggravations of Minnie Ashe," (by Cyril Kersh) Valancourt Publishing, January 2014.

"Sherlock Holmes in Paris," Black Coat Press, January 2013.

Literary Criticism

Review of "Children of the Ghetto" by Israel Zangwill, published on Literary London Society website (provisional date) June 2022.

Review of "Angel Pavement" by J.B. Priestley, published on Literary London Society website (provisional date) March 2022.

"'A Humble M.R.C.S.' The Man behind the Mask," (under "Jim McGrory"), Baker Street Journal, Autumn 2020.

Review of "Fowlers End" by Gerald Kersh, published on Literary London Society website February 2012.

Review of "London Belongs to Me" by Norman Collins, published on Literary London Society website October 2011.

"The Great Perennial Problem: The Religion of Sherlock Holmes," (under "Jim McGrory"), Baker Street Journal, Autumn 2011.

TABLE OF CONTENTS

FOREWORD

"Even after 100 years of study, there is still plenty to write about."

Leslie S. Klinger.[1]

I had been a card-carrying Holmesian for many years, but it was only after attending a series of talks given by the Sherlock Holmes Society of Scotland and reading Conan Doyle's "Memories and Adventures"[2] that I progressed to becoming a Doylean. Conan Doyle's book demonstrated the extent to which his own life experiences were reflected in, and coloured, the stories he wrote. It is, of course, well-known that he fashioned Holmes from the bones of Dr. Joseph Bell (his mentor), but it was fascinating to see this or that character whom he had met in real-life later being transformed into a Peter Carey[3] (the "swarthy, dark-eyed, … beard[ed]" shipmate from his whaling days whose "temper was Satanic"), a Holy Peters[4] (a number of candidates from amongst the "prophets and perverts" he encountered), or a Thaddeus Sholto[5] (the young Oscar Wilde, perhaps – after all, Holmes's languid witticism on the invitation from Lord St. Simon[6] ("one of those unwelcome social summonses which call upon a man either to be bored or to lie") could have come straight from the lips of Algernon Moncrieff[7].

The manner of art imitating life also provided the subject matter for a surprising number of his tales: the affair of the Beryl Coronet[8] was based on an incident that happened to one of the Doyle family; the convoluted and (ostensibly) implausible denouement of Thor Bridge had at least one counterpart in Austrian[9] criminal history ("parallel cases!"); the suicide of Montague Druitt in 1888, whose body was found in the Thames

1

with his coat pockets weighted down with stones, may be where Dr. Watson found the idea for the wharfside scene in "The Man With The Twisted Lip"; and even the Red-Headed League, one of the *apparently* most preposterous, and amusing, inventions in the entire Canon, had its roots in a secret undergraduate Cambridge debating society (the Cambridge Apostles) notorious for their complete lack of earnestness – a trait shared, as we shall see, with the average Holmesian. One of the Apostles' senior members (Henry Sidgwick, the English utilitarian philosopher) imagined a world in which, "... a rich bachelor with no near relatives leaves the bulk of his property in providing pensions exclusively for *indigent red-haired men,* (however much) this might strike us as unreasonable and capricious[10]."

Conan Doyle also had a fascination with the Coptic Church and language, despite having abandoned mainstream religion at one point in his life. He went so far as to visit one of the original Coptic monasteries in the Egyptian desert – a trip which almost had fatal consequences when his party managed to get lost in the searing heat ("the only guide being wheel marks across the sand"), and which inadvertently provided the material for his "Tragedy of the Korosko[11]." He mentions the Copts twice in the Canon, once in a tantalising reference to an unrecorded case. When I sat down to write this book, it was inevitable that I should include a pastiche on the problem which troubled the Coptic Patriarchs.

Having devoured the Holmes Canon, I soon discovered that not only was there a flourishing trade in pastiches (which began in Conan Doyle's own lifetime, and with his characteristically kind blessing), but that there was also an extensive body of Holmesian scholarship stretching back more than a century. As regards the scholarly (or perhaps, more precisely, mock-scholarly) articles on the canonical works, I noticed immediately that this strand of scholarship differed wholly from the usual "appreciation society" endeavour which is generally based on a kind of hero worship. If you look at the societies which celebrate some of Conan Doyle's contemporaries – Arthur Morrison, Arnold Bennet, Stevenson, for example – you will find a rather uncritical, not to say, adulatory flavour. This is truer still when it comes to some of the "classic" authors popular during the Victorian period, take Jane Austen or the Brontës, for instance: "... idolatrous enthusiasm for Jane ... and every primary, secondary, tertiary ... detail relative to her," thundered one literary scholar[12], and a celebrated academic[13] once complained that "there are so many persons to whom speaking lightly about Miss Austen is as bad as 'speaking against the Prayer Book.'" Even Kipling (hardly an arch-iconoclast) fashioned a parody on the "Janeites."

The Brontës fared little better: in the 1950s, the president of the Brontë Society railed against the same "idolatry" which had "a generation ago" spawned a brisk commerce in fake Brontë artefacts fired by "zealous (relic) hunters"[14]: A plethora of bogus handkerchiefs, phoney quills, counterfeit inkwells, and forged letters flooded the market, and there were so many pianos circulating in the West Riding whose ivories were reputed to have been tinkled by Anne, Emily, and Charlotte – and just possibly Branwell, when he was sober enough – that they must have gone through one per month at the Haworth Parsonage.

To my initial surprise it seemed that, far from being offenders against the First Commandment, Holmesians – hammering away in each of the five continents, connected by societies, journals, magazines, posh dinners in swanky hotels[15], and, latterly, the internet – were busily de-constructing, re-constructing, post-modernising, dissimulating, and generally contradicting every single word that Conan Doyle had written on any conceivable point. Every Holmesian worth the name was an avid revisionist; there *was* no orthodoxy!

On the contrary, they triumphantly gloated over each plot hole and mercilessly exposed every inconsistency: how in "The Sign Of The Four" July slips into September and then apparently back again as dawn breaks at 3 a.m. (it *could* have been the Côtes De Beaune which Watson had drunk at lunchtime!); Watson's embarrassing ignorance of the rules of the turf in "The Adventure of Silver Blaze"; the fact that there is no such creature as a "swamp adder," which allegedly killed Dr. Roylott in "The Adventure of the Speckled Band"; Holmes's miscalculation of "obliquity of the ecliptic" in the "Musgrave Ritual," about which he lectured Watson in "The Greek Interpreter"; and how anyone with even a rudimentary knowledge of Victorian railways must have winced painfully when they read about the train departing for the Derbyshire Peak District[16] from, yes, *Euston!*

In addition to those who boldly affirmed that Dr. Watson deliberately lied ("diligently and frequently" according to one scholar[17]), there were those who shamelessly propounded an orrery of blatant and unpalatable heresies from *behind* Watson's written word: Holmes was a woman (and Watson's lover); Holmes never emerged from Reichenbach (that was deutero-Holmes); Holmes was Moriarty (playing a cunning dual role); Holmes never existed in the first place (it was Moriarty all along); Holmes was wedded to Irene Adler (who bigamously married Godfrey Norton, with Holmes, albeit *incognito*, as a witness); Holmes was secretly married to Mrs. Neville St. Clair[18]; Watson was not so much Holmes's Boswell as his Bosie (hence the detective's apparent overreaction in "The Three Garridebs"[19] when Watson is wounded by Killer Evans) and so on.

What a breath of fresh air. This was no secret gnostic sect where only a small circle of the anointed received some direct revelation form the deity or were entrusted with the "true" interpretation of the dogma. On the contrary, the tradition of

Holmesian scholarship afforded a living example of encouraging a hundred flowers to blossom and allowing a hundred schools of thought to contend; not only was a plurality of readings considered possible, indeed desirable, but any illusion of a single correct reading had been dispelled. Moreover, novitiates were positively welcomed and encouraged.

These influences provided much of the inspiration for writing this book (and others), and for some of my own Holmesian mock-scholarship. As Holmes himself says in "The Problem of Thor Bridge": "One drawback of an active mind is that one can always conceive alternative explanations."

The Tragedy of Langhorne Wyke

It was during the long, baking hot summer in the year 1890 that a certain Russian statesman commenced his official visit to England, a diplomatic overture which succeeded the signing of the Franco-Russian Alliance some years earlier. Previously, the German and Italian powers had signed a similar concord with the Dual Monarchy, and the recently enthroned Kaiser was now embarked upon a policy of naval expansion. Great Britain now held the crucial balance of European power in her hands. In my notes from that year, which I have consulted extensively in producing this reminiscence, I speculate that it was due to the magnificent and colourful spectacle of the arrival of that Russian nobleman's entourage in the metropolis that the sinister episode which I am about to relate was largely ignored by our London newspapers. Indeed, it was not until after the conclusion of our adventure, when the remarkable history of the affair finally became known, that the London public became acquainted with the case. For the most part only the Leeds Mercury and that great stalwart of the provincial Liberal conscience, the Northern Echo, made any effort to keep the wider British public informed about this tragedy which had occurred in the North Riding of Yorkshire.

My friend, Sherlock Holmes, and I had been smoking our after-breakfast pipes and sipping coffee in our Baker Street sitting room one bright August forenoon, when we received a terse telegram from an Inspector Barrowclough of the North Riding Constabulary.

"En route concerning Langhorne Wyke–Arrive noon."

"Do you know this fellow Barrowclough?" I asked.

Holmes shook his head, "The name certainly does not ring a bell," said he in reply.

"Arriving at noon, so he has taken the first train down, anyhow, so it must be urgent," I said.

"Had you said, 'the first train *up*,' Watson, that would have been more accurate. It is always 'up' to London."

"Really, Holmes, I had no idea you were such an enthusiast."

"Then your memory must be failing you, for surely only an avid enthusiast would delight in calculating the speed of our moving train by observing the precise time elapsed between successive lineside telegraph posts, as you recorded me doing not so long ago. But your inference is correct; it must be a serious case, for in my experience Yorkshire policemen do not squander money lightly. Anything in the papers?"

"Besides the Russian visit and the threat of the Nihilists, nothing that I have noticed today. I know *'wyke'* is Yorkshire dialect, but beyond that I must confess I am entirely ignorant as to whether 'Langhorne Wyke' might be a person, a place, or a comestible."

"A *comestible*?"

"A breed of moorland sheep, perhaps, with long horns," I said, somewhat flippantly.

"Pshaw! Why should anyone wish to consult me over sheep-breeding, Watson?"

"You have been consulted over far more abstruse matters than that, as my records would show: Take the Colonel Warburton affair, for one thing; and was there ever a more bizarre case than *Señor* Persano's singular polychaete which was believed to induce symptoms of hysteria, even temporary insanity? Still, I suppose there is no point in guessing, the inspector will be here soon enough."

Indeed, at about ten minutes past twelve, we heard a knock at the door, and a few moments later we were joined in our sitting room by Barrowclough himself. He seemed rather slightly built for a policeman and very young for the rank of inspector. Dark-haired, slim, clean-shaven and dressed in a dapper fashion, his bearing was one of quiet confidence. His brow was dappled with beads of sweat, and he gazed at both of us with honest blue eyes.

"I came straight here as fast as I could from King's Cross station," he said in a strong but neither impenetrable nor unpleasant northern accent. "It was quite a dash. I trust you have received my telegram, gentlemen?"

"We did, indeed," replied my friend. "And we must, right away, confess our metropolitan ignorance as to who or what 'Langhorne Wyke' may be, and we look forward to your dispelling our curiosity."

"That is very easily done, Mr. Holmes. 'Langhorne Wyke' would be found in the company of Roger Trod and Bulmer Hole!" the young man replied with a twinkling smile.

"Then 'Langhorne Wyke' *is* a person," I said.

Perceiving our mystification, he continued. "No, Doctor, they are all local beauty spots on our lovely North Riding coastline. I really do beg your pardon for I had thought that, by now, you would have seen an account of the tragedy in the newspapers and knowing your interest in such matters … presumably the story has not reached the London dailies yet. I shall refer straight away, then, to this report from yesterday's Northern Echo:

'Tragic Incident on Sea Cliffs: Foul Play Suspected. A tragic incident occurred yesterday morning on the North Sea cliff path near Scalby on the outskirts of Scarborough, in the North Riding of Yorkshire. The bodies of a middle-aged couple, who had earlier been seen walking in the area, were found at the base of the sea cliffs just north of a point known locally as Langhorne Wyke. The cliff path is a popular spot for tourists who come every year to take the mineral waters of the spa in the town, and to enjoy the bracing sea air. It is not known exactly how the victims, who have not yet been identified, met their deaths, but it seems that two witnesses were on that stretch of path at about the same time. They stated that they heard a cry behind them and turned around to see a man running away from the point on the cliff path near where the bodies were later found. Police are treating the matter as foul play.'"

"Those being the public facts," said Holmes, "I presume if you have come two hundred miles in order to see me, then it is in all likelihood to apprise me of those facts which, for whatever reason, did not find their way into the press reports. Pray proceed."

"As you know, there are always a few things which we intentionally hold back, but first of all I'll tell you a few odd details about the incident which have left me slightly puzzled," he said, shaking his head in mild dismay.

"For example," he continued, "we have had no success in identifying the two victims, who were on honeymoon at the time. All we know, is that they appeared at the Royal Hotel in Scarborough two days ago, gave their names as Mr. and Mrs. Holroyd, and told the proprietrix, Mrs. Hurst, that they had just been married in secret – only a few friends had known beforehand – for they had wanted to get away and have a quiet time of it. They paid her a fortnight in advance without quibble, and as the woman was wearing a very expensive looking wedding ring, Mrs. Hurst had no suspicion about them whatever. They seemed to her a pleasant couple, happy in each other's company as was to be expected, well-heeled but not affected or showy, the very epitome of model guests and, although they kept themselves to themselves and did not mingle much with the other residents, she said she found nothing strange or secretive in their behaviour. When the tragic news was brought to Mrs. Hurst, she gave us the couple's address so that we could make an attempt to inform the relatives. We discovered that the address was a false one and so, probably, are the names under which they signed the register. I can give you their full descriptions."

"How did you manage to ascertain so quickly that they were boarded with this Mrs. Hurst?

"The hotel receipt was in the dead gentleman's pocket."

"Good."

"The man was about thirty years of age, below average height, very sturdily built, square jawed, dark brown eyes, in excellent condition all round, no distinguishing marks. The woman was of a similar age, brunette, slimmer, taller, and darker skinned than the man, with dark, almost black eyes. No other features to note, but she must have been very beautiful in life. We are presently making inquiries along the usual lines and–"

"That's what your colleagues at Scotland Yard usually tell me when they are completely lost and have no idea what to do next."

"Yes, that's right," the young man replied with a slight grimace. "There was nothing in their luggage or belongings to suggest their exact place of origin, although most of their wardrobe was purchased in London and the West Country. However, fortunately for us, the two women referred to in the *Echo* were able to give us an excellent account of the incident."

"Have you confirmed the cause of death?"

"Well, it is pretty obvious ..."

"There is nothing so deceptive as an obvious fact."

"The police surgeon confirmed both victims died from injuries sustained from the fall from the clifftop."

"Newspaper reports are notoriously unreliable; is there anything to preclude the possibility that the man, for example, may have been trying to push the woman over the cliff, and that in the struggle the victim dragged her assailant down with her?"

"Or *vice versa*?" I interjected.

"That was the first question that occurred to me. Yes, the body of the woman was found about twenty yards from her companion at the foot of the cliffs. The newspaper omits to state that the two witnesses clearly saw the woman being pushed off the cliff."

"Who were the two witnesses?"

"Mrs. Coakley, an elderly widow from Harrogate and Miss Daymer, her travelling companion, who had been out for an afternoon stroll on the cliff path"

"An elderly woman you say?" Holmes interrupted. "On a cliff path on a blazing hot August day?"

"Not so elderly, Mr. Holmes – in fact a mere sixty-eight apparently, and quite spry for her age. I should add that the path, which commands astounding views on a clear day across the–"

"Yes, Inspector, we shall consult *Baedeker* should we require tourist information," said Holmes, "please stick to the undisputed facts."

The young man blushed madly and continued.

"I beg your pardon. The path, which is high above the sea, is fairly flat and well-trodden for a mile or two in each direction around the Wyke, before it plunges into a gully to the north. It is actually a rather less strenuous walk than some of the hilly streets of the town itself, for there is a funicular tram which takes visitors from the town up to the cliff top at a ha'penny a head, so that it is popular with all ages and classes, though few tourists stray much beyond the viewpoint by café at the summit. Mrs. Coakley and

11

Miss Daymer had been passed on the path by Mr. and Mrs. Holroyd, who were walking in the opposite direction, that is, southwards towards the town. The couple were about fifty yards behind Mrs. Coakley and Miss Daymer at the time when the incident happened; but the path takes a slight turn inwards just before the Wyke, close to bushes which cling to the cliff top and both parties would have lost sight of each other. The two women became aware of an altercation taking place, then suddenly they heard a loud shout followed by a horrible scream and they hastened back; as they rounded the point, they saw, to their utter horror a man pursuing a woman then pushing her over the cliff. They both swear to the fact it was the same man who had passed them only moments before going in the same direction as the Holroyds. A tall, medium-built, youngish man about twenty-five years old with a light coloured, broad-brimmed hat pulled low over his eyes. They saw no one else on the path at the time."

"The implication is that he had been following the Holroyds, and had chosen this moment to strike?"

"Yes. It seems incontrovertible that he followed the couple, caught them unawares on the cliffs and pushed them off onto the jagged rocks below. It is a sheer drop of a few hundred feet or so – no one would stand a chance. The witness testimony seems to confirm that the man was killed first, and as the woman tried to escape, she, too, was overtaken and driven to her death."

"It seems logical enough."

"But the strangest part of the tale is yet to come, and it gives us our only real clue so far. The commotion was heard by the crew of a fishing boat which was in the area not far offshore; the fishermen call this cove 'Sailor's Grave' due to the dangerous lee shore when seas are high and the wind is in the nor' east. The boat was manned by a local family, the Normandales, whom we know well, and they fairly flew to the scene. As the tide was low and the sea calm, they were able to heave-to close to a spit of rock, whereupon the younger son, William, got out of the boat, waded and clambered across the scars to see if he could render any assistance.

"For the woman it was too late; she was already gone. But the man was, incredibly, still alive, though barely. William tried to raise him but to no avail. He, William Normandale, is prepared to swear that the dying man murmured the name 'Clement.' It is ten-to-one that that is the assailant's name, do you not think?"

"Possibly. Or, at least, the name by which the assailant was known to the victim. Equally, he may have been trying to give his own name – his *real* name – since he was traveling incognito. But it is rather too soon for such flights of fancy."

"And it is likely that he was delirious with shock and pain," I added.

"It is an interesting case, though," my friend went on, "is there anything else?"

"Not very much. The Normandales said that they saw and heard nothing from the boat until the cry rang out, for they were hauling pots at the time and were distracted. This family has been fishing out of the town for several generations, and they assisted us with the recovery of the bodies by boat. I cannot think they have been in any way associated with the incident."

"No, I agree that it seems highly improbable. There was also no sign of robbery, I assume?"

"None. One other small thing: The more Mrs. Hurst thought about it, the more she became puzzled about these two visitors. Holroyd is a northern name, but she would certainly not have identified them as local people by their accents and yet they seemed to know their way around the district well enough; she thought there was something vaguely different about them; small things – the cut of their clothes, their demeanour at table – the sorts of things a woman notices, and she began to wonder if they might have been of foreign extraction even though their English was very good."

"Yet you say their wardrobe had been bought mainly in London and the West Country. This would suggest that, if they were indeed foreigners, then they had been here for some time."

"Yes, I had come to that conclusion too."

"Hmm. That does not advance us much further. Let us recapitulate: your theory is that the victims were followed to Scarborough by this fellow who lay in wait at or near the hotel at which the Holroyds were staying. This couple, on the balance of probability, were of foreign origin but their assailant, going by his description, was possibly not. This assailant then followed them to the cliff and struck when he saw the chance. One wonders if he knew in advance that they were going to be in that vicinity. Did they mention their plans to Mrs. Hurst?"

"No, you will remember that Mrs. Hurst said that they did not mix much with the other guests, so it is unlikely that anyone knew. However, I really must recall your attention to the dying man's words 'Clement.' That does not sound particularly foreign to me," persisted the inspector.

"That is true."

"It is one of the facts which we have held back because, let me tell you, that we in the North Riding constabulary know one Clement Howe very well. He is a blacksmith in Cloughton, a village that lies not two miles across the fields from the scene of the murder; a fearsome man he is too, when in drink. There is scarcely a public house in town in which Howe has not fought and been thrown out of. I should like to have had my hand on his collar many a time for his depredations, but no one could be found who will testify against him because of his violent temper. He is tall and fair coloured – perhaps slightly more heavily built than the description given, but it did occur to me that he may have followed them in the hope that an opportunity would present itself."

"What possible motive could he have?" asked Holmes. "And what possible connection could this well-heeled foreign couple have they have with a village blacksmith?"

"He is known to have a hatred of foreigners, due to his grandfather, a sergeant in the Green Howards, having been killed by the Russians at the siege of Sevastopol. Suppose the unidentified man whom we think may be foreign, was, in fact, Russian. Howe's temper may have already been aroused by all this news of the state visit. Then again, this Clement Howe is one of those low types who is apt to make a bit free with women when he is in his cups, that's one of the reasons for his constant brawling. Perhaps he made some coarse remark to the woman, and a fight broke out with Mr. Holroyd which ended with him throwing them both off the cliff."

"It is essential not to begin by twisting the facts to suit theories, Inspector. How could this blacksmith know whether the man was Russian or not? I could provide you with an equally coherent explanation in which the incident happened whilst Howe was sitting in a local public house all along. So, I should not drag him off to gaol quite yet. If he is guilty, you will forewarn him of your suspicions, and make him more cautious. You have done the correct thing in holding back the facts, though it would be more prudent to inquire discreetly of the other villagers as to his whereabouts on the day of the murder. If you must interview him, allow him to think your inquiries are but routine. Tell me, Barrowclough, once you have finished here, I presume you will want to be on your way to Scotland Yard?" Holmes eyes sparkled with amusement.

"Well … I have not specifically requested their assistance yet … I thought they might be rather too busy keeping watch on the

Russian anarchists and Nihilists to be able to take much interest in a *provincial* case."

"We shall agree to say so for the present," Holme smiled. "There are certainly a number of points of about the case which have aroused my keenest interest. I think there is an express from King's Cross at two-fifteen, is there not, Watson?"

"Then you *will* come back with me?" said Barrowclough with delight.

Holmes nodded, "Lestrade and company are perfectly capable of looking after the London criminal whilst we go on the trail of his northern cousin. I shall send Billy to reserve us a first-class carriage."

The journey north was an uneventful one. The young inspector was quite appalled both at the expense of travelling first class – he had come down by third, he said, and that was good enough for him – and at our decision to call a cab ("for a mere twenty-minute walk!") but Holmes waved away his objections with an amused smile. Much of the journey was spent in discussing a recent unsolved railway murder in a remote part of the Lincolnshire Wolds attended by the most mysterious of circumstances – the "Level-Crossing Mystery" the press had called it. The victim had been the level-crossing keeper, who had gone missing in the middle of his turn one dark December evening, and whose corpse was discovered by an engine driver on top of a twelve-foot pile of coal in the goods yard. There had been no indication as to how the body had got there; the coal had not been disturbed in any way, and the level-crossing keeper's boots were missing and had never been found; moreover, the victim's hair had been cropped very closely and roughly in patches, though whether before or after death was not known. Even more puzzling were the scorch marks on the neck of the victim, the nature of which could not be identified by the police surgeon. Holmes and Barrowclough made speculations as to the possible culprit and motives, and I faintly recall my friend saying, "Why, it is surely obvious that ..." before I nodded off.

When I awoke, they were discussing the causes of the fateful Armagh train smash of the previous year. Barrowclough, it turned out, had joined the constabulary from having been a railway signalman on the North Yorkshire Moors line thus he had the sort of inside knowledge that a layman, even such a well-informed layman as Holmes, had not. In answer to some questions put by Holmes (which showed me that my friend had grasped some of the intricacies of the subject), Barrowclough explained several detailed points of interest on the operation of railways, and for an hour or two they kept each other engrossed with talk of connecting rods, pounds-per-square-inch, and the mysteries of some quaint apparatus known as block instruments. For my own part, most of the jargon went over my head and, although Holmes later insisted that ninety *per cent* of it was merely a matter of gravitational force combined with an electrical charge, I was forced to the conclusion that the North-Eastern Railway Company's signalling was something of an occult dark art, and Barrowclough one of its wizards. Still, it passed the journey pleasantly until it was time to change trains at York for the final leg of the trip to the hilly but charming spa town.

A severe shock awaited Holmes and me when we stepped into the Borough Police Station in Cemetery Road. We were being shown into the inspector's office, when my attention was drawn to a vaguely familiar tall, lean figure standing at the bar conversing with the desk sergeant.

"I say, Holmes, look there. Don't you think that fellow resembles ... by Jove, yes, it *is* Dr. James Mortimer!"

"What a coincidence!" Holmes expostulated, as the doctor spun round at the mention of his name, his keen, closely set, grey eyes peering at us. His face remained quite grave in spite of our animated greeting, and for the second time in my career as Holmes's chronicler, Dr. James Mortimer of Grimpen, Postbridge, Devonshire, caused a shudder to pass through me.

"I am afraid it is no coincidence, gentlemen," he said grimly, showing restrained emotion. "I have just come from the town mortuary where it has been my sad duty to identify the bodies of Sir Henry Baskerville and his wife, Beryl. They were horribly murdered yesterday on the sea cliffs outside the town."

I stammered out the merest semblance of a rejoinder, incredulous and horrified at this unexpected jolt to my senses.

"Sir Henry and his *wife*?" Holmes asked, leaning forward, his eyes glittering.

"Yes, when Sir Henry and I returned from our travels earlier this year, he and Beryl García, whom as you know was by then a widow, re-kindled their friendship; the friendship blossomed into a romance, and thence into matrimony. I was extremely happy for them after all the troubles they had both gone through. And now …"

Barrowclough, naturally, was considerably astonished at the turn which events had taken. "Do I take it, then, that you already know the victims, Mr. Holmes?"

"We knew Sir Henry extremely well and had more than a passing acquaintance with the woman who had become his wife," replied Holmes. "Let us proceed to the privacy of your office, Inspector, and we shall render you an explanation in full."

Once we were seated in the fusty cramped office, Holmes began.

"Last year, Sir Henry Baskerville, who had been living and farming in the Canadian prairies for some time, inherited an estate

18

in Dartmoor, Devonshire, on the death of his uncle, Sir Charles Baskerville. There had been an ancient legend associated with a curse on the family – frankly, some mediaeval nonsense concerning a phantom hound which haunted and harried the heir to the estate. Sir Charles died from heart failure after believing that he had actually *seen* this spectral beast about to attack him one dark night near the moor. In point of fact, the hound had been set upon him by a distant relative, a potential rival claimant to the estate and the title, a man named Rodger Baskerville, a cousin of Sir Henry who had gone about under the pseudonym of Jack Stapleton. It was indeed a huge hound, but perfectly mortal as Dr. Watson and I proved when we emptied the barrels of our two pistols into it one foggy night upon the moor. This Rodger's intention had been to eliminate the incumbents to the estate one by one, in order that the estate should revert to himself. Thus, having eliminated Sir Charles, he then attempted the very same trick with Sir Henry and, but for the intercession of Dr. Watson and myself, may well have succeeded. If Rodger Baskerville had managed to murder Sir Henry in Dartmoor, he would have emerged as the legitimate heir to the title and the estate which totalled almost three quarters of a million pounds. However, following this unsuccessful attempt on Sir Henry, Rodger Baskerville fled into one of the many boglands upon Dartmoor and perished. We followed his trail to an abandoned tin mine where he had kept the beast. Unfortunately for him, there was a deep fog that night and he appeared to have lost his way in the deep morass. In the "Devon County Chronicle," you will find the full report of the coroner's inquest which inevitably concluded 'Death by Misadventure'; this left Sir Henry free to marry Rodger Baskerville's widow, Beryl Baskerville, née García."

"Wait a minute! Do you mean to tell me that he married the widow of the person who attempted to kill him?" asked Barrowclough.

"That is true."

"I have never heard the likes of it!"

"Then you must read Dr. Watson's account of the affair. Now, to return to our case; given the history, it is highly probable that the motive for the murder of Sir Henry relates to the inheritance of the Baskerville estate. Perhaps Dr. Mortimer would be so kind as to tell us all that has happened in Devonshire since we last met?" Holmes asked.

"Certainly. When Sir Henry returned to health after the ordeal of his attempted murder, he re-established contact with Beryl García, who was still living at Merripit House on the edge of the moor. There had been some liaison between these two prior to the incident of Rodger setting the dog on Sir Henry and, although it appeared that Beryl had seemed to have been her husband's accomplice in the murder attempt, we know that she was viciously, one might say sadistically, treated by her husband. She had done everything in her power to warn Sir Henry of the danger beforehand, to the extent of risking her own life. Once the shock had abated, and Sir Henry had fully recovered, he realised that he had judged her far too harshly. Since she was now a widow, Beryl and Sir Henry reformed their attachment which, as I said, led in the fullness of time to the offer of marriage and so to her becoming the mistress of Baskerville Hall. There was a ceremony last week, at which I was a witness, and then off they went together on honeymoon. As you say, Mr. Holmes, this seems to have sparked off another attempt by another member of the family to get his hands upon the estate.

"Why did Sir Henry consider it necessary to use a false name in this part of the country?" asked Holmes.

20

"I cannot, either as his friend or his medical advisor, say precisely why. After the incident on the moor, I can assure you he was never the same man again; the more he brooded about it, the more he persuaded himself that there really was some sort of curse on the family. You will recall how he described it to us in Baker Street: 'an inheritance with a vengeance.' He once asked me about the provisions of English law for formally changing his name. Frankly, I held Sir Henry's behaviour to be preposterous and, as a medical man, verging on the obsessive. I told him so, albeit tactfully, on a number of occasions. I had hoped, and believed, that his marriage, and the prospect of an heir to the estate, would bring him to his senses."

"I suspect it was that very possibility of an heir – since Beryl García was by no means past the age of child-bearing – that may be the reason why another attempt was made on his life," said Holmes.

"Who could possibly have a claim on the estate?" asked Barrowclough.

"The only other relatives went by the name of Desmond, who were distant cousins in Westmoreland," continued Mortimer. "I recall the father was a clergyman who refused to accept anything from Sir Henry by way of settlement. He had held the living at St. Luke's, Yealand until it was decided to merge the parish with that of Burton St. James, and so he retired last year. The family moved back to Rothbury in Northumberland whence they originated. Eventually, the Reverend Desmond did allow Sir Henry to purchase the freehold on his cottage in Rothbury and present it to him on the occasion of his seventieth birthday. He died of pneumonia last winter, sadly. There was one son by the second marriage of the same name – James; he would be in his late twenties or thirties now."

"Then this James Desmond would be the heir to the estate?" asked Barrowclough.

"Given the shock I have just received, I had not got to the length of thinking about what might happen to the estate, but, yes, I presume so. He would, in all probability, inherit everything except, of course, the title."

"Then he has the strongest motive for the murder of Sir Henry," said the inspector.

"I can hardly dispute that."

"Do you think that Sir Henry would have recognised James Desmond had he met him?" asked Barrowclough. I am thinking of your late friend's final word: 'Clement,' which, of course, might well have been the word 'claimant'."

"Of course, Inspector, it was exactly that: *claimant*. Very bright of you. Yes, I am sure that they met at Sir Charles's funeral. Other than that, I know next to nothing about the Desmonds."

"I shall soon remedy that," said the inspector, his eyes aflame.

We were interrupted at this point by the desk sergeant who requested a private word with his superior.

"Incidentally, there is a wryly amusing side-line to this awful tragedy," said Mortimer, as Barrowclough left.

"There usually is," replied my friend.

"It has nothing to do with these tragic events directly, but you must recall old Josiah Frankland from Lafter Hall near Postbridge?" asked Mortimer.

"The elderly crank with a passion for vexatious litigation, the father of Mrs. Laura Lyons?" I replied. "Yes, I spent some time with him last year when he was celebrating his victory in the *Frankland v. Middleton* case. We half emptied a decanter of vintage port in triumph. Why, what has the old reprobate been up to now?"

"You are well-acquainted with his knowledge of ancient and obscure manorial laws; well, he took it into his head to launch a lawsuit against the Baskerville estate under the Stannary Convocation – some abstruse, long dead, decree governing the Devonian tin mining areas dating back to the early Middle Ages – to which, Frankland strongly maintains, the Baskerville lands remain subject. His contention was this: As a foreigner, Sir Henry was legally debarred from holding the entail; therefore, the entail was now null and void; accordingly, the baronetcy should be extinguished and the entire estate falls to be forfeit to the Crown under the terms of the Convocation!"

"But surely," I argued, "those laws are obsolete, overwritten and repealed by legislation."

"I am not so sure. He has not lost a single case yet, and you also will recall that he was able to discover an old manorial bylaw that allowed him to prosecute Sir John Morland – *himself* a magistrate – and his warrener for shooting rabbits in his own private warren!"

"But now that Sir Henry is dead, the case must fail surely," I reasoned, "one cannot prosecute someone posthumously."

"I am afraid not; you see the claim of *misfeasance* was entered against myself as executor of the estate, not against Sir Henry."

"Ah, here is the inspector coming back. Why, what is wrong, Barrowclough?"

The young inspector had returned, looking very pale.

"I am afraid I have some very bad news," he replied with hesitation, "Mrs. Coakley and Miss Daymer, the two women who were witnesses to the murder, have disappeared."

"Disappeared! Under what circumstances precisely?" asked Holmes.

"Sergeant Ricks went around to the George Hotel to speak to them earlier this morning as I had directed him to do. When he got there, the proprietor said the women had just left. Apparently, they had given notice last night. Mrs. Coakley felt their holiday had been spoiled by the awful events in which she had been caught up and wanted to move out of the town. However, they would, she said, only move up the coast as far as Whitby and complete their holiday there. They were to leave on the ten-seventeen train. Ricks then went to the Railway Station where he found the cabman who had dropped them there just before ten o'clock. The booking clerk remembers selling the younger of the two women first-class single tickets to Whitby, and the ticket collector on the platform recalled checking their tickets as they passed through the gate. Although the platforms were busy – it is the middle of the tourist season as you know – he remembered the younger woman asking him which was the Whitby train, following which he directed them to Platform One. Schofield, the train guard on the ten-seventeen, cannot actually recall seeing them; however, as the Whitby trains have to execute a curious manoeuvre when leaving the station, with hand signals exchanged between the guard and the engine driver to back the train out, he could have been distracted.

"Ricks then went up with the next available train and checked at Whitby station – nothing! No cabman he spoke to can remember picking them up from the station, no hotel or boarding establishment within the immediate vicinity of Whitby station appears to have received them; he then stopped at all of the other stations on the line on the way back down; the two women had not been seen amongst the passengers who alighted from the train at any station. Somewhere between Scarborough and Whitby, the trail has gone cold."

"Are the tickets checked on the train?" asked Holmes.

"There is no need to – there are ticket barriers and staff at all the stations including the intermediate ones. It would be impossible to say if their first-class single tickets had been collected at Whitby as there are so many, but had they alighted at any intermediate station with a Whitby ticket it would have been noticed."

"What about their luggage?"

"There is no sign of it."

"Did any of the newspaper reports mention that the two women were staying at the George?"

"Certainly not, we would never give out such information."

"Then, this is very grave indeed," said Holmes. "The culprit presumably knew where the women were staying and must have followed them. And yet one would think that he cannot have conveyed two women away by force in a busy railway station, especially after they had passed through the ticket barrier. He may, of course, have followed them onto the train and attacked them in the carriage."

"But then there is the question of their luggage," I said.

"Had he somehow been able to murder them, it would have been child's play to walk off with the baggage."

"But how could he have disposed of the bodies?" asked Barrowclough.

"This is something of an outside chance," said Holmes, "but are there any places on the route where their bodies may have been thrown from the train, and not yet have been discovered?"

"Is that not rather improbable?" Barrowclough replied.

"Hardly so. I recall very clearly the celebrated case of Briggs, the Lombard Street banker: robbed, murdered, and thrown from a moving train at Hackney Wick without a single passenger noticing a thing."

"Let me think … there is only Falsgrave Tunnel. If they had been attacked there and thrown from the train that may be the reason why Schofield did not see them. The tunnel is as dark as pitch owing to the bend in it; it is generally full of smoke and

25

steam, and it is unlikely that anyone would see a body, or even two, lying in the tunnel cess from the window of a train."

"How often is it walked?"

"Once a week, on Saturday night when the platelayers go through the tunnel with lamps to check the rails and fastenings."

"Then have it examined it immediately."

"But we would need to stop all the traffic ..."

"Then do so! This is a murder case, and you are a policeman now, not a railwayman!"

"Very well. There is a tunnel at Ravenscar too, but it is short and straight so that anything by the side of the line would be easily spotted. Then there is Larpool viaduct over the river Esk."

"Where is that?"

"At the Whitby end of the line, just outside the town. The trains have to slow down there on the approach to a curve; sometimes they are stopped there awaiting other trains clearing the junction."

"He might have chosen such a moment to throw the bodies over the parapet. Is the river tidal at that point?"

"Yes. But it was low water slack at eleven in the morning; any bodies thrown into the river would easily have been spotted in the shallow narrow channel. Besides, it would be an enormous effort to heave the bodies out of the train and over the parapet too."

"Not if the killer had an accomplice. But I agree, it seems very unlikely, at least one of the bodies would have turned up by now. What about the trains which immediately followed or preceded the Whitby train?"

"Ricks questioned the station staff with regard to all of the trains: Hull, Liverpool, Manchester, Sheffield – no one saw any sign of two women of their description. Moreover, if they had boarded any of these trains by mistake with tickets to Whitby then someone would have remembered. Dash it! It is my first big case,

26

and it is going from bad to worse already," Barrowclough sighed. "I ought to have kept those women under surveillance."

"Indeed, but that is past praying for now," replied Holmes.

"One would presume that by reading the newspapers the killer had discovered that these two women had identified him and could swear his life away if he were caught. I imagine that was the one thing he hadn't bargained for," I said.

"Indeed, Watson, it would have been a most unexpected complication for him. I fear you must prepare yourself for the worst, Barrowclough."

"Well, I shall spare no time in investigating this fellow, Desmond," said the inspector, "from Westmoreland you say?"

"No, the family moved back to Rothbury in Northumberland last year," said Mortimer.

"Incidentally, your Mrs. Hurst seems to have a turn for observation," said Holmes. "Sir Henry had spent most of his life in the Canadian prairies as I said, and his wife was of Latin American origin. That would explain their rather un-English manners and accents."

"Not much escapes these seaside landladies, they are as suspicious as cats," said the inspector, "but how could they have known the district so well, as Mrs. Hurst had said?"

"Beryl García had helped her late husband, Rodger Baskerville, run St. Oliver's Preparatory School, near Burton Fleming in the Wolds."

"There is something that doesn't quite make sense to me. If this fellow, Rodger Baskerville, had succeeded in murdering Sir Henry last year in order to claim the inheritance, I am at a complete loss to understand how he could possibly have claimed this inheritance you spoke of," said Barrowclough.

"A difficult question, but one that I shall endeavour to answer. Had he been successful it is an open question, quite frankly, whether, despite the weight of the purely *circumstantial* evidence, a case against him could ever have been brought before a court. After all, we did not actually see him set the dog on Sir Henry; his wife could not have been compelled to give evidence; we do not know whether he had an accomplice who looked after the dog, and so on. That would eliminate the obstacles which might prevent a person convicted of murder from benefitting from a felony. As to how he might have actually claimed the inheritance, this was a question which perplexed us before but, intractable as it seems, it is by no means insurmountable. We do know that he spent some time in Costa Rica, which is where he met Beryl García. Although we believe he fled San José after perpetrating some fraud concerning railway construction company shares, he might possibly have returned there and claimed the estate through British authorities."

"Indeed, Mr. Holmes," said Dr. Mortimer, "from what little I knew of the man or about the affairs of that place, I am sure that, by the astute greasing of official palms, he could easily have inveigled himself back into the bosom of the country."

"Very true, Doctor," said Holmes, "but there would have been other possible means of instituting the claim."

"It is rather a moot point now, of course, since he is dead," said Mortimer.

"Getting back to the murder: whoever the culprit is, it occurs to me that it is possible that he may not have killed these two women," said Barrowclough. "The trains were busy as we know and to murder two women then throw their bodies out of a train would be no mean feat."

"Perhaps he had an accomplice, as I suggested," said Holmes.

"Even so, why should they not scream for help?"

"Perhaps they did and what with the noise of the engine no one heard. Why what do you suppose has happened to them?"

"That he may be holding them *incommunicado* until the heat dies down, then he can escape," said Barrowclough.

"Then how did he decoy them from the railway station? After all he could scarcely have brought two of them to any hideaway under duress. What happened to their luggage? How was it that no one saw any sign of the two women after they arrived at the station? That seems a vital point – no one saw them leaving."

"But no one saw them on the Whitby train either, and there are a number of exits from the station."

"Surely they would still have to come back through the ticket barriers? In which case they would have been noticed."

"Not necessarily. There is a wicket gate halfway down Platform One, which the signalmen use to gain access to the signal box from the street; they could simply open it, walk out into Wendover Road, and disappear."

"But why should they do that? Surely they would have recognised him from the episode on the cliff?"

"Not if he was *incognito*," I interjected. "Barrowclough may have something here."

"It is possible," said Holmes. "In your theory, then, he had spirited them away somewhere and is holding them captive. What should he do next?"

"Once he believes it is safe, he will make a break for it."

"Why should he delay at all? In the meantime, he has to feed and water them and ensure they do not escape or raise an alarm. Which, again, implies at least one accomplice."

"Really, Mr. Holmes," asked Dr. Mortimer, "you do not think this man has an accomplice here with him, do you? Who could that possibly be?"

"Frankly, no, I should say he is a lone wolf. I should lose no time in pursuing your inquiries in Northumberland, Barrowclough, and let me know how you progress. Well, Watson, it has been a busy day. Let us make our way to the George Hotel and pursue our investigations there."

"Don't you mean the Royal?" asked Barrowclough helpfully.

"No, there is nothing more to be gleaned from the Royal," replied Holmes, as we stood up to leave. "By the way Dr. Mortimer, they are likely to have at least one vacant room there if you—"

"Thank you, but I have already engaged a room at the Columbia," Mortimer replied.

"Ah, you were in the area when the tragedy occurred?"

"No, I came straight up from Devonshire."

"I see. Then unless you receive a telegram to the contrary, Barrowclough, meet us at the George Hotel tomorrow morning at ten-thirty."

Holmes and I managed to secure a suite of rooms at the George easily enough. After supper I left him in the sitting room with his old briar-root pipe and went off to bed. I could still hear him mousing around long after midnight, and at one point I heard the night porter arrive, presumably to bring him some tea or a nightcap. The following morning Holmes had evidently been out for his constitutional before breakfast, and after we had dined, we went down to find Inspector Barrowclough and Dr. Mortimer waiting for us in a quiet corner of the smokers' lounge. The latter had been busy putting into effect the arrangements for the interment of his late friends.

"Well, Inspector," began my friend, "have there been any further developments?"

"No sign of the bodies, if that is what you mean," replied Barrowclough eagerly, "which would, of course, tend to favour my theory that these two women have not actually been killed.

More to the point, though, I received a wire from my counterpart in the Northumberland Constabulary."

"Is thy news good, or bad? Answer to that!" said Holmes with a smile.

"From my point of view, it is not merely good, it is most encouraging! I found out that young James Desmond has been on holiday for the last week," said the inspector with an unmistakeable glow of triumph.

Holmes laughed, "I fear that you are about to tell me that not only has he been missing for a week, but that he favours walking holidays, particularly on coastal cliff paths, and that he matches the description given by the two women."

"That's exactly it! Have you also been investigating Desmond's whereabouts?" asked Barrowclough with a look of suspicion.

"Not at all; it is your manner which proclaims as much."

"His passions are walking and fishing, often alone. He is said to favour the Scottish Highlands, the south Pennines, the Peak district and," he paused exultantly, "the North York Moors!"

"Comfortably within a day's easy travel of Northumberland. Excellent! And you traced him to his hotel, discovered he had no alibi, placed him under lock and key, and have extracted a written confession from him."

"Not exactly, no. You see, it is also his custom to sleep under canvas when the weather is fine, but we have put a bulletin out to all stations in the areas I mentioned, and we shall comb the moors until we lay our hands upon him. By the way, we also discovered that he has a depleted bank balance and has a bit of a leaning towards the turf. A rum habit for a clergyman's son, eh? What about you, Mr. Holmes, did you find out anything at the George Hotel?"

"I have had an exceedingly busy time since we last met and followed up on one or two lines of inquiries. Then, first thing this morning I walked the path where the tragedy occurred. It is hardly the sort of spot I should choose should I wish to do away with my sworn enemy, and it seems an incredible coincidence that the hunter serendipitously found his quarry alone and unaware and struck when the opportunity presented itself."

"Well, of course, they were very fond of hill and moor walking," replied Mortimer, "they conducted much of their courtship whilst walking on the remote Dartmoor paths amongst the tors and goyals, so it was ten to one, I suppose, that if they were being followed by someone, such an opportunity would occur."

"Tell me, Inspector," said Holmes, "has anyone else seen a man resembling Desmond, other than these two women?"

"Come, Mr. Holmes, you say *a man resembling* Desmond, can there be any doubt that he is our man? His being away from home at present, his special hobby, his matching the description – surely it is too much of a coincidence?"

"Well, coincidences do happen," I said.

"Or can be contrived to happen," muttered my friend enigmatically.

"To answer your question, Mr. Holmes, no one else has seen him."

"And yet it seems to me an odd thing that he was able to follow them to such a crowded place as a railway station without being noticed by a single person; even odder than the fact that no one saw the women leave the station, so much so that I would be inclined to make that my starting point. I have a few questions to put to you. Did you personally interview Mrs. Coakley on the day of the murder?"

"Yes ... well not exactly, you see Miss Daymer gave me most of the information – Mrs. Coakley had had to go and lie down; she was still very upset at having witnessed a murder."

"In a darkened room by any chance?"

"Yes, exactly, in a cool darkened room – she suffers from the occasional migraine, she said."

"No doubt she did say that. Then you did not see her personally?"

"Well, I went into her room, and she confirmed the details which Miss Daymer had given me."

"She spoke to you then?"

"Yes, well–"

"It was more a series of nods and shaking of the head."

"No doubt the hotel staff told you that."

"In fact, they never mentioned it. I have another question: on your second visit to the hotel, after they had disappeared, did you examine the rooms at the George Hotel which Mrs. Coakley and Miss Daymer had inhabited?"

"No, I must confess I didn't," replied Barrowclough. "I couldn't see what purpose–".

"Ah," said my friend, "then you would not be aware that Mrs. Coakley had inadvertently left her umbrella behind, Inspector."

Barrowclough looked mystified.

"No. Do you regard that fact as especially significant?" he asked.

"I regard all facts as significant until I have decided otherwise," said Holmes suavely.

"And what have you decided?"

"That, on the whole, a return to London would be best."

"Then you think the case is a mere formality now?" asked the inspector.

"I should not quite go that far," replied Holmes with a touch of asperity, "but I think I have done all that I can possibly do in this town. Incidentally, have you ever read Poe's 'Purloined Letter'?"

"No," replied the astonished inspector, looking at Holmes as though the latter had taken leave of his senses. I had often seen this expression before when folk failed to understand the significance of some of Holmes's more Delphic utterances.

"Then it may profit you to do so. Do you have a Bradshaw?"

"I suppose you will be wanting to know the train times and connections for your journey back to London."

Sherlock Holmes smiled at the inspector. "No, in point of fact, I already knew that, but I think that *you* may find Bradshaw useful."

"Not at all, I know all the local timetables by heart," said Barrowclough, looking even more puzzled.

"Well, I have given you a hint or two, but it is up to you whether you pursue them. Allow me to give you another piece of advice: Confine yourself to investigating the murders on the cliff. I should not waste any further time seeking the murderer of Mrs. Coakley and her companion, or searching for their bodies, for I do not believe that you will ever find either."

"You believe that Desmond is too clever for me – is that it?"

"I have said what I have said," replied Holmes evenly, "and unfortunately have no time to explain further as we must dash for our train now. However, I have left an envelope at the police station containing a few further minor points of advice which it may benefit you to consider. You may study them at your leisure. Well, gentlemen, please feel free to contact me if there are any further developments, and now, Dr. Watson and I must bid you both a very good day."

Holmes and I collected our belongings and departed the hotel, much to the astonishment of the staff. The manager was mortified at the thought that our leaving was due to some dissatisfaction with the service or the accommodation; however, Holmes assured him that it was on account of our unexpected necessity to return to London. I confess I was as mystified as the manager at Holmes's sudden decision, but something in my friend's manner made me refrain from demanding an outright explanation immediately. However, as we steamed out of York that afternoon in the quietude of a first-class compartment, I broached the subject of our abrupt departure.

"I perceive, Holmes, that you are unconvinced of the likelihood of this Desmond being the assailant on the cliff. If you have a theory of your own, surely it would have been only fair to have presented it to the inspector. Even *you* must concede that Barrowclough has a strong case."

"On the face it, from the point of view of the motive for the crime, he has an overwhelming case for hunting down Desmond and subjecting him to a most searching examination. After all, he appears to be the sole heir and there is a million pounds at stake, perhaps more. I shall sum up all the strong points in his case: the absence of the young man from home, his likely presence in this area, his probable lack of an alibi if he has been travelling alone, his apparent matching of the description by the two women and so on. Cumulatively, it looks very solid. What he has not done, is to consider either the weaknesses in his own case, or to look for any alternative theory and address it. It is a fault for which I have castigated the official police countless times. I am disappointed in Barrowclough's lack of imagination, and even more so in his inability to grasp the significance of apparently trivial details. How does he explain the sudden disappearance of the two women for example? His idea of abduction is patent nonsense; it is no less than the twisting of every fact to suit a theory. Was the umbrella left behind by accident? What if Desmond is discovered to have been a hundred miles away in the Peak District with a group of friends? What of his theory then?"

"Can you explain these things?"

"I can, Watson, and in the few hours that we have between here and London, I shall, but let me tell you right away that you are seated beside one of the biggest fools in Christendom. I shall explain my train of thought to you, for it is a useful way of testing my chain of reasoning. Last night I slept very little and spent the time tossing around in my head all the facts, or supposed facts, with which we had been presented by Barrowclough and, to a lesser extent, by Dr. Mortimer. I was forced to the conclusion that we had been taking things rather too much at face value due to our familiarity with the history of the case and the people involved in it. So, I am going to ask you to cast your mind back to the events of last autumn in Dartmoor and take a rather more sceptical view than we did then.

"It may astonish you to learn that I have begun to undergo an accumulating sense of disbelief towards the notion that Rodger Baskerville ever perished in the Great Grimpen Mire. A very telling phrase you used, perhaps subconsciously, at the time: you wrote 'much was *surmise.*' And so it was. In retrospect, I must confess that I now consider the 'evidence' of Baskerville's death to be spectacularly unconvincing. No coroner's jury ought to have accepted it, especially after the episode of the hound had become public knowledge. After all, no body was ever discovered, and the wands which marked the path to Baskerville's hideout in the bog had remained *in situ*. How could we have been so naïve as to credit his paltry stratagem of tossing Sir Henry's old boot aside where we could easily find it! How came we to be completely taken in by the whole contrived *mise en scène* in his abandoned lair!"

Holmes leaned forward, "I put it to you, Watson, is it not quite inconceivable that a cunning man like Rodger Baskerville would not have drawn up some contingency or escape plan in the event of failure? I further put it to you that he never perished in that mire for the good reason that *he was never in it!* And that—"

"That it was Rodger Baskerville himself who murdered Sir Henry on the cliff path," I cried, in horror and amazement.

"Indeed. This Desmond fellow has no more to do with it than you or I. It is pure blind chance that he has been on holiday."

"But, then his wife, Beryl, must therefore have been married bigamously to Sir Henry!"

"Precisely. A tangled skein indeed."

"Dear me, this has all the qualities of one of Mr. Hopcroft's third-rate melodramas!"

"Early this morning I despatched a telegram to the postmistress in the hamlet of Grimpen, Devonshire, requesting a few details. I was so encouraged by her first reply that I made a further connection with her by telephone, and there followed a conversation which lasted fully twenty minutes and cost me a small fortune. As you know, no one has greater knowledge of the secrets of a rural district than a postmaster or postmistress. It turns out that the person with whom Rodger Baskerville had had a liaison a year ago—"

"Mrs. Laura Lyons."

"You remember her?"

"I do."

"I rather thought you might for I seem to recall, having read your account of the affair at the time, that you were quite taken with her. Something about 'hazel eyes and a complexion like' … what was it now, ah yes, 'the dainty pink at the heart of a sulphur rose,'" my friend's eyes twinkled mischievously.

"Really, Holmes! There is no need to—"

37

"Laura Lyons left the district some few weeks after the attempt on Sir Henry's life. The local gossip was that the shame of her involvement with Baskerville having become public knowledge was the reason for her leaving, and she could barely hold up her head after being tainted by her friendship with a murderer. More likely, Watson, she was still in cahoots with Baskerville who, as we *now* know, had not only survived the apparent flight to the moor, but was still alive, and managed to find sanctuary not too far off."

"At Coombe Tracey with Laura Lyons? But that is a long way off from the moor at Grimpen."

"Twelve miles or so – nothing to a fit fellow like Baskerville who spent most of his time leaping around on the moor chasing butterflies. Then she, and probably he too, moved away; to where, the postmistress did not know. It cannot have been very far, however, because the burglaries which Baskerville had been suspected of committing at the time still continued. There was one at Westman's Copse where the haul of silver was quite a valuable one, and in another such case the butler or the groom, I quite forget which, was left for dead – the Bachelor's Hall Murder, the press called it. That was only a mile or so from the Grimpen Mire where Baskerville had kept the hound. They were still watching and waiting."

"But if, as you suggest, it was Rodger who killed Sir Henry, why did the latter not recognise Baskerville on the path and raise an alarm? Indeed, why did Beryl not recognise *her own husband* whom she thought was dead?! How came Sir Henry who was a strong, burly man to be overpowered by someone of perhaps barely half his weight?"

"You summarise very well the pertinent questions in the case. I could give you a hypothetical answer to each: Neither Sir Henry nor his wife would have recognised Baskerville had he been in disguise; Sir Henry's strength would have counted for little or naught had he been taken by surprise on the very edge of a cliff path. Once Sir Henry was dispatched, Beryl would be paralysed by fear and shock. In fact, Watson, it was one of your own observations which helped me to see the obvious explanation for some of the puzzling events of the last twenty-four hours through the fog of deception."

"I cannot recall."

"Perhaps you did not do so consciously, but you put your finger on the one factor upon which this aspect of the murder revolves. Yesterday you used the word 'incognito.' When I was out this morning, I managed to obtain from the hotel manager a very full description of Mrs. Coakley and Miss Daymer. Here is the latter's: tall, slim, brown hair, hazel eyes, high cheekbones, pink complexion with freckles. Whom does Miss Daymer's description recall to you?"

"I cannot possibly think."

"Come, Watson, you mentioned her name a few moments ago in connection with Devonshire. Think of sulphur roses."

"Why, Laura Lyons!"

"It was she."

"His accomplice on the cliff … then this old woman, Mrs. Coakley—"

"Was Rodger Baskerville, in woman's attire."

"My word, Holmes, what a cool one! That was why Barrowclough could hardly get a word out of her in the darkened room."

"Yes, even a cunning dog like Baskerville could hardly expect to fool the sharp-eyed Barrowclough."

"Then how were they able to fool the hotel staff?"

"In point of fact they did not, at least not completely. The hotel manager's wife thought there was something a bit odd about the older woman, some harshness of expression, but she could not quite put her finger it. And the two women took their meals in their suite which kept them apart from other guests."

"But why all the rigmarole?"

"To divert the attention of the police to events in Yorkshire, whilst they made their way to London, thence to America to claim the inheritance."

"So, Baskerville and Laura Lyons in their guise as Coakley and Daymer followed Sir Henry and Beryl to the footpath and attacked them! There was never any man in a broad-brimmed hat pulled low over his eyes."

"So I read it; they then reported the matter to the police, giving a description of Desmond as the man they had seen running away."

"How could they possibly have guessed at the appearance of someone they had never met?"

"I don't believe they did. They could easily obtain the Desmonds' forwarding address from the parish in Westmoreland or possibly from Crockford's directory, then a few apparently innocent local inquiries as to what the son, James, looked like – nothing to a man of Baskerville's capability. They knew it would take a while before the police traced the potential heirs, and then discovered Desmond. At that point, the priority was simply to waste police time and divert attention while Baskerville, presumably with his hazel-eyed, sulphur rose in tow, made his escape."

"And Laura Lyons would have had the sweetest revenge on Beryl, the woman who was first presented to her by Baskerville as his sister! Yet how did Baskerville know that they would be on the cliff path at that time? What if Sir Henry had taken Beryl to the spa instead, or an afternoon concert in the park?"

"That is the jigsaw piece which is missing, Watson, although I think know where to find it. They may have had other plans afoot had they not been presented with their excellent opportunity at Langhorne Wyke."

"A poison-tipped walking cane?!"

"It would not be the first time: there were similar cases in such diverse places as St. Petersburg and Charlotte, North Carolina. Of course, as soon as the false trail to young Desmond was discovered, Baskerville knew that suspicion might eventually revert to himself, and his sole aim then would be to get out of the country by the next available boat. But first he wanted to set up a diversion, hence the farce of the two supposed witnesses; it kept the attention of the police fixed on the North Riding – to make them believe the murderer was still there. It was nothing but a ruse to throw the constabulary off guard whilst he slipped away. Of course, he could not possibly know that young Barrowclough would come straight to us; that was a profound miscalculation on his part. The likelihood, as Baskerville no doubt saw it, was that Barrowclough would dither away fruitlessly at least for a few days before calling the in Yard who would blunder around just as hopelessly as he had, by which time he would be halfway across the Atlantic. Hence why we are steaming southwards at our present rate."

"But what makes you think he will go to London? Boats also leave from Glasgow, Liverpool, Bristol, Tilbury, and Southampton. Then there are scores of freighters, leaving from every sizeable port in the country, which carry passengers, sometimes as many as thirty or forty, as a lucrative side line. Why should he place himself right under your nose, as it were?"

"Because that is exactly the type of risky stratagem I would expect him to adopt. You see, he knows we cannot search every boat leaving every port for America: the more boats, the more difficult for us, hence London, where there are literally dozens of shipping lines. It would also satisfy his egotism to be sitting within a few miles of Sherlock Holmes mocking my attempts to find him. And so, you perceive the scale of the task: we have to find these two people from amongst the 4 million teeming in London."

"It will be like searching for a needle in a haystack."

"It will be worse," replied Holmes, "it will be a search for a needle amongst a thousand other needles."

"Do you think they will continue to travel as two women?"

"No, I do not believe so. I should say it would be much safer to travel as a couple, for it would be harder to trace a couple than two women, and it would be difficult even for Baskerville to maintain his disguise all the way to America. It is also possible that he may decide to dispose of Lyons at some point, for he is a ruthless, cynical swine who would not think twice about eliminating anyone who could send him to the scaffold. I honestly feel sorry for any woman in his power, even Mrs. Laura Lyons."

"He has such a magnetic effect on certain women that is quite uncanny. I assume she must have forgiven him for his duplicity over presenting his wife as his sister."

"The postmistress at Grimpen said that she had finally obtained a divorce from her husband, Patrick Lyons, the alcoholic poet, and that may have changed her view, especially now that she is free to marry Baskerville at last."

"Perhaps it is the legacy of a million pounds that has changed her view!"

My friend laughed. "And yet, Watson, there was a hardness and a callousness about that woman; I recall her words at the time when she discovered Baskerville's deception over Beryl – 'a villain,' she spat the words out! She did not strike me as being the sort of woman who had a particularly forgiving nature, quite the contrary." Holmes shrugged, "However, women are so inscrutable, Watson; their motives utterly inexplicable."

"But how did these two manage to escape from the railway station at Scarborough without being seen?"

"I fear you did not grasp the meaning of my cryptic reference to the 'Purloined Letter' either."

"I am afraid not."

"The significance of Poe's story was this – a very valuable purloined letter, used in a blackmail threat, was concealed in a room, a room which the Prefect of Police had searched on numerous occasions with a magnifying glass! Auguste Dupin worked it out – although it amused me to read that he had taken a month to make a deduction which I should have made in less than ten minutes – nevertheless he pointed to the very place where no one would have thought of looking; the letter was stained, crumpled, half torn and scribbled over, and was pinned carelessly to a rack right in the middle of the room along with old notices and other official detritus. The point, Watson, is that the Parisian police believed that the blackmailer would have concealed the letter in a very elaborate hiding place and behaved accordingly. It was invisible to them, for it was *hidden in plain sight.* I had begun to reason that the two persons who gave the evidence to the police were not only alive and perfectly well but had been likewise hidden in plain sight. I imagine that they went to the station as two women, and boarded the Whitby train in plenty of time; Baskerville would have gone to the toilet and changed back into men's clothes and then – as man and woman – left the train on the pretence of having got into the wrong one by mistake; they then took another train, say the Hull train or more likely the Sheffield train, where they could change and make their way to London, having bought the Sheffield tickets the day before. It would not be difficult. He, or rather they, have had a day's start upon us. In fact, he was probably already steaming into St. Pancras when we were walking into Barrowclough's office."

"And what was the significance of the umbrella?"

"Straightforward. Yet another ruse to mislead the police. You can be sure that at what Baskerville considers the right juncture, he will have a note sent to the hotel, purportedly from Mrs. Coakley to say that she will be coming back on her way home to Harrogate to collect the umbrella which she had left behind. The result will be further confusion and delay in the police ranks as they wait for their two prize witnesses to return."

"But why did you not tell Barrowclough about this this morning?"

"Well, you heard me give him enough of a hint for him to be able to work all of this out for himself. But perhaps, Watson, it is no bad thing for the moment if the police think the murderer is still in Yorkshire; the press, of course, will merely follow their lead and it may just induce in our friend Baskerville a false sense of security. Besides, I have another reason – nothing more than a mere intuition at present and one which requires a good bit of working out yet. I need some further, more exact, data to hand to lend some solidity to my theory – a theory which I am disinclined to reveal even to you at present in its partly formed state. However, I shall give you a hint also. Early this morning I took the trouble to verify that the bodies in the mortuary were indeed those of Sir Henry and his wife."

"My dear Holmes! And were they?"

"Yes."

"What did you suspect?"

"That we had already been guilty, as I said, of taking too much for granted in this case."

"What do you intend to do now?"

"We now begin the long slow tedious search for Mr. and Mrs. whatever-they-may-decide-to-call-themselves; of course, if any link in my chain of reasoning is faulty, then we have probably lost them for good. One thing is certain though–"

"They are unlikely to use the name Stapleton or Baskerville!"

Holmes laughed again. "Indeed. We know how audacious he is; you will recall in London he once sent my own name back to me via a cabman! But I believe he will take a severely practical view in this case and will most likely decide that it would be easier to conceal himself until the last possible moment before boarding his boat, which in turn means he will repair to a lodging near the river. Loath as I am to share the case with the Yard, I fear we may need Lestrade's assistance now. There are powers and resources such as only they have."

"Why not send in the Irregulars?"

"I will send them to comb the areas round the docks and the riverside where Baskerville is likely to be holed up awaiting his chance to bolt. But we need a body of men that can legitimately enter private premises and conduct interrogations. Time is very much of the essence, and the difficulty is that we shall have to conduct this search with a very light hand and under some other pretext, for if we flood the area with uniformed constables our prey will simply melt into thin air and make alternative arrangements."

"Then the best plan would be for Lestrade to get his plainclothes men to make ostensibly routine calls on hotels and boarding houses in the dockside areas on the pretext of checking for Nihilists and Anarchists who may have come here in preparation for the Russian visit."

"Indeed, the likelihood of an assassination attempt is high, and I think that such a stratagem would pass without comment amongst the English-speaking population, for they would realise immediately that it was not aimed at them and would not be suspicious by it."

The next morning Holmes had gone out long before I appeared downstairs for breakfast. He returned at dinnertime in the highest of sprits, dressed in seaman's garb and reeking of Demerara rum.

"There is a note from Barrowclough," I said.

He nodded as he tore the envelope open.

"The umbrella stunt, no doubt."

"Yes, that's it, Watson. Also, with a clever little Baskerville twist, listen to this: A note purportedly from the two women to Barrowclough to say that they had again seen the man they had identified on the cliff path and that he had followed them to Whitby! Accordingly, they were terminating their holiday early due to the anxiety this had caused, and they would stop off to collect *et cetera, et cetera*." He tossed the note across to me.

"Barrowclough rather takes this as vindication of his own theory that the two women had not been murdered."

"I have given him my best advice, but he is a rather stubborn young man."

"I believe it is an intrinsic part of the Yorkshire character. You seem in rather good spirits. Where have you been?"

"All the usual spots when I want to find something out about ships and sailors, Watson. In the Turk's Head, the King's Arms, the Duke of Connaught, and the Prince Albert on the north bank; the Armada Beacon, the Three Compasses, and the Prince of Orange on the Surrey side. If I never see another drop of grog again, it will not be too soon! I had initially intended to begin the task of sifting through Lloyd's Register and the Mercantile Shipping Gazette for likely boats leaving London for America within the next few days, but it was an enormous job, quite impossible: we should have required a whole office full of clerks to complete the task. I resolved upon a more direct method and today I had a most interesting conversation with the landlord of the Three Compasses – an old lag now gone straight, or at least as straight as it is possible to go in a place like Rotherhithe. I asked him, in the manner of a hypothetical question, that if I needed to leave London for America very quickly whilst avoiding the scrutiny of the police, what would be the best way to do it: Would I be better to choose a passenger boat where I should be hidden amongst a myriad of other passengers, or take one of the freight boats that carry a passengers as a side line, where the police might not think of looking? He thought for a moment and said, 'Neither! A better idea altogether would be to take one of the small fast mailboats which carry only a few dozen or so passengers. Not many people know about them, and the companies are not too fussy about who they carry. You remember Rathbone in the Bishopsgate case? That's how he got away – on a small mailboat.' There are boats that leave from a number of points north and south of the river and that sounded to me, Watson, just like the very ruse that Baskerville would try to pull off."

"When do these boats leave?"

"The ones that interest me leave on Tuesdays and Saturdays."

"Then, as this is Wednesday, we may already be too late, since Baskerville has already had twenty-four hours start on us."

"In theory, it is so, Watson, but even he could not possibly have known in advance that everything in his plan would go like clockwork; he had probably estimated that he would have had to tail Sir Henry for a few days at least until he had an opportunity to strike. In the event, luck was on his side, but he was not to know that. Now, this is where Scotland Yard comes in. I have sent a note to Lestrade to suggest that he send his men out to carry out an apparently routine check on the boarding establishments in the dockside areas. Ostensibly they are checking the papers only of foreigners, but in fact they are, of course, looking for a couple who fit the description of Baskerville and Laura Lyons. Under this pretext they can go from street to street, ask awkward questions and no one will be any the wiser.

"If they discover anyone who looks like our pair, they are to carry on as though nothing is amiss and report it directly to the Yard. Lestrade will be most annoyed at having let Baskerville escape his clutches in Dartmoor, and I think we can guarantee that he will leave no stone unturned to assist us here. I have also posted a detachment of our Irregular force along both banks with instructions to find out whether there have been any new arrivals at the boarding establishments near the docks. As you know they can go everywhere, see and hear everything, and strike up apparently innocent conversations without suspicion. Wiggins has been well-remunerated in advance and will, as usual, report any developments to me by wire. I expect to hear something very soon."

But contrary to my friend's expectations, there we stalled for a few days: There was no word from Lestrade, nothing from the Irregulars; Holmes became morose, impatient, and quite insufferable, pacing the sitting room from morning until night. One evening rather late, he retired to his room with his violin and scraped away exasperatingly. He had recently been making a special study of the music of the great Celtic harpers and had developed a theory about the relation of the Gaelic slow air to the flamenco of Andalucía and the primitive music of Arabia and India. On this occasion, however, the resulting cacophony could have been titled "torment and death of a feline." Once or twice, he received a wire at which he glanced in a desultory fashion and, muttering inaudibly, stuffed into a pocket. Over and over, he went, through the personal columns of the London newspapers and journals. My patience finally began to be exhausted when he started taking in some of the provincial ones too, notably the Northern Echo, the Leeds Mercury, and the Scarborough Daily Post, which meant that our sitting room became knee deep, rather than merely ankle deep, in newsprint. On one particular occasion he had added the Financial Chronicle, the Corn Exchange Reports and, for some odd reason the Calgary Daily Herald, which made me think he was fairly grasping at straws now. He said not a word to me about the case, however. For all his inclination towards histrionics, his extroversion in playing to the crowd, and his occasional contriving of a melodramatic dénouement, he nevertheless bore a distinctly secretive streak which I had long observed. The upshot was that even I was often left grasping at air when it came to trying to anticipate the lines on which his mind was running; this was just such an occasion.

After breakfast on Saturday morning, I went off to my club in order, frankly, to avoid him, and when I returned at five o'clock, he was gone. Mrs. Hudson told me that he had received another telegram in the late afternoon then he left soon afterwards. When I asked her whether he had gone in his guise as Captain Basil again, she replied, "If you mean in that smelly old pea-jacket and filthy scarf, no he didn't. He looked more like a jarvey in his get up, but you can never tell what he's up to."

I noticed an opened telegram upon the coffee table and sprang at it. Surely this must be the cause of his sudden departure, I thought. Holmes had evidently been delving into the Devonshire connection again for the wire was from the postmistress at the Grimpen, Postbridge in Devonshire. I was thoroughly mystified on reading it for it contained only one word: "Dorothy." Who was this mysterious Dorothy, I pondered? I racked my brains but could not come up with a solution. Could it be the pseudonym that Laura Lyons was now using? Or was Dorothy the third conspirator, the accomplice of Baskerville and Laura Lyons at whom Holmes had hinted in Scarborough? No person of that name had featured in the case going back all the way to our initial involvement almost a year ago. Sir Henry, of course, had had house servants and this Dorothy might be one of those, but even if this were so, why would the Grimpen postmistress be writing to Holmes about her? And why no surname to identify her, after all Holmes would not have known any of the servants personally. Then again, I mused, we knew that Rodger Baskerville was something of a philanderer and so perhaps …

My curiosity and impatience began to gnaw at me. The telephone directory lay on the shelf by the window. Surely, I ought to ring Baskerville Hall and try to find out; it could do no harm, and as Holmes was absent, I was entitled, I reasoned, to act upon my own initiative. On many such occasions in the past he had entrusted to me this authority. Very well then, I noted the number of the Hall and went straight along to the post office to use the telephone. It was Barrymore, the late Sir Henry's butler, who answered, and naturally I began by offering him my sincere condolences.

"Condolences, Dr. Watson? I am afraid I do not understand."

"I am dreadfully sorry, my dear Barrymore, I should have thought you and Mrs. Barrymore would have been informed by now."

"Informed of what, sir? Has something untoward occurred? If so, we have heard nothing."

"I am very sorry to bring the bad news to you like this, but I now find myself placed in a quite impossible situation. I am afraid I have to tell you that your master and mistress were murdered only a few days ago. It was a perfectly brutal murder, and you must prepare yourself: They were thrown from a cliff in Scarborough by Rodger Baskerville."

"How awful! My wife will take this very badly, sir. Rodger Baskerville – do you mean the man with the hound?"

"Yes."

"I knew it!" he swore under his breath.

"You knew what, Barrymore?"

"That he was still alive. It was not my place to say, sir, but in my heart, I never believed that man was dead, although I spoke not a word to Sir Henry lest it should make him uneasy."

"Then you have been proven correct in your belief."

"I did mention it once or twice to Dr. Mortimer, however, when he was up at the Hall. He spent much time here assisting Sir Henry with his affairs, particularly the Canadian wheat business; in fact, he had gone out there for a month back in May of this year. We saw rather a lot of him at the Hall, but he refused to take my concerns seriously and he swore me never to mention it in Sir Henry's presence. And I did not, for he made me feel very foolish about it: 'Death by Misadventure,' he repeated severely, 'that was the verdict by twelve solid, hard-headed, moorland countrymen.' The implication being, sir, that I was a soft-headed butler."

"Speaking of whom, I fail to understand why you have not had a telephone call or at least a telegram from Dr. Mortimer."

"Indeed, sir, nor have we seen anything in the newspapers, though I am thankful that my wife did not find out about Sir Henry's death in that manner. As you know it had been our intention to leave Baskerville Hall and retire, but we were persuaded by Sir Henry, may God rest his soul, to remain. At least I can break it to her as gently as possible. As for Dr. Mortimer, perhaps he wanted to speak to us face to face, as it were."

"Perhaps. I am sorry to trouble you further, but may I ask if you have, or recently had any servants called Dorothy?"

"No, sir, never in my time here."

"Or anyone from the village by that name?"

"No, and we have lived in the neighbourhood for some twenty years. But I am sure I have heard that very name mentioned in conversation between Sir Henry and Dr. Mortimer on more than one occasion."

My ears pricked up at this. "You are absolutely sure of this?"

"Certainly – I would swear to it in court if it came to it, however I can remember nothing else about it."

I came away from my conversation with the butler of Baskerville Hall more intrigued than ever. For me, there was always an aura of melancholy and inscrutability about the man Barrymore; his appearance, his saturnine demeanour, his self-conscious understatement – I thought of Holmes's earlier reference to Poe, and it occurred to me that Barrymore would have made for a great character in a gothic novel. And yet he had seen through Baskerville's deception on the moor which had taken in both Holmes and myself. I could understand why Mortimer might ridicule him over his conviction that Baskerville was still alive, but why did he not convey Barrymore's misgivings to us in the police station at Scarborough? And why had he not mentioned his trip to Canada in connection with Sir Henry's farming affairs? And yet, Barrymore *had* heard the name Dorothy, and moreover, the postmistress at Grimpen had confirmed that very name to Holmes in a telegram. What part did Dorothy play, or had she played, in this intractable affair?

It was then that I spotted a note from Holmes jack-knifed to the mantelpiece and went across to open it. As I did so, I heard a familiar tread on the stairs, the sitting room door opened, and in walked Inspector Lestrade of Scotland Yard. I was certainly glad to see the man, for there was much that I wanted to discuss with him, but I noticed straight away that there was something odd about the manner in which he was dressed. He was attired in a very slovenly fashion for a man who was normally quite dapper and smart; as I had not seen him for some months, I had at first a vague concern that he might be taking to drink, and recalled that that was often one of the first signs of serious intemperance in patients, perhaps more obvious at the outset than any physiological symptom.

"Very propitious timing, Lestrade," I said motioning him to a chair. "I was just about to read Holmes's note."

"Go on then, open it," said the inspector, grinning, "you'll get a bit of a surprise."

"Ah, I see now why you are dressed as you are! No doubt you have received similar instructions: be at Brunswick Wharf at eight-thirty tonight looking like a wharfside loiterer."

"Indeed. I looked up the boats: We are to be there for the departure of the Union Mail Line's *Dominion Star* for Quebec."

"Then Holmes has found Baskerville?"

"So, it would appear, though as usual he's very close with his information and hasn't said so exactly. I suppose we just appear as a couple of dockside idlers," Lestrade said, "the sort who carry the luggage up the gangway for the passengers for consideration of a couple of bob, then drink it away in the nearest public house."

"Quebec? It seems a rather long way round to reach Costa Rica. I suppose for Baskerville it holds the advantage of seeming to shake us off his trail a bit, for no doubt he would expect us to be looking for boats to Panama for a connection to San José. By the way, do you know anything about this Miss Dorothy?" I showed Lestrade the telegram. He shook his head and declared himself as mystified as I was.

"Never heard that name in connection with this case," he answered.

"We are to be armed and ready too, he says, and I see he has gone out of his way to remind you not to wear your police boots;

I am to remember to slouch about and not stride like a guardsman, and we both must keep both hands in our pockets."

Lestrade chuckled, "Always the dramatist is Mister Holmes! If it were up to me, and I knew this fellow's hideout, I'd have had the whole place surrounded, but you know what he is like, Doctor, he loves playing to the gallery and he won't be gainsaid."

"And we are to do nothing until we hear the words 'Sherlock Holmes!'"

There was still plenty of evening light in the sky as Lestrade and I stepped into the cab taking us eastwards. We alighted a few streets from the wharf itself, by the Lansdowne public house, since it would have looked somewhat suspicious to have arrived by hansom in our current dishevelled and ostensibly impecunious state. The *Dominion Star* was berthed by the Customs House as was the practice for boats carrying the mail. We could hear the distant clanking of trains arriving at the terminus station on the pier, and there were little knots of people dotted here and there on the quayside, along with the usual sellers of souvenirs and odds and ends."

"I assume Mr. Holmes is amongst this crowd already."

"Perhaps, he is already on the boat," I suggested.

"If I know him, he will be ensconced in the captain's cabin hobnobbing with the officers over a glass of rum."

The occasional hansom or growler arrived from time to time, depositing its passengers bound for a fresh start in the New World, and causing a flurry of activity amongst those jostling on the quayside hoping to make a few pence helping with the mountains of luggage. Lestrade and I, our dirty caps pulled down to avoid recognition, hung to the outside of this little knot of people. We had no real plan of action, but waited expectantly. Presently a cab drew swiftly up almost as far as the jarvey could get to the edge of the gangway. Lestrade muttered something under his breath about nearly running over his toes. The jarvey was a garrulous Cockney of the falsely subservient type, yes-sirring and no-sirring away in a most ingratiating manner to the bearded man and the blonde-haired woman whose luggage he was unloading, in the hope, no doubt, of receiving a substantial gratuity. Lestrade nodded to me to move away from this vulgar lout whose loudness was beginning to attract unwelcome attention, when we heard the jarvey say in a mock jocular manner to the man who was descending from his cab.

"I don't suppose you'd like to know the name of the fellow as drove you here tonight, sir?"

The impatient looking gentlemen to whom he addressed the remark merely grunted something inaudible in a dismissive manner. Then, in a familiar voice, the jarvey went on, "Well, Mr. Rodger Baskerville, I think I really ought to tell you that it was Sherlock Holmes!"

The bearded passenger to whom the remarks were addressed merely stared in astonishment, at which point I suddenly recognised the voice. For a moment or two Holmes's words hung in the air. In another instant my friend had quietly clapped his gun to the man's head. The woman let out a scream and began to reach into her bag but by this time Lestrade had moved closer and checked her in the act; from the bag the inspector retrieved a miniature pistol.

"Well, Inspector, I suppose you hardly need an introduction to Mrs. Laura Lyons and Rodger Baskerville," said Holmes. Turning to the woman, he continued, "You may be interested to know, Mrs. Lyons, that we have arrested your lover and co-conspirator."

The woman glanced briefly at Baskerville, and I recall thinking that it was an inanely obvious remark for Holmes to make under the circumstances: Then he delivered his *coup de grace*.

"No, Mrs. Lyons, I do not mean the man you have known variously as Jack Stapleton or Rodger Baskerville: I mean, of course, Dr. James Mortimer!"

It is difficult to say which of us was the most astonished in that little company, for I must confess that Lestrade and I had been as amazed by Holmes's words as Baskerville was.

"Dr. Mortimer was arrested by Inspector Barrowclough yesterday as he left the post office in Scarborough after receiving your message," Holmes went on. "He was, as you know, on his way to meet you on this very boat tonight under an assumed identity. By the way, Baskerville, did you know, that you would never have reached the other side of the Atlantic? The deceiver deceived I am afraid – for there was to have been a tragic accident on board. You would never have claimed that farm in Alberta; you would never have held the Baskerville estate; you would have seen nothing of the million pounds; your *friend* Mortimer would have had all that. You see, you were merely a pawn in their game, or at least in their endgame, however things may have started out. Ironically, I have saved you from certain death at the hands of these two; nevertheless, it gives me great satisfaction to hand you over to the certainty of a similar, but more ordered, fate."

Amazement and murderous anger fought for supremacy in Baskerville's features as he was handcuffed and disarmed, and he uttered a string of oaths that would have shocked a fish porter as he turned his vitriolic gaze upon the woman whom he now realised had thoroughly betrayed him. Lestrade blew his whistle, and a number of uniformed men began to pour out from the Customs House building to the curious stares of the onlookers who had begun to gather round the gangway. Lestrade motioned to them to take the two away.

"Dr. Mortimer? Well, I am amazed," I said. "Though some things are beginning to fall into place now."

"I know criminals come in all sorts," said Lestrade after the two prisoners had been led away, "but I would have staked my life on such a straight, respectable fellow as Mortimer. As I've heard you say before, Mr. Holmes, education never ends, for I hadn't the slightest suspicion of him."

"Neither did I, until a few days ago. A mere suspicion plus purely circumstantial evidence – and fairly flimsy at that. I say it again, attention to detail! That's where most criminals go wrong. Fortunately for them some of your colleagues at Scotland Yard have a similar aversion to minutiae! However, there is a tale to be told, and I have asked the dependable Mrs. Hudson to have something choice tomorrow evening at Baker Street. Lestrade, I hope you will honour us with your presence. Barrowclough too, is on his way to join us; he deserves his moment of glory for sticking to the task which I set him."

Holmes could play the part of the epicurean host exceedingly well, and the gleam of silverware and the rattle of the fine china on the spotless, starched white cloth in our brightly gaslit dining room boded well for a convivial evening. His idea of something choice turned out to be lobster thermidor, followed by a remove of game, succeeded by a gorgonzola that could have been smelt across the street. The Puligny-Montrachet and Gevrey-Chambertin were exquisitely chosen too, but we waived the dessert course in favour of coffee and Curaçao. It was close on midnight by the time Mrs. Hudson had cleared the plates away, and at last our little party was at last able to relax; a decanter of Holmes's best whisky made a circuit of the table pursued by the gasogene.

"Well, Mr. Holmes," said Lestrade, once we four had settled down, "not only have you astonished us yet again, but we now have three villains in custody for the price of one."

"I had my own reputation to think of as well as yours. Otherwise, Sherlock Holmes would have been proven to be an ass for having got himself mixed up in a story concerning spectral hounds, and Scotland Yard's reputation would continue to decline."

"How on Earth did you come to suspect Dr. Mortimer, of all people, so quickly?" asked Barrowclough.

"I have a question too," I added, "who is this shadowy Miss Dorothy? We have heard nothing of her yet."

"Very soon you shall know everything there is to know about Dorothy."

"Cherchez la femme!" said Lestrade with a wink, beginning to revel in the gaiety of the occasion.

Holmes laughed. "Oh, there was a *femme fatale* behind this all right, and a very shrewd and dangerous one too, but I am afraid it is not your Miss Dorothy."

"Then who is she?" I asked.

"I am afraid there is no such person," replied Holmes with a smile.

"But who –"

"Let us begin at the beginning," said my friend. "And I think we must start, Watson, by admitting to our two colleagues here that you and I hardly covered ourselves in glory last year in Devonshire. We were remiss in several respects, not least that, on the night of Sir Henry's attempted murder, we completely failed to anticipate such an elementary factor as the possibility of a deep fog on the moor, and we were nearly undone by it. We undoubtedly saved Sir Henry's life on that occasion, having first endangered it by our own folly of consenting to his crossing the moor when we knew that the hound was loose on it. We also failed, and I must blame myself for this and set it down against our present success, to properly understand the ambivalent role of that self-effacingly humble M.R.C.S. as he called himself, Dr. Mortimer. No one was better placed than he to play the false friend to Sir Henry and yet the warnings were there if only we had read them. With the benefit of hindsight, I could point to a plethora of statements and actions from Mortimer which sit at odds with his status not only as a medical man and a man of science, but also as a friend to the Baskervilles."

"I distinctly recall you saying at the beginning that the Baskerville case was 'full of obvious things which nobody by any chance ever observes'!" I said pointedly.

"*Touché,* Watson! In truth, I failed to observe most of them myself. To begin with, Mortimer breached a cardinal rule on client confidentiality when he told Rodger Baskerville of Sir Charles's heart condition – knowledge which allowed the former literally to terrify Sir Charles to death. As not only a scholar of craniology but also an authority on atavism, how could he possibly have failed to recognise Rodger Baskerville's physical resemblance to the family portraits in Baskerville Hall? Watson will tell you that it was quite the first thing that struck me when I walked through the door; how could he have failed to observe the symptoms of what he himself called 'the old masterful Baskerville strain,' that is to say, in plain language, an atavistic propensity to violence? Why did he not recognise the extreme racial differences between the apparently blood-related Stapleton 'siblings' – the neutral tinted Rodger and Beryl, the dark South American beauty who posed as his sister. Each on its own should have been suggestive but taken together these characteristics should have been quite conclusive In fact, to do Watson justice, he noticed and commented upon it at the time. As a 'man of science' Mortimer constantly pressed the claim of the supernatural and told us that several people had seen a creature upon the moor which corresponded with this Baskerville demon. The only explanation for this is that he must have been part of the plot from the outset, and that the cunning which I had originally ascribed to Rodger Baskerville was, in reality, Mortimer's."

"But why on Earth did he drag you into the case at all, Mr. Holmes?" asked Barrowclough.

"I believe his arrogance drove him to do it. He presumably felt that no one, not even I, could touch him, and after he had arranged Sir Henry's death on the moor, he would have been able to say, 'I took the case to very highest authority in the land—Mr. Sherlock Holmes himself, but even *he* was unable to prevent it.' I mean, of course, the highest *private* authority," my friend added, with a placatory glance at Barrowclough and Lestrade.

"At first, I believed he was a mere co-conspirator; however, I began to develop a more audacious theory, albeit one for which I had no manifest supporting evidence at that stage, which was that Laura Lyons had a long time ago been disabused of Beryl's pretended status as Rodger's sister by none other than Mortimer, and that these two were now in league. I am sure that when she discovered that she had been betrayed and saw that the plot on the moor had failed, she was then taken up by Mortimer whose supposed wife, incidentally, no one ever seems to have seen. No doubt the two became intimate, and from that point onwards Rodger would do all the dirty work and run all the risk while the other two sat aside. Between them, they could easily dispose of him at some stage, probably on the journey to America, and posthumously dispossess him of the estate which, of course, included the Canadian wealth too. I must confess I did not realise any of this on our arrival in Scarborough. But one thing above all stood out when I thought about what Mortimer had told us in the police station. He made a fatal error on one very minor point, which was initially lost on me as one dramatic event after another crowded in on us in quick succession: the realisation the murdered man was Sir Henry, the sudden disappearance of the two witnesses, the probable flight of Baskerville to London; all these pushed my detached tranquil contemplation aside for the moment. However later that night, when I slowly turned everything over in my mind it became obvious that at least part of Mortimer's version of events was a complete fabrication."

"How exactly?" asked Barrowclough.

"I had some assistance."

"From Dr. Watson?"

"No, from a man you will know well: Bradshaw! Hence why I directed your attention there. Not only could Mortimer not possibly have heard the news since that news had not travelled even as far as London, as you discovered yourself when you crossed the threshold at Baker Street."

"Dash! What a fool I was – I ought to have spotted that."

"Mortimer could also not possibly have travelled up from Devonshire in the time he stated as there are, as I soon discovered, no trains from mid Devon that would bring him to Yorkshire so quickly. 'I came straight up by the first train,' he said. He would have had to have read a London newspaper to discover the murder, then pack his bags, then find a trap to take him to the station; half the day would have been gone by then – impossible! The next day I checked at the Columbia Hotel – he had already been there for a couple of days. Once I discovered Mortimer's deception, I began to formulate a theory of his part in the conspiracy."

"But you had no proof at that point," said Barrowclough.

"Precisely. I can tell you that one of the first things I try to do is do refute my own theory with an alternative explanation of the facts. I assure you, Inspector, as a habit of mind it will always repay the effort. A possible theory remained that Mortimer's behaviour could be ascribed to his protective attitude to Sir Henry; that he was secretly, in order not to upset or alarm his friend, keeping a careful watch on this couple; perhaps after their deaths he realised that this furtiveness may not have exactly put him in a good light when it came to a charge of murder. That may *hypothetically* have been one reason that he did not disclose the full facts to us right away. Nevertheless, I noticed Mortimer's rather suspicious reaction to my suggestion that Sir Henry's murderer may have had an accomplice and, as my suspicions were already aroused, I asked you, in the letter I left at the police station, to keep a watch on him and especially note any visit he made to a post office or messenger office. After my departure it appears that Mortimer somewhat relaxed his precautions."

"And walked straight into the trap which we had laid for him!" said Barrowclough. I thought the "we" was rather fine but said nothing to dispel the spirit of the occasion.

"It will be obvious by now that it was Rodger Baskerville and Laura Lyons, in disguise, who carried out the murder on the cliffs. The rest will naturally fall into place: their 'disappearance'; the ruse with the umbrella; the direction Mortimer gave you on the likelihood of the murderer having have been James Desmond, and of whom he gave you such a clear account, despite somewhat disingenuously claiming that he knew little about the Desmonds. I will not rob you of the pleasure of the telling of the next part Barrowclough."

"I read the note which you left for me, and I followed Mortimer one day, then Sergeant Hicks followed him the next, just to make sure he didn't keep seeing the same face."

"Excellent!"

"Mortimer did nothing suspicious for a day or two. He went walking on the promenade, went to the spa for an afternoon concert, took a day trip to Whitby– "

"Whence, no doubt, he sent that note informing you that they had seen the man they had identified on the cliff path in Whitby."

"Of course! I saw him go into a post office but thought nothing of it at the time. However, he did arrange a rather hasty burial of the remains of his late friends in Scarborough, and not in the family vault in Devon, which I did think was rather odd. The funeral took place as soon as was legally possible."

"I believe that was because he did not want to return to Baskerville Hall again," said Holmes. "His reasons for doing so are not entirely clear, but it is certain that he wanted to get away on the earliest possible boat. I have a vague idea that the butler, Barrymore, a far shrewder man than he looks as I have learned from Watson, may have begun to have suspicions about Mortimer and I think he simply wanted to avoid him."

"Hicks followed Mortimer one day to the post office in the outlying village of Burniston where he picked up some mail. Now that *was* suspicious, because he had to pass three post offices in town to go there. Secondly, the mail was sent to him under a false name. We were unable to ascertain the address of the sender, but the letters were postmarked Poplar, East London. I spoke to the postmistress in Burniston, whom I knew well, and impressed it upon her that should this gentleman return, she was to contact me immediately and on no account to forward any letters or send any telegrams from him until I had seen them first. I made sure that she understood that this was in connection with the murders on the cliff – the difficult part was in getting her to keep her mouth shut, but I warned her that she must not speak a word to anyone. When Mortimer returned the next day, she did exactly as she was asked. Hicks and I were there within the hour, and that is how we obtained the address of the place where Baskerville and his woman were staying: a commercial hotel called the Steam Packet in Naval Row not far from Poplar High Street – under false names, of course. We arrested him as he was leaving the Columbia Hotel. He had the boat and train tickets in his case, but what was curious was that he had boat tickets for *three* people from London, via St. John's to Quebec, but only two train tickets, for a male and a female, again under false names, from Quebec city to Calgary. So I wired to tell you that."

"And this is where your Miss Dorothy makes her entrance, Watson. Mortimer had, in point of fact, been quite legitimately conducting the Canadian affairs on behalf Sir Henry for some time. Indeed, I had already suspected that that was precisely where he was heading–"

"And not as we had originally thought to Costa Rica?" Lestrade asked.

"No. I believe even Rodger realised that he had finally burned his boats in South America, although you will recall that Mortimer attempted to misdirect us with some nonsense about Baskerville inveigling himself back into Costa Rican society. Sir Henry was a modest man as you recall, and when he said he had been farming in Canada, he did not mention that he owned the entire chain of production from growing and harvesting the grain on his farm on the prairies, transporting it to the railroad towns, right down to selling it at the wheat pit in Chicago. The value of Sir Henry's wheat business would bring the value of the estate up to one and a half million pounds! So, I had good reason to believe that Mortimer was making not for Costa Rica, my dear Watson, but for the Canadian prairies; in fact, for the headquarters of the Baskerville Grain Company in the town of Dorothy, Alberta."

"So that is how Barrymore had heard the name!"

"When I spoke to the postmistress at Grimpen, she apprised me of the details of the Mortimer's mail traffic, and it was obvious then that he had been running the business quite openly. It struck me as strange that Mortimer had sought to conceal that from us. The obvious reason was that he was preparing to escape there after the murder. The postmistress had omitted to tell me the name of the town – she had merely mentioned Alberta, which is a very large province – so when I asked her to be more specific, she replied with that rather terse telegram which you found, Watson."

I must confess I felt rather foolish at this simple explanation, but Holmes's next astounding statement soon dispelled my chagrin.

"When I then wired to the manager of the Baskerville Grain Company, a Mr. Paul Hammond, he told me quite definitely that he had had a visit from Sir Henry's English cousin, Rodger, earlier in the year! I was convinced he must have been mistaken so I wired again. No, there was no mistake whatever. A chap called Mortimer had been helping to run the affairs from England for a while, he said, but wasn't he only a country doctor after all who had no head for business. So, Mortimer had wired to inform him that Sir Henry wanted to share the inheritance within the family and would be transferring the business to his beloved long-lost cousin, Rodger, whom he would be sending over. He asked Hammond if, when Rodger arrived, could he please make him familiar with the business, show him around the grain elevators, introduce him to the people and so on and so forth. As you might imagine this put my head in a spin; but I rallied and wired yet again for a description of this cousin, Rodger. It came back, 'Very tall, thin, ascetic looking, a long nose, prematurely round-shouldered,' and so on."

"Nothing like Baskerville!" I exclaimed.

"No, but it fits Dr. Mortimer exactly."

"What the deuce!" expostulated Lestrade. "Was Mortimer up to tricks with the funds in Canada?"

"Not at all. It would have ruined the entire scheme if either Sir Henry, or Hammond, had had the slightest suspicion of that. No, even though by this point Sir Henry's only involvement was in reviewing the quarterly accounts, which could easily have been falsified or substituted, Mortimer's dealings there were scrupulously honest. He never took a single cent from the business and for good measure, he also gave Hammond to understand that he would be retained as the manager once the business was transferred to Rodger, and he gave the rest of the staff a sizeable increase in salary. The game was this: Mortimer went to Dorothy in May this year and passed himself off as Rodger with the intention that, after the murder, he would return as the bereaved, but soon to be richly endowed, relative. What could be more natural? Of course, Canada being a British Dominion, it should make the entire process of claiming the estate much more straightforward than, say, Costa Rica, and he now had a number of quite respectable citizens in Dorothy who would be prepared to absolutely swear to his identity as Rodger Baskerville."

"Surely it cannot have been so simple?" asked Lestrade.

"I am afraid it was. And had it not been for this young man having had the foresight to visit me in London," he indicated Barrowclough, "the plan may well have succeeded. On Saturday, I received Barrowclough's telegram which informed me of the address to which Mortimer had sent a note to the two fugitives. It was on Lestrade's list and had already been visited by the police, who for some reason did not manage to elicit the fact that there had been two new arrivals. I immediately dispatched some of my Irregulars – that's to say, for your benefit Barrowclough, some young gentlemen of the street who occasionally carry out some surveillance work for me – to the scene. They set up watch and were told to follow our two friends wherever they went with the proviso that, if they split up, both would be trailed. However, they barely left the hotel and then only to correspond with Mortimer. It was odds on that they were waiting for a boat from Brunswick Wharf which was only a few hundred yards away, though I could not be certain, but when I discovered there was a sailing to Quebec

– *voilà!* Barrowclough's note later confirmed that they had tickets for the boat. I decided to borrow the cab from our friend, Jacobs, who had assisted us once before in the Soho case. I had just enough time to leave a note for my trusty Watson, scribble one to Scotland Yard, dash over to Brompton Road for Jacobs's cab, then be back to the docks. I waited in the area just off Poplar High Street near the Steam Packet, confident that Baskerville would send for a cab to take him to the dock."

"What if Baskerville had already arranged a cab?" asked Lestrade.

"It was possible, but unlikely, as he would not have wanted to give anything away in advance, not even the remote chance of some loose-tongued jarvey talking about the fare he was going to pick up. In any event, had Baskerville not taken my cab, I would still have been able to follow him a few score yards behind and I should have caught up with him as he arrived at the dockside. As it happened, he sent one of our boys, who appeared to be playing innocently in the street outside, to fetch a cab for him, and the rest you saw and heard."

"And you think that Mortimer would have simply done away with Baskerville *en route*?" I asked.

"There can be no doubt. Once Barrowclough had discovered that there were only two train tickets onward from Quebec, and I put that together with Paul Hammond's description of 'Rodger,' it was the only plausible outcome. I imagine that Mortimer would have had no intention of returning to England, and very little interest in the estate *per se*. He would sell the Canadian business, claim the estate and sell it too, and then simply disappear. Should the worst come to pass, and he was pursued over the death of Sir Henry, the close proximity of southern Alberta to the United States, with whom we have no extradition agreement, would be quite felicitous."

"Then who will inherit the estate now?" asked Barrowclough.

"Once Baskerville and his two accomplices have been tried – and I see little prospect of anything other than a guilty verdict and the gallows – the estate ought to revert to young James Desmond, once the case has gone to probate."

"In saying that, Mr. Holmes," replied Lestrade, "we still have to prove exactly who struck the final blow. No doubt Mortimer will have a strong alibi for the time when the murder actually occurred, and a clever lawyer might be able to get him off on the charge of being an accessory. As you said yourself, he might use the argument that he was maintaining a protective watch on Sir Henry; he could now throw his co-conspirators to the wolves and argue that he was unable to prevent the murder, had seen through the escape plan and was intending to denounce the other two once he had arrived at the boat on the night."

"He certainly denied everything when I arrested him," said Barrowclough.

"Indeed," replied Lestrade, his eyes bulging in wrathful indignation, "he said to me that we had completely misunderstood his intentions and that whilst he not been entirely honest with us, the real reason for that was that he was concerned that we might bungle the case as *we had done in Dartmo*or! And he said, quite bluntly, that he had now been proven correct as we had bungled it again. What a nerve he has! And yet, we may have our work cut out to get a jury to disbelieve him."

"Who knows what the prospect of immunity through turning Queen's evidence may bring about?" said Holmes. "I have an idea that the perpetually disappointed Mrs. Laura Lyons may be useful to us a second time."

Holmes had judged it correctly as usual. Mrs. Laura Lyons, though she found herself committed for two years for withholding evidence and obstructing the police, was at least spared the gallows. The other two were not. Baskerville was found guilty of premeditated murder and Mortimer, though he wriggled like an eel, was found guilty of being an accomplice before the fact, which carried the same penalty. Young James Desmond, who had eventually been discovered fishing on a river in Perthshire with a party of friends, finally and to his utter astonishment, inherited the Baskerville estate. He was able to pay off his trivial gambling debts and in time showed the same philanthropic qualities as his father and his distant uncle, Charles: he pensioned off the Barrymores very comfortably, sold off the Canadian business, at a knockdown price, to Mr. Paul Hammond, and turned the hall into a refuge for impoverished and orphaned children. The last Holmes and I had heard of him, he had begun a campaign to restore the Lindisfarne Gospels to Holy Island, which had been one of his father's unrealised ecclesiastical ambitions.

As I write these final words on the double tragedy which occurred at Langhorne Wyke, it is to be hoped that the Desmonds enjoyed their legacy in peace and tranquillity. But given the grisly history of that family, it is uncertain what the future holds for the Desmonds: not for nothing did Sir Henry Baskerville, perhaps with some premonition of his own fate, describe it as "an inheritance with a vengeance."

END

The Mystery of The Thirteen Bells

For more than a decade I have narrated the exploits of Mr. Sherlock Holmes and, whilst I have relished publicising his abundant and admirable successes, I trust I have been equally assiduous in recording those, admittedly exceedingly rare, instances where even *he* met with failure. As regards the latter, the publication of those cases was generally at his own behest, for my friend's cold, dispassionate nature would have stirred in protest against any attempt on my part simply to ignore his less-than-successful efforts to bring villains to justice; on the contrary, he often insisted, with characteristic intellectual honesty, that I set down a complete and truthful account however unflattering to his person or apparently injurious to his reputation. Aside from those very few instances in which Holmes was roundly defeated, there were a number of cases where his reasoning had been awry from the beginning but where he nevertheless managed to bring the case to a satisfactory conclusion: chief amongst these was our adventure at Norbury which, it may be remembered, involved the complicated but, happily, resolvable domestic upset of Mr. Grant Munro.

There were also cases where his deductive powers were sharp enough and his practical application quick right from the outset; where he alone was able to penetrate the shroud of mystery which confounded others, but where, ultimately, he took upon himself that awesome responsibility for meting out his own form of justice to the culprit. In a very few instances, his sympathies residing with the perpetrator rather than with the victim, this amounted to a *de facto* acquittal, and once even resulted in a blunt refusal to assist the official police in tracking down the murderess of a particularly repugnant blackmailer. Indeed, I have already recorded that, on that occasion, he stood silently by and allowed private revenge to take its lethal course.

The tragic events which I am about to relate constitute yet another category entirely, although I should spoil the appreciation of the story for the reading public were I to provide any further elucidation at this point.

The case began one very foggy November afternoon, soon after we had returned from France where my friend had been involved in a complicated affair which had involved the attempted robbery of a priceless jewel and had made international headlines. Holmes had been tipped off in advance by one of his underworld contacts, one Fred Porlock, who provided details which allowed us to prevent the theft which had been planned by that arch-criminal, Colonel Sebastian Moran, whom Holmes had once described as the second most dangerous man in London.

On this day, Holmes and I were lolling indolently in the Baker Street sitting room after lunch hoping, in vain as it turned out, for some remission of the murky weather. I had begun a half-hearted attempt to bring some order to the notes which I had made of my friend's unpublished cases from the year 1895, which included the affair of the Shadwell Nightingale, the depredations of the shadowy Montgomery Turf Syndicate, and a case of embezzlement from the Chimney Sweeps' Benevolent Fund and subsequent abscondment of the culprit – when Holmes broke in on me in that ostensibly offhand manner of his.

"I perceive, Watson," he remarked, indicating the newspaper he held open, "that there has been an unprecedented increase in the number of executions at Newgate this year for wife-murder and infanticide."

"Really, Holmes? I was quite unaware of that," I replied, "and yet, in some ways, I am not entirely surprised to hear it."

"And why is that?" he asked.

The year had seen an ominous rise in the usual scale of both human tragedy and of rupture in the settled order of the natural world, which so often seemed to me to coincide. There had been a disastrous earthquake in Celebes, a calamitous tidal wave in Japan; in England and America there had been mining disasters and railway smashes; in April, from one London stretch of the Thames alone, over a score of infant bodies had been recovered in various stages of decomposition; in the late summer, a gigantic sea creature had been found washed ashore in the Azores, which no scientist or natural historian was able to identify; and the German Kaiser's new naval policy had cast the chill shadow of bloody war, once again, across the entire European continent. With such portents in mind, I had drawn myself up to make a suitably allusive reply, when there was a light, brisk tread on the stair and a knock upon our door interrupting what may or may not have turned out to be an illuminating discourse as to why domestic life had suddenly become so perilous and why Billington, the Newgate hangman, was being kept so busy. Billy the page entered with the afternoon post, and since I was not accustomed to receiving a large correspondence, this was a daily ritual which I took little interest. As usual, all the letters were addressed to my friend, and he began to go through them one by one, finally tossing each of the official-looking envelopes upon the table without opening them. My friend's unanswered question remained hanging in the air, when at this point a second untimely interruption was brought to bear upon us.

This time, Mrs. Hudson appeared at the door with a visitor whom I immediately recognised as one of our neighbours, a Mr. Stanley Holles, the proprietor of the Baker Street Bazaar across the road. Some time previously, he had been instrumental in bringing us a most extraordinary, and for Holmes rather lucrative, case which was connected with the mysterious fire at a tavern in

Stepney Green where the owner lost his life. Holles was every inch the middle-aged, complacent London shopkeeper: pleasant-featured and easy-going; stolid looking; bespectacled; hair greying to white; dark, baggy, pin-striped trousers; black frockcoat; heavy topcoat; and billycock hat; a beige waistcoat and a watch with chain completed the ensemble. He had that ineffable pomposity of the self-made man, and I could picture him as an elder at a dissenting tabernacle and leading morning prayers before the bazaar opened.

"Foggy morning, what!" he said loudly, removing his hat. "Do you remember me, Mr. Holmes, from the Addleton Arms business – about a year ago?" he continued eagerly and, without waiting for an answer, plunged into an explanation.

"See here, I've had one of these anonymous letters delivered to me by the midday post. No idea who sent it. I think you will agree there's a rather sinister tone about it and, seeing as it is about something happening at seven o'clock tonight, I thought I'd best come here right away."

"You acted very sensibly, Mr. Holles. Pray take a seat and we shall examine this disturbing epistle. Naturally, I recall your case very well, and I remain obliged to you for bringing to me such an interesting and rewarding problem."

"Oh, I did rather well out of it myself; there was the reward for one thing, and then all the publicity – free publicity – in the press for the bazaar. You wouldn't believe the number of people who came to gawk at us, and of course, most of 'em bought something as a kind of souvenir."

"Unfortunately, Dr. Watson has not quite got around to publishing that remarkable story yet."

"I confess I have been somewhat remiss," I added, "though may I assure you, Mr. Holles, that it is not through lack of any intrinsic merit for it was certainly one of my friend's most instructive cases, and quite unique in many respects."

Thus mollified, our visitor handed over the offending communication which read:

"Here, we are but shadows. 7 p.m."

Our neighbour sat upon the settee with his head thrust forward, looking from one to other of us in a quizzical fashion, whilst Holmes turned over the note. He was undoubtedly gratified at the impression he had made upon us and reverted to the subject of his visit.

"Can either of you tell me what it means?" he asked eventually.

"I suppose you know nothing about any tryst at 7 this evening?" my friend asked.

"That is correct," our visitor replied, "the shop is generally open until eight so I should never have made any such arrangement. Unless the sender means that he is coming to see me. All the same, I don't quite like the look of it."

"Nor do I," said Holmes darkly.

"You've brought the envelope as well I trust?" I asked.

"Yes, here it is," he replied, digging it out of his waistcoat pocket and passing it to Holmes who looked at it, frowned, shook his head slowly, and passed it to me. I noticed that it bore a Surrey postmark.

"Do you have any friends or relations in Surrey? I asked.

"Not a living soul."

"Business acquaintances, perhaps?"

"No. I know no one there."

"I agree that it looks rather menacing," said Holmes, "indeed, I have come across this sort of thing before on a number of occasions, and I am sorry to say that, at first sight, it occurs to me that it might be a precursor to some species of blackmail."

"Blackmail? Ha!" Holles chuckled away merrily. "I should very much like to know what anyone might blackmail *me* about."

"I am sorry to be obliged to be intrusive, Mr. Holles, but if we are to get to the bottom of this, you must be perfectly honest with us: Do you owe anyone any large sums of money?"

"Not at all, I have a healthy balance in the *City and Suburban*. Enough to retire on if I fancied. A few business expenses outstanding perhaps, but nothing that may give rise to concern."

"No jealous husbands?"

Mr. Holles laughed unabashedly for a few moments, "Why, Mr. Holmes, I shall take that as an extreme compliment!" Indeed, he did not strike me as any sort of Lothario.

"Where do you live?"

"11 York Mews-south, not far from the shop."

"And you have remained unmarried since we last spoke."

"Indeed, a confirmed and very happy bachelor."

"Nothing … *untoward* with any of your shop girls or domestic servants?"

"I assure you not. I have no women working in the shop. As for domestic servants, I have only one elderly widow who comes in each day, and if you had met Mrs. Dalton," he raised his eyebrows and smirked conspiratorially, "you should not have to ask that question!"

"Not interested in the turf, by any chance?"

"Wouldn't know the fetlock from the withers."

"Nor drawn to drink?" I asked.

"Total abstainer," he smiled back at me, "and chairman of the Camden and St. Pancras Temperance Association."

He certainly did not take offence easily this upstanding neighbour of ours, around whom an aura of mystery was beginning to form. I looked closely again at both the letter and the envelope and then it struck me.

"Holmes, I believe we are barking up the wrong tree. Look at the address: the first line has been badly smudged either when it was written or at some point in transit. Does it not strike you that what looks vaguely like 'S. Holles, Esq.' may originally have been 'S. Holmes, Esq.'? See how the third and the fourth characters of the surname merge into one another, and into the 'e' too. And in the second line, the number of the street could easily be '221b', not '224'."

"By Jove, I believe you are correct. I see now that the postman has read my name and address incorrectly and delivered it to the bazaar by mistake."

"Then the letter wasn't meant for me, after all?" Holles asked, looking relieved, but also it seemed to me, a little deflated.

"So, it would seem. You are quite unaccustomed, I imagine, to receiving such apocrypha in your morning mail, Mr. Holles."

"I am indeed, though I receive plenty of bills to make up for the lack of such interesting correspondence. Well, that is certainly a weight off my mind. I had best be on my way, so I thank you and am sorry to have needlessly taken up your valuable time – and time is money, sir, as we both know! Just send me an invoice for your fee."

Holmes waved away the suggestion as our visitor departed, and then he returned with curiosity to the extraordinary missive which our neighbour had brought us, though the future would show how ominous this was to be.

"Well, Watson, this is a sow with a different snout! What do you make of it?" he asked, turning to me with an amused expression.

I shook my head. "Is it some sort of cipher?"

"I think not; as you know, there are few ciphers which I am not able to decode with ease."

"I'm afraid I can make nothing of it. *Shadows*. What is meant by that? And who is this innominate 'we'?"

"I cannot say, my dear fellow," he replied with a shrug, "but let us take another look at the envelope. Surely, we shall fare better with that."

"Posted from Horsell in suburban Surrey," I remarked. "A quiet, nondescript little village if my memory serves me. Both letter and note are by the same hand, it appears; a fairly educated hand too, and unless I am mistaken, the writer has not taken any trouble to disguise his handwriting, and thus has no concern as to the possibility of it being recognised by you. Therefore, despite being phrased somewhat cryptically, and sent to you anonymously, I should nevertheless conclude that it is bizarre rather than sinister."

"I think all inferences may be permissible," said my friend, "but we shall return to that. Anything else?"

"Hm. Done with a pen with a narrow-pointed nib."

"Excellent! You are improving."

"Postmarked yesterday at eleven thirty-seven."

"Ah, I have it now, Watson!" my friend interjected.

"You have worked out the identity of the sender already?"

"No, I am afraid I have been unable to add sorcery to my list of accomplishments, Watson. 'We are but shadows' – it's from an Ode by Horace, is it not?"

"Ah yes, so it is. *'Pulvis et umbra sumus'* is the full quotation. You are well up in your Classics, Holmes."

"Book Four I think, though I should not wager much upon it. Horace, I recall, writes at one point about his fellow pupils being crammed with Latin and flogged for idling; it seems little has changed in two millennia!"

"Proof that our man has had some classical education."

"Perhaps, though Horace is common enough; even the Board schools teach Latin."

"And ought we to assume it is, in fact, a *he*?"

"Indubitably; it is a distinctly masculine hand. In any case, no sensible woman would waste paper and ink on such arcana. She would either come straight to the point if it were a matter of material interest, or alternatively employ a litany of euphemisms and evasions if it were an unresolved *affaire de coeur*. Unless it were a case of revenge, of course, in which case she would have knocked Mrs. Hudson's front door down, instead of sending a letter. You will recall the histrionic entrance of Madame Vavasseur when she believed she was being usurped by her governess."

"Only an educated man would know–"

"Now then, Watson, you are getting ahead of yourself. No doubt you already have a mental picture," my friend's eyes twinkled as he spoke, "of some pompous, sardonic, middle-aged professor of Classics amusing himself by scribbling out obscure verse as a prank in order to mystify that famous detective Mr. Sherlock Holmes; following which, this pretentious self-important old fool arrives this evening, promptly at seven, explains his little joke, and presents us with a singular, perhaps slightly abstruse, conundrum entirely free of any criminal connection."

"I must confess, Holmes," I replied, musing how transparent my thought processes often seemed to him, "those were the lines upon which my mind was running. I was at first not sure whether it was a warning or … I suppose *eccentric* was the word that occurred to me."

"Well, I am sorry to disarrange your little *tableau,* but let us start with the paper. Surely you can see that it is not quite the size and shape of standard headed notepaper. In fact, it has been cropped by a sharp knife, not scissors, to eliminate the heading – so that we cannot trace him. However, as it bears the Whitman watermark – the shield is unmistakable – it is likely to be of the type that is more commonly used by a company than an individual, so I should say that there is a business concern of some sort connected to the sender; the envelope is almost certainly from the same stationer since it has the identical watermark. The white laid Whitman, the ink, and the narrow-pointed pen are all of the commonest types, thus I fear your middle-aged professor must vanish into the air Watson, for no self-respecting academic would permit such mediocre stationery to besmirch his study. Unfortunately for us, the very commonness of it will possibly make it all the more difficult for us to trace."

My friend continued, "Would that this were indeed some harmless eccentricity, as you suggest; I detect something menacing in this note; terse as it is, it carries a sense of challenge or defiance. The fact that the sender has not gone to any trouble upon to camouflage his handwriting may equally mean that we are not meant to discover who he is."

"Then why should he ask to meet you at 7 p.m.?" I asked.

"He will send an envoy, perhaps."

"Unless a postscript arrives with further detail."

"I suppose we must entertain that probability." My friend glanced at the clock, "We have five and a half hours in which to labour upon the answer. Now, it is clearly a reference to a place which the sender well knows we can reach by the time stated. Incidentally, a rather sinister aspect of this derives from the fact that he has assuredly taken the trouble to ascertain that Sherlock Holmes is in fact at home."

"You mean we have been watched?!"

"I think it is inevitable. Unless he is a complete crank, then he is unlikely to have sent this invitation without being sure that I am at Baker Street. He cannot know that unless he, or an accomplice, has been observing us. Look at the brown oily fog swirling outside; how easy it would be for all but the most inept bumbler to dog our footsteps, unseen and unheard." I felt something of a shiver at Holmes's words and glanced towards the window, where the houses opposite were barely visible.

Holmes followed my gaze. "There is no point in looking now, he will have departed long ago. It is also surely self-explanatory," my friend continued, "that he thinks we should have little difficulty in finding the place for ourselves."

"Horsell?"

"I think not, rather too obvious. Much closer I should say."

"We are but shadows," I repeated. *"Actually, it should be dust* and shadows. *'Pulvis et Umbra Sumus'*."

"A place where we are but dust and shadows."

"A cemetery?" I suggested.

"Eternally literal, Watson, you should have been a lexicographer! It cannot be that, for there is no indication as to which one amongst all the cemeteries in London."

"In fact, though, he only uses the last two words. There may be some significance in that."

" *'Umbra Sumus';* we have seen that inscription somewhere, have we not?"

"Indeed, I am trying to recall exactly where and when."

"I have it now, Watson! You must surely remember the murder of *Señor* Bracamonte by the Paradol Chamber – it was during our peregrinations in that affair."

I nodded, remembering it only too well though some time had passed, for it had concerned the apparently motiveless killing of the music hall *artiste* Aaron Brauchmann, or Bracamonte by stage name, and I had only recently completed my, as yet unpublished, account of the affair. The tragedy, I recall, was compounded by the fact that it transpired to be a case of mistaken identity of the victim.

"Then you must recollect passing the old Huguenot church at the corner of Fournier Street and Brick Lane," Holmes continued. "Indeed, it was you who pointed out this very inscription above the sundial and the date, 1743, upon it."

"Ah yes, so it was; and you remarked upon your Huguenot forebears who had come to England around that time."

"I believe that is where our man wishes us to be this evening at seven o'clock."

"A strange place for a *rendezvous*."

"Come, Watson, we have had far stranger than that! Remember our meeting with Thaddeus Sholto and his mysterious coachman; think of the hair-raising night at the lock house in Bow Creek."

"What can be behind this?"

"It is impossible to theorise, although I do not anticipate that the appointment has been arranged for social reasons."

"But it is unlikely to be a dangerous affair, surely? After all, no adversary with ill intent should be likely to warn us thus in advance."

"Your logic is impeccable, Watson, yet it is as well to be safe. There is more than a touch of arrogance in his assumption that this curt summons will so overwhelm every other consideration of mine, that I shall simply drop everything and go."

"And yet we cannot ignore it – we are *bound* to go!"

"Yes, we are. All the same have your service revolver at the ready, Watson."

With this dramatic rejoinder, my friend laid down his pipe, sprang out of his chair, and departed the sitting room only to return a few minutes later with a purposeful demeanour, bustling into his overcoat and hat.

"Going out, Holmes?"

"Yes, Watson, and it would be as well for you to be ready to leave at a moment's notice, too."

"But surely seven o'clock is–".

It was too late, for my friend had already disappeared onto the landing. Knowing his habits of mind and his illimitable energy once he had been stirred to action, it was therefore with little surprise that I received the following telegram an hour and a half later:

"Come at once, armed. 3, Heneage Street."

I knew the district of Spitalfields only vaguely and surmised that Holmes had gone to there to reconnoitre the field, though I was baffled as to why he had summoned me so far in advance of our appointment. The street was a turning off Brick Lane and was barely narrow enough to admit the hansom; the fog still hung thick and heavy, and there was little sign of life at that time of day, save for an old rag-and-bone man with his cart. On alighting, I noticed immediately that number 3 was a dingy-looking shop belonging to a beer and spirit retailer, one James Stewart the sign proclaimed, and I began to wonder if this were a hoax. There was, however, a gap between numbers 3 and 5 in the street which turned out to be the entrance to a disreputable-looking terrace yard belonging to a rag merchant's shop, next door to a German wholesaler of string and paper bags.

My first instinct was to race after and recall the cab which was trundling away; after all, I could not be certain that it was Holmes himself who had sent the message, and we had evidence which suggested that 221b was being closely watched. At least I was armed. I began to ponder whether it might have been our unseen, unknown watcher, and not Holmes, who had sent the note when I sensed a movement behind me and a familiar voice whispered, "This way, Watson, and quickly."

I followed my friend through the narrow yard entrance, and along a damp, gloomy, ill-smelling cobbled lane, turning first to the right, then to sharply to the left, finally halting outside the back door of a shop.

"We are now at the chandlery owned by John McCarthy, a thoroughly reliable and trustworthy individual," said Holmes. "You may recall, we rendered him some small service in the episode of the Tired Captain."

"Yes; he said afterwards that you had saved his life."

"He exaggerated somewhat; he was in no mortal danger for I do not believe that Ainsworth would ever have carried out his threat."

"I assume you thought it was to our advantage for us to lie in wait here, so that we should have a view of our adversary when he arrives?"

"Not *we,* Watson, y*ou* shall have the covert view of our adversary."

"Where shall you be?"

"Standing in the open street, waiting for our friend. I do not believe he or his agent will appear until he has first verified that I have turned up to the appointment. All the same, I intend to employ some subtle means of following our man without attracting undue attention, which was why I summoned you to remain behind after McCarthy closes for the day. I have already surveyed the area, including all the approaches to the lane, from the window of a growler and I am convinced that there is no one watching the place at present. Still, it does not do to take chances, especially in these conditions."

"The fog seems to be lifting, though, which ought to make it easier to shadow him."

Despite Holmes's mention of the favour which was implicitly owed to him by the shopkeeper, I had no doubt that he would have commandeered the premises at a handsome remuneration.

"From the vantage point of the shop, which has a large front window and so gives an excellent view of the place, you can observe the lane and the street opposite. It occurs to me that the *rendezvous* point may have been chosen with the express purpose of ensuring that I can be observed by our friend or his accomplice. You will notice how the church door is very well illuminated by the lamp standard opposite. It may be, of course, that he will invite me to join him in a cab in order to repair elsewhere for the continuation of our interview. I cannot anticipate what transaction may occur, nor what turn the events might take, but should I require your assistance, I shall remove my hat, and mop my brow with my handkerchief as a signal.

"After my interview with this party is over, I shall turn on my heel and walk briskly away down Fournier Street without even a backward glance. At that point, I shall leave it entirely to your discretion as to how best to follow our man; but whoever he is, wherever he goes either on foot or by cab, he must not elude you. I have my jarvey friend, John, whom you will recall from our adventure in the Neville St. Clair case, standing by in the yard of the Seven Stars across the way – you see the passage to the right? He has his dogcart and a fresh horse, and he will follow any vehicle as far as you need him to. Use your initiative Watson, I know you will not fail me."

I demurred slightly at this, but Holmes clapped me reassuringly on the shoulder and I endeavoured to display a confidence in my errand which I did not feel. The dusk had already fallen, and it had just gone six o'clock when I took up my position by the front window of the quiet, darkened, and now empty shop. Through the gauze curtains the windows of the chandlery commanded a perfect view of the narrow street opposite; the church where the *rendezvous* was to take place was in fact no more than thirty paces from the shop entrance. I was, as Holmes had said, able to observe every means by which an approach could be made on foot or otherwise. Unseen, I could see all; unheard, I could hear all; I held, or seemed to hold, every advantage as an auxiliary force.

At a quarter to seven I saw Holmes appear, sauntering to the corner where he stopped to light his pipe under the gas lamp. In the darkness and silence, I sat expectantly amongst the tea chests, trunks, ropes, candles and tackle, my eyes riveted upon the street without, my ears cocked for the slightest sound which might herald the arrival of our mysterious correspondent or his agent. I heard only the mice pattering and squealing by the wainscoting. It occurred to me suddenly that, if our mysterious adversary had chosen to arrange matters so, it would be no difficult task for him to pick Holmes off with a single shot and then disappear through the darkness of the lanes and back courts. I hardened my heart and fingered my revolver thinking that, should the worst come to pass, and Holmes were attacked, at least he would not be unavenged. I crept closer to the shop door and listened, my hand on the doorknob, ready to spring.

The bells of Christ Church rang seven, and then the quarter; still no one had appeared. When I had started off on my journey from Baker Street that afternoon I had felt that familiar thrill of anticipation I had experienced on many similar occasions, but I must confess that I now began to be suffused with a feeling of anti-climax at the monotony, and I could sense Holmes's own impatience, though he appeared outwardly calm. Then, as the half hour struck, his hat came off, out came the white handkerchief, and seconds later I was at his side.

"There is no doubt that we shall have to call it off now, Watson," my friend said, "there is little point in remaining here much longer. I am sorry to have brought you out on such a fool's errand."

"I have endured much worse, Holmes. A dozen things may have happened which have caused our man to postpone the meeting. He may have decided for some reason that it was too risky and taken cold feet; or he may have been aware of our preparations to follow him."

"It occurs to me that it may have been our interpretation of the note which was at fault. Perhaps it will turn out to have been nothing more than a prank after all," he shrugged, "a few weeks of this unrelenting foggy weather can play tricks with the imagination."

"One moment, Holmes, you do not think that he may have meant *inside* the church?"

"What an idiot I am, Watson! No one has gone inside in all the time we have been here, and it now dawns upon me that there may well be another entrance at the rear through which he could have entered."

"Shall I return to the shop?"

"No, it is too late, you have exposed yourself now, so you may as well follow me."

The door turned out not to be locked. We stood for a while inside until our eyes become accustomed to the darkness. The church looked derelict; at least, it was evidently not in use, for the pews had been removed in the lower floor and there was a dank smell. It lacked that distinctive odour of incense and candlewax that one always associates with such places; however, Holmes, who had been asking questions of McCarthy, told me that the place had been used by a nonconformist congregation for some decades and was now about to be sold to the Machzikei – a Lithuanian Orthodox group – to be transformed into a synagogue.

It was clear that we were alone, and just as Holmes was about to light his pocket lantern to illuminate the stairway to the gallery, we saw it. The sky had been full of low heavy cloud, which had been gradually clearing, and now a half-moon peeped through the windows and bathed the nave of the church in pale light. At the base of the pulpit by the south wall, there lay a shapeless bundle which looked like a large drugget. On closer inspection it turned out be a tarpaulin.

"What have we here?" my friend whispered.

"Take care Holmes, it could be booby-trapped. I have seen such things done by the Pashtuns in Afghanistan."

Slowly and carefully, Holmes peeled back the edge of the sheet with his walking stick and bent over to look more closely.

I heard a sharp gasp and then he said with an edge to his voice, "This is no prank, Watson."

My mounting sense of foreboding was confirmed, for I saw that the bundle contained a bloodied human torso from which the head and limbs had been rudely and gorily hacked. The shock abated quickly, and I examined the corpse with a professional eye.

"I should say the murder was fairly recent and the dismemberment has been quite crude; it was no doctor who did this," I said.

"Nor even a moderately competent butcher," Holmes agreed in a darkly sardonic tone, "it is quite atrocious."

I mused on the words of the message sent by the killer: *shadows*. It seemed to me now to be eerily apt for this poor fellow who was but now, indeed, a mere shadow.

"Shall I run for a policeman?" I asked.

"There is no rush," Holmes answered, and handed me a whistle. "Go outside and blow this. John will appear from the

Seven Stars. Send him to Scotland Yard and tell him to bring Lestrade back at once." Then he drew out his tape measure and sternly set about his task.

Once Mrs. Hudson had deposited the tea tray on the table and departed, Inspector Lestrade began his report.

"Middle aged, no distinguishing marks, 'Caucasian' it says here, but that's an overly broad description: could be Mediterranean, Levantine, Hebrew, or a sallow-skinned Englishman," said the inspector, in answer to my friend's question. "Dr. Bond is certain that the limbs and head were removed after death."

"Well, that is some consolation," I replied.

"What was the actual cause of death?" asked Holmes.

"Here, I'll read it out:

'I beg to report that I have read the notes of the murder, I have also made a post-mortem examination, at 7:40 this morning of the mutilated partial remains of the man found yesterday inside the derelict church in Fournier Street. All the circumstances surrounding the murder lead me to form the opinion that the limbs and head were removed after death. The separation was conducted by a person lacking not only in basic anatomical knowledge but lacking even the knowledge of a butcher or horse slaughterer, though the instrument used must have been something like an exceptionally large and strong butcher's knife. There appears to be no evidence of struggling; death has not been caused by any injury visible on the corpse, nor, by an examination of the stomach contents and major organs, by the administration of any *known* poison. I cannot form any definite opinion as to the time that had elapsed between the murder and the discovering of the body, but it is certain that the man must have been dead more than twelve hours and the contents of the stomach would indicate that no food had been digested since the previous evening.'

"Impossible to say, therefore, what the cause was," Lestrade went on, "but since there was no poison and the major organs were intact, the likelihood is a blow to the head or strangulation. My colleague, Mr. Gregson, and I had a little discussion about this earlier today. We agreed on one point: you don't normally find male victims dismembered, that's quite unusual; severed head, yes, to avoid identification, but rarely cut up like this. Sadly, gentlemen, it's usually a certain poor unfortunate class of woman that this happens to, and you will no doubt recall what the press called the Thames Torso Murders from seven or eight years ago – they were all women, and going further back the Whitechapel case.. Now, I've brought the list of persons recently gone missing, as you asked. It's surprising the number of reports we get in a week."

"Yes," replied Holmes distractedly, "we shall never know how many murders go undetected and how many murderers go unpunished. London is, amongst many other things, a city of the disappeared." I forbore to add, thinking of his own case, *"and of the reappeared."*

"Leaving aside the obvious cases," said Lestrade bringing us back to earth, "people whom we know are fleeing from justice or from debt, or the ones who've eloped with the barmaid from the Rose and Crown – most of the missing people, perhaps ninety-per-cent, are never found alive. A large proportion are fished out of the Thames, and the Regent's Canal gives up about half a dozen a year, though it can sometimes take a few weeks, sometimes even months, for the bodies to show up in the river due to the tidal movement, by which time proper identification is well-nigh impossible."

"Indeed," I said, "as a medical student I was shown *The Book of the Dead* in the River Police Office at Wapping; it tells a heart-rending tale."

"Three middle-aged men have gone missing in the past couple of weeks: There was the sudden disappearance of Major Maurice Cholmondley of Bleeding Heart-yard, Holborn, who was last seen a fortnight ago in the buffet at St. Pancras Station on his way, allegedly, to a hunting party in the Peak District; he was unmarried with no family, and no debts to his name, at least no official ones. Tenor with St. Etheldreda's Church choir, seems to have been a steady enough character, excellent record in India, no insanity or scandal in the family. Vanished without trace.

"Then there is Dr. Sinclair, the celebrated academic and eccentric, of Hackney Wick. He is an authority on the pagan religions of the ancient Britons and carries on the work begun by the Reverend Duke on the alignment of prehistoric monuments and medieval churches," he shrugged comically, "well, it takes all sorts. Sinclair is known to have a fervent interest in the mystic arts, and he was last seen leaving John Watkins's occult bookshop in the Charing Cross Road one day last week. We've had our eye on him for some time. He's a member of The John Bellingham League—"

"John Bellingham?" I said in surprise. "The fellow who assassinated the Conservative Prime Minister?"

"Yes, they have a society that honours his memory once a year for, as they would have it, 'rendering an important service to the country'!" Lestrade chuckled. "Sinclair was one of its founders and wrote its constitution. A bit cracked, but he seems perfectly harmless. I've kept the best one to the last, gentlemen. The third, and most recent, disappearance is a Mr. James Phillimore, a retired accountant and something of a recluse, with no known relatives in London. Another complete eccentric, he left Bavaria some thirty years ago after doing his military service and had anglicised his name from Jacob Pflaumer; he was last seen on Friday morning by a neighbour, a respectable furniture dealer, Julius Malden, who keeps a warehouse in Princelet Street, near Phillimore's flat which was in Spelman Street."

"*Aha!* A mere street away from where our torso was found?" said Holmes.

"Exactly. Malden says that on the day that Phillimore was last seen, he, Malden, had stepped outside the warehouse to smoke a pipe; he then wandered down to the street corner to stretch his legs, where he met with an old acquaintance outside the Alma public house, and they stopped to talk. They both saw Phillimore come out of the house at number sixty-four, gaze up at the sky as though to gauge the weather and then promptly go straight back inside, presumably to collect his umbrella. Malden finished his pipe whilst talking to his friend, but neither can remember seeing Phillimore coming out again; in fact, he has not been seen since. But here's the oddest thing– I often think over your little sermons, Mr. Holmes, and I know you reckon we fellows at the Yard don't pay enough attention to *apparently* trivial details, but last Friday, the day that Phillimore stepped back inside to collect his umbrella–"

"It had not been raining, nor had any rain been forecast."

"You don't miss much!" Lestrade laughed. "I should say, of the three, Phillimore looks the most obvious candidate going by the description: There's his age, his general build, and skin colouring for the other two are English."

"Possibly. There is the question of motive, however," said Holmes.

"We know about a certain type of killer who will select a victim at random, rather than out of personal animosity – for no logical reason whatever. Sheer sadistic pleasure. With that kind, it's the lack of any connection with the victim that makes them so hard to trace."

"Very true. You say Phillimore was a recluse."

"A very eccentric one, as I said; some of these reclusive types often turn out to live quite, *ahem, colourful* lives, which is one reason why they seek obsessive privacy. We have some files down at the Yard, Mr. Holmes, that would turn your hair white to read them. This Phillimore may have a darker past than his neighbours suspected. You see, we entered his rooms after his reported disappearance and found some very odd things."

"What sort of things?"

"He had a collection of old newspapers, journals, and books in something like twelve different languages, ancient maps marked with strange symbols showing obscure journeys around some of the queerest parts of London. Quite the strangest of the lot, though, were his papers on the Qabbala, an ancient Hebraic mystical tradition which claims to be able to turn base metal into gold and bring inanimate objects to life. This may be some sort of link to this Machzikei crowd."

"How, precisely?" asked Holmes.

"The 'upholders of the law' they call themselves, they are very strict. The fact that the body was left in their synagogue could be the result of some internecine dispute or punishment for transgressions," replied the inspector. "It certainly seems an incredible coincidence."

"The annals of murder, my dear Lestrade, are positively riddled with coincidence; the difficulty is in distinguishing between those which are genuine and those which point to the solution."

"In the absence of any other clue, I think it is a reasonable assumption."

Holmes shook his head. "I cannot agree; for one thing, it has not yet been consecrated as a synagogue," he said. "Secondly, what do we know of the Machzikei? Is this how they settle disputes – by dismembering corpses? It stretches credulity."

"We know extraordinarily little about these foreign groups," said the inspector doggedly, "or what might make them resort to murder. Perhaps Phillimore had broken some sacred taboo or violated the code – you remember what happened to Molesey a few years back when he fell foul of the Bessarabians."

"But this is no ordinary murder, after all. And why should his assassin involve me in the case personally?"

"It is just the very same trait that compels these characters to send letters to the official police, boasting of their actions and defying us to catch them. There have even been cases where they have warned us in advance what they intend to do next – we're always *just* too late to catch them red-handed. Some of these gentlemen are very clever, even if they are insane. If they get satisfaction from goading Scotland Yard, then think how much more they would get from baiting the renowned Sherlock Holmes! Phillimore certainly didn't lack any education, and you thought the sender of the letter was an educated man – isn't that another link between killer and victim?"

"He was certainly educated enough to be familiar with Horace. Yet apparently not affluent enough to use decent stationery."

"Some of Phillimore's indecipherable scribblings were in a language and an alphabet that no one has been able to identify, and which he appears to have invented himself. And his rooms showed that he was living in dire straits: there you have it, erudition and poverty."

"You have an answer for everything," said Holmes judiciously. "Very well then, suppose we take it to be Phillimore as a working hypothesis … ah, I believe our next instalment is about to materialise," said Holmes, as the page interrupted us bearing a small sheaf of letters.

"Thank you, Billy, I was expecting this one."

My friend quickly selected a small white envelope from the pile.

"You may have the honour this time, Inspector."

Lestrade examined the envelope carefully before opening it.

"Surrey again; Woking, this time," he said. "Postmarked yesterday at eleven-twenty. I should think it was a hoax if I didn't know it was from our suburban murderer." The inspector tossed the white sheet on the table, shaking his head in perplexity. The paper's watermark and the handwriting were identical to the previous note, and it read:

"Here, they groan'd aloud."

"I notice he gives no time on this one," said Lestrade.

"By which I take to mean that the goods have already been delivered," I replied.

Holmes nodded grimly in agreement.

"But what does it mean?" asked Lestrade. "He says 'they' – do you think there has been more than one victim?"

"It is something we cannot rule out at this stage," replied Holmes bleakly.

"Another corpse! Good Lord, I hope we are not going to have a whole string of them as we did over the Soho business," I said.

"Or in '88, which was even worse, for we never got the man, though we knew who it was. Is this a reference to the victim's groaning? Does he torture them before killing them?"

"It is impossible to say, though it may be nothing quite as literal as that. What do you say, Watson?"

"I saw no signs of any torture or mistreatment on the torso we found, but who knows what we may find on the limbs or head. Our man is certainly flaunting his learning," I replied.

"Indeed. The quotation, though, is quite straightforward," said Holmes.

"From Blake, is it not?" I asked.

"Yes, it is about Druidic sacrifice: 'they groan'd aloud on London Stone, they groan'd aloud on Tyburn's brook.' Therefore, the allusion could be to the stone or the brook. The Tyburn brook is now culverted over, of course, and runs below ground but the reference may well be to Tyburn as a place of execution: 'Albion's Fatal Tree.'"

"Tyburn? That's near to where Marble Arch is today, isn't it?" said Lestrade. "Yes, the Tyburn Tree and public executions – I know my criminal history! It must be there that he means surely."

"Not necessarily; you see, Blake envisaged the London Stone as a Druidic altar of human sacrifice so it could be either."

"Highly appropriate! But there are no Druids nowadays, and what on earth is the London Stone, and more to the point, *where* is it?" asked the inspector.

"You have never heard of the London Stone?" asked Holmes in surprise.

I must confess that Holmes continually astounded me, not so much by the breadth of his learning – for although a true polymath, his *lacunae* were as remarkable as his store of knowledge – but more by his accumulation of out-of-the-way facts. I mused, however, as I recalled his words on the subject of Scotland Yard detectives: "Given that their profession is one of, essentially, constant inquiry," he had once said, "policemen are generally remarkable for their complete lack of curiosity."

"It is a block of limestone forming part of the foundation of ancient London, thought to date from before the Roman occupation to the time of the Druids," Holmes continued. "It was believed to have had some military significance, perhaps as the exact centre of what was then *Londinium*."

"These notes raise almost as big a puzzle as the murder itself," said Lestrade, looking at Holmes in mixed incredulity and admiration.

"The London Stone is also rumoured," I put in, thinking of the missing Dr. Sinclair's interests, "to have had occult connections going back beyond mediaeval times."

"I have no doubt," said my friend acerbically, "that in a hundred years' time some future Dr. Sinclair will draw a line connecting all the District Messenger Offices in London, discover a pentagram, and assert that there had been some occult significance in their location. Now, to return to our practical problem: the London Stone is presently encased in the south wall of St. Swithin's Church."

"The one in Cannon Street?" asked Lestrade.

"Yes, no doubt you have walked past it many times without realising it."

"Then it's either there or at Marble Arch we need to be."

"That is my interpretation, and so it will be quicker to divide forces. I shall send Billy for two cabs right away: one to take you and Watson to the Arch, and I shall make haste to the City on my own."

We set off in our respective cabs on this grisly reconnaissance, the inspector and I following Holmes as far as Oxford Street, whereupon his hansom bevelled off in the opposite direction towards the City. The thick fog had again descended on the city streets and our cab crawled slowly through the murk. Lestrade and I considered where we should direct our search once we had arrived at our destination, but we were unable to come to any definite conclusion. We soon stood at the front of the great marble edifice, then passed beneath the keystone of the central arch. A crowd was milling around the newspaper boys who were bawling out the headlines of the "Torso" story in the midday editions, and a costermonger was packing up his barrow at the finish of the morning's business. Surveying the scene, we saw nothing resembling the package which we were expecting. Off to our left, however, was a stone terrace fronted with seating. Behind this was a shallow raised area where low, thick bushes grew. Lestrade nodded in this direction, and we strolled across and climbed through.

"Seems as likely a place an anywhere else," he said, but despite combing the area for a quarter of an hour we did not find what we were looking for. We withdrew, to some queer looks from passers-by, and I noticed immediately that the costermonger had abandoned his barrow.

"Under the cart," I said, pointing. "Look! He has left something behind."

There was a bundle wrapped in brown paper beneath the axle of the cart. Lestrade knelt down and slashed at one end with a penknife; as the package unfurled, we saw that it contained a hirsute male arm. It was a hundred to one that the limb was from the torso which Holmes and I had found the previous night. I hurried off to fetch a uniformed constable and caught one easily enough by Hyde Park Corner. Once Lestrade explained to him how he should deal with the incident, we made straight for the City to inform Holmes of our find.

It turned out that we need not have rushed, for a similar discovery to ours had been made just before Holmes had arrived at Cannon Street, parcelled up in the same way as the arm and torso we had already found. It had been spotted in a dark corner of St. Swithin's church just prior to the midday service by the warden who raised the alarm at once. The morning newspapers had been full of the "Torso in the Transept" case – albeit, as Holmes, ever pedantic, pointed out, the church in Brick Lane *had* no transept – so that the warden had entertained little doubt as to the likely contents of the strange bundle and had called the police immediately. The City constable, Humphreys, who had been summoned to the scene of the outrage was overwhelmed. Before the poor man had had time to collect his thoughts far less report the discovery, the celebrated Sherlock Holmes had descended upon the scene, soon followed by Scotland Yard. Humphreys, in turn, had called in his inspector from the City force. Lestrade's condescending demeanour towards the City men, and his pompous remarks to them about "prior information received from an exceptionally reliable but completely confidential source," were almost comical to see and hear. The policemen and I waited and watched as Homes took a brief measurement of the arm and then made a quick note in his notebook.

"Well," said Lestrade with a wry smile when Holmes was finished, "the doctor and I have our own little tale to tell. To put it shortly, our suburban friend delivered the other arm to us in a nice little parcel up at the Arch. I had to send it to the city morgue so you had better come along with me and examine both arms there, though I suspect they will merely confirm what we already know."

It was some time before the mortuary van arrived to remove the gory relic from the church, by which time St. Swithin's Lane was beginning to throng with onlookers. The press too had begun to arrive in packs, and we three slipped away, leaving the unfortunate City inspector and his constable to confront the curious public.

At the mortuary, an attendant produced the arm which Lestrade and I had discovered earlier; a slight mottling was now evident due to the time elapsed since death; Holmes, characteristically, had no qualms about examining the hideous objects minutely. He was busy for a few moments with the tape measure and magnifying glass, then he turned to Lestrade.

"It would be especially useful," he said, "if we could obtain further, more accurate data on this man Phillimore. I recall that you told me that he was an accountant. I should say that this fellow has done a fair degree of manual work in his day, a weaver or something similar; I can tell that from the roughness of his hands."

"He may have done manual work before that, or while studying for the examinations, and then went on to become an accountant afterwards," I pointed out.

"That is certainly possible."

"It certainly cannot be Major Cholmondley, since he would be highly unlikely to have done any manual labour."

"Or Dr. Sinclair, surely?" I added

"I am not so sure about Sinclair. Although a qualified doctor, he has never practised as such. Something of a Bohemian, he has been known to take menial jobs apparently by choice to eke out a living. He has worked in bookshops and taverns, he was a jarvey for a while, and has been known to handle a shovel. We cannot rule him out," said Lestrade. "Anything else?"

"Although having been a manual worker," Holmes continued, "this fellow's physique is not, overall, a particularly athletic one. Therefore, I would suggest a sedentary occupation. The callosities which I have observed on his hands, are somewhat faded, which might support a theory that he may have changed his profession but could mean equally that he has been out of work, or at least out of his own line, for some time. The pattern would suggest to me either a tailor or, just possibly, a sailmaker; the former is a common trade in Whitechapel and Spitalfields and the latter in the dockside areas. If he had been a sailmaker, then he was he was of the landlubber type, and not one that sailed with a ship for there is nothing to suggest a life at sea; therefore, he may have been attached to, or worked for, a ship's chandler.

"On the whole, though, the balance of probability inclines towards his having been a tailor at some point in his life. There is a suggestion that he was left-handed, going by the more calloused epidermis of the left index finger and thumb as a result, I suspect, of repetitively handling a pair of cloth shears. I should say nothing publicly in the meantime, Lestrade, but have your plain clothes men make tactful inquiries in the districts I mentioned. Find out what Phillimore did before becoming an accountant and a photograph of him would be useful too. However, allow the press to believe that you are still completely in the dark as to the victim's identity."

"What of the sender of these messages, Mr. Holmes, do you take him to be the same person as the murderer?"

"Undoubtedly."

"He has some peculiar traits, has he not?" I said. "He is classically read, for he knows Horace; perhaps a dissenting strain, for he has read Blake; egotistical to the last degree."

"A madman, surely?" said Lestrade."

"Possibly, possibly not. If he is a lunatic, then he does not lack method; but I do predict that this unrestrained egotism of his will tempt him into a fatal error at some stage."

"Someone from the criminal underworld surely?"

"It is difficult to be certain. Burying the body in wet concrete or in some disused railway tunnel is a more likely end to the typical underworld murder, than the public baiting of Sherlock Holmes; but then everything about this case puts it well beyond the typical. Most murderers want to hide their victim's corpse, but here …"

"We know that the notes were sent from two adjacent villages in Surrey," said Lestrade, "but I am undecided as to whether this is a blind. In all probability, he lives somewhere on the other side of London, and the Surrey postmark is designed purely to mislead us."

"Normally, I should be inclined to agree with you, Lestrade, but there is an arrogance and narcissism about his correspondence; in making no attempt to disguise his handwriting, he is saying to me, 'I need not worry, for Sherlock Holmes will never find me.'"

"Do you suspect there *is* some connection in Surrey?"

"I think it is likely that his choice of post box is determined more by expedience than anything else, although it is noticeable that he appears to have avoided sending his notes from exactly the same place two days running."

"Then I shall make my way out there directly," said Lestrade.

"There is more to come," I said, "we can only await the morrow."

"Indeed," replied Holmes, with a rueful frown. "'To-morrow, and to-morrow, and to-morrow'."

The next day's post did indeed rouse us from our petty pace and presented us with the most difficult conundrum yet. The note, posted in Byfleet, Surrey, at ten-forty simply read:

"Here, the thirteenth bell never pealed."

Holmes looked at me with a wry smile.

"The same paper and handwriting. It may or may not be significant," he said, "but, unless my geography fails me, the sender's point of despatch is getting closer each time."

"That is correct, Holmes, I know the area fairly well, as I have a few cricketing friends down that way. I notice too that the postmark times are a slightly earlier each day."

"Indeed. Well, I am afraid our correspondent has the better of me this time."

"The Thirteen Bells sounds like a public house does it not? Or, perhaps, like Seven Dials, it may be a local by-name for some district," I said.

"In fact," said Holmes, "there is a public house called the 'Ten Bells' not a hundred yards from the church where we found the torso, but I know of no 'Thirteen Bells' or more correctly, 'Thirteenth Bell' and my knowledge of London is not only quite complete, but pretty exact and up to date too."

"Then what?"

He paused to light his pipe before answering and sat for a few minutes in studious silence, the smoke from his old clay pipe curling up to the ceiling.

"Come, Watson, it is obvious in which sort of building we should find thirteen bells, is it not?" he said at length, as a smile of enlightenment illuminated his features.

"The Whitechapel Bell Foundry."

"Very good."

"It is in Plumber's Row, which is only a few streets from–"

"Yes, but does it hold exactly thirteen bells? Not twelve, not fourteen?"

"I see what you mean."

"But if I were to ask you, where do the bells cast in the Whitechapel Bell Foundry usually end up?"

"In a church, of course."

"Exactly."

"Another church! Do you think there is some religious or ritual element to this?"

"It is still rather early to draw any definite conclusions. But the question is, how do we determine which bell the sender of the message indicates?"

"It may be the thirteenth bell which the foundry had produced or something of that nature?"

"I think that is a possibility. Only a trip to Plumber's Row will determine that."

The manager of the foundry, Mr. Alfred Lawson, shook his head vigorously. "I am afraid it doesn't make any sense to me. It would be impossible to say. You see, the thirteenth bell which this foundry produced could have been as long ago as the reign of George III. The records possibly do not go that far back, and I shouldn't know where to find them if they did exist. Why do you want to know?"

Holmes gave a brief but informative reply and continued, "What if I were to ask you about the thirteenth bell you produced this year?"

"I could look in the sales ledger, I suppose," said Mr. Lawson, "give me a few minutes."

He returned to the office a short while later with some jottings on a sheet of paper. "Dead heat for thirteenth place," he remarked drolly. "A whole instrument of twelve was despatched to St. Mary's Episcopal Church, Philadelphia, on the same day as a new six hundredweight tenor went out to St. George-in-the-East in Wapping. That's only ten minutes down the road from here."

As I have noted elsewhere, Holmes kept what he called his "uncommonplace book": a collection of the city's unexplained occurrences and strange discoveries, often suppressed by officialdom, many of which had passed into folklore. One of the entries concerned reports of a secret passage beneath London, now abandoned, linking the churches designed by Hawksmoor, one of which was St. George's. *En route* to the church, he mentioned the missing Dr. Sinclair in connection with this.

"I made it my business to hunt down some of Sinclair's obscure writings. He certainly has an obsession with the darker side of church-building and seems to believe, using Hawksmoor's buildings as examples, that there are elements within the designs which go beyond the use of Hebraic symbolism for aesthetic purposes. So far beyond it, that he reads the codes and sigils as a veritable palimpsest of the covert conflict between two factions struggling, as it were, for ascendency: the ideals of the enlightenment and the pagan anti-intellectualism of the occult."

"Surely a bit far-fetched, Holmes."

"I am not so sure: despite his eccentricity his research has certainly yielded some interesting questions: how does one explain the six sacrificial altars on the roof of St George's, for example? The obelisks and pyramids in his other church precincts? The pagan temple of Bacchus in the church in Bloomsbury? Where is the cross of Calvary amongst all this? It is nowhere to be seen."

"It is certainly difficult to reconcile such imagery with traditional Anglican belief and yet, Hawksmoor was perhaps the most acclaimed sacred architect of his age."

"The greatest evil, Watson, comes often from the corruption of good; Lucifer was an angel; Judas was an apostle. It occurred to me that, as the murder has a connection with three churches, it is at least reasonable for us not to eliminate Sinclair as a potential victim quite yet."

"But what would be the motive in this case?"

"It is impossible to say. There are several orders of *illuminati*, small clandestine hermetic sects whose members are continually in discord over arcane dogma. Sinclair's interest may have inclined him towards one of these secret cabals. Occasionally, they enforce discipline in the ultimate manner. Equally, as an outsider, he may, during his research, have stumbled across some secret that they wish to preserve."

We were unable to speak to the rector at St. George's, the Reverend Turner; however, one of his curates made us welcome once we had apprised him of the reason for our visit.

"I am afraid this church has had its share of brutal murders over the centuries," he began, "not least its association with the appalling Ratcliff Highway outrages. The members of the Marr family are buried here, including the three-month-old child who was butchered. The parish never lived down the reputation, I am afraid; the former rector once showed me some of the newspaper clippings in his scrap book from 1811. One said, 'God has left Wapping': so it must have seemed at the time. If what you suggest is correct, this will evoke agonizing remembrances, and I hope it is not the beginning of another orgy of murder."

"It is impossible to say at present," replied Holmes, "so far we only know of one death. Is the church open during the day?"

"It is always open for those who have need for it."

"Then perhaps we should …"

The curate led us into the cold damp church, where the three of us examined every inch of the place for the best part of an hour but found nothing. Holmes suggested searching the crypt next; however, the curate explained that it had, since the days of the Burkers, been made as secure as any bank vault, and it was impossible that anyone could have entered through several locks without the sexton, or someone else, noticing.

"Unless I am mistaken," said my friend at last, "the church tower is topped with six sacrificial Roman altars, is it not?"

"That is correct; they are rather famous and attract scores of visitors, including many from abroad, especially from the eastern states of America."

"A somewhat curious choice for an Anglican church," I said.

"Yes. Surely you don't think ..."

"It occurred to me, given the nature of the crime we are investigating, that a sadistic murderer might see it as an apt place," said Holmes.

It was a steep climb up the narrow steps, and I realised how out of condition I had become as I arrived breathless on the roof above the tower. On a clearer day there would have been striking views, up and down the river, with Parliament Hill to the north and the undulating North Downs looking southwards; but on this dull foggy morning one could not even view the pavement below. There was nothing for us to see on the bare white altars, though Holmes persisted.

"I noticed on the way up," he said, "that we passed a door just above the level of the bell tower. What is it used for?"

"It is a tiny room actually, and it is unused. No one knows for which purpose it was built; I think it may have been more architectural than practical, though I suppose you would need to consult the original plans drawn up by architect himself to find out. No one ever goes there, and I have never actually been in it myself. It has no lock, so let us take a look."

As the curate had said, the chamber was very small with barely standing room, though it was well lit by semi-circular windows from roof to ceiling. But it was empty. Again, as at the foundry, we had drawn a complete blank, and Holmes apologised to the curate for having disturbed him.

"Do you not think we ought to have forced the issue and examined the crypt?" I asked Holmes as we sat in our cab later heading westwards.

"You may be right, Watson, and in the event that we do not discover this thirteenth bell, that must always be our last resort, including, if necessary, recourse to a legal warrant from Lestrade.

Our assailant has used opportunistic means to find places to leave us his gory relics; so far, on every occasion he has used places which are open and public. To get into St. George's crypt he would need several keys. No, I think we have misinterpreted the message this time, but not wildly. It now occurs to me that the wording indicated a place where, for some reason, one of the thirteen bells had never rung."

"You still believe it relates to a church?"

"My imagination may be failing me, but apart from a foundry I can think of no *other* place that might have thirteen bells.'

"Then how can we find out which churches have thirteen bells far less one that didn't ring?"

"By taking a lesson in campanology," Holmes said with a smile.

"Of course, there must be some sort of gazetteer of churches ... I'm sure I've seen it, yes, the Bell Ringers Guild has some sort of reference book. I seem to remember Thurston mentioning it once."

"'Betterton's Belfries,'" he interjected. "That should have been my first port of call, instead I have wasted a whole morning looking for a mare's nest."

"'Betterton's Belfries,' that's the one, Holmes! We ought to consult it, then. We can ask the jarvey to drop us in the Charing Cross Road, or that little bookshop in Church Street, so that we can buy a copy," I said reaching for the trapdoor to redirect the cabman.

"I think we can do rather better than that, Watson."

"How?"

"By repairing to the parish church where we may catechise the author on his knowledge of campanology."

"The *author?* You mean Mr. Betterton himself?"

"I mean Gabriel Betterton, a prince amongst change-ringers. There is scarcely a church bell in the diocese which he has not personally rung: Plain Bobs, Quarter Peals, Grandsires, and Cinques are as the air of life to him, and his knowledge of church history is immense. He is presently gathering subscriptions to establish an organisation, the Bell Ringer's Guild, and he has penned a number of historical works including one which traced the origin of bell-ringing right back to the early Celtic church. His 'Campanologist's Companion' is every bit as renowned as 'Betterton's Belfries' throughout the English-speaking world and beyond, and every bell-ringer worth his salt has a copy of the manual. A man after my own heart insofar as dedication to his art goes and, what's more, he is an old friend of the Holmes family."

I gazed at Holmes in amazement at this new revelation. Our cabbie dropped us on Marylebone Road in the chilly, smoky, November smog as Holmes recounted how Betterton had been a school friend of his father, Sheridan Holmes.

"They were both born the year after Wellington's crushing of Bonaparte's forces at Waterloo, went to school together, and never lost touch until my father's death. Betterton's health had failed in early manhood and, almost crippled at one point by heart trouble in the wake of rheumatic fever, he had never recovered sufficiently to complete his studies in divinity, nor to attain his ordination. He has, nevertheless, remained close to his calling by combining the responsibilities and duties of churchwarden, sexton, and verger at St. Mary-Le-Bourne, in addition to his role as the captain of the bell ringers."

At the corner of Marylebone High Street the newsboys were shouting out the latest headlines: "Arms Found in Torso Case," and at Oldbury Place we turned into the precincts at the rear of the parish church and found the sexton tending the church gardens. He was an elderly man of bright complexion with that eternally boyish look about him, which is so often the case with persons who have been sheltered in the bosom of the church away from the trouble and bustling toil of secular life. A tall, spare man, with a very erect bearing, his hair was completely white and though now approaching eighty, to observe his carriage and demeanour, one would have guessed sixty-five at most. He welcomed Holmes like a long-lost son, with twinkling eyes and a childish delight.

"My dear Sherlock, how simply *wonderful* to see you again. The last time, let me see ... it was over the Cleveland Street case. And this must, of course, be Dr. Watson, very pleased to meet you." He wrung my hand with surprising strength for a man of his age.

"I have read all of your wonderful stories, Doctor, though I confess I should not have recognised you from the photographs. But what brings you to our humble parish, Sherlock?"

"I believe you may be able to shed some light on a most difficult case," said Holmes.

"*Ex tenebris lux!*" he chuckled. "Splendid! Well, it would be more that I could wish for to be able to assist in yet another of your celebrated adventures. It must be this headless corpse in the church business? I saw the headlines in *The Globe* the other evening. Abominably wicked. Is it to do with the connection to the church, or rather the two churches?"

"It is precisely about that, Gabriel, perhaps a third church."

"Can you tell me whether the murder was actually committed in St. Swithin's? The newspapers were rather vague about that."

"I am as certain as it is possible to be that it was not."

"Then that is some small consolation. You see, the church would have to be re-consecrated if that were so and my good friend, Godwin, from the Worshipful Company of Parish Clerks at St. Swithin's, would have been quite distressed. In what way do you think I could assist?"

"It is a rather curious inquiry, Gabriel, for I am trying to discover whether there is a church in the London Diocese which has thirteen bells. As you are the most knowledgeable and eminent person in the field …"

"Thirteen bells? In the Diocese of London?" he shook his head firmly, "No, there is none. An unusual number; apart from anything else it might be considered by some to be unlucky too."

"Even by clergymen who are not supposed to entertain pagan superstition?" asked Holmes impishly.

Betterton laughed. "The number of bells in the tower would normally relate largely to the size of the belfry, obviously, and at one time, to the status of the church. Until the eighteenth century, few churches would have had more than five or six, such as you would expect to see in a small church today. A larger church such as St. George-in-the East or Christ Church would have a peal of eight; there are ten in St. Dunstan's, and St. Paul's and Southwark Cathedral have twelve each. Of course, they would all have separate service bells, but there are few tower captains who could boast twelve or more bells at their disposal. But why do you ask – is the number of bells of some special significance?"

"Yes. It may be a clue to where some more body parts are hidden."

The old sexton looked pained, and his brow clouded.

"This person seems to have an almost diabolical obsession with churches. But what exactly is this clue?"

Holmes handed him the note we had received.

"Pealed," Betterton said, "*past tense*. You said a church in the London Diocese, but I see now that you spoke geographically, of course. Yes, there once was a London church noted for its thirteen bells: It had a standard twelve bells with an additional tenor added, which was actually too large to be rung by one person. That may be the meaning – that bell never *pealed* as we bell-ringers would say, it *chimed*; that is, it had to be struck with a mallet; that might very well be your thirteenth bell. You mentioned pagan superstition: The bells, intriguingly, were rung *widdershins* – that is, anti-clockwise, which is also unusual. It was the Ulrika Eleanora Swedish Church which was built by the High Church Lutherans in the Wellclose precinct in 1729. The Swedes retained greater use of ceremony and ornate furnishings than their more traditional Scandinavian counterparts, hence the lavish provision of bells. You have surely heard the name of Emanuel Swedenborg?"

Holmes shook his head.

"I have heard that name, Swedenborg," I replied. "I seem to recall it from my undergraduate days. I am sure that he published some of the very earliest works on the cerebral cortex."

"Yes. And he lived in the Wellclose precinct, worshipped in that church adjacent to the square that now bears his name – the one with the thirteenth bell – and was buried in the churchyard."

"He was thought to have been a century ahead of his time," I said.

"Indeed, he was at one and the same time both a century ahead of his time and several centuries behind it! He had written numerous learned treatises on medical subjects, including the one to which you refer, as well as predicting the invention of such things as automatic guns, submarine boats, and flying machines. Although something of an eccentric in theological matters, he was nonetheless well regarded by his peers in the scientific community. He was a man of mighty visions and believed that God spoke to him personally. Of course, that is not entirely uncommon in the more, *ah*, chiliastic denominations. He also, by his own account, visited heaven and hell, conversed with the archangels and the devil, and once took a trip round the solar system. But that is a story which we shall keep for another day."

"May the public visit this church at Swedenborg Square?" asked Holmes.

"I am afraid that would be impossible."

"Why?"

"Because it was demolished some years ago, at the time when the Scandinavian community began to move away from the area to the wealthier suburbs of the west. Indeed, many of them returned to their native land."

"That rather disarranges our theory, then."

"Ah, but the churchyard remains as it was, although I believe it is, indeed, an unweeded garden that grows to seed and is rank with nettles for there is, sadly, no one in the community to tend it any longer. It is full of old neglected crypts ..."

Holmes sent a wire to Lestrade from the post office in Upper Wimpole Street, and then we hailed a cab on Marylebone High Street, arriving just as the fog had begun to deepen, snaking wraith-like up towards us from the river. The gas lamps were being lit, and by what little light they threw it was just possible to make out the roofs of the dark, sooty, weather-boarded buildings, mostly seedy looking lodging houses, which enclosed the square, now deserted except for a wizened old woman with a shapeless bundle on a cart who looked as though she might be going to the public wash house.

Where the church had once stood in the middle of the square, there was but an empty, overgrown plot of clayey soil and broken brick to be seen, interspersed with faintly visible broken and flattened tombstones. On entering the churchyard from the west side, I noticed that many of the tombs were lying open and empty, and I was assailed momentarily by the shocking idea that the place had been desecrated by grave-robbers. Holmes reassured me, however, with some amusement on his part, that it was rather more likely that the remains from the crypts had been transferred for re-interment. All the same, it made a dismal impression upon me, for the whole place was damp, fusty, and unkempt, with many of the headstones overturned, lending it a desolate and abandoned air, and at our approach, two long, plump greasy-looking dark-bodied rats scurried across the path in front of our feet and slunk into the undergrowth. There remained just enough daylight to see by, and it did not take us long to find the grisly object of our journey. By a derelict crypt; in a corner, obscured by the deepening gloom, lay the, by now, familiar-looking package.

"We may as well go ahead, without waiting for Lestrade," I suggested.

Holmes set about the grisly chore and sedulously unwrapped the folds of the canvas to reveal a pair of human legs.

"Adding together the measurements from the torso," he said eventually, putting away his tape measure and consulting his notebook, "and assuming no unusual features of neck and head, I should say height about five foot ten."

"Which tallies with Phillimore," I replied; "Sinclair is rather taller. I notice you measured both–"

"Firstly, to confirm that the legs were from the same corpse – one should not make unwarranted assumptions – there may be more than one victim, as Lestrade has already suggested. And secondly, to see if there were any discrepancy in the length of the legs which would give rise to some irregularity in gait through which he might be identified."

"The legs do not appear to be of the athletic type," I said, "which is consistent with the sedentary occupation you mentioned, but there are no further indications."

"What do you think of the feet, Watson?"

"Fallen arches, quite pronounced."

"I noticed that. It would argue against his having done military service."

"Not necessarily, as he may have developed them in later life."

"Good point. Well, we have seen enough here."

I looked in vain in the area to find a telegraph office in order to send a wire to Scotland Yard and, in the end, I resorted to asking the landlord of the Blue Anchor in Ship Alley to send a messenger. I then returned to wait in the dreary deserted churchyard. As darkness fell around us and the fog thickened, it was a grim wait and a cold one, and I was glad of my hip flask. Eventually we heard the hooves and wheels of a carriage and horses, then Lestrade emerged from the darkness with a small entourage to take charge of the proceedings. He had been able to procure a rather out of date photograph of Phillimore which he gave to Holmes. There was little else to say, and we decided to leave him to his task.

"We shall know soon enough whether or not it is Phillimore," said Holmes, "the greatest is yet to come,"

"The final instalment," I murmured.

"A most extraordinary affair," said Lestrade dolefully, looking glummer than ever. "Never seen nor heard of a case quite like it,"

Holmes shook his head. "It has all been done before: James Greenacre, the Camberwell murderer, hanged in 1837. Body parts concealed on both banks of the Thames, in Edgware, in Cold Harbour Lane, and in Regent's Canal; and Fanny Adams, Hampshire, 1867, dismembered, disembowelled, and strewn across a hop garden, a flower meadow, and the banks of a river," was my friend's parting shot to the amazed and speechless Lestrade.

It was very late by the time we arrived back at Baker Street. An envelope, which bore the hallmarks of the preceding correspondence, albeit somewhat bulkier in size, had been placed on our sitting room table. There was no postmark, so it had been delivered by hand. Mrs. Hudson denied all knowledge of it and said that she had been out most of the evening at the music hall and had just returned which meant, of course, that 221b had been empty for a period. Our watcher must have taken his chance then, knowing we were at the deserted churchyard. Holmes proceeded to extract the contents. There was the usual handwritten note, but in addition there were four very hazy photographs which had obviously been taken in poor light. Though badly blurred, it was not difficult to pick out the figures of Holmes and I standing at the opening of the passage in Heneage Street; Lestrade and I beside the costermonger's cart at Marble Arch; Holmes outside St. Swithin's in Cannon Street; and finally, most chilling of all, Holmes and pausing at the gate of the churchyard near Swedenborg Square. It is not often that I have seen my friend struck dumb, but he was lost for a single word on this occasion.

"My dear Holmes, our instincts were correct all along; he *has* been watching us, dogging our footsteps," I remarked with a shudder of horror, for I felt as though this invisible adversary were deriving as much perverted gratification from our discomfiture as from the murder itself. "Perhaps he is near us now, somewhere – laughing at us."

"There is little doubt about that, Watson."

"And yet his campaign of terror cannot be directed against us personally, after all, he has had ample opportunity, had he wanted, to finish us off with a rifle or revolver shot if that were his object; I thought as much when I sat watching you from McCarthy's chandlery; he could have booby-trapped the bundle in the church and blown us both to pieces." I strolled across to the window and peered out but saw nothing. "If only we could lay our hands on him, yet what can we do in this yellow smog! It is impossible even to see the houses across the street at night."

"He has certainly enjoyed all the advantages of the terrain," Holmes said, philosophically. "Of course, our Thames fogs have been shrouding the nefarious activities of London's felons since Roman times: There is nothing new under the sun."

"What can his object be in drawing you into this intrigue?" I asked.

Holmes shrugged. "His motive continues to elude me. Well, let us see what little puzzle he has for us now." He looked at the note and passed it across to me with a grimace.

"Here, five ancestors sleep."

"Well, Holmes, I think he may have us beaten this time. I have not the ghost of an idea what he is getting at."

"Nor have I."

"One's ancestors 'sleep' in a graveyard or in a churchyard do they not? More churches and graveyards ... should we find it in the Bible or the almanac?"

"I am not sure. Perhaps neither. What relevance do ancestors have?"

"We worship them, do we not?"

"Less of the 'we,' Watson."

"I was speaking of the human race as a species. Many primitive peoples still to this day perform such rituals, even in Europe. Very grotesque and sinister practices too, and I can certainly recall tales from my days at the diggings in Victoria which would shock the average Englishman."

"Historically, as you say, it is almost a universal trait."

"And yet this is London, Holmes, the epitome of civilisation and progress. We have no aboriginals here, few Africans, few primitive American peoples."

"But we have a throng of Asiatics in the dockside areas: Chinese, Indians, and Malays, most of whom are seamen. There are whole districts given over to them: Lascars in Shadwell and Wapping; the Sailors Home for Asiatics, Africans, and South Sea Islanders in the West India docks; Chinese in parts of Limehouse and Pennyfields. No, Watson, I think we shall eliminate Whitaker and your book of Holy Writ and take a more practical line. Have you ever heard of Elphinstone's Riverside Emporium?"

"Never."

"I am surprised, for it is one of the queerest spots in London even by the standards of the riverside. It is part menagerie and part curiosity shop; you can buy a tiger cub or a cheetah, an anaconda, a scorpion, even a bear. If your tastes do not run to cohabitating with animals which can eat you, tear you limb from limb, or cause you a slow excruciating death through paralysis, you might be satisfied with a shrunken human skull, a two-headed calf, elephant tusks, or a heathen relic which is either unlucky, dangerous, or fatal to possess; not to mention some of the strangest substances known, or more interestingly, unknown, to man. Much of Elphinstone's stock in trade originates with sailors bringing these things from one or other tropical outpost of the Empire. If Elphinstone has not seen it, or heard of it, it probably does not exist, and he has a knowledge of curios and semi-forbidden lore that would astound most academics in the field. His shop is off the Ratcliff Highway and if you are game for it, we can be there first thing in the morning."

The Riverside Emporium was exactly as Holmes had described. Tucked away amongst the colossal warehouses at the bottom of New Gravel Lane off the busy Highway, its broad front was one of a row of brightly painted shops which included ships' chandlers, rope-makers, butchers, pawn-brokers, tripe-sellers, bakers, musical instrument makers, tailors, and carpenters catering to the maritime population. It was a district I remembered well for Holmes and I had had a brush with death in a basement in Cinnamon Street during the affair of the Amateur Mendicant Society. There was a chalk-written list outside the door; I provide only a brief example:

> *"Tigers £300*
> *Elephants £300*
> *Lions £100*
> *Zebras £100*
> *Baboons £80*
> *Ostriches £80*
> *Giraffes £40*
> *Polar Bears £25*
> *Camels £20*
> *Leopards £20"*

I may say that the denizens of the emporium were certainly in character with the merchandise. We were greeted by a small, humpy, bespectacled fellow in a brown dustcoat, whose thick black hair seemed to sprout from everywhere: from under his cloth cap, from the collar on his neck, from his nose, from his ears, and from the backs of his hands which were like a monkey's paws. His manner, however, was bright and friendly, and he had a wonderfully piercing pair of eyes. He bore the air of someone who wanted you to know that he had seen everything and dared you to shock or surprise him.

"Well, gennelmen, what c'n I do you for today?" he said briskly, slipping his pencil behind one very hirsute ear.

My friend introduced himself and the odd little man stared back at him.

"Sherlock 'Olmes, did you say? You 'avin' me on? I've read orl abaht you in one o' them illustrated papers – 'Ound O' the D'Urbervilles, or summat. Funny thing is – I didn't know you reely existed!" he said in surprise. "I thort you was one o' them literary detectives aht of a novel, y'know like Martin Yewitt or 'Orace Dorrington."

Holmes smiled sardonically, "And, yet here I am! My existence has been cursed by many but never actually doubted," he said, handing over his card, which the man read:

Sherlock Holmes Esq. M.A. (Oxon)
Private Consulting Detective
221b Baker Street
London, England

"'Ere … this ain't an 'oax is it?" the man replied, peering at Holmes suspiciously. "It ain't young Lemmy up to 'is ol' tricks again? You should 'ave seen the one 'e pulled on us wiv the Egyptian mummy. Nearly gave me and the missus an 'eart attack when it got up an' walked abaht durin' the night – we live above the shop, see, as Mr. Elphinstone 'as to 'ave somebody on the premises at orl times in case one o' them lovelies aht the back escapes," he nodded towards the cages outside.

"I suppose you will not be troubled by burglars, then," I replied.

"No, we got the opp'site problem. We 'ad a tigress escape once, grabbed a small boy, she did, and off she lopes up the 'Ighway wiv 'im. I fahnd an iron crowbar is an uncommon good argument against an 'ungry tigress, so the boy was orlright; well, more or less. Cost us a bob or two to 'ush the thing up, mind you. Then there was a chimpanzee got out and stole the parson's 'at an' stick an' strolled into 'The White Swan' like one of the customers goin' for a jar – 'onestly. And, o' course, bein' eddicated gennelmen, you must 'ave 'eard of the poet 'oo wrote an elegee abaht the wombat we sold 'im wot died. Nah then, what you arter?"

"Some information."

"That's easy given and free too – no charge for advice. You'd be surprised at some the things we get arsked about: 'Ow much does a full-grown lion eat; 'ow do you tame a baboon; do we 'ave an antidote for cobra bites, an'," here he paused for effect and winked, "'Ave we got any poisons wot the p'lice don't know abaht!"

"We are looking for something much more prosaic: It is an allusion which we think may have some connection to the Orient."

"I s'pose you mean the place an' not the football club?" he grinned. "Go on."

"It is a reference to 'five ancestors': where they sleep."

"I've 'eard that expression somewhere before, definitely sounds sort o' Chinese, maybe Japanese, not sure. But I'll tell you the man 'oo *will* know exackly – Dr. Bower-Dalton, 'e's one o' them china-ologists."

"A sinologist," I put in helpfully.

"Any roads, 'e's the one you want. 'E's bought a few things 'ere, curios an' the like; anything Chinese comes in, we let 'im know right away, first refusal y'know. Good customer, pays regular, money no object."

"Where can we find him?" I asked.

"Dahn the 'Ighway 'alf a mile or so, get to 'Orseferry Road turn right, then sharp left. Keep on a bit, then a couple o' doors past *The Bunch O'' Grapes* – y'know the one wot Dickens made famous – number 88, nice big 'ouse. Folk there always makes us a nice cup o' char when we drops the doctor's deliveries off.

Funny sort o' stuff, lapdog sampan or summat, comes in a bowl an' always tastes as 'ow someone's forgot to put the tea in; still, it's the thort that cahnts."

"Thank you, you have been most helpful."

"Don't mind if I keep this, do you?" he held up Holmes's card at which he gawked, "or the missus'll never b'lieve I've ackshally met you!"

We wandered on by tall narrow terraced houses that leant at impossible angles, and past wild-looking taverns half hanging over the river, through streets which resounded to the sound of cartwheels and hooves, for it was congested with horse-drawn traffic and handcarts. The fog still hung low over the river, and the pavements thronged with hordes of filthy looking children who cheeked the passing carters and jarveys, and who clung on to the backs of carts until the lash of the carters' whips drove them off laughing. Past canals and dry docks, by railway lines which sometimes blocked the street traffic at the crossing gates; as we walked eastwards the coal yards, timber yards, tall cranes, sawmills and soapworks gradually gave way to smaller workshops, laundries, and Chinese shops and cafes with their exotic interiors, providing a counterpoint to the otherwise grey, dull surroundings of Limehouse.

The house was one of those stolid Georgian houses which would have been owned by a well-off ship's captain or merchant in the days when that class of person was not too conceited to live by the docks and amongst the people who made them their money. The servant of Dr. Bower-Dalton brought us into the house, took Holmes's card, and showed us into a room which was furnished in the most impeccable oriental style. The celebrated antiquarian joined us a few moments later.

"Mr. Holmes, and Dr. Watson – how pleasant to meet you. To what do I owe this undoubted and unexpected honour?"

Holmes explained our errand and how we had come to know about him.

"Yes, it is a fascinating place, Elphinstone's. A remarkably cultured man, self-taught, of course; his knowledge of Japanese art, or Chinese pottery, for example, is quite outstanding. I am not so much interested in the flora and fauna, you understand – frankly, I can see no use whatever for an Indian pangolin or an Australian cassowary – but some of the articles that fetch up there are complete rarities. Of course, the sailors who bring these things back often have no idea of their value and sell them for few shillings once they have drunk or gambled away their pay – or worse. The chap you spoke to was Fred Spurgoen. I'm never quite sure when he's being serious and when not. If Elphinstone's ever fails, which I should doubt, I always think Spurgeon would at least have the music halls to fall back on. Now, the five ancestors, yes, I can tell you something about them, but it might make it easier if you say precisely what it is you want to know and why."

"It is a delicate subject and related to the so-called 'Torso Murder.'"

"Yes, I'd read about that. But what is the connection exactly?"

Holmes explained how the locations of the body parts had been sent to him in a sort of code.

"That is bad, very bad" his brow clouded. "Yet, I should be astonished if any of the Chinese societies is mixed up in this. If they are, I must say that you may as well abandon your search right now as it will be fruitless. No white man will get a word out of them. They have an iron code of *omertà* that would make the Sicilians seem positively garrulous. You should be wasting your time."

"Frankly, I am not sure that they have had any involvement in this. It is more to do with a place where I think one of the body parts may be concealed – the place where the five ancestors are said to sleep."

"I think I may be able to help. There are, in point of fact, two distinct populations: the Shanghai Chinese who have settled around Pennyfields whose numbers are very small; the Chinese from southern China and Canton tend to be found, in greater numbers but still not particularly numerous, around the Limehouse Causeway and Three Colt Street. I would hazard a guess that it is there that you want to go. This ancient legend of the five ancestors or the five elders of Shaolin as they are often known, is one which is known to every Chinese person. There are two societies that might interest you in Limehouse; they both have a sort of shrine to the five ancestors, with incense, dragons, and lanterns and such paraphernalia: there is the Chee Kong Tong, on the Causeway itself at number 48. They are a sort of Chinese equivalent of a friendly society, or Freemasons, and generally quite above board as far as I am aware, although one can never be quite certain, of course.

"There is also Yau Lee's place. He runs a slop shop and store in Limehouse a few doors away from the Carpenter's Arms just off Gill Street which, while it has a respectable front, is also a gambling club *cum* opium den. That may be the allusion to 'sleep' in your note. Lee's is unique in Limehouse in that they allow no white men, or for that matter, women, to cross the threshold to the back premises. They very wisely keep themselves to themselves and, like all the other foreign populations, settle their own affairs. Despite what you might read in the penny dreadfuls about the 'yellow peril,' the customers are generally harmless fellows who drop in for a pipe or a game of fan-tan. They do not look for trouble and try to stay clear of the law. Lee's place is known unofficially as the five ancestors club, and it is signified by

Chinese character for five," here he scribbled on the back of Holmes's card: 五.

"You will see it above the shop. It is often the first place that the Chinese sailors come to when they land, usually without a word of English, hence the sign which they will recognise immediately as indicating a friendly welcome. The store also handles mail and parcels for the Asiatic populations in Limehouse and Pennyfields so it may profit you to ask there. Lee's premises are in 42 and 42a; the legitimate premises to the front and the other at the rear. Incidentally, when you get there, it may be as well if you tell Lee that I sent you."

The final leg of the journey was a short one. We strode on past Limekiln Wharf with its strings of small lighters and chalk barges, the quayside suffused with the sharp tang of hops from the Barley Mow Brewery, overlaid with the unmistakeable musky scent of hogs from Milligan's piggery; towering over all, and barely visible in the fog, the colossus of St. Anne's clock tower, ball, and ensign. In a few minutes, beyond a public house, we saw above a shop door the sign 五. As we entered, my senses took in that peculiar *mélange* of new clothes, dried fish, and aniseed, overlaid with a faint odour which I recognised from our episode in the Bar of Gold in Paul's Wharf. At the end of the counter, was a tank of silver slithering eels and beyond that, on hooks, a row of shiny brown ducks looking as though they had been flattened by the treads of a heavy dustcart.

Holmes did as he had been directed by Dr. Bower-Dalton and explained his errand succinctly, whereupon the proprietor disappeared swiftly through a bamboo curtain and returned with what looked like a small tea chest. He refused to accept any money for his having been thus put to trouble, and seemed very disdainful of us and yet, as far as I could see, he had no reason to be. He seemed to associate Holmes and I with some heinous transgression, almost as though he knew the contents of the chest. But he would not be drawn on the subject.

"I suppose there is little point in asking for a description of the man who delivered these?" I asked.

Mr. Lee shook his head. Once outside in the street, Holmes and I looked at each other in silence and consternation.

"I assume he knew what was in here," I said, indicating the chest.

"He may have guessed, though it is unlikely that he is in any way mixed up with this. I suppose to do Lestrade justice, we ought to take a cab straight to Scotland Yard."

On our arrival at the Yard, the inspector's visage fell when he saw the object of our visit.

"There was something else we picked up about this Phillimore character," he said, "One of his neighbours told us that he used to take midnight walks through Epping Forest. Do you know what else? He used to take a spade with him! It would be no surprise that he met his end in such a manner, if it turns out to be him."

Lestrade glanced ominously at the box; his customary jauntiness and assurance had deserted him, and his sharp features were creased with distaste. Holmes removed the cover, drew back the hessian on the top of the chest, and suddenly uttered a soft cry of recognition.

"No! This is my doing!" he expostulated, following with a bitter curse.

"Whatever can you mean?" Lestrade gasped. My own thoughts were a maelstrom.

"Neither of you will recognise this man," my friend said. "It is not James Phillimore; it is Fred Porlock! I am to blame for this"

I gazed at the ghastly relic: a swarthy face with greying hair and beard; lifeless eyes, the straw packing speckled with dried blood. I turned the object and saw, as I had anticipated, the gory hole at the back of the skull was which told us that the man had been shot.

"There is some blackening which suggests that the pistol was held close to the head when the shot was fired, also the wound is small," I said.

"A judicial execution for treachery," said Holmes.

"From what we saw of the rest, at least he appears not to have been tortured," I said. "A wound of this nature suggests that death would have been instantaneous."

"Gruesome as this is, Watson, we have been spared a far worse climax. From the outset, as soon as I began to understand the nature of the case, I have been haunted by the appalling presentiment that this final instalment, as you described it, would be delivered to 221b. Can you imagine Mrs. Hudson's horror?"

"Good Lord, Holmes!"

"I see it all now, Watson, though I have been culpably slow. Well, Lestrade, I do not know how well up you are in my continental exploits, but last month Fred Porlock tipped me off about the theft of the Nebrodi Sapphire in Paris which was masterminded by Colonel Moran."

The British public will recall the case of the disgraced Colonel very well. In September 1894 Colonel Sebastian Moran, lieutenant of the late Professor Moriarty, was acquitted on the charge of murdering the Honourable Ronald Adair, a series of events which I recorded contemporaneously in "The Adventure Of The Empty House". The acquittal obtained by Colonel Moran's defence counsel was founded entirely upon a legal-procedural technicality, and not due to the lack of material evidence – for it was Holmes himself who brought the man to justice. Following Moriarty's death, Moran had assumed the leadership of what was the most efficient criminal organisation in England, and the latter was rumoured to be even more ruthless in maintaining disciple over his people. My friend continued.

"Afterwards, I became convinced that Moran had intercepted our correspondence. I made discreet, *very* discreet, manoeuvres to ascertain the whereabouts of Porlock to try to discover whether he had remained at his post. I met a blank wall of silence. No amount of money, no threat or inducement would loosen anyone's lips. I had feared this might happen, but I could not contact Porlock directly for our communications, I was sure, were being opened and he was never out of sight of his accomplices. And now, this is the result of it, and it is I who am to blame."

"I thought you said you had never met him," said Lestrade. "How can you identify him?

"I said I had promised that I would not try to trace him, and I did not. However, circumstances alter cases, and once I realised our correspondence was being intercepted, I made it my business to try to find out if he were still alive and somehow try to warn him. Having shadowed him from the post office in Camberwell one day, I found myself sitting beside him in a carriage in the Underground. I also noticed that he was being followed by someone whom I assumed was one of our late professor's close associates although I did not recognise him at the time."

"And Porlock did not recognise you?" asked Lestrade.

"My dear Inspector," Holmes replied witheringly, "do you not suppose I might have taken some trouble to make myself unrecognisable? I managed to slip into his pocket a note warning him not to return home but to flee immediately, to an address in Marseilles where he would be safe, along with some money in order to facilitate his escape. I then managed to waylay his pursuer, who regrettably suffered a trifling accident ... well, I can hardly tell you about that, Inspector, but I manged to delay this fellow long enough to allow Porlock to get clear away, or so I had thought. I had expected that he would be somewhere on the Continent by now, and so did not connect him with the murder victim. He seems to have hesitated just long enough unfortunately."

"Then there can be no doubt?" asked Lestrade.

"None whatever."

"I will require to have you sign a formal identification. And you believe Colonel Moran is behind it?"

"As ever Lestrade, he will have remained in the background while others did the dirty work. This is the work of one of his agents."

"Which one?"

"I am unable to say, but believe me, I will move heaven and earth to find out."

Inspector Lestrade, when he returned the following morning to Baker Street, was very sceptical about both Porlock's connection with the late professor, and of the late professor's own connection with the criminal underworld.

"The photographs that were placed here during our absence surely indicate that this was no amateur effort," said my friend. "Watson will tell you that right at the outset I felt sure we were being watched by someone, but he has been very subtle. He was in all likelihood the man with the rag-and-bone cart in Heneage Street; the costermonger you saw at Tyburn; he would have mingled with the crowd at St. Swithin's, and he was almost certainly the old woman with the bundle of laundry by the churchyard near Swedenborg-square. In the latter case, at least, I ought to have apprehended the deception and given chase."

"That would have been difficult, even for you Mr. Holmes; you see, the back lanes and alleys thereabouts are labyrinthine and unlit; often our men are confounded in pursuit of some wrongdoer, for the boards and planks which cover the holes and ditches are pulled up behind the fugitives in the manner of a drawbridge, leaving yawning traps for the pursuers."

"Well, my dear Lestrade, you must now recognise that this entire operation was well beyond the means of any ordinary criminal organisation, and the fact that the campaign was also directed at myself confirms that this act of revenge – of which Moran, to do him justice, openly warned me – emanates from one man only."

"He warned you personally, did he?" asked Lestrade incredulously.

"At least he let me know subtly that he had intercepted the mail between myself and Porlock and had cracked our protocol. It came to the same thing. As I have said before, and it gives me no pleasure to repeat it especially under the present circumstances, the man behind this is more than a match for the official force. Do not take that amiss for, after all, I am bound to admit that in the present case up until now, he has been more than a match for Sherlock Holmes."

"As you know, Mr. Holmes, since the Adair case we have never had the slightest vestige of evidence which would connect Moran with any form of criminal activity. Now, this Klesmesh Porloch," Lestrade went on, reading from the official report, "I'll give you that Mr. Holmes – you have got the name correct, or almost. Known locally as Fred Porlock, as you said. Fifty-eight, a Russian Jew and former tailor of Princelet Street, well-known in the district but a noticeably quiet character, apparently, no close friends or family. Made his living by doing odd jobs here and there. Now, as to the *post mortem*, this will make more sense to you, Doctor, than it does to me. *'Bullet entered at the back of the neck, slightly to the left of the third vertebra; embedded in the zygoma to the left. Bullet passed through the trapezius, fired at point-blank range.'* Most of the locals we spoke to were astonished at his murder – they thought he was the type who would have had no enemies."

"Now we have established that he had at least one implacable enemy!"

"The fellow has been assiduous in concealing his links with the underworld for there was nothing incriminating upon the premises – and certainly nothing which would connect him either with this late professor of yours or with Colonel Moran. There are certainly plenty of Russian criminal societies in the area: the Odessans; the Black Cossacks; the Aldgate Mob – again we found no evidence. There are, no doubt, smaller fry but it would be a complete waste of our time to pursue further enquiries amongst the Russian immigrants for they have an ingrained terror of any kind of police or authority – even a private detective."

"A terror which is wholly justified, as I learned first-hand," said Holmes.

"Anyway, my colleague, Inspector Larsen, who makes a speciality of the Russian communities in Whitechapel and Bethnal Green, told me that this method of killing is generally reserved for those who have impeached upon one of the societies or collaborated with the police. It reminded him of the killing of the former Tsarist policeman, Gavrilovitch."

"Indeed, I thought immediately of the Trepoff case, for when I was in Odessa it was a hotbed of anti-Tsarist dissent, but in this case, I know precisely whence Porlock's persecution derived."

"Bring me the evidence, Mr. Holmes," said Lestrade with a smile, "and I shall have the colonel under lock and key within the hour!"

"Very well, Lestrade, I perceive that I shall not convince you. Still, we have a number of points, do we not, from which we may draw some inferences: There is the watermark on the notepaper which suggests that the sender of the notes has a connection with a trade or business, one that requires headed correspondence; there was the lack of skill evident in the dismemberment; there is the connection with three villages in suburban Surrey – which, admittedly, may be a blind.

"Let us reconstruct the events and see where these clues lead us. First, Porlock is murdered – was he murdered in his home or was he lured to the killer's own lair?"

"To break in and kill him in his home would be very risky, surely, in such a densely crowded neighbourhood?" I said.

"And yet depending on the time of day, perhaps not. It is a busy, noisy neighbourhood. There are factories, warehouses, tradesmen constantly at work at this or that task, with tools, equipment and ladders – all of this might cover the sound."

"None of the neighbours heard a thing," said Lestrade, "surely someone would have heard a gunshot? And there was no sign of any blood in Porlock's house. How could a murder like this have been committed and a corpse dismembered without leaving any bloodstains or bullet holes?"

"Then he was lured to a *rendezvous* and killed. The assassin or his accomplice would then have had to dismember the corpse then transport it piece by large piece. The torso must have been brought in through the rear door of the church – under the cover of darkness, no doubt, but it is still no mean feat to transport a corpse through the metropolis; it would require a great deal of nerve to dodge the beat constables, albeit their rounds are generally predictable. But what if he should be stopped by a plainclothes man? How does he explain the body parts if he and his vehicle are searched?"

"He may have been prepared to shoot his way out of it, if he had a gun," I suggested.

"Worse and worse. How could he know that the crack of a pistol would not bring policemen running from every quarter? Even after the torso was left in Spitalfields there were still the head and limbs to dispose of. I merely point out at this stage, that they must have had some fool-proof method, or as fool-proof as possible, for moving the body parts without the risk of being disturbed by curious policemen, and that the whole affair was well thought out in advance."

"We commandeered the costermonger's barrow that he brought the arms in," said Lestrade, "and discovered that the thing had been stolen from the yard of a well-known, firm, Carteret & Sons, in Covent-Garden. They hadn't noticed that it was missing until our constable turned up with it, and I'd say they have no involvement in this."

"I am sure that you are right," said Holmes. "Moran is a professional, and neither he nor any of his agents would take such ridiculous chances as relying on amateurs for the success of his mission. Now, Inspector, you said you would take a run out to Surrey."

"Yes, well I've not been letting the grass grow under my feet," said Lestrade. "I questioned the three postmistresses myself at Horsell, Woking, and Byfleet. I didn't want to depend on the yokels out there."

"Excellent, pray continue."

"I was relying on the possibility that the sender might have had to go into the post office to buy the stamps or that someone might have noticed a letter being posted by a stranger in the village. That depended on there being a post box *inside* the post office. Unfortunately, we drew a blank at Horsell – the woman doesn't remember selling stamps to anyone on the day in question and says she was too busy; and in any case, the post box there is out on the street. The other accounts, from Woking and Byfleet, agreed on two points: a man whom they didn't recognise bought a stamp and posted a letter around the time we were interested in, and he was tall, youngish, fair, and very formally attired; 'looked a right toff,' the woman in Woking actually said – she remembered his top hat; the other woman, in Byfleet, said she didn't remember any top hat but remembered he was dressed 'a bit sombre like.' Not a lot of help, but we know our man was there."

"Yes, I fear it is not much in the way of data, yet we proceed do we not? A tall, fair, formally dressed youngish man. On his way to his office in the city or to his club for lunch perhaps. A gentleman in other words, is the suggestion is it not? And yet that would sit at odds with the cheap stationary."

"Which could be a blind."

"Perhaps. The two women couldn't say in what sort of vehicle he came?"

"No, I asked them that too," said the inspector, "they saw none."

"And yet dressed *like a toff,* it is unlikely he walked there. Well, thank you for the information. I fear I must now retreat into solitude and ponder the details of the case. I shall keep you abreast of any developments."

Once the inspector had departed, I left my friend to his desired seclusion and went for a walk in the park. Having bought some of the early editions, I stopped at a small café near Portman Square for a pot of coffee. The press was now reporting the matter as "the mysterious murder of a Russian tailor" and made several inane speculations as to the motive, which included references to Russian secret societies, the Nihilists, the Fenians, and the East End protection rackets. I went back to Baker Street at lunchtime expecting to find Holmes in one of his black moods; instead, I found him with an unmistakeable gleam in his eye.

"Anything in the 'papers?" he asked chirpily.

"The usual tosh," I replied, tossing the newspaper on to the table. "Nothing of any interest."

"Tell me, Watson, what connection do you think there could be between Horsell, Woking, and Byfleet?"

"I'm sure I cannot say. I have walked an odd time on the moor and common at Horsell, and you will recall my old school friend, Percy Phelps, who once brought us on a case to Woking; but I cannot think of any connection in particular between those two and Byfleet."

"I mean a physical one."

"Ah, of course, the Basingstoke Canal?" I ventured.

"An inspired and clever, but unfortunately slightly out-of-date answer, Watson. I am afraid there is, in fact, no longer any such connection. There was a serious breach at Crookham some years ago which not only left the canal dry but flooded some of the farmland in the vicinity. The canal company was liquidated as a result of the lost traffic and the compensation claims."

He pointed to the map on the table.

"I think you have hit upon the right idea, though," he said. "The canal connected these three places when it was built in the eighteenth century; what connects them today, Watson, in the nineteenth?"

"The railway!"

"Good. Which one?

"The London and South Western Railway to be precise."

"Let us leave the London and South Western Railway to one side for one moment and recall our discussion regarding the difficulty in transporting a corpse, even a dismembered one, through the city. We foresaw, as no doubt did Moran, the risk of the assassin or his accomplice being stopped by the police. But what sort of person might legitimately transport a corpse through crowded City streets without raising the slightest suspicion. Think on what the two postmistresses said."

"What was that?"

"A man with a top hat, *sombrely* attired."

"Why, of course, an undertaker!"

"Excellent; a funeral director, to give him his proper title. Or a member of his staff. At least, that is a probability worth exploring, is it not? Now let us return once more to the railway. Which part of the London and South Western Railway do you think a funeral director might take an interest in?"

"I really could not say."

"Of course you could. Remember that rather bizarre little station with the delightful inscription which we passed on Westminster Bridge Road on the way home from the Oxshott case? *'Mortuis quies, vivis salus'* – no *mortuis quies* for friend Porlock, I am afraid."

"Of course, the Necropolis Railway at Waterloo, transporting the coffin trains to Brookwood! Thurston told me that they built a lunatic asylum there too – what a strange institution."

"A citadel of the mad and the dead, Watson."

"I recall reading a rather droll article in the 'Gentleman's Magazine' some time ago, an invective damning the entire operation as grotesque and inhuman, concerned with the possible mixing up of the carriages of the dead with those of the living."

"I read the same article, though I must say I was left with the distinct impression that the author was rather more dismayed at the prospect of mixing first-class passengers with third-class ones. Nevertheless, I believe you have it: the Necropolis Railway."

"As a cover for criminal activities, I suppose no occupation could be more useful for disposing of the bodies of victims!"

"Indeed not, one can imagine what skulduggeries may be achieved with double sized coffins."

"But amongst the hundreds of funeral directors in London how does one begin to narrow the probabilities even further?"

Holmes picked up a heavy volume from the table.

"Here is the trade directory for London," he continued, "I had no idea there was such a demand for their services; from Aldgate High Street to Zanzibar Terrace, there are a hundred and seventeen funeral directors. Then there are those situated in the neighbouring counties of Kent, Middlesex, and Surrey."

"Good gracious! We cannot possibly visit each of those surely …" I groaned.

"Indeed no. Hand me the Bradshaw, if you please. Now, listen to this, though! At eleven thirty-five, Monday to Saturday, a funeral train departs the Necropolis Station in London for Brookwood, arriving at Necropolis Junction where it leaves the main LSWR line at twelve twenty-five. The train returns from Brookwood leaving the Anglican station at two-fifteen and the Nonconformist and Roman Catholic station at two-thirty p.m. and is back in London by three twenty."

"Brilliant!"

"So, our enterprising undertaker arrives with his legitimate cargo at Westminster Bridge Road the night before and leaves the coffin; next day he has to meet the train at Brookwood and convey the remains of the deceased on the final leg of its journey; this leaves him ample time to pop into one of the villages *en route* and post his letter, then arrive to meet the train in good time and complete the service. Equally, he could post the letter on the return journey. Of course, he is dressed fairly conspicuously and travelling in a hearse, but the villagers there are no doubt used to seeing such traffic to the cemetery day in and day out that they barely notice. It would be no more remarkable than seeing a fishmonger's cart at Billingsgate. Nevertheless, he avoids going to the same village more than once, so as not to attract attention.

By virtue of his profession, he is practically free from police scrutiny, for how many constables would have the impiety to stop and search a hearse?"

"Since he posted letters on three subsequent days, we have only to find out which of the undertakers officiated at funerals on Monday, Tuesday, and Wednesday, and we have the answer?"

"Here we have yesterday's newspaper, from which we can start to make a list; I had sent Billy round to the newsagent for Monday's and Tuesday's editions. I shall ring for lunch now, then we can make a start afterwards."

It took us several hours to go through the newspapers, checking and double-checking the entries with the object of making a list, but by the finish we had discovered that only two firms had officiated at Brookwood on all three days.

"A. Braithwaite, Undertaker, Funeral Furnisher, and Monumental Sculptor," said Holmes, "Established 1850. Funerals to Suit All Creeds and Classes – First, Second, and Third Class available on application – admirably egalitarian! Situated in Clare Market. And the other is McCabe and Son, Breffni Funerals, Roman Catholic only – more select, though they also cater for three social classes; they are located in Crimea Road, Aldershot, Hampshire. Braithwaite had a third-class funeral on Monday and Wednesday, and a second-class one on Tuesday. The Breffni company did two third-class funerals on Tuesday, with one each on the other days."

"So, either is equally likely."

"Perhaps. However, Aldershot lies in the opposite direction from Brookwood to the three villages from which the letters were sent, so our Breffni man would not pass the three villages; he may of course have made a deliberate detour, but why? Whereas Braithwaite's hearse would pass the villages on both the outward and return journeys – always assuming that the hearse has to return to the Clare Market premises."

"In which case Braithwaite is the marginally more likely one."

"More than marginally, I think, Watson; look at the times postmarked on the letters, they are all consistent with morning funeral times, whereas on Wednesday the Breffni company had one in the afternoon. As Braithwaite's premises are closer, it would make sense to start there."

"And the names give you no hint?"

"I know no one of either name in Moran's establishment, but in any case, it will be a false one. I feel that I have a sudden pressing need to bury a deceased relative, which nothing but a visit to Clare Market will satisfy. In fact, no, I have it! A recently deceased *parishioner* of mine needs a burial, and you, Watson, shall be the solemn, lachrymose, recently bereft husband."

"Shall I get Billy to call us a cab, then?"

"Good Lord, no! The very last thing we should want to do," replied my friend cryptically. "We'll pick up a growler or a hansom at the cab stand at the station."

Holmes's impersonation of the nonconformist clergyman was exquisite: he had played this part once before in the Irene Adler case and his dress, his speech, his demeanour, were such as could not have been equalled by the real thing; the moment he put on the clerical neckband he *became* the man. With myself at his side, dressed in deep mourning and summoning all the false solemnity that I could muster, surely the proprietor would entertain not the slightest suspicion as to the reason for our errand. Holmes asked the jarvey to drop us at Lincoln's Inn Fields for some reason and we made our way on foot from there, negotiating the ill-lit crowded lane behind the Royal College of Surgeons; every roadway and cobbled thoroughfare seemed to be choked with butchers' and costermongers' carts.

"We seem to have picked the very worst time of day," I said.

"Indeed, Watson, that was my intention," replied Holmes mysteriously.

The yellowing shade of a gas lamp above a shop doorway in a row of smoke-blackened two-storied buildings proclaimed the parlour of "Albert Braithwaite," and there was a courtyard entrance to the side at the corner of New Inn-passage to facilitate the hearse vans. There could be few dirtier or noisier spots, and fewer poorer populations in London.

"It seems an inauspicious spot for one of Moran's crew," I remarked to Holmes.

"It is a mere façade. It would hardly do to proclaim one's wealth in the midst of such a hovel. Now let us see what Mr. Braithwaite has to offer the grieving widower and his spiritual adviser."

The shop bell announced our presence and very shortly a tall, fair-haired, fresh-faced, young man in dark clothes appeared behind the counter. Holmes explained our business and before long we were going through the rigmarole of discussing prices for this and that standard of coffin, what purvey could be provided and when, and, inevitably, the specifications for first, second, and third-class funerals by train. The young man was very well-spoken, and at no point did his eyes desist from sharp scrutiny of us.

"We are very grateful for your assistance, young man," said Holmes at length. "I am afraid I have a terrible memory for numbers, and, as you can see, my friend is quite incapable at present. If I could trouble you to write down just a summary of what you have told us ... on your headed note paper, if you don't mind; you see, we shall need to make it official-looking as we have to submit a claim to the insurance company. No need to have it typed out, as we are in rather a hurry, just the brief details and a signature at the bottom. Ah, thank you, Mr. Braithwaite."

"Well, Holmes, did you recognise him?" I asked as soon as we were ensconced in the cab on our return to Baker Street and had the trap door closed against the possibility of the driver eavesdropping.

"Yes, it is Mears; he is but a minor cipher in Moran's organisation and was involved in the murder of John Vincent Harden earlier in the year. I did not know much about Mears at that point, but as Harden's body was never found, it now seems obvious how it was disposed of and by whom; the case never came to court, as you know. I assume it was Mears whom I saw following Porlock at Camberwell on the occasion which I mentioned to Lestrade, but I certainly did not recognise him then. He would appear to have a talent for disguise and I have no doubt it is he who has been shadowing us throughout.

"He comes from an excellent old county family, or at least an offshoot of one, which included an archdeacon and a famous explorer and navigator, replete with Eton and Oxford education – hence his familiarity with the classics. Like many of his ilk, he went to the bad partly through his cosseted and privileged upbringing. He is a fairly recent recruit to the Moran establishment, and no doubt he was given the job of eliminating Porlock in order to test his mettle. That is how his chief operates."

"A wily fellow, though – did you notice the looks he gave us?"

"He never took his eyes off us for a moment, and at one point I thought the game was up. I think we have pulled it off, though."

"How can you be sure he is the culprit?"

"I cannot, at least not yet. But once I have compared his handwriting with the notes … well, here they are. I call your attention to the little flourish under the "y" and the peculiar sloping of the number 7. Well, what do you think?"

I nodded in agreement. "Identical. What do you intend to do?" I asked.

"I should be failing in my civic duty were I not to inform Scotland Yard of the identity and whereabouts of the man upon whom my suspicions have fallen. Of course, it is obvious that any incriminating evidence in the shop at Clare Market will have been disposed of by now. These fellows are, after all, hardly amateurs. I should be interested to hear your own view, Watson."

"I think it is beyond any reasonable doubt that he was, at the very least, involved in the murder, but I cannot see how you will ever obtain the evidence which would necessarily satisfy a jury."

"Excellent, Watson, that was exactly what I wanted to hear. You see, once I discovered the victim was Porlock, it was never my intention that this case should go anywhere near a jury," my friend replied, somewhat to my confusion.

"What! Are you leaving?" I asked as Holmes threw up the trap door and shouted to the jarvey to pull up.

"Only to stop off briefly at the post office *en route* to Baker Street," was my friend's enigmatic rejoinder. "You can tell Mrs. Hudson that we will dine at seven-thirty as usual, Watson."

I was not entirely surprised when Lestrade appeared in our dining room the very next morning. We had hardly sat down to breakfast when the door burst open upon us. He looked more harried and fatigued than I had ever seen him, and I felt sure that the savage characterisations in the press concerning the incompetence of the official police in the conduct of the case must be affecting his customarily indomitable spirit. He immediately engaged my sympathy but Holmes, I felt, seemed curiously off-hand on this occasion.

"Pray sit down and take a cup with us," said my friend, waving him to a chair. "I take it something has turned up in the Porlock case, then?"

"Turned up, Mr. Holmes? Why, that note you sent me yesterday, naming Mears as the murderer–"

"You have arrested him already, then."

"The undertaker's *dead!*" the inspector blurted out, apparently incapable of savouring the delectable irony of his own pronouncement. "He committed suicide at his premises in Clare Market during the night!"

"How exactly?"

"He shot himself in the back of the head."

"Did he really?" replied Holmes with a stifled yawn. "How very strange don't you think? An incredible coincidence, is it not, that he dies by exactly the same method as his victim? Now, here is a cup and saucer for you. Milk and two sugars, isn't it?"

"The very man you put the finger on is dead within twelve hours, I'll say it's strange. But it's no coincidence, Mr Holmes!"

"No?" my friend replied, looked mildly alarmed. "Why do you say that?"

"I reckon he knew we were on to him, and he would rather face death at his own hands than stand justice. *Cheating the gallows*, they call it."

"Ah, indeed, I have read that very expression in the Newgate Calendar; that will be one job fewer for Billington who, as Watson and I discovered recently, has been sorely pressed this year. Did Mears leave a written confession, by any chance?"

"No, he didn't. Usually, once they get overcome by remorse, they spill their guts. He did write a suicide note, though, saying he died by his own hand."

"But with no reason?"

"None, but, as I say, it looks very much as though he knew the game was up."

"Then you are satisfied?"

"Perfectly, the case is wrapped up. Why, Mr. Holmes, you don't sound convinced."

"I am bound to point out the weaknesses in your case. The natural thing to do, if you had intended to kill yourself would surely be to put the gun to your temple; shooting oneself in the back of the head seems to me a rather awkward way to do it. And unless you have an informer in your ranks, Mears could not possibly have known that the police were, as you say, on to him. Only we three knew that, and the telegram which I sent you yesterday was, as you will recall, not only discreetly worded in order to avoid explicit reference to the case but also carried a rider to the effect that it should be opened only by yourself. Moreover, I should say that he had absolutely no reason to fear the gallows for the game was by no means up."

"Why do you say that?"

"Because you had not, and still have not, sufficient evidence to bring a conviction for Porlock's murder – you can be sure that anything vaguely incriminating would have been disposed of long ago. Since you reject my theory of a connection with the late Moriarty's gang, where is your motive? Have you anything to connect these two, the victim and the assassin? You do not, in which case you may even have found it difficult to have proven him to be an accessory. Any half-decent defence counsel would have torn your case to pieces. I doubt if you could have proven even the much lesser charge of being in unlawful possession of a corpse, or prevention of the lawful and decent burial of a dead body."

Lestrade looked crestfallen "But you are certain he was the man who killed Porlock?"

"Neither Watson nor I have the slightest doubt, but I did not suggest for a moment that we could have proven it in a court of law."

"But the suicide note–"

"Do you happen to have it?"

"Here it is."

Holmes glanced at it superficially.

"It is as I expected. Compare the handwriting there with the original notes he sent to me. There is no similarity whatever, it is not Mears's hand," Holmes said dismissively.

"Come, Mr. Holmes, you don't suppose he asked someone to *write* the suicide note for him?" Lestrade asked warmly.

"I don't suppose anything. I am merely bound to call your attention to this as a singular discrepancy, and to point to the general weaknesses in your theory of suicide. Have you found any trace of gunpowder on the hands of the deceased?"

"Well, the test is rather uncertain. We have the gun, of course, and the bullet which will almost certainly match the wound. And we have further evidence, Mr. Holmes, evidence that you cannot possibly be aware of," the inspector continued somewhat haughtily, "that he was visited by a clergyman and a gentleman in mourning dress several hours before he died."

"A gentleman in mourning dress … is that not to be expected in an undertaker's?"

"Perhaps but I think they were impostors."

"Excellent idea! Did you get their description?"

"Yes, we have one reliable witness; a workman stuck in the traffic with his barrow saw them quite clearly going into the shop and coming out again some ten minutes later. He swears he would recognise them again if he saw them."

"Capital! Go on."

"Both middle aged: the padre was tall and thin, high cheekbones, bit of a hook nose, right odd-looking chap, apparently; the other was middle sized, square jawed with a moustache and – why Dr. Watson, what is wrong with you?"

"Watson has been having trouble all morning with a ticklish throat. This foggy weather doesn't help. I have suggested that he see a doctor, but he will not hear of it. I am afraid those descriptions of yours are not very much to go on."

"Hm, perhaps not. I think they must have picked the very busiest time of the day to call at the shop in Clare Market, for the place was bustling and positively heaving with carts. The workman who saw them was stuck there for half an hour. Apart from him, no one else saw them, and we haven't been able to trace a jarvey who either dropped them there or picked them up."

"Of course, they may have alighted on another street nearby in order to put the cabman off the scent, and then walked the remainder of the way to the premises."

"Dear me, Doctor, that *is* a pretty awful cough. Good point, Mr. Holmes, I shall follow that up. Very suspicious, don't you think?"

"Extremely so. In fact," said Holmes, "I agree they were most likely a couple of impostors."

"And they must be implicated in this, don't you think?"

"Up to their necks in it."

"My theory is they were sent to give him some sort of warning."

"From the Porlock faction possibly, bent on revenge?"

"Of course, I hadn't thought of that! But if Mears's persecution came from these two impostors, it doesn't say much about your theory of Porlock's link to this professor's organisation."

"Doesn't it?" said Holmes languidly and reapplied himself to his buttered toast.

"Please, no more of your professor's gang, Mr. Holmes!" said Lestrade laughing, "Well, thank you again, gentlemen, for your valuable assistance; as usual it has been a privilege to work with you and bring another case to a close. Incidentally, Mears seems to have written another of those queer little cryptic notes, but instead of sending it to you, he must have decided not to post it."

"It had my address on it, then?"

"No, it didn't strangely enough. In fact, there was an envelope with *his* address on it, but there must have been something else in that. The note was in Greek, this time. He had crumpled it and thrown it into the wastepaper basket. Here it is – you might as well keep it as a *memento*, as it has clearly nothing to do with the case."

"If anything else comes up, be sure to let me know."

Lestrade's footsteps died away on the stair.

"Come, Holmes, there is more to this than meets the eye."

"Well, you heard me give Lestrade a hint or two."

"Rather more hints than were comfortable in my view, Holmes," I said keenly. "You almost gave him the entire solution, wrapped up like a present."

"At least, Lestrade cannot accuse me of withholding evidence."

"Of course, it was no suicide. But how ..."

"I'm afraid I was forced to complain to head of the organisation for having my intelligence insulted. I pointed out to him that if he wished to retain his reputation as the most dangerous man in London, he should not be so incautious as to appoint an agent who, through his shallow egotism, allowed himself to be traced through something as elementary as his postmarked letters. Pride cometh 'ere a fall – and in an effort to impress his master, Mears rather overplayed his hand. A man in Moran's position cannot and must not afford to brook incompetence, even in one so useful to him as Mears. It seems to have the desired effect; when he read from my own hand how the incompetence and arrogance of his agent had led me straight back to him, I knew that he would step in himself to put matters right. As I have said before, Watson, there are certain felonies which the law may not or cannot redress and which, therefore, may justify private revenge."

"Then that is how the presumed suicide note was not written in Mears's handwriting."

"Of course."

I looked at the note Lestrade had brought:

ʼΝέμεσι! πτερόεσσα βίου ροπά, κυανῶπι θεά, θύγατερ Δίκας!

"I could never master the Greek I am chagrined say, Holmes: what does it mean, and how does it come into this?"

"It's from the immortal lines of the Cretan poet, Mesomedes:

'Nemesis! Wingèd balancer of life, daughter of Justice!'

I sent it myself."

End

The Adventure of The Sixty Steps

Chapter 1

One of the most dramatic adventures which occurred to my friend, Sherlock Holmes, began in the winter of eighteen ninety-seven. December was drawing towards a close when I was unexpectedly forced to make one of the most difficult decisions in my sixteen-year association with Holmes. I have already placed on record how busy a year this had been for my friend, for he had recently been involved in a number of capital cases in quick succession that year, two of which, the case of the *Edmonton Horror* and that of the *Devil's Foot*, bore more than merely shades of the grotesque; another affair – the abduction and tribulations of Ebenezer Calthorpe, the Quaker prison reformer – occupied Holmes for several weeks on end and had driven him to the point of nervous exhaustion.

Moreover, Holmes had been the defendant in a particularly acrimonious libel action, the circumstances of which I have alluded to in my notes of the Eugenia Ronder case, and which concerned a certain well-known, and scandalously indiscreet, Conservative cabinet minister. His detestable debaucheries in one of Soho's most notorious night-clubs, "The Lighthouse," with what was euphemistically known in the *demi monde* as a "trained cormorant," are now a matter of public record, as are his accomplished swindles in awarding lucrative government contracts to friends and family. The enquiring, and unfastidious, reader may view the libel proceedings in the Law Society records under the Queen's Bench division (*Chamberlain, Hickman, & Sykes vs. Holmes),* which stand as a cautionary tale to those honest, but naïve, citizens who fail to understand the distinction between law and justice.

Although his Lordship, Justice Maberley, found against the three appellants and dismissed the case; nevertheless I was concerned that, under the strain, my friend's health would degenerate to the sorry state it had been earlier in the year when we had been forced to obtain the ministrations of the famous Harley Street specialist, Dr. Moore Agar. I had absolutely insisted, as his friend and as his medical advisor, that Holmes take himself off to some remote spot in order that he might recharge his system. Despite his protests, I succeeded in persuading him to take a fortnight's recuperation in a village near Fulworth where, I had hoped, the quietude of the forest, the wide Sussex skies, and the bracing air of the towering sea cliffs would restore his overwrought nerves.

Above all, I reminded him sternly, he was to avoid overtaxing himself, and he should give himself up solely to the appreciation of the *flora* and *fauna* of the district by day, and in the long evenings should continue to labour gently upon his *magnum opus* – *The Whole Art of Detection* – a theoretical and practical compendium which he had begun to compose in the weeks immediately following our involvement in the Lady Brackenstall affair.

I recall the evening in Baker Street before he set out for Fulworth, when he aired, for my benefit, some of the ideas which would form the kernel of his seminal work containing both theoretical and practical elements. He had, he told me, succeeded in synthesising the logical systems of Boole and Schröder in his thesis on the distinction between deductive and inductive reasoning. I must confess that this was on a rather too ethereal plane for my own dull, pragmatic intelligence and limited academic range. He had also made a special study of the more practical work of Stanislavsky, the famous Russian actor-theorist, whom he had met in his younger days, and to whom he paid great tribute as a mentor in the art of disguise.

"Whether masquerading as a mendicant vagabond, a drunken sot, or as a fortune-telling Gypsy woman," he had said to me as we sat in our little sitting room in front of a roaring fire with a glass of nutty Verdelho on that cold winter evening prior to his departure, "I have never seen anyone who could quite capture the essence of a character so well. Stanislavsky did not simply act the part, Watson, he *lived* the part; he absorbed the character; he underwent a transfiguration and *became* someone else. It was uncanny. And yet, it must be admitted, he had a peculiar, indeed almost perverse, theory regarding his own method: 'When you play a saintly man or a hero,' he once told me, 'you must discover where he is bad or weak and accentuate *that*; when you play the villain, find out where he is good and decent, and draw it out in the character!' *Dialectics*, he somewhat grandly called it. And as you have had good cause to observe, Watson, that advice of Stanislavsky's has stood me in great stead in my many guises."

"Indeed," I replied, "then your actor-theorist is responsible, albeit indirectly, for putting many criminals behind bars."

"Very well put, Watson."

I recall that I had been making my own preparations to visit some medical associates in Southsea to bring in the New Year, and my intention had been to then visit Holmes a day or two afterwards at Fulworth. However, I was now being forced to abandon these plans since I had been presented with a truly remarkable case which, as the reader will see, united a number of disparate points of significance and demonstrated both Holmes's intellectual faculties and his singular ability to deploy those powers to practical ends. It was with no small degree of mortification that the very next morning after his departure from Baker Street, I found myself seated in a draughty deserted carriage belonging to the London Brighton and South Coast Railway rattling over the Grosvenor Bridge across the river as I followed in his trail. I had planned to complete the last two miles by the station fly, over the steep road on the escarpment of the South Downs to the isolated cottage overlooking the English Channel where my friend was staying.

My present dilemma was a painful one, for I had, only the previous afternoon – indeed a mere two hours after Holmes's departure – received a missive from an old school friend and countryman, Mr. Crawford McIntosh, begging me to prevail upon Holmes to look into what appeared to be a *prima facie* serious miscarriage of justice. McIntosh, whom I had not seen since my college days, was the solicitor acting for a client who had been apprehended as a suspect and charged in a Glasgow murder case which was subsequently tried at the High Court.

After reading McIntosh's précis of the trial, it seemed even to a layman such as myself that the case against the accused had been so extraordinarily weak that it was no wonder that McIntosh and his advocate had been confident of establishing their client's innocence before a jury. But the verdict had unexpectedly gone against them, and the man now stood convicted of murder without recourse to appeal under Scots law. The statement from McIntosh, which contained only the salient facts without the least resort to the rhetoric of advocacy, convinced me that the situation was rapidly becoming a desperate one.

As matters stood, the accused would certainly face the gallows unless the case against him were meticulously demolished point by point and his innocence established beyond any legal doubt; in order to achieve that, however, the affair must be brought swiftly to the attention of those persons in exalted circles with the power to act upon the injustice. There was, of course, only one person whose multifarious experience of the history of crime and criminals, and whose influence in the highest official channels, would be equal to the task. Either I would have to coax a probably very reluctant and still unwell Holmes out of the exile to which I had banished him or stand by while an innocent man was executed.

Of the fact that Holmes was glad to see me when I appeared unexpectedly on his threshold, I had not the slightest doubt, though his welcome was not especially effusive; after all, I had interrupted his rather tardy breakfast. I had barely crossed the lintel, however, before that formidable old reasoning machine had cranked itself into action.

"I had thought at first that you had decided to come down here some few days early in order to see me, but I now perceive that your visit is a professional one and not a social one," he said.

"You are as sharp as ever, Holmes!"

"Well, the absence of any luggage is rather a giveaway; the fact that you have kept the fly waiting outside in the lane–"

"I asked him to wait in the lane that is true. But how could you possibly know that? You cannot conceivably either see or hear the lane from this back kitchen."

"No, Watson, but I can still reason, nonetheless. The station fly appears over ridge of that hill which you can see from this room. Five minutes elapse, and it does not reappear on the return leg of the journey. There is only one habitation on this road, therefore its driver had been bidden to wait, albeit out of sight and earshot, which suggests that you intend me to return with you immediately. Which means, of course, that my much-vaunted recuperation must come to a sudden and premature end."

I believe I had caught him of two minds; his desire for continued peace and solitude in his Sussex cloister wrestled with the prospect of intellectual stimulation. If pushed to it, I would resort to the extreme ends of begging a personal favour but there was, as it turned out, no need for me to go to that length. His eyes twinkled with amusement at my chagrin as he continued.

"It is clear that you have travelled here by the first available train from London, which indicates the urgency of the affair; I know that only a matter of capital importance would bring you here."

"It is quite literally so, Holmes," I replied, "and a very singular one at that."

"Excellent," he answered brightly, "the more singular the better! What exactly is the problem?"

"I will speak very plainly: It is the grossest and plainest miscarriage of justice I have ever had the misfortune to come across in my entire life, Holmes – and you know that I do not commonly resort to hyperbole. An innocent man will die on the gallows unless someone can act to prevent it."

"Well, then, you had better sit down. Help yourself to a pipeful of ships', and I shall pack immediately."

"Good. I am in hopes that we can leave today."

"Indeed. I perceive that you have, in any case, already made your own arrangements."

"How so?"

"Here," he indicated my waistcoat pocket from which peeped the merest margin of a slip of paper. "Passengers' Luggage in Advance," he continued, "the numbered ticketing system of the London North Western Railway is unique and unmistakable."

"Yes, I did send my luggage off to the station but surely, Holmes, not even you can have memorised every single railway company's crest."

"True, Watson, but in recognising this particular one, I now also realise that I may have kept you in ignorance of one of my recent cases – inadvertently, of course. I believe you were on a golfing trip with Thurston at the time. Anyhow, this was the

Fitzreynolds disappearance case. A comfortably off stockbroker had disappeared having drawn out his entire balance of two hundred pounds from the bank. He had been staying at the Northumberland Hotel, and it was originally assumed by the police that he had been done away with for the sake of the money. His family members were not satisfied and had contacted me to solve the matter. Fitzreynolds had been out for the evening, returned to the hotel, changed out of his evening clothes – which he left in his room – then simply disappeared. He was never seen again."

"In similar circumstances to the Blenkinsopp disappearance," I replied.

"Except for the fact that there was no woman involved in the case. You see, although no one saw Fitzreynolds leave the hotel, a resident in the adjacent room declared that he remembered hearing him moving about before midnight. I wrote to the family to say that he was evidently somewhere in Scotland. And I would venture to suggest that is where you are dragging me off to now – either Edinburgh or Glasgow, probably the latter."

"My dear Holmes!" I laughed, "I am afraid that you cannot take me in this time. My friend Crawford McIntosh must have written to you separately regarding the case. You cannot possibly have deduced that–"

"I can assure you Watson, that you until mentioned the man's name I had no idea that you had such a friend. I never heard the name before in my life."

"Really? Do explain."

"Well, in the Fitzreynolds case to which I referred, the deduction was simplicity itself. Here was a man who had clearly made plans to disappear, otherwise why empty his bank account. He had left his hotel around midnight – making sure first to divest himself of his evening dress for no doubt that would draw attention to him. After midnight, when the last of the theatre crowds have gone, the hotels close their doors and one can only egress by getting the night porter to open the door. He clearly wanted to slip away quietly, but where could he go after midnight? His choices are few: another hotel, perhaps, but why? He was using a false name and was therefore already concealed. He went, of course, to either King's Cross or Euston to catch one of the overnight Scotch expresses. As he wished to disappear, it is unlikely that he would have alighted at three in the morning at some provincial station, such as York or Crewe, and thus make himself conspicuous. Some guard or porter would have spotted him, for railway people are as suspicious as policemen when it comes to noticing things like that. No, he went on to the terminus station, which can only have been either Glasgow or Edinburgh, and then lost himself amongst the crowds of a big city.

"My deductions were similar in your case. You have not made any attempt to rush me back therefore the train you have in mind cannot be leaving very soon. By the time we get back to Baker Street, allowing time for me to repack my suitcase and collect a few professional necessities, it will be late evening. Since you said you wished to leave today and already have a ticket, the overwhelming likelihood is that we are taking an overnight express, and we, like Fitzreynolds, presumably do not wish to be dumped in an unhospitable provincial town in the middle of the night. It might, of course, be Edinburgh, but as I recognised the company crest of the London North-Western Railway then Glasgow obviously holds the balance of probabilities."

"It *is* Glasgow, in fact," I replied.

"*Ultima Thule!* I have never visited the place; from what I have heard of the inhabitants, I shall need to purchase a vocabulary book."

"You will have your trusty Watson to effect any necessary translation and act as a native guide if you wish!" I replied, rather warmly, somewhat torn between resentment at his light mocking of my countrymen and gratitude at his acquiescence in answering my plea. He seemed not to have taken offence, so I continued, "We have two first-class berths on the overnight train, so we should arrive fresh in the morning."

"When we reach London later, you ought to wire ahead to tell your friend, McIntosh, that we are coming."

"I had already done so, Holmes, I knew you would not fail me."

Chapter 2

We dined leisurely at Simpson's, sitting at one of our favourite front tables by the window, then took a cab to Euston. As soon as we were settled in the sedate comfort of the Pullman carriage with our nightcaps, I reverted to the object of our journey north and explained the contents of the letter I had received from McIntosh.

"As to the crime itself," I said, beginning a discourse that would last until we reached Rugby, "it appears commonplace; it concerns the murder of a seventy-five-year-old spinster who lived alone with her young maidservant. On the evening of Saturday, October 16th last, Miss Maureen Gilbert, known to relations and those few friends she had as "Maisie," was sitting alone at home after sending this aforementioned servant, twenty-two-year-old Miss Agnes Morgan, or Nancy as she was generally known, out on an errand. The house, which is in fact a flat, is situated in a quiet residential district in a very comfortable, but not ostentatiously wealthy, part of Glasgow known as Kelvinside.

"Colloquially, the area is known as the Sixty Steps owing to the fact that many of the byways are connected by steps, since the street levels vary quite considerably due to the hilliness of the terrain. Some of these stairways and their abutments have colourful nicknames from long-forgotten places and events: there is the Giant's Walk, the Schipka Pass, and the Redan – redolent of Windham's campaign in the Crimea. The street in which Miss Gilbert lived is connected to an adjacent lower thoroughfare, Queen Margaret Road, by these Sixty Steps, the largest and steepest of the stairways in the that district, and one of the city's famous landmarks: it is named Millbrae Terrace due to its pre-eminence over an old flint mill and lade by the river Kelvin. The subjects consist of three large rooms roughly corresponding to a living room, a drawing room and a dining room, with a further two bedrooms, a bathroom, and kitchen which includes servants' quarters. This flat occupies the entire first floor of a tenement three storeys in height and is reached by a stair accessed through a short common passage or lobby leading from the street known as a close. This entrance, numbered 8, is common to the first and second floor inhabitants, while the ground floor flat which occupies the entire ground floor and basement – with the exception of the area displaced by the common close – is numbered 6, and has its own private main door leading directly from the street immediately adjacent to number 8. The flat above Miss Gilbert had been vacant for six months at the time of the murder and has remained so. The old lady and her servant, who lives *in*, were therefore the only persons resident at number 8."

Holmes took a long pull at his pipe and nodded for me to continue.

"Miss Gilbert was for her age apparently very sprightly, mentally and physically, and, it may be said, differed somewhat from the typical elderly Scotch lady of Free Presbyterian persuasion. She had retained, from her younger days, a passion for precious stones and she continued to add to her collection of jewels; these she purchased mainly from a well-known Glasgow firm with whom she had dealt for twenty years, but also, it appears from time to time, from other sources. The collection was valued at more than three thousand pounds. For some reason, these jewels were kept amongst her clothes in her bedroom wardrobe – not in any safe or bank. Not surprisingly, Miss Gilbert was nervous about burglars and lived in a constant dread of her house being broken into, though it seems to me quite significant that she appears never to have entertained any particular fear for her own person."

"What brings you to that inference, Watson?"

"It appears she often wandered, invariably alone and without concern, around some of the rougher parts of the north side of the city, disbursing items of charity, mainly food and clothing, but occasionally money on behalf of the Kirk."

"Excellent, pray continue."

"She was most assiduous as to the fastening of not only the door of the flat, but also the door of the common entrance close, which was always kept locked. If she were alone for any length of time; then in addition to a chain on the door of the flat, she had two separate mortice locks and one warded lock, and also a heavy bolt operated from within. These details may be important in understanding how difficult it was for a stranger to gain access to the flat. Apart from her charitable rounds to which I alluded, she seldom travelled much further than Kelvinside Free Church, or to her doctor, to her solicitor, or to her bank in Great Western Road some half a mile distant. She was in the habit of going to the country or the coast for a month or so at a time, at which point her valuables were generally despatched to the bank for safe custody until she returned. The house on the ground floor, number 6, is occupied by a family by the name of Butler which consisted of the widowed mother; two sisters, Violet and Alice, both teachers of music; and a son Arthur, a concert musician who is often at sea playing in a ship's orchestra, but who happened to be at home on this occasion.

"Miss Gilbert, though kind, was not an especially friendly person it seems, for although these households had been neighbours for many years, they were not upon visiting terms. In point of fact, Miss Gilbert's wealth meant that she was substantially, but not affectedly, the social superior not only of the Butlers but of most of the residents of the street. Nevertheless, she seems to have been greatly liked by her downstairs neighbours, so much so that she had made an arrangement with them that, if at any time she was alone and required assistance, she should knock upon the floor of her room, and on hearing this signal one of them

– especially Arthur if he were at home – would go up to find out the cause of the trouble. This arrangement, once instituted, had never in fact been initiated until the night of the murder. On the evening in question Miss Morgan had left to go on the first of what would be two separate errands: on the first errand she had taken a penny to buy a newspaper which would cost a ha'penny, and had left behind on the dining room table one half sovereign for the subsequent trip."

Holmes interrupted, "What reason was there for not completing both errands at once?"

"Apparently the old lady liked to read the newspaper in peace and quiet while the girl, who was bit of a chatterbox, went out, and it was, as far as can be ascertained, quite common practice for her maid to return with the newspaper and then go out again. On her way out to purchase the newspaper at about ten minutes to eight, the girl met a policeman whom she knew, standing at the police call box in Queen Margaret Road near the bottom of the steps, and they spoke briefly, so that the time can be established with a very high degree of certainty. When she returned not more than ten minutes later, she found the close in turmoil.

"During the period of her absence, the Butlers in the flat below had heard what they thought sounded like the pre-arranged distress signal from the old woman, so that Arthur was despatched immediately by his sisters to go and find out the cause. When he left his own house, he was initially surprised to notice the door of the close ajar – Morgan was supposed to close and unlatch the door behind her for safety – and when he mounted the stairs and arrived at the flat door, he rang the bell. There was no answer, but through the stained-glass panel of the door he could see a light burning inside, and thought he heard the servant girl chopping sticks to kindle the fire, so he returned downstairs. However, as neither Violet nor Alice was satisfied with this account, they ordered him back upstairs again. As he went towards the close for a second time–"

"One moment," said my friend, "presumably Butler had unlatched the close door behind him?"

"He seems to have done so, yes."

"Then how did he consider that he would regain entrance?"

"By ringing the bell, I imagine."

"The Butlers had not keys, then?"

"It appears not."

"Then the entire arrangement was worse than useless, was it not? For it provided an illusion of comfort when there was none. If there had been a genuine emergency – let us say that the old woman had taken a fit of some sort and was partly immobilised, how would anyone rushing to her aid get into the house? They do not seem to have taken account of that."

"Indeed, so it occurred to me too. However, as soon as Butler set out a second time, he noticed that Morgan was returning, which took him aback for he knew then that old woman would not possibly have been chopping her own firesticks in the kitchen. He met Morgan at the close-mouth and told her of the situation, but she did not seem to be alarmed, and suggested the noise the Butlers had heard may have been something falling in the house, rather than a distress signal. They had, she said, recently had trouble with a kitchen pulley which had fallen down once or twice. Then Morgan and Butler then went up to the flat together."

"My apology for interrupting again, Watson, but did not this young man explain to the girl that he had found the close door ajar when it should have been shut?"

"Yes, apparently so, but he did not pursue the matter further at the time. He seems a rather muddle-headed and timid young man though his faculty for *observation* is quite remarkable as you will see. Morgan then opened the close door with the key and up they both ascended to the flat. The girl opened the flat door and entered; all seemed normal at first. Butler, observing protocol notwithstanding the circumstances, had remained uneasily on the threshold by the open door pending an invitation from Morgan to enter. At this point, however, there occurred something very queer and unexpected, something which has never yet been explained: Morgan made her way towards the kitchen which is on the left of the hall at the farthest end, and when she had gone past the grandfather's clock which was at the midway point also upon the left, from the direction of one of the bedrooms on the right, a man – hatted, gloved, well-dressed, clean and sober looking – appeared and walked very quietly and calmly through the hall. Not a word did this man say, not a glance did he spare towards either the young man or woman, no sign of recognition did he make; then he hurried downstairs to the close-mouth and disappeared. He was not known to either Butler or Morgan, allegedly, and his precise description seems to be a matter of some contention between them."

"You mean to say that neither person made any attempt to ascertain this apparent stranger's identity nor his reason for being in the house, despite Butler attending what he believed to be a distress call."

'So it seems."

"A distress signal followed by the discovery of a stranger in the house! What is their explanation for that?"

"They have none. Butler, after all, was a virtual stranger himself. And you must consider the social etiquette of the situation: it would hardly do for a servant to question her mistress's visitors, however odd the circumstances. Neither Morgan nor Butler knew at this point that there was anything seriously amiss, of course. The latter's recall of the scene is remarkable. He gave a very full description of the man in the hall:

a sharp-featured man of about twenty-five, an unremarkable face – as he put it, clean shaven, dark, not well built, and not tall; he also gave a full and coherent description of the clothing worn by the man. There had been some speculation as to whether the man in the hall may have had an accomplice who escaped by the window – "

"If there were an accomplice, then why should he not simply walk out as calmly as did the other?"

"Indeed, Holmes. There are a number of explanations which will occur to you: that the accomplice was possibly known to either or both young persons and had to leave unseen; or the accomplice had some peculiarity of dress, gait, or appearance such as to make his subsequent identification easier. Now to the gruesome part. Inevitably, the body of the old woman was eventually discovered in the dining room, where Morgan had last seen her. She lay in front of the fire and had been beaten almost to death and was insensible but still alive, though her life hung by a thread; by the time a local doctor had been called, he pronounced life extinct. The *post-mortem* examination revealed a series of blows to the head by a very blunt instrument, and it seems incontrovertible to me that those blows were delivered either by the man whom Morgan and Butler saw in the hall or an unknown accomplice."

'Steady on, Watson, we have no proof as yet that there was ever *any* third party in the house! Did either Butler or Morgan notice any bloodstains on the mysterious visitor?"

"None at all, and yet Butler's description of the man, as you heard, was quite detailed. Those are the immediate facts surrounding the murder. The old lady kept her jewellery in the bedroom, some pieces being kept in a locked wooden box, the rest of the collection being kept with the clothes. A small diamond brooch of modest value appeared to have been stolen from the box, therefore the initial assumption was that the motive for the burglary had been robbery. However, the brooch was by no means the largest or most valuable piece in the house, and there was some money lying around, including the half-sovereign on the dining room table, none of which was taken. The box, by all accounts, was small enough to be carried away, though of course someone carrying the box may have attracted attention or comment. It is not known whether it had been locked.

"Now, as to the suspect. Some days later the police picked up a man known as Osip Stoller, a thirty-two-year-old German Jew whose real name is Lehrer, and whom, it must be declared, is a known receiver of stolen property. His appearance did not even vaguely resemble the initial description given by Morgan, even less the one given by Butler for that matter, but he was known to have pawned a brooch, similar to the one apparently stolen. When Stoller was picked up he was in the process of packing to leave for New York – evidence which initially appeared to suggest an escape attempt. In point of fact, Stoller had received an invitation from a countryman to go America and mentioned it to many people in the weeks prior to the murder. However, it was subsequently discovered that Stoller's brooch had been pledged some time before the murder, and he had a ticket which proved the predating. The pawnbroker in question – a Mr. Allan McLean – also averred that the description of the brooch missing from Miss Gilbert's was nothing like the one which Stoller pledged to him: he still had the brooch and showed it to the police. Stoller was found to have a small hammer in his house which the prosecution claimed he used to commit the murder. In point of fact, however, Dr. Corbett who lived locally and attended the flat within several minutes after the murder was committed, testified to the police that the instrument used was probably blunter and heavier than the hammer produced, and deduced from the bloodied state of an armchair leg in the living room that, in fact, *that* was most likely the murder weapon. The bloodied state of the fender around the fire also attested to the likelihood of this as the murder weapon and it was believed that the old woman was bludgeoned to death as she lay on the floor."

"If the victim had been lying on the floor that, to some extent, would explain the absence of bloodstaining on the person in the hall – assuming, of course, that the unnamed visitor *was* in fact the murderer. But why use a thoroughly awkward object such as a chair leg if he had a cosh or a knife to hand? Indeed, why harm the old woman at all, why not simply gag and bind her?"

"Does not that suggest some degree of personal malice towards the old woman?" I asked. "

"It may suggest a number of things, Watson, the most obvious being that there was no thought of murder or even assault in the culprit's mind beforehand since he had not come armed; also, that there are reasonable grounds for believing that the old woman would have been able to identify the murderer – hence why he acted as he did."

"A family member perhaps?"

"Not necessarily, because that begins to suggest that the presence of the old woman was thoroughly unexpected. If it were a family member, it is odds-on that he was acting in concert with Morgan; if he were acting in concert with Morgan, he could not possibly believe the house to be empty! Perhaps we are beginning to theorise rather too much ahead of our data," he said, "pray revert to your story."

"Morgan later positively identified Stoller as the man she had seen in the hall, though her identification is contradicted by the testimony of Butler who would say no more than that Stoller *resembled* the man he had seen – sallow skin and dark-haired – but with two exceptions: one, which was that the man he saw was of medium height and build, whereas Stoller is small – five foot five; and, most importantly, Butler *absolutely insisted* that the man he saw was clean-shaven; Stoller sported a heavy dark moustache of several weeks' growth. Butler's and Morgan's various descriptions, taken down at the time vary quite widely. Butler said that the man he saw wore a felt hat such as a commercial traveller might wear; Morgan mentions a cloth cap. By McIntosh's account Stoller is a bit of a fop, very particular about his dress, and would never be seen in either a cloth cap or felt hat. Stoller attests that he has never owned a fawn-coloured overcoat which Morgan said he wore – Butler mentioned a brown worsted overcoat – and a police search of Stoller's house failed to find anything resembling any of the clothes mentioned.

"The prosecution produced two other witnesses who depose to seeing someone *resembling* Stoller on the night of the murder at or near the scene of the crime: a Mr. John Armour, an employee of the Glasgow Central Railway who says he thought he remembered selling a man who looked like Stoller buy a ticket at Botanic Gardens Railway Station just after the time of the murder but he could not positively identify him; and a Miss Mary Duncan, who said she definitely saw a man alighting from a train in a most agitated state at Stobcross Station on the same line – she also could not positively identify him. Neither of these two witnesses knew Stoller beforehand. There is little agreement in any of those four original descriptions of Stoller. However, Morgan alone picked Stoller out at a parade in which *he was the only foreigner* amongst a cohort of fair-skinned, clean-shaven Celts, so he should have stood out whether he was a Frenchman, Ottoman, or Greek.

"Stoller who lives in Blythswood Drive, said that he never went near a railway station on the night. As regards his alleged movements, neither of the stations he is alleged to have been seen at would make any geographical sense. For example, to go to

Botanic Gardens Station from the Sixty Steps he would have had to walk half a mile away from the actual direction of his domicile; and the station which he is alleged to have alighted at would have taken him even further away from it and would entail a walk of over a mile back to reach home. As against that, a number of Stoller's acquaintances and friends who regularly played cards and billiards with the man, depose that Stoller, who has a dark complexion and jet-black hair always wore a thick moustache. They are Aaron Rolfe and Simon Aumann – we may discount those as his friends and countrymen, but there is also William Cameron Reid, a bookmaker; Charles Gibb, a billiard marker; Joseph Kempton, a grocer, and Bernard Schultz, his tailor – who incidentally deposed that he had never sold Stoller a light raincoat; and, finally and most notably the barber who had recently shaved him – Andrew Nichol. None of these is especially friendly with Stoller and none of the latter, apart from Schultz, is a countryman. All of them testify not only to Stoller's thick black moustache but also remember him mentioning the American invitation quite openly long before the murder took place – Rolfe and Aumann had both actually seen the letter and could quote the address in Bronx, New York."

"The question of identification is always a vexed one, Watson. I can recall two highly instructive cases: the case of Beck in London and that of Foster in Nürnberg. Beck, entirely innocent, was actually arrested twice on false identification and almost hanged on each occasion – what mental torments he must have gone through! According to Feuerbach, the eminent German jurist, Foster, who was almost certainly guilty, refused to confess and escaped the gallows solely through the absence of any eye-witnesses to the murder he had committed. I am coming around to the view that no jury should ever convict on witness identification alone, so unsafe is the practice."

167

"Another local shopkeeper, a cheesemonger, George Sillem, actually deposed that he nodded to Stoller, whom he knew well and to whom he had occasionally sold produce, as Stoller passed the shop on the evening of the murder. This was just as the church by the bridge began striking the third quarter – five minutes before the girl Morgan left to go out. Sillem, a man of excellent character with an exemplary military record, has a shop at in Great Western Road, about half a mile from the Sixty Steps, and at the time he saw Stoller, the latter was walking *away* from the direction of Miss Gilbert's house. If true it would have been physically impossible for Stoller to be the murderer, but Sillem's evidence was also, unaccountably, not led in court."

"How long had Stoller been in Glasgow?"

"Six months."

"May I take it that there is nothing to connect this small-time crook with a wealthy, highly respectable, elderly Christian spinster, or more importantly perhaps, with her housekeeper?"

"Nothing at all; at least, not until the City of Glasgow Police set to work on the case."

"To recapitulate, then. The prosecution case was that this man Stoller somehow obtained information as to the contents of the house, and then on the night of the murder managed to gain entry thereto. In doing so, he must have held the key to at least three locks or have been let in by the servant or the mistress herself. Having first paraded himself in front of his cheesemonger in order to establish an alibi, he sprinted the entire half-mile back to the house – an action liable to draw immediate attention. Then he murdered the old woman quite noisily, broke open – or unlocked with yet another falsely obtained key – the jewellery box on the spot rather than carry it with him, after which he selected but one piece, and a modest piece at that. Then having managed somehow to make his full black moustache invisible to the one witness who

168

appears to have an eye for detail, he calmly bade good evening to the neighbour and servant on his way out.

"Finally, although Stoller had the presence of mind to dispose of all the spare keys to the house and the fawn coat and whichever hat he was wearing on the night of the murder, and adopt a most circuitous route home, he did not bother to drop the murder weapon into the river which your map proclaims he crossed not once but twice; instead he took the hammer home with him, cleaned it up, and tucked it neatly into a cupboard for a clever policeman to come along and find easily."

"You sum it up precisely, Holmes."

"A remarkable performance!" said Holmes witheringly. "Especially since it would have entailed the police, by the operation of the purest and wildest coincidence, having managed to arrest the right man by having followed up the wrong clue with the wrong pawnbroker at the wrong time. Surely a set of coincidences even beyond the bounds of Mr. Dick Donovan's fantastic creations."

"Well, those are the essential facts which I have recounted to you," I replied, "and McIntosh hints at other more esoteric things in his missive, but I fear they must keep until morning for we had better get some rest. It is not difficult to see, though, why my friend McIntosh must have been confident of his client's acquittal."

"Indeed, Watson, the standard of police work in Glasgow begins to make Scotland Yard look like a school for geniuses."

Chapter 3

I am afraid to say that I did not sleep well on the journey north. Our compartment was towards the front of the train and my berth was unfortunately positioned right at the end of the carriage. The screaming of the steam whistle, the rattling of the wheels, and the swaying of the carriage over junction points all conspired to keep me from sleep. I had also, foolishly, drunk several cups of coffee after our excellent dinner in the Strand. When I finally drifted off it was into a fitful doze, for the exertions and excitements of the day and the enormity of our task had begun to play upon my mind. I have vivid recall of an anguished dream in which I saw the cold, damp stone wall of the gaol, a prison parson in requiem robe reciting the *De Profundis*, and the knotted hempen rope and stark triangular geometry of the waiting scaffold, before the cabin attendant woke me abruptly with a cup of tea.

Like Holmes, I had never visited Glasgow. On the approach to the town that cloudy murky morning, we saw from the carriage window mile upon dreary mile of high sooty tenement houses huddled at the feet of lofty factory chimney stacks; overall there hung a pall of damp sooty vapour which the city folk assured me, in their well-nigh impenetrable dialect, rarely dispersed. As the train snaked through the junction into the station, we caught a glimpse of the dark river with its many balustraded spans, choked with tugs and strings of barges. My first impression of the place was that it was, if anything, noisier, smokier, and dirtier than London; a thing I had not thought possible. And much colder too, for we had dropped at least ten degrees of Fahrenheit overnight, and a raw damp wind seemed to blow in the face and chafe the skin no matter which point of the compass one was facing. We deposited our luggage in the Station Hotel and then we set off up the steep hill to McIntosh's office in Blythswood Square, where he shared a floor with a stockbroker and a repairer of fountain pens.

My lawyer friend was delighted to see us and welcomed us warmly. Stout and jovial as ever, he was now bespectacled and heavily bearded too. Inevitably, there was an exchanging of the sort of reminiscences which might be imagined from old schoolfellows who had not set eyes on each other for twenty-odd years: recollections of rugby games, cricket matches, and the half-remembered *bon mots* and savage sarcasms of our college tutors followed one another in quick succession. McIntosh had been a brilliant boy at school, carrying off every prize for debating, and possessed a pawky and irreverent sense of humour; iconoclastic and ever popular at college, he had been constantly in brushes with authority, often over trifling matters. Indeed, I recall one of the history dons telling him that he "would have made a great Roundhead"; it was not intended as a compliment. When I heard that he had given up medicine in favour of law, and intended to specialise in criminal defence, I felt an inward delight that he had chosen a profession far more suited to his temperament, for he had as fine a way of putting ordinary people at their ease as any doctor I ever knew.

"Words cannot express my sincere gratitude to you, Mr. Holmes, for taking such great pains to make this journey north. I am sure our provincial problems must seem like trifles to a man of your remarkable achievements, but I can assure you that, in this case, it is quite literally a matter of life and death, and your particular, indeed unique, talents will not be wasted."

My old school friend's accent had hardly changed, and I noticed with a little thrill, that his intonation of the word "particular" still gave away his Aberdeenshire roots. Holmes afterwards said that he had reminded him of Inspector MacDonald of Scotland Yard with whom we had worked in the Birlstone affair.

"There are two people I should like you to meet, both of whom may be able to assist us in the case: the first is Rabbi Jacobs who is, if you like, my client's spiritual guardian, if, indeed, anyone can claim to be such. He is the custodian of the benevolent fund which has been set up by some Hebrew gentlemen in the city to disburse the expenses entailed in Stoller's defence."

"By all means," said Holmes warmly, "anyone is welcome who can provide us with useful information."

"The other is Detective-Lieutenant James Thomson Carlyle of the City of Glasgow Police."

"The City of Glasgow Police?" Holmes repeated incredulously.

"Why, surely," I cried, "they are the last people who would be likely to help us!"

"Aha! Watson, I beg you reserve your judgement until you hear what he has to say," replied McIntosh who rang a bell; a few moments later a young assistant led in the grey-haired, pleasant featured old rabbi followed by a tall, slim, and athletic looking fellow whose appearance and demeanour were as unlike those of a middle-ranking policeman as could be imagined. He carried a worn and dented bowler hat, wore a rather outdated suit, and had a thin, black, waxed moustache which emphasised his slightly melancholy smile. My lawyer friend completed the introductions.

"I believe I can claim your acquaintance by association, Mr. Holmes," said the rabbi. "You looked after my old friend Mossy Abrahams when he was threatened with his life by the dreadful Maksimienko. You remember Abrahams? From Shoreditch? He was to have been a witness in the Yiddish Music Hall murder trial."

"Ah, yes, I remember the case well. Abrahams was saved the trouble of testifying – Maksimienko did not survive to face the judge as it happened. He had a difference of opinion with yet another old foe of mine, the garrotter Merridew. We never yet found his body."

"Who lives by the sword!"

"Rabbi Jacobs has provided me with invaluable assistance in the case," continued McIntosh, "for instance, in uncovering evidence which would otherwise never have seen the light of day. It was he who found the shopkeeper Sillem who was standing smoking at his own shop door and who recognised Stoller clearly when he was alleged to be at the scene of the murder, and also the barber, Nichol, who averred that Stoller was wearing a full dark moustache. One thing I must explain to you first of all, Mr. Holmes, and I'm sure the reverend gentleman will understand, and excuse, my forthrightness in this matter: we cannot conceal from you that Osip Stoller is a denizen of the criminal underworld. He was living partly off the immoral earnings of his mistress, partly from resetting items of jewellery; he frequented illegal gambling dens where he was a notorious cardsharper; he has convictions for a number of minor crimes. He has left a string of creditors in towns and cities the length and breadth of Britain whom he has neither the ability nor the inclination to repay. When not engaged in some form of criminal activity, he was generally to be found playing billiards for money. And even then, I cannot swear that he did not use twisted cues and elliptical billiard balls, for his reputation was that he never seemed to lose a frame. So much so that he was banned from a number of billiard clubs and private card clubs. To complete the picture, he left Silesia in order to evade military service. So, there you have Osip Stoller: a perfect specimen of pimp, thief, fence, shyster, cheat, and coward."

"And Jewish to boot," added the rabbi, with a wry smile, "though frankly, I doubt he has been in *shul* since his bar mitzvah. Nevertheless, I try to find good in all men, even in Stoller. I visit him every day in the prison – do you know that he can hear the prison carpenter building the scaffold outside his window? Believe me he is a very frightened and chastened man, and I can tell you that if he receives justice, he will never again commit another crime. But, cometh the bad to the worst, I will accompany him to the gallows, and say *kaddish* over his body. Three hundred pounds I have managed to scrape together. Were he not such a *schmendrik*, were he a respectable tailor or a merchant, I should have raised several times that amount. From these funds I can disburse yours and the doctor's fees. If you would be so good as to give me some indication–"

"That will be a very simple matter," Holmes interjected, "we waive our fees entirely, though we may require the disbursement of a few expenses for I foresee that we may have – to put it quite bluntly – to grease the odd palm in order to loosen tongues."

"Then you are a saintly man, as well as a very wise one, Mr. Holmes. My son, Daniel, tells me that you do not know the meaning of failure."

Holmes smiled. "In truth, I have failed on a number of occasions, as Watson's chronicles will show. Perhaps the most tantalizing one was the case which was referred to me by an eminent detective agency in London. The head of a well-to-do family had died, and exactly one year to the day after his death a letter was received addressed to him. It bore the postmark of a quiet northern provincial town. The family opened the envelope and found nothing but a blank sheet of paper; they sent it to the agency who, finding they could extract nothing from it, passed it on to me. I submitted this blank sheet to every conceivable chemical and physical test known to science, with no success whatever. A fortnight of exhaustive inquiries in the provincial town in a variety of disguises produced a similar result. The paper remains to this day locked away in Watson's trunk awaiting, perhaps, some further advance in science to unravel the mystery! Now, to return to the case, I should like to speak to some of the witnesses."

"I am afraid you might find that rather difficult. Butler is gone back to sea; Morgan has returned to live with her family in Holytown and refuses to speak to anyone about the case. Indeed, the Crown witnesses, generally, have a disinclination to speak to anyone, even the press, and one can scarcely blame them after what they have been put through in the witness box."

"Well," said Holmes with a wry smile, "I relish a case where everything is against me from the start. I am at a distinct disadvantage here, for I do not have my underworld contacts, nor do I have a Lestrade or a Gregson to open official doors for me. I have heard the main points of the case from Watson. I readily agree that it is one of most blatant injustices with which I have become acquainted and one which cries out to be righted. The depravity of the victim's soul does not come into it."

Whether he sought his prey in the purlieus of seven dials or in the high towers of Hampstead, whether the person in distress spoke with vowels of the East or the West End, it was always my friend's way to recognise no social or racial distinction.

"I have many questions to ask," Holmes continued, "and should also like to see a transcript of the trial if you can provide me with one. We are lodging at the Station Hotel if you would be so good as to send it over."

McIntosh nodded and scribbled a note inside the file he had placed upon the table.

"I'll have it sent over this afternoon."

"The first thing that struck me was the number of inconsistencies in the evidence," Holmes continued. "The differing descriptions of the suspect by two people who had stood within a few feet of the probable murderer; the unlikelihood, as stated by the first doctor who attended the scene, of Stoller's hammer having been the murder weapon; the fact that Stoller's brooch had been pawned before the murder; the identification, effectively an alibi, provided by the shopkeeper, Sillem. I am also, quite frankly, astounded and appalled that neither the doctor nor Mr. Sillem was called by the defence."

"As am I, Mr. Holmes, as am I! You understand my position, of course – the solicitor has no real influence over the advocate once the proceedings have begun. We can but advise and suggest. If my counsel is ignored, as it was in this case, I have no legal or moral redress unless the advocate breaches the rules of his profession."

"It would have been open to you, would it not, to dispense with the advocate's services?" I asked.

"Frankly, I *was* minded to discharge McKinnon on the very first day of the trial but, as you will understand, changing horses in midstream is an extremely risky business when a man's head is at stake, for it may have the effect of signifying to the jury that there is a weakness in your case, and they are apt to adjudge accordingly."

"I should like to hear anything you wish to add to the bare outline of the case which I have heard," said Holmes.

"Indeed, you shall! But I fear the statement of this case may take up a good part of the morning, Mr. Holmes. Aye, what a tale I have to tell you and my old friend Watson!"

"Then proceed without delay," said Holmes, rubbing his hands.

"First of all, I shall tell you of a rather unusual, indeed in my professional experience unprecedented occurrence, which immediately followed the passing of the verdict upon Stoller. It came about in this way. On the morning after sentence of death was pronounced, I received a visit from this young man," he nodded towards Carlyle. "He had initially been involved in chiefly routine aspects of the case, such as obtaining minor witness statements and checking alibis and so on. He informed me that he had taken a statement from a Miss Margaret Healy – the niece of the old woman and – *nota bene* – a potential legatee. Go on, tell your story, Lieutenant Carlyle."

"Nancy Morgan had asked the police if she could leave the house to tell Miss Healy that her aunt had been murdered," began the young man, whose overwhelming impression was one of sincerity and conscientiousness. "It was authorised, since they knew Healy to be a close relative and the news was now travelling fast all over the district, as you may imagine. Miss Healy deposed to me that Morgan had arrived, still in a state of the most terrible shock, and told her the whole story. When asked by Healy whom she thought had done this thing, Morgan said it was one of Miss Gilbert's nephews! Miss Healy deposed to me that she asked Morgan, 'Was that the man in the hall?' following which Morgan answered 'Yes' and burst into the most violent hysterical sobbing and would not stop. I noted this at the time in the presence of Healy, Morgan and my colleague, Constable Gavin Duncan, and I then submitted the notes in the normal manner as formal evidence. Prior to the case going to court, but unknown to me, Healy retracted her statement, Morgan also denied ever having said those words, and Constable Duncan, who had accompanied me, appeared to have no recollection either."

"But surely those notes of yours were produced as evidence?" said Holmes animatedly.

"My superintendent, Mr. Stevenson, avers that he never received any notes in evidence though I can assure you I posted them in the evidence box provided in his office."

"How can this be?"

"I cannot say. The evidence box, or rather all the live evidence boxes, are in a kind of anteroom to prevent the superintendent being disturbed too often and allow him some privacy. Unless the evidence is urgent, the papers are posted in the boxes which are opened every morning by one of the desk sergeants and each item of evidence is placed on top of the correct file for the case, or a new file is opened and delivered to the superintendent personally, which he then signs for. My report, you must remember was merely routine – it was a check on the whereabouts of Margaret Healy who, although she had no alibi, was never at any time a serious suspect. Only uniformed policemen and detectives may gain access to the anteroom where the box is kept and *only* we have keys to the box. In fact, anyone going into the superintendent's room has to pass a police clerk who is on desk duty continuously, but no one seemed to have remembered seeing me going into the anteroom. That alone would prove nothing, for there is a constant traffic of constables and sergeants, uniformed and in plainclothes, delivering official papers there for signature. And on that particular night in question, the station was buzzing like an upset beehive due to the murder, and also to the fact that it was a Saturday night with the usual drunks and ne'er-do-wells, and arrests for brawling at football matches."

"Dear me, this is quite serious," said Holmes, looking quite perplexed. He ruminated for some time.

"I know what you are thinking, Mr. Holmes," said McIntosh with a glint in his eye. It was one of my old friend's qualities to be able to read the thoughts of even so inscrutable a character as Holmes. "It is the word of three witnesses and a senior policeman

178

against a junior colleague. No doubt you are beginning to wonder what kind of record Lieutenant Carlyle has."

I cannot say that Holmes actually blushed – he is incapable of such a reaction, but he took some time to recover himself and then looked inquiringly at Carlyle.

"I shall answer for him," said McIntosh. "He has an outstanding record and a character which is without blemish. He is not only the youngest person ever to have held the special rank of Detective-Lieutenant, but some months ago went down to Buckingham Palace to collect the Queen's Gallantry Medal for Bravery, from Her Majesty, no less. He also rescued a drowning boy in a swirling ebb one murky night from a tidal stretch of the River Clyde, and once entered a burning house to save a blind woman's dog. And here is something which will perhaps bring the matter within the scope of your own *métier,* as well as touching the fabric of the present case – he was instrumental in getting a young American off on a charge of murder two years ago in Dundee.

"To cut a long story short, the young man who was suspected by the police of killing an elderly woman had no alibi but averred that he had been travelling in Europe and that on the very day of the murder, he had pawned his waistcoat in Antwerp. He produced what he claimed to be the ticket, although the police disbelieved this, for following the offer of a reward, there came forth the inevitable drove of witnesses to identify him. He obtained this ticket from the accused man, took a part of his annual quota of leave, and travelled to Antwerp, much to the scorn and amusement of his colleagues. He returned several days later, having found the pawnshop and redeemed the pledge, and he presented the waistcoat to officer in charge of the murder case. Aye, at least one American citizen has reason to owe his life to our young friend here, and I'll say that for bravery, intelligence, and commitment to justice at any cost, you would travel a long day before you would find a man to equal Lieutenant Carlyle of the Glasgow City Police Force!"

He was beginning to impress me more and more this young man and I felt almost as though we ought to have stood and applauded McIntosh's histrionic eulogy; I have no doubt that that was the sort of effect that he was, with ease, used to producing in court.

"After the arrest of Stoller," Carlyle said, "I began to perceive the striking resemblance between the Antwerp case and the Gilbert case and the collection of unreliable identification witnesses."

Holmes nodded, "That was perspicacious of you; but to return the subject of the missing evidence, how do *you* account for its disappearance?"

"I cannot, Mr. Holmes," he said quietly, "but the day after my visit to this very office I was suspended indefinitely from duty by Superintendent Stevenson!"

Even the normally impassive Holmes looked dumbfounded, and it was certainly rare for me to see him lost for words. I began to wonder even at this early stage, how many further twists and turns this dramatic case might yet take. Carlyle's bland but intriguing statement, which we had no cause to doubt, recalled to me the words of an American client of Holmes who once said during a case that he thought he had "stepped into the middle of a dime novel."

"Do you mean to suggest, then, that Stoller's conviction is not simply the result of mere incompetence upon the part of the police and the Crown?" asked Holmes. "Are you suggesting it is the result of some sort of conspiracy, which includes interfering with evidence?"

"I should not go so far as that," said McIntosh. "Lieutenant Carlyle was suspended from his job with full pay and has been charged with the disciplinary offence of disclosing facts to me which are police and Crown matters. As his disciplinary case is *sub judice*, he is for all purposes *incommunicado* – at least officially. Of course, Lieutenant Carlyle's version of events directly implicates the superintendent himself in the missing evidence and it is not difficult to see why the superintendent acted as he has done. Perhaps it is a subtle punishment for breaking ranks in the Dundee case; it will have the effect of keeping Lieutenant Carlyle silent until ..." here he hesitated with a glance at the rabbi, "until the due process of law runs its full course."

"You mean, by which time Stoller will have been hanged?" asked the rabbi.

"I did not wish to be brutal, but, yes, that is what I mean," said McIntosh.

"And when is that fatal date?' I asked.

"The sixth day of January is the last day that Osip Stoller will walk this earth,' said the rabbi grimly. "Unless ..."

"What is the cause of their antipathy, is it the fact that he is a Jew?" I asked the rabbi.

"I am not certain," said Jacobs, "this is not France, after all. Six people on the jury did not think him guilty, and not all of the people who have made subscriptions to our campaign are Jewish, nor are all of the twenty-thousand or so who have signed our petition. They are concerned about justice, whether Jew, Gentile, or Mohammedan. This girl Morgan, was she malicious? I believe so, but it is difficult to say whether she was prejudiced. As for the police and the judge, ah, well that is a different matter, but impossible to prove. Someone described Stoller in court as having 'a Jewish nose,' but otherwise the word was not used during the trial but, you know, there was a little sly hint here and there about

181

'aliens.' Stoller was generally described in the press as 'German,' but of course, since the Jameson affair[20], there has been no lack of hostility here towards the German race either for that matter!"

"There was, without a whit of doubt, a vein of prejudice running through the entire affair," said McIntosh. "Let me read you just a few words from the trial judge's summing up: *'Stoller has maintained himself by the ruin of men and on the ruin of women, living for years past in a way that many blackguards would scorn to live'* – how's that, gentlemen, for judicial independence?!"

"It certainly surpasses the usual platitudes from the bench," I replied.

"Aye, Watson, that was from Lord Guthrie – one of our fire-and-brimstone teetotallers. The legal establishment had their man, and they would allow nothing and no one to stand in the way of a conviction and an execution. I believe that the real reason why Lieutenant Carlyle was suspended was that he was able to cast some doubt upon the Crown case."

"Why did you not come to see Mr. McIntosh before the trial?" Holmes asked Carlyle.

"I did not, and could not, know at that point that my evidence – which pointed not to Stoller but to a family member – was not only not being called, but had never seen the light of day."

"Frankly now, do you believe that Superintendent Stevenson destroyed the evidence?"

"No, I do not," replied the young man forcefully.

"Nor do I," added McIntosh, with similar emphasis.

"Then how …"

"That is the question which I am in great hopes that *you* will address Mr. Holmes. You have the vision, the perspicacity …"

At that point, we were brought our morning coffee by the office boy and the discussion was curtailed while my lawyer friend handed round the cups.

Chapter 4

After Carlyle had departed, McIntosh resumed his story.

"There are number of aspects which did not come up in court, some of which you may deem irrelevant, but I shall bring them to your attention in any case and you shall form your own judgment, dismissing them should you see fit. Prior to the murder, Miss Gilbert was given a dog as a present from one of her nephews on her birthday, around the time she had returned from her September holiday in the Trossachs area. The purpose of the dog was to allay Miss Gilbert's fears on the few occasions when she was left alone – such as on the servant's day off or her holidays. The dog, it appears, was poisoned about two weeks before the murder."

"The exact date being?" asked Holmes.

"The third week in September is the nearest estimate, and from that point forward, some rather odd things seemed to happen in the vicinity of the Sixty Steps. The close immediately opposite number 8, number 13, which has a landing window at the front of the building – facing Miss Gilbert's drawing room – had its gas stairlight turned off on a number of occasions in the early evening. This had never happened before, nor has it happened since."

"The beginning of the campaign," said Holmes, rubbing his hands. McIntosh nodded and continued.

"Several people, around twelve in number, have deposed to seeing a strange man loitering about the area, invariably near the wall at the top of the flight of steps, between the end of September and the night of the murders. That is an area which is fairly busy at certain times of the day as it is the nearest route to the main thoroughfare in the district and to the cab stand by Walker's Bridge in Queen Margaret Road. This man was seen smoking and loitering in the same place, often staring towards Miss Gilbert's house. I should have been inclined to discount those reports which were made after the event. However, five of the witnesses mentioned the sighting to another person *before* the murder, and one witness, a Mrs. Corbett – the wife of the doctor who attended the scene just after the discovery of the crime – had gone so far as to actually report the man's presence to a beat constable some four days *beforehand*. The constable later confirmed this: he recorded it in his notebook it at the time, and said he would keep a look-out, though he never did catch sight of the man himself."

McIntosh drew some papers from the file and continued.

"Here are the corroborated depositions of those five people who had described the man in some detail: Mrs. Corbett, of whom we know; Mr. Fraser Neilson, a senior railway clerk; Mr. Thomas Jackson, a publican; the Reverend Jocelyn Emmet, rector of St. Mary's; and Mr. Angus McNevin, a legal assistant who spotted the man on a number of occasions from the rear window of his flat in Queen Margaret Road. All thoroughly respectable and reliable people, most of whom are in positions of trust. Now, here is a plan of the area showing the house and the steps.

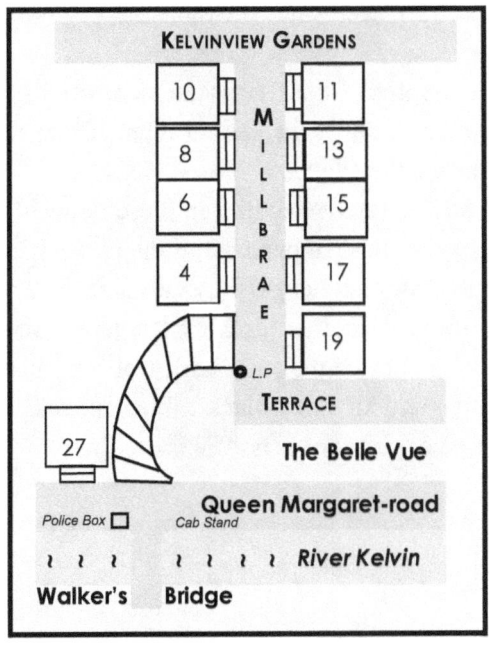

" ... a plan of the area showing the house and the steps."

"There is a lamppost at the top of the steps by a low wall encircling a terrace that is called the Belle Vue; this is where the man stood, and from there he appears to have been watching the close of number 8 in an attempt, we assume, to note the coming and goings of the occupants of Miss Gilbert's flat.

"I'll hazard those sightings of this man were always at approximately the same time as the murder was committed on the night."

"Quite correct."

"Do the descriptions of this watching man tally with that of Stoller?"

"They are nothing like them."

"Or the stranger in the hall?"

"No."

"Then the assumption is that this was an accomplice of the murderer, not the murderer himself."

"That seems a reasonable inference."

"Has this man been seen since the murder?"

"No."

Holmes then applied himself to the depositions to which McIntosh had referred, and then passed them to me in turn. At length, Holmes broke the silence.

"Something strikes me as peculiar in these depositions," said Holmes indicating the sheaf of papers, "of the five reliable people who saw this watching man, as we may call him, loitering in the street at the top of the steps, there is complete unanimity as to his outfit; each states a short light coat, dark trousers, black shoes, checked cloth cap – and all agree black leather gloves."

"Yes, it is to be expected is it not?"

"Perhaps, but the thing that is odd," Holmes continued, "is the fact that while is complete unanimity as to his mode of dress, the body and facial descriptions are quite discrepant are they not? Three say quite clearly that he was tall and sallow skinned, dark hair, sharp features; the other two state, just as emphatically, that he was slim or athletic, medium height, and lighter coloured."

"Aye, it is just as you say," said McIntosh.

"It is the first indication I have received, that this might be even more complicated than I had first thought."

"More complicated!" gasped the rabbi, almost oversetting his cup. "It was not complicated enough?!"

"Anything else?" asked Holmes.

"Yes. Stoller was arrested by the police at his home. His mistress and his servant both say that he arrived at home about eight o'clock – consistent with Sillem seeing him when and where he did. It is understandable that his mistress was not called in court, she is, after all, already his *de facto* partner in crime, and would be expected to lie in order to save her man from the scaffold, but is it likely that a mere paid servant would put her neck in a noose, as an accomplice to murder?"

"I agree it is highly unlikely."

"Yet she was not called as a witness either; nor was the pawnbroker who averred that the brooch Stoller pawned had been in his possession some two weeks before the murder."

"So I understand."

"There was a box which may or may not have contained jewellery but nothing, it appears, was taken other than the brooch; and yet it is by no means certain that it had actually been stolen, because no one can apart from Morgan can remember seeing it. A further three hundred pounds was concealed, but not particularly well-concealed, in the wardrobe from which the box was taken, and there were other small amounts lying about the house, none of which were taken. A suggestion that–"

"That the intruder may not have been after either jewels or money, but was after something else which he believed to have been contained inside the box? Quite plausible, on the face of it is it not – yet, if not money or jewels then what was he after?"

"Some speculation has been made to the effect that the box was rifled because of the contents or suspected contents of a possible will and that, of course, would naturally implicate the relatives. Miss Gilbert had four male relatives, all nephews; two are successful men and very comfortably off. They are the Findlaters: Archibald, in fact, is a legal brother of mine; Lennox is a very successful doctor, and it was he who gave the old woman the dog. Both are at the heads of their respective professions, and Lennox is about to take up a position as a Head of Faculty at St. Andrew's University. I should say it is highly unlikely that they have had anything to do with this."

Holmes nodded.

"There are two other nephews: Austin Birrell and Winton Healy. The latter are sons of Mrs. Josephine Healy, now deceased, Miss Gilbert's late sister who re-married after the death of the father of Mr. Birrell, that is, Austin Birrell's father. As far as we know, Winton Healy died some time ago in New Zealand, around 1886 during the long depression there. His younger step-brother, Austin Birrell, had also not been heard of for some time, and did not attend the aunt's funeral. However, inquiries were instituted, and the Glasgow police received this from their counterparts in London who managed to run him to earth." McIntosh handed us a slip of paper from the file which read:

"Telegram received from London Metropolitan Police, Limehouse [23 October, 1897; 1.49 p.m.].

To Chief Supt. City Police, Glasgow.

Re: Murder of Maureen Gilbert and Whereabouts of Austin Birrell.

It has been ascertained that Austin Birrell was at his place of employment, Greenwich Gasworks, on the evening of 16th inst. Confirmed to me personally by Geo. Hescott, Esq., Manager, South Metropolitan Gas Company.

Signed: Inspector J. Bradstreet, 'R' Division, London Metropolitan Police."

"I think you will agree that rather clears Austin Birrell and Winton Healy of any likelihood of being implicated in the old woman's murder."

"Austin Birrell, yes; but I should like more details in order to be absolutely certain about this Winton Healy. In my experience, presumed deceased relatives have a disconcerting tendency to reincarnate in probate cases, especially where there are large sums at stake. As it happens, I have a correspondent in New Zealand, Mr. Silas Spragg, of the 'Auckland Daily Herald' with whom I shall confer. What about the female relatives?"

"Mrs. Healy's unmarried daughter Margaret, the one whom Carlyle interviewed, lives nearby and is the only niece, the sister of Winton and step-sister of Austin. There are no other surviving relatives, only those five. Incidentally, Miss Margaret Healy had no alibi on the night, but there appears to have been no suspicion thrown on her at any time. It is certainly difficult to cast her as the one who hammered the old woman's brains out with the leg of a chair."

"Indeed, had she been the murderess it is more likely that she would have used some form of poison."

"Although the surviving Healys and Birrells are not all wealthy or even comfortably off, they are certainly of sufficient education as to understand that merely to destroy the *client's* copy of a will, would have no legal or practical effect."

"And what were the provisions of the will?" Holmes asked.

"Miss Gilbert left all her worldly goods and her money to Mrs. Kate Sutherland, *neé* Scott, who once occupied the position in her household subsequently held by Miss Nancy Morgan."

Homes raised his eyebrows, "How very singular!" he said.

"Of all that is fanciful!" I remarked. "I had always believed that inheriting a fortune from a stranger was one of those things that happened only in the works of Mr. Dickens and other harmless fables."

"Not so, friend Watson. Though Mrs. Sutherland was hardly a stranger, having been in service with the old woman for many years. She has inherited the estate to the value of twelve thousand pounds, which includes the house itself, the three thousand pounds worth of jewellery and the cash which was in the house; of course, the probate case has yet run its course and the will could be challenged. Mrs. Sutherland was domestic servant to Miss Gilbert for many years before her marriage to an engine driver on the North British Railway, a William Sutherland. Miss Gilbert paid for the wedding, and when Mrs. Sutherland's own eldest daughter was born, she was christened Maureen, and was called 'Maisie' after Miss Gilbert. Mrs. Sutherland was a regular visitor to Millbrae Terrace after her marriage, and in fact was there just two days before the murder."

"A strong bond indeed," said Holmes, "Did they know of the impending legacy?"

"It was no secret; for all her eccentricity, Miss Gilbert seems to have been a kindly woman and had wanted them to know that they would be financially secure after her death."

"Then, at least in theory, they may have had a material interest in, shall we say, hastening her departure from this earthly demesne."

"In theory, yes; in practice, however, the Sutherlands wanted for nothing, and William Sutherland went to work solely out of manly pride. Incidentally, he was driving a train to Dundee on the night of the murder and his wife was at home at her cottage in Callander with a neighbour. They were already enjoying their legacy in advance – as it were – and, frankly, it would require a quite monstrous conspiracy for the Sutherlands to have been in any way involved in the murder of Miss Gilbert."

"Well, I could tell you of for more monstrous ones, formulated in order to gain far less than twelve thousand pounds."

"Yes, but if this box had been rifled because of the contents of the will, that would hardly put the Sutherlands in the limelight, as they stood to benefit *in statu quo*; in point of fact only a *codicil* to the existing will, negating the former effect, would have been of any interest to them."

"It occurs to me that that is precisely what Mrs. Sutherland and Miss Gilbert may have been discussing on the visit two days before the murder!" said Holmes.

"It is possible, but we are entering the realm of speculation. In fact," said McIntosh, "given Morgan's obvious prevarication, I had not entirely ruled out the possibility of some collusion between the two young neighbours."

"If there were any collusion, it is more likely that the descriptions of the stranger in the hall would have tallied right down to the shirt buttons. But, surely, one of the vital points was that of the man seen in the hall was identified as the nephew of the murdered woman. Who was it – which nephew?"

"The name of the relative was, apparently, never disclosed by Morgan to Healy in Carlyle's presence therefore, he cannot say with any certainty to whom Morgan referred, he merely reported the facts which he had discovered. I hesitate strongly to deal in gossip, Mr. Holmes, but there is no use in my pretending that I do not know the name of the man who has been implicated. It is whispered behind hands in every Masonic Lodge and every private club around the fashionable parts of the city. It is Lennox Findlater."

"The doctor!" I gasped

"I am sorry to say so. All the more so, since he is the brother of a legal colleague. I cannot possibly believe he has had anything remotely to do with it. He looks nothing like the man described either by Morgan or Butler, but Lennox Findlater appeared on the doorstep within minutes of the alarm being raised – his laboratory, where he was working that evening, is only a few minutes from his aunt's flat – he said he had been there when the murder took place."

"How was he able to get there so quickly?"

"His medical colleague, Dr. Corbett, who was the first doctor on the scene, knew that he was related to Miss Gilbert, and walked round to tell him. Indeed, he invited him to come to the house, and I am sure it is this sudden appearance of his which led to the rumour. However, whether he is or is not the person identified by Morgan, it appears that there has been a concerted effort by the legal establishment to keep his name out of it. It is as unfortunate as it is inevitable that many people find it difficult to read anything other than guilt into that."

"You have had no communication, I take it, with Archibald Findlater on the subject since the trial?"

"None. An uneasy truce obtains; after all, as far as he sees it, I am defending not only the man who murdered his aunt but also the man who has, albeit inadvertently, spread the rumour about his brother."

"But Carlyle did not actually name Lennox Findlater?"

"No, but it may amount to the same thing as far as his brother is concerned."

"We had better speak to Archibald Findlater directly. Also, I should very much like to examine the house and visit the street where the murder was committed at a similar time of evening."

"I will collect the keys from the estate agent – the house is being sold, as you might understand – you will easily pass for a couple of gentlemen interested in a west end property."

Chapter 5

Archibald Findlater was a small, thin, dapper man, sharp-eyed and alert. He had a dazzling, disarming smile and a tendency to speak very quickly but precisely, marshalling his words to good effect. He reminded me of one of our great flyweight boxers, shifting nimbly, picking his punches shrewdly and cleanly, and one could easily see how he would make a most favourable impression in a court of law. However, much we may have surprised him by our visit, he fairly astounded us with his opening words as he motioned us to a couple of chairs.

"Mr. Holmes, by all that is wonderful! I have heard of your great powers, but I had not heard that clairvoyance was amongst them," he said his eyes sparkling with wit and intelligence. "I mean, of course, that you could not possibly have seen my telegram."

"Your telegram?" Holmes shook his head, "No, I'm afraid that you have the advantage of me."

"I dispatched a telegram to your address this morning to enquire as to whether you would take up the case–"

"Of your unfortunate brother, in relation to the slanderous rumours about the tragic death of your aunt."

"Then you did see it!"

"No."

"Then how …"

"I had better explain. We have come to Glasgow in response to a summons from your colleague, Mr. Crawford McIntosh, in connection with the same case."

"Ah, then you will be aware of the circumstances of the case. McIntosh is, of course, acting for Stoller and the disgraced policeman. No doubt you have eliminated Stoller as the culprit and have now turned your attention to the immediate circle of the

194

family in order to identify an alternative candidate. You are aware of the speculation surrounding the will, have heard all the rumours concerning my unfortunate brother, how the police have covered up for him by browbeating a servant, framing a detective for an offence he did not commit, and attempting to hang an innocent man in the bargain. There is, I am told by a fellow club member, a variant of the rumour, originating from some cretin of a journalist, which had both Lennox *and* I climbing in the windows in order to murder our aunt and steal the will! Lennox, in this version, had the decency to stay behind to allow me to escape via the roan pipe. If you have come to ask me if I think Lennox is the murderer, the answer is no, I know he is not.

"Quite apart from anything else, you may or may not know that we are not blood relatives, for my mother, you see, was already the widow of Miss Gilchrist's brother, when she met my late father. We could have had no possible claim on the estate at law on any consanguineal basis. I am sure you do not imagine that we would jeopardise our careers and our reputations, not to mention our lives, for the sake of what would amount to a few years' salary to us both. If you do, then you clearly do not possess the great analytical powers with which you have been attributed."

Holmes was slightly taken aback by this forthright opening sally; however, he merely smiled.

"It was obvious me from the outset, Mr. Findlater, that if your brother had had anything to do with this, he would have concocted a rather more convincing alibi than that he was working alone in his laboratory all evening. No, I am as convinced of his innocence as I am of Stoller's and had come here merely to ascertain whether you or your brother have any information whatever which might shed some light on the case. If you can assist me in finding the real culprit then that will dispel forever the rumours which have attached themselves to your brother, will it not? I think that is the best way that we can be of service to you."

Findlater nodded, which Holmes took as a sign to continue.

"One thing puzzles me, so, let me begin there. Have you any idea why your aunt should, as it were, cut out her entire family, and so grandly endow someone who was, after all, merely a paid domestic servant and a former one at that?"

Findlater's eyes shone brightly as he laughed.

"Let me assure you, Mr. Holmes, that if you had spent as many years in probate as I have, then you would have come across far stranger wills and precatory orders than that of my aunt's. Did you ever hear of *Breckenridge vs. Jenkinson*? Or *Cheverton vs. Roche*? No? The former cut out his entire family and left half a million pounds to his pet bird, a fine Lesser Antillean macaw. Look them up! You'll be amused, enlightened, and astonished all at once. I'll confess that I was mildly surprised myself at the identity of the legatees, for I had thought that Aunt Maisie would have left most of her estate either to a cat and dog home or possibly to the Kirk to disburse as charity. In truth, she had little in common with her only surviving blood relatives who have been content to live in a kind of feckless, drifting, genteel poverty. Now, I assume you will want to speak to Lennox at some point too, Mr. Holmes, for I am aware of your view that a doctor is the first of criminals, as you have put it."

Holmes shook his head emphatically. "No, not unless absolutely necessary."

"Good, I do not see how he could be of any practical help to you, and he has suffered enough. Lennox is not very ... worldly. If I am to be honest with you, Mr. Holmes, I think it is partly his own diffidence which has exacerbated the dreadful rumour. Rather than denying the allegation, and making some effort to counter it, his tendency has been simply to regard it as absurd. He

196

has shown an innocence about the affair that is almost childish. '*Of course,* people know I didn't kill my poor aunt Maisie!' he merely says. He does not even seem to bear any resentment against whoever begat the rumour. 'Oh, people will gossip anyway, so what's the use,' is all I have got out of him when I try to rile him into action. He has no idea what these people are saying behind his back."

"As regards your aunt's wealth, may I ask how she came about it?"

"She inherited it from her father – and thereby hangs another tale! Old Willie Gilbert was the proprietor of one of the leading furniture retailers in the city."

"Ah, trade, not profession."

"Indeed, though the distinction would be somewhat less weighty in Glasgow than in, say, Edinburgh. He was self-taught, raised himself from relative poverty, and sold the business in order to retire, or so he thought, to a life of leisure. First of all, his wife died after a long illness within the first year of his retirement, then the following year he himself started to deteriorate quite rapidly with some wasting disease and, despite a couple of false rallies, he too yielded up the spirit."

"How long ago was that?"

"Thirty years ago – April 1867 I believe. Only Maisie, the youngest, stayed with the father until the bitter end, and bitter it was too, believe me. William, who could be cantankerous and harsh, not to say slightly vindictive, left everything to Maisie – cut the other three siblings out without a penny. Although Maisie was the favourite daughter, her father was of the old stern Calvinist type, and I believe there was a story at the time that he had forbidden her to marry during his lifetime on pain of disinheritance. It came to nothing in the end since, as far as I could see, Aunt Maisie had little fondness for the male species and yet, perversely in view of the present circumstances, she had something approaching affection for Lennox. He seemed to have more patience than the rest of us with her rather eccentric ways, and of course they had a shared interest in religion – he is a lay preacher – although Aunt Maisie remained of the old Free Kirk persuasion. In many ways, she is her father's daughter."

"I assume there was some dissension in the family as regards the settlement of the will?" I asked.

"Dissension, Mr. Holmes?" Findlater laughed, "There was merry hell! In short, the other three siblings never spoke to Aunt Maisie again."

"Are they still alive?"

"No, they are all dead, and perceiving the direction of your cross-examination and anticipating your next question, I can tell you that, apart from the late Mrs. Healy – the mother of Austin, Margaret, and Winton – they all died unwed and childless. I suppose, knowing probate as well as I do," he said with a smile, "I should say *apparently* unwed and childless for it is not difficult to conceal these things."

"And you know of no other relatives?"

"Other than Birrells and the Healys, none at all."

"Have you any personal contact with them?"

"Very little, I hardly know them; they are not blood relations, as I said. Winton Healy, the younger brother, who was always a bit of a ne'er-do-well, went off to the antipodes some time ago and was never heard of or seen again; he is believed to have died about ten years ago. Austin Birrell came to me professionally a few years ago when he was at a low ebb. His business had failed badly, and I handled his bankruptcy for a reduced fee. I later helped to establish him in writing – I have a few contacts in publishing, you understand – the best I could do was to find him an occasional column in an evening paper. He began writing detective stories for

The Globe, which has traditionally been a place for writers beginning their careers.

"Like many authors, he has alternating fits of inebriation and sobriety – *present company excepted,* Dr. Watson! I am a scribbler like yourself and have produced a few volumes of humorous legal anecdotes and a novel about a thoroughly unscrupulous lawyer. If a doctor is first in criminal leanings for nerve and knowledge, as you once suggested, Mr. Holmes, then a solicitor would surely be a very close second. However, I digress. I last heard of Austin in London when, somewhat against my better judgement, I signed a testimonial for him to take up a post as a timekeeper in the gasworks in Greenwich. I reasoned that even a feckless chump such as he could hardly do much harm in such a post. However, that was some time ago and I have not heard from him, or of him, since then. Otherwise, my path does not cross with those of the Birrells or Healys, I am happy to say."

"Are there any other legatees apart from Mrs. Sutherland?"

"My aunt left a sizeable sum of money to buy an annuity for the James Johnston Trust, which as I recall, is a Christian organisation which administers the funds on behalf of the Society for the Welfare of Indigenous Children in New Zealand. Aunt Maisie had visited the place at some point in her early life as part of a missionary campaign and was moved by the plight of the impoverished native population. She was a great believer in the three virtues, especially charity, though I should point out that she was not one of the Mrs. Jellyby type: she well understood that charity begins at home. I know she liked to live within walking distance of the Kirk where she did much great charitable work for the poor and elderly. That used to amuse Lennox – some of the 'elderly' were at least a decade younger than she! But on these trips, she was mingling with some of the lowest classes and, respectable though the Sixty Steps undoubtedly is, it is shoulder to shoulder with some of the worst slum districts in the city. Full of ill-kempt, half-starved children and yet there are a hundred public houses to the square mile. I suppose I should not be surprised at what has happened."

"Do you know who this James Johnston is and whether he is still alive?"

"Other than that he appears to have been the founder of this Trust, I have no idea. I could ask Lennox, I suppose."

"Please do, it is always important to hunt up apparently trivial clues, for one never knows where they may lead. You see, we now have a second connection with New Zealand, which is where Winton Healy went. When two people who have such a close link to a murder victim travel twelve thousand miles to end up in the same place, I am naturally suspicious."

"Yes, I quite see that now."

"There has been some speculation that the assailant may have been after important documents. Do you have any idea what they might have been?"

"None whatsoever, though I had not given the matter any thought. Frankly, the unjustified slight upon my brother has cast the whole thing in a different light, and though not wishing to sound callous or disrespectful to the memory of my late aunt, my concern has been for the living rather than the dead. Obviously, it was not the will, nor can it have been the title deeds, or bank accounts, all of which were in my aunt's name and lodged with me, since I acted as her solicitor. To steal copies of any of those would have been absurd. It remains a mystery to me."

"Thinking of the girl Morgan and the discrepancies in her testimony, do you know of any reason why she might want to shield anyone?"

"None at all, nor could she have had any possible motive for murder, for it will have thrown her out of what was, notwithstanding my aunt's eccentricities, a rather easy berth. Nevertheless, I would not trust that girl an inch, Mr. Holmes. McKinnon, for the defence, referred to her as unscrupulous and untruthful, perhaps that is to be expected, but the presiding judge described her as an unreflective girl of small mental capacity – I believe he was being kind; even the prosecuting counsel, Fraser Woods, told me some time later that he found her cunning and duplicitous. It must be obvious that she was the one who mentioned Lennox's name out of pure spite, and that she has wilfully misidentified Stoller as the man in the house, whether through her own avarice – such as a desire for a share of the reward – or through subtle pressure applied elsewhere, I am unable to say."

"The police, perhaps?"

"It is entirely possible. They are certainly no angels; in fact, I feel I ought to warn you that the prospect of an English private detective arriving here to undo the clever work of the Glasgow Police and make fools, not to say knaves, out of them will not be appreciated."

"To return to the main beneficiaries of the legacy, the Sutherlands, are you satisfied that they had nothing to do with the murder?"

"Professionally, you take me out of my depth for criminal law is not my *métier*. But the Sutherlands have always seemed to me to be a decent hard-working family, and Kate was certainly a very faithful servant to my aunt in her days in service. Without wishing to be condescending, I think it would be fair to say that the Sutherlands live in a degree of comfort far beyond their means to provide, and it must be pretty obvious where that money comes from. Aunt Maisie visited them on many occasions, and she also took them on holiday twice a year, generally to the island of Arran in summer and to a village in the Trossachs, Callander, where Kate was born and returned after her marriage.

"Neither I nor Lennox grudge the Sutherlands a single groat of that inheritance, for my aunt could be rather more than merely eccentric at times; to put it mildly, she could also be downright carnaptious, a word used in these parts to describe a particular species of cantankerousness. I also seem to recall that my aunt was treated by Dr. McDonald for a problem with overwrought nerves two months before her death. Kate came back to live with her at that time and nursed her through her illness."

"What if the will were to be challenged by one of the surviving relations, say Austin Birrell or Margaret Healy?"

"I should say it would be the quickest way to bankruptcy for the plaintiff, Mr. Holmes; we have all read of the fictional but cautionary tale of Jarndyce *versus* Jarndyce! And in real life, suits in Chancery do not come cheaply. The will is perfectly sound as things stand, and though it might be challenged by a consanguineal relation, I should certainly not advise it professionally, for the terms are pretty clear and it was amended and re-endorsed relatively recently – on the 16th of August to be precise. Of course, any claim that the benefactor was either insane or mentally unstable or was placed under any kind of duress at the time the will was made would be a different matter."

"Why was it amended?"

"To provide Mrs. Sutherland's daughter, Maisie, with a share to be held in trust. Previously, there had been small shares for each of the two nephews and the niece, but I heard that Margaret Healy went so far as to make some none-too-subtle references to an expected share of the legacy in her presence some years ago, and knowing the old lady as I do, this would have vexed her greatly. Then one of the nephews, I believe, tried to touch her for a few pounds and he was sent away with a flea in his ear. She saw the whole lot as lazy, grasping and presumptuous – frankly with much justification–and didn't hesitate to tell them. I only wish I had been there at the time! Anyway, she cut them all, Healys and Birrells, right out of the will."

"That is most interesting, I was not aware of it."

"I am sure there is a lot of which you may be unaware. Lennox would know more about my aunt's medical condition, although he was not her family doctor. Like many old folk, she was a bit hard of hearing, and she had also developed a minor renal complaint, nothing to be vexed about, just old age catching up. In fact, she had received a letter from her own doctor explaining the diagnosis, but I know that she had not wanted to look foolish, so she asked Lennox for an explanation since it was couched in that quite inscrutable medical jargon that medical men … my apologies Doctor, for we legal men love our jargon too! Pardon me for asking, but have you drawn any preliminary conclusions?"

"You have provided me with six crucial pieces of information and, although it is rather too early to say, there are certainly aspects of this affair which bear a strong resemblance to the Mile End Murder."

"One of your celebrated cases?"

"No. In fact, it was much before my time and Watson's too, but the old wheel turns round again and again, and history often repeats itself. Well, I have already pledged Mr. McIntosh, that I should not abandon this case until I find your aunt's killer. I pledge you the very same, and now," said Holmes, rising, "we have taken up enough of your time,"

"By the way, there is one more thing, Mr. Holmes. Lennox told me something about Morgan that I found quite inexplicable; he said that on the night of the murder when he saw the girl at first, her eyes were practically jumping out of her head, she was shaking visibly, teeth chattering, and was rambling and incoherent. So much so that he remembers wondering to himself how the police could possibly rely on anything she said in her testimony. More ominously, he also told me, and you will no doubt bear in mind that he is a qualified medical man whose specialism is that of the mind, not the body, that his strong and immediate suspicion was that she was not so much paralysed with the shock of her mistress's death as with fear for her own person."

"Thank you – you have now provided me a seventh clue."

Chapter 6

After dinner that evening, we made our way along with McIntosh to the Sixty Steps, the jarvey dropping us by the police box at Walker's Bridge at just after seven-thirty. There were already broad wraiths of mist rising in the chilly air from the river behind us. From the foot of a gentle slope, lit dimly by a gas lamp, the imposing staircase climbed steeply in a gap at the end of a row of red sandstone tenement buildings, and the abutments of the adjacent terrace rose up sheer like that of a fortress. The steps were lit by a pair of decorative lamps at the bottom, one at each of the two half-landings, and one at the top; the central balustrade followed a distinct curve to the right, so that someone standing at the bottom would not necessarily have a clear view of the top. Holmes seemed to be mentally noting these details as he stopped at the foot of the steps for a moment or two and gazed up.

"The entire area bore a distinct and pleasant atmosphere of *rus in urbe.*"

Ascending, we found the misty gloom even deeper; an extremely ornate lamppost, mounted on a plinth which itself formed part of a low wall, provided the only illumination at the top of the steps. This wall extended round the curve of Millbrae Terrace, to what the locals called the Belle Vue – a narrow, stepped terrace of tall, dense, dark green shrubbery which, through a break in the stonework framed by low stone columns of Greek design, gave on to a panorama over the south and west of the great city. Below lay the shallow brown purling stream with its lade, flint mill, lime kiln, and outhouses. The entire area bore a distinct and pleasant atmosphere of *rus in urbe*. For the urban wanderer on a clear day, a starry night, or an autumn evening at sunset, it would have been a truly fascinating vista from the bench on the Belle Vue, with a forest of mill and factory chimneys, the tall masts of freighters and stark shipyard cranes, and, towering over all, the great Gothic bell tower and ornate spire of the University: *Labore et Scientia* indeed.

As for Holmes, the poetry of the cityscape was lost on him as ever. With his accustomed nonchalance he scoured the pavements, the buildings and, especially, the terraced shrubbery. He walked from one end of Millbrae Terrace to the other, at its intersection with Kelvinview Gardens, then he turned back up the street and stopped outside number 8. He gazed at the ground and then at the fronts of the houses, and finally he traced his footsteps back to the lamppost at the top of the steps and stood there with a discontentedness that he was unable to conceal.

"What it is, Holmes?" I asked.

He pointed back up the street toward the house of death.

"I am thinking of the reported behaviour of this elusive 'watching man.' Imagine I am supposed to be making a secret or at least *unobtrusive* reconnoitre of Miss Gilbert's house. What am I doing wrong?"

McIntosh gave a loud laugh, "Why, almost everything, Holmes!"

"Exactly!"

"That's right. Although we can see the close-mouth from here," I said, "we certainly cannot see inside the house or even the windows. And we are standing in the gaslight right under the lamp where every passer-by can see you clearly."

"Yes, *everything* is wrong. We could see just as much whilst either partly concealed in the shrubbery behind me, or at the other end of the street in the shade of the overhanging trees. Instead, our man stood under the revealing halo of the gas lamp and recklessly risked recognition, when he could have taken but ten paces to the rear or fifty paces forward and have been barely visible in the winter gloom."

"What do you make of it, Holmes?" McIntosh asked.

"I make it that it is a fair wonder that there were only twelve witnesses. This watching man was not only *meant* to be noticed, but also to be remarked upon, discussed, and reported. As, indeed, he was."

"What!"

"I pointed out to you how the man's mode of dress was always the same, but how his personal description varied with the witnesses. It is now obvious to me that it has been a different man on some occasions, but for some reason always wearing the same or very similar clothes."

"Very clever! I quite see that now. But why on earth would anyone do such a thing?" asked McIntosh.

"Frankly, the entire episode sticks out as a blind, and rather a crude one too."

"But a blind for what?"

"I cannot yet say."

We debated whether it was within the bounds of propriety to call on the Butler family without notice, but Holmes argued the urgency of our quest. We walked back up the street and knocked on the door of number 6. The mother was out visiting, but the son, Arthur, and elder daughter, Violet, were at home.

Arthur was a short, fair, thin, bespectacled young man with an open honest face and a pleasant talkative manner. He explained that he was home on shore leave at present, and his boat ought to have left two days previously, but had suffered engine trouble which necessitated a repair, and it now lay in dock. Violet appeared to be a year or two older than he, with very different colouring, especially in her dark eyes, and abundance of jet black hair. Although somewhat garrulous, she gave the impression of being a deal sharper than her brother and was certainly forthright in her answers to Holmes's questions. My friend posed the delicate question of whether Arthur would be prepared to accompany us to the upstairs flat; not only did the young man readily agree, but his sister also volunteered to come, though whether in the spirit of helpfulness or out of ghoulish curiosity, I was not certain.

Upstairs, Holmes halted, and bent down for a short time in front of the door, which he then unlocked using the several keys. I looked at him inquisitively.

"Confirming there has been no question of a forced entry," he answered, "there is not a scratch."

We went inside to find a very roomy hall with several doors leading off.

"Now, please just stand exactly where you were on the night of the murder, Mr. Butler," said Holmes, "and tell us precisely what happened, right from the beginning."

Arthur walked across and stood outside the open doorway, then recounted the scene.

"I was stopped right here and after Miss Morgan opened the door–"

"Stop there. You can see there is one warded lock, and two mortices," my friend pointed to each in turn. "Can you remember, how many locks did Morgan open on your return – one, two or three?"

"She was standing in front of the door so that I couldn't *see* exactly but I only remember her putting her key into the warded lock, not the mortices. I only heard one lock turn."

"Pray continue."

"I was standing here, and the stranger came out of that first room you can see to the right, he did not close the door behind him; then he passed Miss Morgan side to side, then he passed me, where I am standing now, face to face. I saw clearly that it was *not* the man they arrested, I told them so," he said quietly but insistently, "but the police ignored my words, and so did the jury."

"Did it not strike you as strange that someone should leave the flat just as you were entering, and that Miss Morgan should say nothing to him? Either she knew the person and would therefore surely have acknowledged him, or if that person were unknown to her, surely she ought to have challenged him?"

Arthur seemed very hesitant, but his sister came to his aid.

"You might as well tell the man, Arthur," she said, "It's bound to come out at some point, and it can't do any harm now that she's dead."

Arthur flushed red, "We knew the old lady had a jewellery collection. I didn't really think it was worth very much until I read about it afterwards in the newspapers. She, Miss Gilbert that is, used to buy pieces here and there and ... well, some of the dealers who used to call ... there was a shady character or two amongst them. It wasn't unusual for these men to turn up from time to time with stuff to sell ... but we mind our own business here."

"There were all sorts of daft stories," said Violet. "That the old lady used to hide her money and jewels under the floorboards; that she had a gun. I never believed them, but the stories would get round; most of the serving girls in the street would gossip about it. Everyone would have known about her jewels."

"Had this man Stoller ever been there?"

"I had never seen him but then I am at sea for long spells," replied Arthur.

"Nor I, Mr. Holmes," said Violet, "I had never heard his name until I read it in the newspaper."

"Who were these men who came to sell her jewellery?"

Arthur looked tongue-tied. "I'm sure they had nothing to do with her death."

"I'll tell you, if Arthur won't," said Violet. "I saw Packie Nolan here, Morgan's old fancy man, on a few occasions, the Moudie they call him."

"The Moudie?" asked Holmes.

"They say he looks like a mole or a moudie as we would call it: long, dark and ferrety looking. And Colm McHale – Cauld Kale is his nickname. It means cold cabbage or old hat. He was here once with another one that they say is a cat burglar – I don't know his name."

"And this man you described in the hall, Arthur, was none of those?"

"No. I've seen all of them," said Arthur.

"But Miss Morgan was neither surprised to see this man nor questioned his presence in the house?"

"I hope you will not drag Miss Morgan's name into this, I know she has nothing to do with it."

"You seem very keen to protect her–"

"He is besotted with that hussy," his sister interrupted hotly, eyes blazing.

"How dare you!" he replied angrily, flushing up, "Mr. Holmes hasn't come here to listen to your spiteful gossip, he is trying to–"

"Then tell the truth, Arthur!" she said, turning to Holmes, "Morgan knows more about this than she is letting on. Take my

211

word, Mr. Holmes, she *knows* who did it, and she *knows* it wasn't Stoller."

"That is what we are trying to establish, Miss Butler, but to come right to the point, merely asserting that will change nothing. It is imperative that we discover the facts and are able to produce evidence that can be presented and tested in a court of law. A man's life depends precisely upon that."

"Very well, then, *I'll* tell you a few things that didn't come out at the trial. It was said that Miss Gilbert must have known the murderer because she opened the door to him. She didn't open the door, I can tell you that, because I'd have heard the knocking on the door, and I'd have heard whoever it was shouting through the door because the old lady was half deaf. My music room is right below her dining room and there wasn't a sound from the flat after Morgan left until I heard a kind of bump, then a few moments later what sounded like the old woman knocking."

"Is there anything else you can remember, Mr. Butler?"

The young man closed his eyes for a second or two, then he said, slowly and carefully, "When Miss Morgan went to check the kitchen pulleys, I noticed over her head, that the kitchen window lay open by two or three inches at the top; I also saw that the gas lamp in the hall had been turned down very low – it seemed even lower than when I had attempted to look through the stained glass in my first occasion."

Then he took a step or two forward and continued, "The coal scuttle was in the hall ...it was right there," he pointed, "And some of the coal looked as though it had been split."

"You seem very definite," said my friend.

"He has a great memory Mr. Holmes, you can rely on it," said Violet. "I always say he should go on the stage –'The Memory Man' is a great drawer in the music halls."

He certainly seemed be one of those individuals who has an almost paranormal ability to recall acute detail.

"Do you know why it was outside the dining room door, when it ought to have been inside by the fire?"

"No."

"I do." said Violet. "They also said at the trial that the locks hadn't been forced; if Miss Gilbert didn't open the door, and I *know* she didn't, what does that mean?"

"Go on," said Holmes encouragingly.

"That the door had been left open for him by Morgan – as the close door had been too. I'll tell you what Nancy Morgan used to do. The lazy besom used to wedge the door slightly off the latch with a tiny lump of coal at the doorstep to save her the trouble of doing and undoing all the locks. All the skivvies do it from time to time."

"Mr. Butler," asked Holmes, "when you went up the first time – was the flat door completely shut?"

"Yes, if it wasn't, I'd have noticed."

"So, if this intruder had gained entrance by means of the door having been wedged open by a piece of coal, he only had to remove the coal, and close the warded lock behind him once he was inside, but he would have been unable to lock the mortices. That would explain why Miss Morgan only had to use one key on her return.'

"I don't believe she has anything to do with this," said Arthur stubbornly.

"If she was innocent," interrupted Violet, "how could she let a strange man walk out of the door and not a word about her mistress! The reason she made a bee-line for Blythswood Street to see Healy on the night of the murder, Mr. Holmes, was because she was afraid of being caught out. Maybe the man she let into the house wasn't supposed kill the old woman; maybe he was just meant to do the burglary then get away."

"Why should she not visit Healy, after all it was the old woman's niece?"

"Because they couldn't stick the sight of each other, and Healy wouldn't look the road she was on for her only being a skivvy. Morgan used to call her '*Old Bagface,* '" said Violet, mimicking a country accent, "'*Conniving after her auntie's money.*' No other reason why Morgan would go there of all places. Of course, everybody knows that she blurted out the nephew's name – the doctor. Then there was a kind of cover-up."

"Do you have any idea why Lennox Findlater's name should be mixed up in this?"

"No. Why would he kill his aunt for money, when he has plenty? It was Morgan who put it about, I'm sure."

"But why should she name him?"

"I could not say. But even if she was covering up for one of her cronies it was madness for her to pretend it was Lennox Findlater. A servant's word against a doctor and lay preacher! I wouldn't have thought even *she* could be that daft."

"Is there anything else you can tell us about Morgan?"

"Only that she knew she wasn't being treated by the old woman the same way as Kate Scott, as we still called her. Morgan rarely spoke of the old woman save with truculence and resentment: '*She doesnae take* me *on holiday wi' her,*' she used to whine, '*I'm no' good enough, I'm on'y a skivvy.*' Perhaps the old woman was suspicious of Morgan who, I can tell you, slipped her fancy man, Nolan, in on a few occasions when the old woman was out. And a few other fancy men besides."

"Meaning that this Nolan would know his way about the flat?"

"And what was in it."

"Does either Nolan or McHale resemble the man Stoller?" Holmes asked McIntosh.

"No. Nothing like either of them."

"Your accounts have been remarkably lucid and I am most grateful to both of you. Should anything else occur to you, perhaps you would be so good as to contact myself or Dr. Watson at the Station Hotel."

Holmes locked up the flat and as we retraced out steps to the cab stand in Queen Margaret Road, Holmes turned to me with a hint of amusement in his voice, "Well, Watson, what do you make of Miss Violet Butler? Is she pointing us animatedly toward the truth or is she blustering in order to keep us from discovering it?"

"There was an unmistakeable spite about her account; jealousy perhaps."

"No, not jealousy, Watson," said McIntosh. "She is exasperated at her brother's fixation with the Morgan girl whom she no doubt mistrusts."

"Snobbery, then! She doesn't like the idea of her brother consorting with a slavey," I persisted.

"Perhaps, but there is also something of genuine concern about her naïve brother being trepanned by, to her mind, so obviously a wrong 'un. Strange is it not, how such a meek, sensible young man can be dazzled by a character like Morgan?" said McIntosh.

"Some of the most lethal criminal partnerships of our own age have begun like that," said Holmes, "I can recall a number of such cases."

"Then you think they might have–"

"I think nothing yet, Watson, though Morgan is clearly implicated; the more likely candidate for her accomplice is this Nolan character not the bumbling Arthur. Violet Butler is a very perceptive young woman and seems well enough disposed towards us. Her eyes and ears, not to say her wits, are as sharp as her tongue."

"Where to now?" asked McIntosh, when we arrived at the cab stand.

"Let us have a walk by the riverside, shall we? Watson will tell you that I like to steep myself in the atmosphere of a place. I should not like to leave right now. Tell me, this Nolan character whom Miss Butler mentioned, do you have professional knowledge of him?"

"Yes, he is a small-time bookmaker and gambler, well known in the criminal fraternity but completely harmless. But why do you ask?"

"May I answer your question with another?"

"Go ahead, Mr. Holmes."

"Do you think either this Nolan or any of his cohorts might have committed this murder, allowing for that fact that they may merely have planned to commit a burglary and then were caught up in something that went dreadfully, fatally wrong?"

"No, certainly not. He and McHale are not burglars, though they may do a little bit of re-setting, that's to say reselling of stolen property, from time to time. They live mainly by their wits, or at rather by the lack of them in others. They do have a friend – James Inglis, the Acrobat as he is known – a skilled cat burglar, the one Miss Butler referred to, who works only in the dead of night. You would never find him in premises at any other time. I strongly suspect if the Acrobat had been there, he would have had the snibs off the windows and no one would have heard a pin drop. He is no bungler, in fact he has never been caught. He once broke *into* a prison at midnight, in order to help an associate escape! As you know Mr. Holmes, criminals, especially petty ones, rarely change their habits, and none of these three has any record of violence."

"This is a bit of a long shot, admittedly. Please think back to the personal descriptions of the so-called watching man," said Holmes. "And this time, ignore the clothing."

My Aberdonian struck his head with his palm, "Good Lord, Holmes! I have been blind. Blind as a moudie in fact," he laughed, "those two descriptions are Nolan and his friend McHale to a tee – the tall dark one and the shorter, thinner fair one."

"Indeed. The entire charade was set up to demonstrate that a stranger was watching the house which, of course, would be the best cover possible for what my colleague in the official force, Lestrade, calls 'an inside job.'"

And yet, McIntosh was not wholly convinced.

"Well, here is the clinching argument," continued Holmes. "If it *were* an outside party who set the job up through intelligence from the sentinel, then why, having watched the house for weeks on end, did they strike during the ten minutes when Morgan went for her first errand, rather than the half hour she commonly took for the second one? Or indeed, why not on her afternoon or evening off?"

McIntosh nodded. "Very good. Yes, that is a key point, but there is a problem with your theory – McHale and Nolan were in police custody at the time of the murder. The 'Hole in the Wall,' a public house in Abington Street not far from here, which runs illegal gambling in a back room, had been raided on the afternoon of the murder and they were held in the station until they went to court next morning. Well, *there's* a cruel irony," went on McIntosh, "I happen to know that Stoller is more than an occasional visitor there, and had he been there on that afternoon he would have received a ten shilling fine instead of a death sentence."

"Unfortunately for your client," said Holmes, "this now means that the police might be able to prove that Stoller, McHale, and Nolan all know each other – there is a link between them."

Still McIntosh demurred. "I would stake my professional reputation on it, and I have been in criminal defence many a long year, that neither of these two would be involved in anything quite so dangerous. It is simply not their line of work."

"In order to settle the matter, do you think I could get these two parties to speak to me?" asked Holmes.

"It is possible, but you would have to be very tactful about how you handle your suspicion that it was they who watched the house."

"Perhaps a few sovereigns will loosen their lips. What about this 'Hole in the Wall' place?" I persisted.

"It is just possible … yes, I suppose I could take you there and introduce you. Your speech and dress will mark you out as strangers, so folk will be very suspicious, though they do have quite a few toffs there, brought in by Stoller no less, who was a bit of dandy himself. And, occasionally, there is a well-dressed fence there looking to do a higher class of business, so if you behave discreetly, you might just pass muster."

"Then let us stand not upon the order of going," I said to McIntosh, who laughed.

"You have not changed a bit, Watson," he said. "Impatient, naïve, energetic but always brave! I am afraid it is not as simple as that. The Glasgow criminal may not be quite as wily as his Cockney counterpart, but he does not allow any Tom, Dick or Harry off the street to simply barge in on his private gambling den!"

"Then how shall we

"We must do things properly and observe due process," he said, with mock solemnity. "Come with me, but not a word out of you until I say so."

Chapter 7

A walk of twenty minutes along the barely lit river path, then by dark tenemented streets of perceptibly decreasing affluence, brought us out near a rather rough-looking thoroughfare known as the New City Road. There was a public house at each corner of the crossroads: McIntosh indicated the dingiest looking one, which had a miniature Tramcar above the door, in place of a sign. He placed his finger against his mouth, led us into the tiny snug bar, and ordered three special whiskies. The curate returned with the glasses and McIntosh passed three half-crowns across the mahogany bar and said, "The same again, please."

"Seven-and-six for three glasses of whisky?" I whispered under my breath, "in this low dive!"

"For three glasses of cold tea, actually."

"What?!"

"I have just given him our password and entrance fee, and we seem to have passed the selection test ... ah, here we are now," – a younger curate had appeared and nodded us towards a door which we went through and then out into what looked like back yard. Some short distance ahead of us in the darkened court was a dim glow through the bare bones of a fanlight, and we walked towards this. The curate who had led us rapped the door and when it was opened, gestured us inside and I noticed that McIntosh had slipped him a coin. The 'Tramcar' was a palace compared to the 'Hole in the Wall,' which had partitioned wooden booths and brass spittoons that reminded me of the American frontier saloons I had seen in pictorial magazines. Most of the denizens seemed to be drinking a cheap fortified red wine purchased in bottles, rather than by the glass, and which had numbers in place of a name on the label. We quickly found a spot in a quiet corner of the drab smoky room. McIntosh went to the bar and spoke with the curate for a few minutes before returning with the glasses.

"It's the real McKay this time," he said, raising his glass. "And you may speak freely now."

"Wait though," I said, "we are taking something of a chance, are we not? Our arrest as denizens of an illegal gambling club would certainly complicate matters. I am not concerned for my own reputation, but for Holmes's. Perhaps you had better leave in case the place is raided again?"

"You needn't worry about that, Watson," said my old school friend.

"But how can you be so sure?"

"Because these things are stage managed," said McIntosh, grinning. "The landlord always receives advance information that the premises are about to be raided. He arranges for a certain number of folk to be present and when the police arrive they are caught *in flagrante delicto*. The police get their men, the men plead guilty and are fined, the landlord then pays the fines of the guilty men plus a bit over for their inconvenience, and justice is seen to be done. Somehow, the landlord manages never to lose his licence for contravening the gambling and licensing laws."

"Advance information?" I asked. "From whom?"

"From the police, Watson!" he laughed. "Anyway, as this place has recently been turned over, we shall be safe enough for a while yet."

Two of the customers had strolled over to our table and sat down, then McIntosh introduced everyone.

"Aye, the London detective and the Edinburgh doctor. We've heard about yis," said one of them whom I presumed to be Nolan by the descriptions we had been given. There was more than a trace of Irish in his accent which was not unpleasant.

"Well, Mr. Nolan," said Holmes, "did you enjoy your time in Australia?"

"How do ye know I was in Australia?"

"It is my business always to know with whom I am dealing."

"Who said there would be any dealin'?" he asked mischievously.

"I can give you my word that neither of these gentlemen has anything to do with the police," said McIntosh. "You may trust them. Indeed, at present it might be said that they are on quite the opposite side to the police."

"How would that be then?" said McHale.

"We are presently concerned with a miscarriage of justice," said Holmes.

"Which one would ye like to take first?" asked Nolan sarcastically.

"Osip Stoller."

"And that's what puts you on the opposite side of the peelers?" asked McHale.

"Until the injustice is righted, yes."

"So, ye knew about me bein' in Australia: What else d'ye know?"

"You were in one of the cattle stations."

Nolan nodded. "Aye. Go on."

"In one of the ranches near Ballarat?" asked Holmes.

"Further north, Bendigo – where all the Paddies used to go."

"I'll say you made plenty of money there?"

"An' blew it was well."

"Gambling?"

"The lot: women, drink, an' the de'il's books as they call them here. Made myself a fortune in the stations an' drank and gambled it clean away in the Shamrock Hotel. Came home as poor as I went out. Like many a man before," said Nolan.

"What can you tell me about Stoller?" asked Holmes.

"He used to be a regular here, and he rarely lost a hand," said McHale with a wink. Some of the boys here was getting a wee bit suspicious, so maybe it was time for him to be shifting, anyway."

"'Twas a couple o' bent peelers that fitted him up, take my word for it, an' it looks like he'll swing for it too," said the other.

"I am convinced that he will not," replied Holmes. "And that is why I am here. I spoke of a deal: In return for any information that you can give me that helps to overturn the case against Stoller, McIntosh here will apply to the campaign defence fund to reward you for your assistance. Moreover, I guarantee that I will keep both your names out of the case."

The two looked startled; Nolan recovered first.

"*Our* names, Mr. Holmes? An' how could our names possibly be mixed up in the case? Sure, we were in Camperdown Street police office when the murder was committed. Just roun' the corner, a few minutes' walk from here. We could take you there right now if you like an' you can check up on us. Sure, it was Mr. McIntosh himself that defended us. I thought you said you made it your business to know who you were dealin' with?"

"Aye, if you want to bluff," said McHale with a sly smile, "we can just get the cards out and have a wee game of brag."

"There is no bluff on my part, gentlemen. Shall I read you out a description of the two men who watched the house at the Sixty Steps in the weeks running up to the murder? One was tall, dark–"

"Awright," said Nolan, raising his hand. "But we had nothin' to do wi' any murder."

"I know that perfectly well," replied Holmes, "which is why we are having this discussion here instead of in a police station."

The two men remained silent.

"Let me give you an account of what I believe to have happened and you may correct me if I go wrong. Nancy Morgan gave you some cock-and-bull story which resulted in you two gentlemen parading yourselves around in front of the house in Millbrae Terrace. Neither of you knew anything about any burglary that was being planned, and you were shocked, perhaps even outraged, when you heard that a murder had been committed. As you have since had time to reflect, you probably now realise that it was lucky for you that you were caught up in the police raid here on the afternoon of the murder, or you might have ended up facing a capital charge, at the very least as an accomplice. Especially, once the police had established your connection with Stoller through this place."

Nolan spoke first. "We've been a couple o' eejits, Mr. Holmes; we don't need ye to tell us that. Nancy told me that there was this character – an admirer, but an unwanted one – who was pesterin' her. He was turnin' up to wait for her at the time when he knew she'd be goin' out on an errand and she asked me as a favour, ye see, her an' I used to ..."

"I know about that, go on."

"She asked me to hang about the place, an' scare this fellow away if he turned up. She was a wee bit anxious that he could be the type that might molest her on a dark night: It can be very quiet down be the river. On the days when I couldn't make it along, Colm here stood in for me, wearin' the same clothes. She wanted this fellow, whoever he was, to think I was waitin' for her to walk out with her."

"And turning off the stairlights across the street ..."

"That was a signal to say I was leavin'."

"You now realise that you have been a tool in her hands?"

Nolan grimaced. "Aye, well. But ye've admitted that ye know we're innocent. The question is," he said warmly, "what do ye intend to do about it? Don't play cat and mouse wi' us!"

"At present I intend to do nothing. The police do not employ me to rectify their deficiencies; therefore, I am entitled to a free hand."

There was palpable relief on the faces of the two men.

"We don't know who did it," said Nolan. "It wasn't the wee Jew man, queer fish that he is, him and that trollop of his, but it's a cryin' shame what they done to him, Christian or pagan or Jew. It wasn't any of the Glasgow crowd either as far as we know. Not one of them would go knockin' an ould wife's brains in."

"We've heard nothing on the bush telegraph about the Sixty Steps case," said McHale. "As Packie says, it wasn't a Glasgow job."

"It is pretty clear though," continued Holmes, "that your erstwhile paramour is implicated, is it not?"

"I've been made a fool of," said Nolan resignedly.

"It is also clear by her wilful misidentification of Stoller that she is shielding someone, is it not?"

"Aye, but I've no idea who that can be."

"Can you throw any light on why Morgan might have said that the man in the hall was Lennox Findlater?"

"Naw. Sure, the nephew is a holy roller! I know some o' them is the biggest rogues goin', but the Findlaters are drippin' wi' money; they'd have no need to do anythin' like that."

"Who are these 'bent peelers' you mentioned?" asked McIntosh.

"You see this Carlyle, he's an honest copper, right, one of the very few, so is his gaffer, Stevenson. Hard but fair, you know the type," said McHale. "But Carlyle's mate on that night, Gavin Duncan, is as bent as a corkscrew. Drunken Duncan some call him; others call him 'The Farmer' – he's that good at planting! Get my meaning? Bigger crook than half o' them that's in the big house in Duke Street. I'll tell you what they say about the polismen in Glasgow, Mr. Holmes – one polis turns to the other one and says, 'Lend me ten bob until the shops are shut!' That's no joke. Well, there's a wee dodge going on and whose snout is to be found right in the middle of that trough? Sergeant Duncan's, that's whose!"

Holmes was leaning forward, eyes ablaze with interest.

"Know the big jewellers' arcade in Argyle Street?" McHale continued. "There's been a few jobs done there recently. Somehow the peelers discover who has the loot, though *supposedly* they can never find it themselves; but then they have a bit of a parley with the crooks to have it returned, no names, no pack drill; there's a deal done, and three thousand quid's worth of jewellery is handed back for, say, two hundred and fifty or three hundred, and who gets the reward? The peelers! Aye, somehow, it's always the same men that are always at the very place of the crime within minutes. And, maybe they just help to make sure the crooks get a nice clean getaway."

"But how does Carlyle come into this? I asked.

"My guess is this: Carlyle was getting wise to what was going on, and if I know him, he wouldn't play along with it; it's my belief that he was waiting his chance to sink Duncan and his crony, Madden – the other one that's involved in it. But *they* sunk Carlyle first."

"But how, in what way?" Holmes asked.

"I don't know anythin' about polis routine," said Nolan, "but I smell a rat – a big greasy rat called Duncan. Supposin' it was him that somehow managed to make Morgan's deposition about Findlater go missin' so that it looks as though Carlyle is calling his governor a liar because he says he submitted the evidence and

Stevenson says he never saw it; so he takes him off the job *sine die,* as the lawyers has it."

"Then you think the two women actually did make the statement and then retracted?"

"Not a doubt of it," said McHale. "A peeler of Carlyle's standing wouldn't make a mistake like that, and he wouldn't tell lies in a murder case."

"But why did the other two change their minds?"

"Maybe it's Findlater's money that shut them up, keep his name out of it – you know what these rich folks is like," said Nolan with a shrug, which rather led us back to where we had started. At that point we left, Holmes disbursing "something on account" to the two men first. As we made our way back in our cab to the city, we discussed with our Aberdonian friend what we had just been told.

"He said nothing directly to me about it," began McIntosh, "but he did mention something about compromising his position in a case with which he was not involved officially; it was clearly nothing to do with the Stoller case, that much I do know. It seemed to me that he was almost on the point of telling me something then changed his mind. It may well have been this jewellery business. As it happens, my friend, Mr. Donald Crosbie, is the manager the Dalriada Insurance Company who insures all the thirty-odd jewellers, silversmiths, and diamond merchants in the arcade. Their cover is entirely dependent upon them using only officially approved alarm apparatus which is checked on a regular basis by an independent party appointed by Dalriada. In addition, the area is patrolled heavily at night, with a beat policeman passing on average every quarter of an hour. So, it was rather a tricky job whoever did it."

"But not if the beat constable were implicated in the job?" I asked.

McIntosh laughed. "The corruption in some of the lower ranks would make your Metropolitan Police look like amateurs."

"Do you know which type of alarm is used?" inquired Holmes.

"No, they are all quite novel and I am afraid that sort of thing is beyond me. Something to do with batteries and solenoids and what have you – Watson here will tell you I was never any use at physics!"

"It is beyond my present understanding too," Holmes replied.

"But Crosbie could give you the details no doubt."

"By the way, McIntosh, is not the insurance company somewhat suspicious?" I asked. "After all, three burglaries in the same place ..."

"One of those incidents was actually in another part of the city, but I take your point. However, recovering the goods with a small reward means that the insurance company doesn't have to pay out the full amount for the missing valuables. Business is business after all. In fact, there was another robbery done in the Arcade only in the last week or two."

"Can you scribble down the exact dates of the burglaries? I assume this last one was after Carlyle had been suspended?"

"Indeed. To the best of my knowledge, the negotiations are still going on in with a view to returning the property for a reward."

"With the usual *dramatis personae*?"

"Yes."

"Do you think that Watson and I could offer to assist the insurance company in some way? Say, by aiding in them in the investigation of the circumstances *et cetera, et cetera*, with a recommendation from yourself."

"Are you serious, Holmes?"

"Perfectly."

"I think my friend would grab the opportunity. I could send a boy round first thing tomorrow with a message."

"Yes, tell him we will drop in on him very soon. We are certainly moving into the active phase of the investigation, McIntosh. The day after tomorrow I shall be taking the night train to London."

"London, eh! You're not giving up on us, surely?"

"On the contrary, friend McIntosh," replied Holmes, "I am pursuing it with singular determination."

"But Stoller is due to hang in ten days!"

Holmes held up his hand. "And that is precisely why I need to go to London. I have given the matter some thought, and I fancy I can see a way out of the present impasse. I am afraid that is all I can say at present; Watson will tell you that I like to keep my cards close to my chest. I shall return again very soon, and with good news."

Later that evening, I left my friend by the blazing fireside, studying the five hundred pages of closely typed official court proceedings on the case of Osip Stoller in McIntosh's file and, despite the chill, went out for my evening constitutional. I wandered through the city and found there a raucous vibrant life in the markets and bustling streets, especially those near the riverside where the public houses and colourful human traffic nearly rivalled Bermondsey or Wapping. There were some very grand theatres and a few, perhaps rather less than salubrious, music halls with an assortment of tragedies, comedies, burlesques and farces, with varying degrees of allurement, though I must say I was not enticed by the fare. When I returned, Holmes and I shared a nightcap before turning in – a very old and distinguished single malt Scotch whisky with which my old friend McIntosh had presented us on the day we had arrived.

"Well Watson, we have handled some tangled and intricate affairs and solved perhaps far more inextricable mysteries in our time, but seldom have I come across such an unspeakable hotchpotch of a case."

"Did you find anything of interest?" I asked.

"Not a whit," he answered with a rueful smile, tossing the papers aside. "It is a very rare thing not to be able to place a whit of reliance on the court proceedings, not to say something of a handicap."

"Incidentally, how on earth did you know about Nolan's time in Australia?" I asked Holmes.

"Oh, that was simple, Watson – 'Moudie' is distinctly Australian slang for an overseer or a supervisor in the shearing stations – the concordance with his mole-like appearance is, I am sure, purely coincidental."

"Ah yes, I recall now that I had heard the expression before, at the diggings in Ballarat."

"It was intended to put him on his mettle for I had no idea how he would react at that point. Of course, now that we have met him it probably means that everyone in the entire criminal fraternity knows we are here. I fear we may be called into action sooner rather than later."

"How soon?"

"Tomorrow."

Chapter 8

We had a hearty breakfast the next morning in the Station Hotel, although Holmes had cavilled somewhat at the previous night's dinner of haggis which he claimed had given him indigestion and insomnia. He also opined that the breakfast kippers had been slightly overdone.

"We covered much ground yesterday," he began, "and now hold all the data which it has been possible to collect in the very short time available to us. We have plenty of material though there is still much that is dark to us. We are agreed, are we not, that the motive for the murder has to do with the legacy, and that the whole idea of robbery was a blind from the word go."

I nodded in agreement, as he drew out some papers along with his notebook. "Let us let us take the dates:

16th August – the will is changed; is this significant? Perhaps, perhaps not.

Middle of September – the dog is poisoned; this clears the way for the burglar to get into the house.

28th September – first robbery in the arcade;

4th October – appearance of the watching man; this provides the artifice of the house being watched by a 'stranger'.

14th October – second robbery;

16th October – murder of Miss Gilbert;

24th October – Arrest of Stoller;

13th December – Stoller found guilty;

14th December – Carlyle suspended for duty; this clears the way for the following day's events.

15th December – third robbery in the arcade.

A neat little pattern don't you think? What set this frenzied activity in train – is it the change of the will? Or did the assailant anticipate yet another new will, written but not yet witnessed."

"Hardly likely, but something to do with it at any rate."

"Exactly. In theory, any consanguineal relative is a potential suspect: However, Margaret Healy certainly did not strike the blow, and Austin Birrell has been cleared by one of Lestrade's colleagues; now, look at this which I received earlier this morning."

I glanced at the note from my friend's Auckland correspondent, which read:

> "At your request, I have made an extensive search but can find no death or burial record for a Winton Healy in any of the records offices. N.Z. Criminal Records show that Healy completed two spells in gaol: one for the perpetration of some minor frauds, the other for assaulting a cabby in a dispute over a fare. A colleague in the '*North Otago Times*' managed to track him down to an address in the dockside in New Plymouth some seven months ago, after which there is no trace of him.
>
> – Silas K. Spragg,
> Auckland Daily Herald,
> N.Z."

"Healy is not dead after all!"

"I never believed he was. And 'seven months ago', allowing for the long journey to England, brings us to around the time of the poisoning of the dog."

"You think it is possible that he came to Glasgow?"

"Via London, of course. I have wired Spragg back to ask him to check the passenger lists on New Zealand Shipping Company and the Dunedin Line during the period we are interested in. I have also asked him to examine the James Johnston Trust for any possible a connection with Healy. However, that may come to nothing, so it is incumbent on us to consider alternatives, for example that there is a possibility of another person presently

232

unknown to us who may have a claim and so at some point, we shall be compelled to inspect the records in the Registry of Births, Deaths and Marriages and delve into the lineage of the Gilberts."

"You think there may be a skeleton in the family cupboard."

"I am convinced there is something, or more likely someone, that we do not know, which may be found there. You recall my mention of the Mile End murder and the parallels with our present case: There was disputed legitimacy, a very complicated genealogy, even bigamy was insinuated, such that the probate actions pursued by the hopeful claimants resounded through the courts of Chancery for quite ten years after the old woman's death. There too, it was in all probability with a final view to the inheritance, rather than immediate gain, that the fatal blow was stuck. The impediment for the police at the time was that the sheer number of claimants, some genuinely plausible and ultimately successful, made it difficult to narrow down the question of motive to a single suspect, or even to one family of suspects."

"Could Healy have been the nephew whom Morgan saw in the hall, not Lennox Findlater?"

"I am certain of it.

"But how would Healy have known her?"

"It would not have been difficult to scrape up an acquaintance with her by all accounts; he may have been one of the other 'fancy men' about whom Miss Butler talked."

"But how would he dislodge Mrs. Sutherland's claim, a claim which a leading lawyer like Findlater believes to be sound?"

"You have picked upon the point, Watson, on which practically our entire case turns at present. It seems incontrovertible that the murderer was searching for some document or documents which would nullify the claim of the present incumbent. If, however, the murderer had been unable to find such a document, his only other option would be to remove

Mrs. Sutherland from the scene so to speak. And I am sure she is quite oblivious to the sinister web that has been woven around her, and to the danger in which she now exists. As indeed I was until I saw the note from Spragg. Let us be clear, only one life now stands between the killer, be he Healy or anyone else, and the legacy; that life is Kate Sutherland's."

"My dear Holmes!"

"It may seem, Watson, that I am acting precipitately, but in past cases I confess I have been culpably slow to act – I refer, of course, to the Hilton Cubitt affair last year and to that of young John Openshaw some years back. I should not wish my conscience to burdened with a third death."

"What do you intend to do?"

"Go straight there after breakfast I have had a wire from her to say that she is quite prepared to meet us. There is a train at ten-nineteen according to Bradshaw. Even if I have misread the situation, it may be useful to question her; having known the old lady intimately for a considerable time it is just possible that she may have some piece of information which can be of use to us."

"Shall we be gone overnight?"

"I am afraid so. And remember to bring your service revolver."

We shared a pot of coffee in the station buffet at Buchanan Street, then settled in the corner of the carriage. After the sooty dreariness of the city, the bright snow-laden hills, valleys, and forests seen from the train on such a fine afternoon were a pleasure to behold. Holmes, now in excellent spirits, prattled away about Rob Roy's birthplace, the grand novels of Sir Walter Scott, and the importance of preserving the Gaelic language and the highland pibrochs; one would scarcely have thought he was on the trail of a brutal murderer.

Mrs. Sutherland, a pleasant-looking woman with the bloom of the countryside on her cheeks, was waiting for us as we steamed into the quiet rural station. She brought us directly to her delightful little cottage, and plied us with tea and scones, such that I began to feel quite guilty about intruding on such decent folk, though I realised Holmes had good reason.

It was clear that the Sutherlands, as Archibald Findlater had said, had been the recipients of Miss Gilbert's generosity. I tried very gently to tease a few details out of her about Miss Gilbert's family: She had met them all at various points: the Birrells, the Healys, the Findlaters – and she was rather shocked to hear about the rumour concerning Lennox and refused to believe it. We naturally asked if she knew of or had heard of anyone else in the family who might have an eye to the inheritance. Perhaps Holmes laid it on rather thick when pointing out that if any consanguineal relative had a claim to the legacy, this might impinge on her portion, but she seemed completely unconcerned.

"We are trying to think of anyone who might have had a motive in killing Miss Gilbert?" I said, feeling the clumsiness of my words.

"I couldn't think of anyone," she said, calmly. "I thought that it was a burglary – nothing to do with the will, though I am certain that this poor man Stoller is innocent. I have signed the petition … you would think that might carry some weight."

"Do you have in your possession, or know of any document in existence, which might be of use to anyone who might try to disinherit you?" my friend asked.

"No, none at all," she replied sincerely.

"Miss Gilbert seems to have taken to you from an early age and, on your part, you named her first child, 'Maisie,' after her," said Holmes.

"She was so pleased, and Maisie is such a lovely name for the child; it suits her to a tee," said the woman pleasantly. "And of course, she had no daughter of her own, being a spinster."

"Yes," said Holmes, nodding, "though that was quite a departure from tradition was it not, where the first female child is traditionally called after the maternal grandmother?"

"Aye, well, it was a wee bit, I suppose, for my mother's name was Jeanette. But, you see, my own mother had been long dead at that point, and Miss Gilbert had always treated me like one of the family."

"There is something about which we must be perfectly honest with you. We have reason to believe that the murderer is one of Miss Gilbert's relatives – which one we cannot say, until we have clearer proofs. Indeed, it may be someone of whom we have never heard – such persons often appear in probate cases. But this impression is strongly supported by evidence we have uncovered in the last few days. We do not mean to alarm you in any way, but it will be obvious to you that only one person stands between this person and Miss Gilbert's legacy."

"*Me!*" she said turning quite pale with sudden shock. Holmes nodded.

"I am afraid I only came to the realisation this morning that you might be in any danger. However, I should not bring you a problem without offering a solution. Where is your husband at present?"

"He is visiting his relatives in Glasgow and will not return tonight. He has a very early start for some turns, and he often does that."

"Then as soon as it gets dark this evening, I would ask that you and the rest of the family retire upstairs and lock yourselves in your rooms until morning. Dr. Watson and I shall occupy the downstairs part of the premises. But we shall have to ask you to move out tomorrow morning until the matter is resolved – this should only take a few days at the most. May I suggest that you arrange to lodge with your Glasgow in-laws?"

The poor woman was quite staggered, but she was able to perceive that the situation Holmes had described to her was a dangerous one. When she collected herself, she went off to make us some supper. I should not have let the long-suffering Mrs. Hudson know it for worlds, but Mrs. Sutherland – once she had recovered from her shock – produced the best roast beef dinner I have ever had. Perhaps it was the advantage of being out in the country and having fresh produce. Afterwards, when we were settled by the fireside, Holmes lit his pipe and looked across at me inquisitively.

"I trust you haven't forgotten your service revolver."

"Yet it seems incongruous in this of all places, one of the quietest, sweetest, spots in the country."

"It is certainly one of the quietest that is what makes it dangerous. Mrs. Sutherland has been fortunate, for months she has been treading on the edge of an abyss."

"You think Healy will make an attempt on her life?"

"Frankly no. I think his first step will be to try to find whatever he was looking for in Millbrae Terrace, failing that ..." Holmes shrugged.

"But we cannot remain here indefinitely."

"That is why I have arranged for two of my former associates, Barker and Mercer – whom you will recall assisted us in the Soho case last year – to replace us tomorrow. They should arrive by mid-morning. They will take it in shifts to hold the fort until I call them off. Now let us see – in an hour's time we should consider taking up our positions for I suspect a quiet village like this is quite dead long before midnight. My favourite spot for an ambush would be in the hut by the wicket gate leading in from the back lane. It's ten to one that he will avoid using the front entrance, though we must not gamble on it, so one of us will need to take cover outside and stay well-concealed."

The cottage in which the Sutherlands lived was in the shape of an **L** facing on to the street and to the kirk and kirkyard opposite where one of us would remain; a lane which led to the back garden and the rear entry, was in complete darkness. Beyond that, the lane ended at a fence by the copse at the foot of a hill. Anyone attempting to enter the cottage by the front door would be easily seen, and should anyone go down the back lane, he was trapped between the sentinel in the hut and the other in the kirkyard. We took up our positions, Holmes electing to take the front of the house whilst I went into the hut. The air was still and cold, I had to muffle my nose and mouth to prevent my steaming breath giving me away; the cloud cover was complete, and it was difficult to see further than a few yards.

When the public houses emptied, the village went deathly quiet, though once or twice a fox barked, an owl hooted, or a tom cat howled. There was not a light in the cottage, and in the pitch dark, one could hear a mouse creeping. It was not long, perhaps an hour or so, before I heard a steady, stealthy rustle which told me that someone was making his way through the lane towards the garden. The rustling ceased for a spell and then, presumably reassured by the utter silence, our intruder moved forward again. I heard the low scraping of the wicket gate being opened and suddenly, I smelt rather than saw a pocket lantern and at the same time heard footsteps passing the door of the hut, so I withdrew as far back as I could.

Through the door space, I picked up a vague shape as it flashed past: a man's broad hat; a heavy looking dark coat or cloak; dark trousers; he was making his way directly towards the house. I emerged from the hut and with a start, I suddenly felt a hand touch mine – it was Holmes letting me know that he was at my side. We followed the indistinct shape until it crouched down by the cottage door, then we heard a click and saw a glint of light; his hands were shaking either with excitement or fear, for circles of light flickered and wavered across the threshold. A bumbling amateur, I thought to myself; my heart was thumping now for we had him completely cornered; then Holmes nudged me forward sharply. Rushing him now, we would have the advantage of two against one and in this stooping posture, he would be further handicapped. It was a gamble which almost paid off.

Unfortunately, in the dark, neither Holmes nor I had seen the stick which he must have carried with him and had then laid to one side. As I leapt forward, I fell clattering over it noisily and went down heavily like a steeplechaser at the final hurdle. It was enough to give him a warning. From my position on the ground, I heard the man utter a curse, saw him turn swiftly and, with an oath, hurl the lantern straight at Holmes, who dodged it easily enough; but in that split second before the lantern went out, I was certain I had seen a glint of steel.

"Watch out for the knife, Holmes!" I cried, as the two went down together and rolled on the path for a few moments. By the time I had regained my feet, the attacker had managed to throw Holmes off and scramble away. Rarely have I seen a man run as did our assailant on that occasion and Holmes went after him like a hound coursing a hare. Though I had my revolver with me I had not dared use it for fear of wounding the wrong man, and now I should have had difficulty in justifying, both to my own conscience and on a point of law, shooting a retreating man in the back. By instinct, our man had run into the copse instead of towards the village and although I followed after them as fast as I could run, by the time I caught up with Holmes, he had lost his quarry. We were the bumbling amateurs I reflected with mortification, to let such a prize elude us.

"It's no use, Watson, he has vanished completely. We had dashed bad luck then," he said, puffing heavily. "What happened?"

"I am afraid I tripped over his stick, or whatever it was, just as we were about to pounce."

"Well, we may make something of that if we can find it. Did you manage to get a glimpse of his features?"

"None whatever. All I could say was that he was of medium height and build. I did hear a sort of rending sound when you and he were in the clinches; I think you managed to tear his clothes."

"I certainly felt something give way. Let us go back and search."

When we arrived back at the spot, we relit the pocket lantern that our assailant had discarded and found not only a piece of lining that had been torn from his coat, but also saw that it was soaked in fresh blood. Since neither Holmes nor I had sustained any wound, the man must have gashed himself with the knife that he had drawn when he had grappled with Holmes and then fallen. We also found his hat, which had rolled some few yards away, and his stick and so we bore our spoils of war back to the cottage.

"Let us see what we can gather, Watson."

"The cloth lining has the name, 'S. Lewtas' on the tab, a fairly common name, I imagine, in the tailoring world. No address – that part is missing, but the letters 'o-w' are visible, and I assume 'Savile Row' is the address."

"Excellent, Watson."

"More importantly, there is just a fraction of the material of the coat adhering to the lining, a brown woollen worsted. Nevertheless, we should be able to trace it. This stick is perhaps less easily traced as it has few distinguishing marks."

"No, it is a cheap one, which may indicate that its owner was never in sufficient funds to be able purchase anything more of a piece with the Mayfair coat, which would appear to be rather an expensive item. Therefore, putting the expensive coat and the much cheaper stick together, I should say the coat was probably purchased second hand, the more so since–"

"There are a couple of minute pinholes in the lining which suggest that a pawnbroker had pinned a ticket on the lining."

"You are quite scintillating tonight, it must be the cold clear air. A number of pawnbrokers, to be precise. In which case, tracing the garment back to the tailor might be futile and trying to find the pawnbroker almost impossible. The colour of the coat, though recalls Butler's description of the man in the hall, does it not?"

"Yes. And the hat?"

"Felt. From a branch of Harris Cohen and Sons, 94 West India Dock Road. Healy probably bought the coat and hat in East London, after he disembarked at the docks *en route* to Glasgow."

"Indubitably."

"It appears your theory has been correct then, but what was your object in questioning Mrs. Sutherland about her daughter's name?"

"You can be remarkably obtuse at times, Watson. Is it not obvious to you that this Kate Sutherland is *not* the Scotts' daughter?"

"No. Whose daughter is she?"

"Why, Miss Gilbert's, of course! And the child, Maisie, is the old woman's granddaughter. There is no mystery in that."

"Good Lord!"

"It would be no great feat to pass off such a thing of in a country district like this."

"Do you mean to say that this quiet, gentle, unassuming countrywoman has played us for complete fools?"

"If you mean Mrs. Sutherland, no – I believe she is unaware of that. However, the pretence has been comfortably maintained for thirty years, and obviously Kate's father and mother must have been complicit in the deception. I only began to suspect so myself recently. I cannot come up with any other theory which fits the facts."

"But surely as Miss Kate Scott, as she was, would have required an extract of her birth in order to be married?"

"That is the difficulty which we shall have to clear up when we visit the records office tomorrow, though, frankly, the forging of such details was no difficult feat thirty years ago."

Chapter 9

Our relief picket, Mercer and Barker, arrived the following morning, after we had escorted Mrs. Sutherland and her two children to the station and seen them safely off. He explained to his two colleagues about the intrusion the previous evening and remarked that he did not think it likely that our assailant would return. Harry Mercer was a former pugilist from the East End, a safecracker now gone straight; suffice to say that I might almost pity any intruder should he by any chance fall into Mercer's hands. Barker was an old university acquaintance of Holmes's whose association with my friend reached back even before the Reginald Musgrave affair. Although to some extent rivals, they had nevertheless worked together on a number of cases. I had no doubt that the cottage would be in very safe hands when we left.

Holmes and I set off to the Registry Office and explained to the official that had been retained by a client in a probate case – he had heard of Holmes vaguely, he said, and went to great lengths to assist us in making our searches. I must say it was dull, dispiriting drudgery and reminded me of my cramming for exams as an undergraduate, and I wondered, perhaps uncharitably, why any sane man would ever want to take up the study of genealogy. We went there on the confident expectation of finding a case of illegitimacy; to our surprise we found nothing of the sort, quite the contrary, in fact. Holmes it was who uncovered our first shock.

"Have a look at this," he whispered, placing a transcription before me. "Our so-called Miss Gilbert was married to one James Johnston in January 1867."

"One of Miss Gilbert's legacies was to the James Johnston Trust in Auckland, New Zealand. Unless it is a preposterous coincidence, it must be the same man."

"I have no doubt that it is."

"Why should she conceal the marriage? Was there something disreputable about this Johnston character?"

"I have not got that far yet, though I may say that I doubt it. I believe the obvious reason that Miss Gilbert concealed her marriage was that she feared her father's wrath, and her subsequent disinheritance, should it come to light. The fact that her father died a short time after the marriage – April, Findlater told us – probably indicates he was in his final agonies when the marriage took place."

"But why not wait those few months more and avoid any risk of disinheritance?"

"We shall never know for certain, but I should say that the imminent departure of her fiancé to set up this trust was the likely reason, the assumption being that his new wife would follow him after the death of her father, which was imminent, with the legacy intact, of course. The fact that the annuity is going to the trust and not the person suggests that James Johnston was no longer alive when the will was drawn up, and since there is no indication that Miss Gilbert ever went out there as a married woman, this might suggest that the husband died soon after her father."

"Or he may have simply abandoned her for some native woman – I saw it happen often enough in India."

"No, had he done so, she would hardly have bequeathed a legacy in his honour."

"True."

"How have you fared?"

"I have not found anyone by the name of Catherine Gilbert who would correspond to our 30-year-old Mrs. Kate Sutherland, nor in fact any other of a similar age which could account for the child being registered under the father's name. However, a Catherine Scott is registered by Mr. Andrew and Mrs. Jeanette Scott born on 18th November 1867. From what you have told me, this happened to be ten months after the marriage of Miss Gilbert and Mr. Johnston and therefore eight months after the death of the latter."

"I am convinced it is the same child. It must be Miss Gilbert's – or rather Mrs. Johnston's – daughter after all, and in all likelihood a legitimate one, but registered deceitfully."

"Is that really possible?"

"Let us ask the opinion of the registrar."

Holmes called the fellow over and put the question to him.

"It is perfectly possible," the man said, "it would be easy enough to do, but it would give rise to a criminal charge if discovered. The penalty would not be too severe, unless, of course, the false entry was made in order to perpetrate a fraud. Here, that's not the Scott records you're looking at, is it?"

"Why do you ask?"

"Only there was another gentleman in here yesterday, looking up the same record, asking the same questions."

"Did he mention the name James Johnston, by any chance?"

"Yes, he was hunting up references for his family tree, he said. It's going back a while, but this James Johnston was from Callander. I remember it well. He was going off to somewhere in the Colonies, but he had a serious accident on his way out; he was brought back here and never recovered. I can show you the entry for his death, I had it out the other day."

"By the way, did this other gentleman give you a name?"

"No."

"Was he of medium height and build, sallow skinned and dark hair?"

"That's him, all right, you must be an acquaintance I suppose?"

"We were in his company only last night in fact."

The registrar brought us back the transcript: James Johnston, husband of Maureen Johnston, née Gilbert; died 18th March, one month before the death of her father

"But why all this deception if the child was legitimate?" I asked my friend.

"Let us reason it out: Mrs. Maureen Johnston, as she then was, foresaw very well what she had to do. In order to avoid being disinherited, she had concealed her marriage in the entirely reasonable belief – as the dates show – that her father had, as it were, not long to go. When her husband died suddenly, she found herself with child – it was unexpected as she would be by then 45 years old. This left her in a quandary; she could continue to conceal her marriage easily enough, but she could not conceal the child – or could she? A common practice in those days, even in well-to-do families, was to give up an unwanted child up for adoption; but this would mean that she would never see the child again. She therefore did the next best thing; she made a false declaration and farmed the child out to the Scotts, whom she knew from the village. She saw them often, as we know, and in the fullness of time managed, in a sense, to claim the child back when she took Kate into service with her at thirteen years of age."

"She had not her sorrows to seek, this quite remarkable woman, in the spring of 1867."

"No. But I believe Miss Gilbert had intended to reveal this to Kate after her death perhaps there was a letter alongside the will."

"It is obvious now that Healy must have had some inkling of the entire story."

"Yes, but there must have been another document in that box that he was looking for on the night of the murder; whatever it was, its abstraction was intended to further weaken the claim of the Sutherlands. He may have believed that Kate Sutherland had this other document in her possession, though he may have come here simply to physically eliminate her."

"At present that is purely speculation."

"Of course, but we have made a good innings today,' he smiled triumphantly. "Our difficulties begin to clear like the mist of a summer's morning. Although I must leave for London tonight, I think you may make the best of your time here, Watson, by beginning to draft your account of how we saved an innocent man from the gallows, for I am in great hopes that very soon our fortunes will begin to turn."

And turn they did. The morning newspapers in Glasgow were full of the story of the commutation of Stoller's death sentence to life imprisonment: "Sixty Steps Murderer Cheats Death" cried the Morning Post somewhat ghoulishly; the Glasgow Herald was more civilised and had, apparently, dispatched its Berlin correspondent to Beuthen in Silesia to inform Stoller's parents of the news and conduct an interview.

Anyone who knew Holmes as well as I did would have little difficulty in understanding the series of events which would have brought this about. To the outside world, Mycroft Holmes was a minor clerk in government employ at Whitehall; to those who knew him, he was one of the most indispensable cogs in the entire governmental apparatus. It was not the first time that the Prime Minister, guided by brother Mycroft, had graced our modest rooms in Baker Street and besought Holmes to pursue some affair of vital national or even international importance. I pictured the discreet meeting in the Stranger's Room at the Diogenes Club; the dignified persons in the highest echelons of government; the august individual who was indebted to my friend for having saved his career, his marriage, and his reputation as a gentleman; and the confidential, understated assurance that would have been uttered to the effect that *the matter would be looked into* by the Secretary for Scotland. Nevertheless, it was a remarkable feat, given that we had no legal recourse to appeal.

"It was statesmanship rather than law," was how my friend later described it.

My reverie over, I dashed down my breakfast as quickly as was consistent with healthy digestion and made my way straight to McIntosh's office, where I had to push and butt my way through the curious citizens and the rabble of pressmen on the steps outside. Rabbi Jacobs, having heard the news, had arrived some time before me and had apparently made a short speech to the crowd which was very well-received. He was in a state of excitation that bordered one moment on utter joy and the next on abject sorrow. Whilst he was in great relief that his countryman had been spared the gallows, nevertheless, as things stood Stoller was condemned to a slower lingering death in Peterhead prison, for that was what his commutation would now mean unless we found the real culprit.

I endeavoured to assure him, however, that Holmes was by no means at his wits' end as far as the case was concerned and that, although sworn to secrecy in matters of detail, I could promise him that we had picked up a number of promising lines of inquiry in the last few days. If anyone could move mountains, it was Holmes, and I told him that when my friend returned, we should be pursuing the matter with a renewed intensity. The case against Stoller, I opined, was unravelling by the day and the commutation of his sentence was merely the first holding position until we were able to pin the crime on the real culprit.

When Holmes arrived back in Glasgow that afternoon, he looked pale but exultant.

"We have quite a busy round of calls today, Watson," he said, rubbing his hands in anticipation.

248

"Lead on, then."

"I feel we are on solid ground now; I am quite ready to take the bull by the horns."

"Meaning?"

"Superintendent Stevenson. The interview can be put off no longer: We have begun to right one injustice; I feel I am quite ready for a second. Firstly, though, we must fulfil our promise to McIntosh regarding his friend at the Dalriada Insurance Company."

Mr. Crosbie very warmly welcomed us into his office and sent the boy to make coffee. Holmes reminded him succinctly of the purpose of our visit and referred to the affair of the Bognor Prestidigitation Circle, a similar case in which he had been successful the previous year.

"Yes, I heard about that from a colleague in London," said Crosbie, "Pinkerton's had been engaged by one of the insurers with respect to a spate of robberies at the small banks in the city. You assisted the Pinkerton fellow, what was his name now ... Abberline, and there was a murder involved in it too. One of your more unusual cases, surely."

"It was unique in some respects, most instructive."

"According to McIntosh, you have reason to believe that a fraud, perhaps a number of frauds, have been perpetrated against our company in the matter of the return of valuables for reward."

"That is correct."

"And you believe that the police are somehow–"

"A *certain* policeman," interjected Holmes, "with perhaps one accomplice – and I must bind you to silence on that. There is no suggestion that anyone else in the force is involved."

"Thank goodness for that. And yet while I admit we seem to have been very naïve about the entire affair, I did wonder if there were any reason why had this not come to light before now? Until after the third burglary, that is."

"A very reasonable question and one that is difficult for me to answer at present, but I believe that your cooperation would assist us in not only in catching the culprits but perhaps also seeing our way to ensuring that any monies previously, and unlawfully, claimed as rewards are repaid to you. If you could arrange a meeting exactly as you have done before with the ostensible purpose of having the proceeds of the robbery returned for the usual reward, we should be happy to be present and advise you. I am sure we can bring the matter to a conclusion there and then."

"*Ostensible* purpose, I don't quite see–"

"There will be no requirement for any reward, you may take my word for that."

"Your fees then–"

"Will be waived in this instance, we are pleased to undertake this commission *pro bono publico*."

"That is remarkably generous of you Mr. Holmes, but we can't allow that, I am afraid. We should need to make some gesture, a nominal sum at least surely."

"Perhaps later. However, one thing I do require from you is a letter of introduction, on your headed notepaper, to say that I am assisting you in the inquiry to recover the stolen jewellery."

"By all means, that is easily done." He rang a bell for his assistant and gave the boy the order.

"And If you could favour us with a list describing said valuables too."

"In fact, only one object was stolen in the most recent robbery at Stenson's – it was the most valuable piece in the shop, of course! It was the Traquair necklace, worth five thousand pounds. An old heirloom which the family was forced to sell – hard times,

Mr. Holmes, come to all of us. It hardly needs describing for it is very well-known in the trade."

As soon as the boy had returned with the typewritten letter, we were on our way again.

"I wish you luck in discovering what happened to the stolen necklace," said Crosbie, as we left.

"I shall have no need of luck, sir, I know precisely what happened to the necklace."

"You know where it is?!" he expostulated.

"There has never been any doubt about that," was his riposte, leaving the affable Mr. Crosbie and myself somewhat bewildered.

"Now for the lion's den," said Holmes as we left the insurance office. As it turned out, his wariness was well-founded, for we received very cold treatment at police headquarters in Low Green Street.

"The only reason I have granted you this interview," began the superintendent icily, "is because my London colleague, Mr. Lestrade, had written to me to explain that you had managed to get yourself mixed up in the Stoller case. I was unaware of the Yard's collaboration with private detectives and thoroughly disapprove; it will never happen here under my jurisdiction. However, Inspector Lestrade assisted us with the routine checking a suspect's alibi, albeit not an especially strong suspect."

"I have been retained by–"

"Mr. Crawford McIntosh, the lawyer in the Stoller case, and you believe there has been a miscarriage of justice; yes, I read about them every day in the newspapers. If every criminal who claimed to have been the victim of a miscarriage of justice were set free, we should have no need of prisons. I am aware of your reputation – in England and under English law, of course.

"Justice is the same in any civilised country, surely."

"You've a lot to learn, Mr. Holmes. I chose my words carefully. I spoke of law, not justice which is a highly subjective definition of an intrinsically undefinable entity. However, I know exactly what you are implying. You ought to be aware that in our criminal justice system there are checks and balances designed to prevent autocracy and to limit the absolute power of the state, some of which, I may point out to you, do not exist in England. The police case is submitted to the procurator fiscal; if he does not consider the evidence against the accused strong enough, the case goes no further. The last thing any fiscal wishes to see is a succession of cases thrown out of court by the judge or jury. A further check exists in whether the presiding judge believes that there is a case to answer at law – there are many instances where the defendant is assoilzied – the judge simply throws the case out. Furthermore, the jury has to agree on the defendant's guilt – they may decide to acquit, regardless of the strength of the evidence, that is their prerogative.

"We have a further safeguard in this country, where the jury is not forced to take a black and white view of the case; even if they believe the defendant may be guilty, it is open to them to deliver a 'not proven' verdict if the counsel has not provided sufficient evidence of that guilt. It is also perfectly well-known that some jurors will not convict in a capital case, since they do not hold with capital punishment. Again, those are the jury's privileges, none of which I should ever seek to revoke. The case which we presented in court, Mr. Holmes, survived every single one of those challenges."

"I should like to begin by stating that it is not my intention to attempt to persuade you to my point of view, but I may say to you that I believe I have the evidence, absolutely clear and incontrovertible evidence gathered together in a coherent sequence, that Stoller is innocent."

"Your friend McIntosh believed that; the jury thought otherwise."

"Unlike McIntosh, I believe can produce the real culprit."

"Then do so, Mr. Holmes, do so! And you shall have my fullest support."

"In due course, I shall not only produce the culprit but will make you a free present of the evidence in order that you may claim the credit. Firstly, however, what I was about to say was that I am retained by Mr. Crosbie of the Dalriada Insurance Company, and I should like to discuss the apparent jewel robberies – here is a letter from them confirming the same. In fact, that was the miscarriage I wanted to speak about first."

"No doubt you want to make complete fools of us in that case too."

"I could very well retort that you seem to have achieved that without any assistance from me; however, I did not come here to trade rhetoric."

"Then, you also have the culprit for that one?"

"Yes, and I will produce him tomorrow morning at the meeting. I have come here to request your permission for Lieutenant Carlyle to be present there."

"Under no conceivable circumstances. This man has publicly called me, his superior officer, a liar. What's more, he did not even have the gumption to say it to my face!"

"In point of fact, he has neither said nor implied any such thing."

"There are three witnesses, one of whom is a fellow police officer."

"Let us leave the three witnesses aside for the present. There has been a highly abnormal set of circumstances which has conspired to bring about the impression that Carlyle has called your honesty into question. This is not the case, as I will show, but we shall return to that in the fullness of time. I believe, however, that Carlyle has vital material evidence in the Argyle Arcade business that will establish the case against the persons responsible. "

"Impossible. Carlyle was not even involved in this case."

"And for that very reason, he was taking an arms-length interest."

"In any case, we have the resources to catch the men ourselves. It may take some time I admit but –"

"With the greatest respect, Superintendent, I do not believe you can."

"Why not?"

"Because, you do not know what crime you are investigating."

"By thunder, Mr. Holmes! You have a rare cheek on you."

"Then what *are* you investigating?"

"A series of jewellery thefts, man!"

"No, there has been no theft."

"No theft! I am not sure whether to have you thrown out or have you arrested for wasting police time!"

"On the contrary, I am offering my assistance," Holmes replied patiently. "I shall begin by asking you a question or two to put the matter in context. How long are you prepared to put up with this charade of your officers receiving rewards for recovering apparently stolen property? How long before the gentlemen of the press suddenly realise what is really going on, and you find yourself hunted by the pack? I can assure you that *that* day is not far off, and when that Pandora's Box is opened, you can well imagine the consequences. If you would show some forbearance, I guarantee you that I shall provide incontrovertible evidence that will clear up this whole business once and for all."

Stevenson exhaled noisily, then stood up and strolled over to the window. He gazed out over the hoar-frosted Glasgow Green for a few minutes, then he returned to his desk and faced us, his steely glare having softened somewhat.

"I have never been entirely reconciled to the current practice, which is by no means illegal in Scotland, you must understand, and which has the *practical* virtue of returning the property to its rightful owner. However, ..." he paused judiciously, "as you suggest, it would not be difficult for, say, an enterprising journalist of the rabble-rousing type, to put a different construction on the strict ethics of the conduct of these cases. You implied that you have evidence ..."

"Irrefutable evidence which I can demonstrate to you, but I emphasise that if any single person has been responsible for bringing this to a head, it is Carlyle."

"Very well, you may bring him along. My instincts tell me that you are an honest man, Mr. Holmes, but I give you fair warning,' a flash of the steely glare returned, "that if you have misled me in any way ... well, we shall see what happens tomorrow."

Our final call for the afternoon was a visit to Stenson's in the Parisian style Arcade in Argyle Street where the most recent robbery had taken place. Holmes showed the letter from Crosbie to the owner, John Stenson, and he brought us into his tiny office at the back of the shop and introduced us to the manager of the firm, a Mr. Alleyne.

"I regret to say," said Holmes by way of introduction, "that we have been instructed by our client at Dalriada to inspect your alarm system to ensure that it is up to scratch."

"By all means," said Stenson placidly, "although it is a bit late for concern about that as we are expecting to have the goods returned to us soon. Mr. Alleyne, please show these gentlemen everything they need to see."

"But it has already been examined by the police," said the latter with some annoyance.

Holmes smiled indulgently, "I am sure that it has; however, how many policemen do you think understand the intricacies of cells, relays, and solenoids?" he said.

"Well, I can tell you it went off all right on the night of the robbery," he replied truculently.

"I should not doubt it; nevertheless, we must check to make sure that all is correct; it is a purely routine matter and will only take a moment, and after that we shall be on our way."

"Well, here's the control box," said Alleyne leading us to a cupboard below the stairwell. "I suppose you know what you are looking for."

"Yes, it is quite straightforward. Ah, could you possibly provide us with a light, for it is rather difficult to see under here?"

I thought this a strange request as Holmes usually carried a small pocket lantern, but I forbore to say anything. As soon as Alleyne had departed, my friend dived under a shelf in the stairway and began fiddling about with something which I could not see. Then I heard a grunt of satisfaction, and he resumed the perpendicular just as Alleyne returned with a lighted candle.

"Here you are, sir."

My friend again bent under the shelf and this time shone the candle around within the space. He hummed and hawed a bit, then withdrew his head.

"Did you reset the alarm yourself after the burglary?" Homes asked.

"Yes."

"That is fine, then."

"Is all in order?" asked Alleyne anxiously.

"It was exactly as I expected," replied Holmes coolly.

"Will you be putting that in your report, then?"

"Most certainly."

"Anything else you'd like to see?"

"Only the Traquair necklace," said my friend, at which Alleyne gave an uneasy laugh, though I was left slightly discomfited at Holmes's rather crass attempt at humour.

"Come along, Holmes, you were bluffing, were you not?" I said when we reached the street.

"Not at all, Watson. I rarely do so. It can be a dangerous habit to attain and a difficult one to get rid of."

"But you said you knew nothing about alarm apparatuses."

"I didn't when McIntosh mentioned the subject in his office, but after a conversation with your friend Lomax in the London Library in St. James Square this morning before my train left, I now consider myself practically an expert. I fancy I could set up in business. And, of course, you will recall the instructive episode with young Inspector Barrowclough some time ago in the Langhorne Wyke case, when he educated me in the finer points of the railway signalling system – the principles are identical, and I rarely forget the merest morsel of useful information, as you know."

"Then what was that remarkable performance all about?"

"You know my methods. Apply yourself to them, it is not difficult."

"Well, three jewellers have been robbed in fairly short order; no culprit has been apprehended despite all three premises supposedly being alarmed; one connection to all of these cases is the same alarm apparatus supplied by the same alarm company. You suspect that the company has been selling faulty or substandard alarm systems to gullible customers?"

"You shall understand all the better when we return to Stenson's later tonight."

"Tonight!" I said with surprise. "Whatever for?"

"Why, Watson, to burgle the place, of course," he replied calmly.

"Really, Holmes, illegal gambling dens and now burglary – what other criminal activities do you have in mind?"

"Since you ask, let me see now: withholding evidence in a murder case; deliberately misleading the police; failing to report a vicious assault with a knife and an intended burglary; and a spot of perjury, if it came to it – albeit purely to protect the innocent. All in a day's work for the private consulting detective," he retorted with a mischievous laugh.

Chapter 10

We left the Station Hotel just before midnight. Holmes had his dark lantern, his drill, and his jemmy concealed under his cloak, so our nefarious intentions were well camouflaged. The difficulty was that, unlike London, Holmes did not have the intimate knowledge of the byways and lanes and we had been forced to reconnoitre the area, particularly the adjacent buildings and lanes, in daylight, which restricted the scope of our activities. Nevertheless, we had a fair grasp of how the land lay and made towards the general direction of St. Enoch's Station; in the unlikely event that we should we be stopped and questioned, our pretext for wandering about at such a late hour was that we were meeting friends arriving on a late train, and as strangers to the city ourselves, we had manged to get slightly lost. In the event, we were able to linger at the corner of Buchanan Street, near the side entrance to the Arcade, without being noticed in the misty, empty street. Eventually, we saw a constable coming down the hill checking the shops and warehouses and so we crossed the main street as though heading towards the station, then pulled into a doorway, and surreptitiously observed the constable as he approached the side entrance to the arcade. He shone his lantern into the dark void of the arcade's main passage, checked the lock on the side entrance door, then sauntered around the corner to carry out the same routine performance on the Argyle Street entrance.

"According to McIntosh," said Holmes, "we ought to have a clear fifteen minutes between visits. Mark the time – seventeen minutes past."

"Given the number of burglaries which have taken place, I am certain there will be no slacking in the constable's routine."

"My own thoughts too, Watson, indeed I should not be surprised if the patrols had been increased."

"Dear me! What if they have been or if our man should return unexpectedly, while we are trying to get through the door?' I asked.

'Should the constable make an unscheduled return, then in extremis, I suppose we could set up a commotion which will delay him until at least one of us is safely removed from the scene."

While the other receives two, perhaps three, years' imprisonment for burglary, I thought, answering myself silently.

"Would it not be safer to wait until his next round?" I asked.

Holmes nodded agreement. We remained hidden in the doorway waiting for the constable's return and saw him return as expected and repeat his earlier performance. Them, we re-crossed Argyle Street swiftly and noiselessly and arrived the side entrance; we had a clear view up Buchanan Street which was now completely deserted and quiet. Holmes produced a prodigious assortment of skeleton keys from the voluminous pockets of his cloak.

"At least, we shall be able to avoid the use of force; once we are inside, the rest will be plain sailing," he said jiggling hastily with the lock for a moment or two, following which the door slid noiselessly open and we were inside with the shut behind us. It was difficult, however, to find the shop we sought since only a little street light filtered through and it would have been utter folly to use even a pocket lantern in the L-shaped passage. Finally, our eyes grew accustomed to the poor visibility, and we found ourselves at Stenson's. This time, Holmes was able to take his time with the lock on the shop door. I touched his sleeve and whispered: "Have you no means of ascertaining whether the alarm has been set? I mean, if they had discovered your ruse or decided to examine it after we had gone."

260

"None at all, Watson, but we said nothing to give them any cause for such suspicion. Why should they expect a second burglary?"

Once inside, we calculated that it was safe enough to light his pocket lantern.

"Can you remember the layout, Watson? I am looking for Alleyne's desk."

"It was in that side office," I said pointing to a door, which as it turned out was not locked. The lantern shone into a corner of the office and there was the desk. In no time, Holmes had every desk in the drawer opened but found nothing.

"It cannot be so," he said, puzzlement ranging across his features. "Ah, no! I have it now."

He lay on the floor with his head under the desk and gave an exclamation.

"A false drawer!" I said.

"I ought to have suspected it."

I looked over his shoulder and saw that he had extracted a long slender shiny black case.

"It was here all along," I said, the truth dawning on me, "what a paltry ruse."

"I did not doubt it from the first, for I reasoned that while the police would have searched Alleyne's house after the robbery, it would never have occurred to them to search the shop."

"But if you remove it, surely it will be noticed in the morning?"

"Do you think I am such a bumbling fool, Watson, that I should not have anticipated such a possibility and brought a replacement?" he replied acerbically, withdrawing a tight white paper packet, from which he withdrew an object that I could not quite see. He quickly made the switch then repositioned and locked the drawer.

"Carlyle managed to procure for me a copy of the necklace. It was the best we could come up with in such a short time."

"Will it pass?"

"If my view of the case is correct, the culprits will want to get this off their hands as quickly as possible. It will not occur to them to re-examine it, but if they do so, they can hardly call in the police. We have them in checkmate."

Making our escape was rather easier than we had expected: we waited for the glare of the constable's lantern, the rattle of the door, then the darkness and silence which followed to give us our opportunity.

"We shall have some sport when we meet the superintendent," said Holmes, when we were safely back at the hotel. "I should not do anything to injure his reputation publicly, but he has been somewhat off-hand with us, and he deserves a Roland for his Oliver."

The next day at the appointed time we assembled in the police headquarters: Superintendent Stevenson; Sergeant Duncan; the owner of the shop, Mr. Stenson, and his manager, Mr. Alleyne; representing the Dalriada Insurance company were Mr. Crosbie, Holmes, and myself. When Carlyle arrived, the young man's frosty reception from his two police colleagues was impossible to ignore. Mr. Crosbie asked Holmes to open the proceedings. There was a discernible strain in the air and, before we began, my friend intimated that he wished to make a point of clarification.

"We are agreed, I take it," said he, "that the precedent has been established and that whoever produces the Traquair necklace – providing, of course, that it is the genuine article – will not be subject to any questioning as to how, or from whom, it has been obtained."

The shop owner, Mr. Stenson, bristled somewhat at the word "genuine" as did Sergeant Duncan – the latter no doubt resentful at the implication which Holmes's words may have introduced. Nevertheless, the point was admitted, and the superintendent replied judiciously, "As in the previous two cases, there shall be no question of police proceedings against the person who has recovered the necklace, always provided that they did not either steal, or conspire to steal it, and it can be shown that they have made no attempt to keep the stolen goods back from their lawful owner."

Duncan seemed to be mollified at this.

"Fair field and no favour, then," said my friend enthusiastically as he scribbled a note on his pad, "let us proceed: May I ask you now to hand over the piece, Sergeant Duncan."

"With great pleasure," replied Duncan, clearly relishing the moment as he reached into the recess of his jacket, withdrew the black case I had seen the night before and passed it across Holmes.

"You have no objection to Mr. Stenson examining it, I suppose?" said Holmes.

"Of course not," replied the sergeant in a cocksure manner and with something of a smirk, "if it satisfies you, Mr. Holmes."

Holmes remained impassive as Stenson took out his eyepiece and laid it aside on the table, opened the box, and brought out the contents. The seconds seemed to crawl by and, as Stenson continued to handle the jewellery with a puzzled frown, I felt the tension begin to mount. At length, the shop owner looked up at us in pale consternation.

"I quite recognise that I am under obligations to all of you gentlemen here," said he, "but I must regard this as either a rather silly prank or an insult, if not something worse."

"Whatever do you mean?" asked Mr. Crosbie.

"I mean that this is a fake!" he exploded, flinging the piece on to the table derisively, "and not a particularly clever one for I had no need to use the eyepiece to see that. Why, a child would not be fooled by this." There was a tense lingering silence followed by an uproar which ensued for several minutes, as Crosbie, Stenson, and Duncan all clamoured to speak, until the superintendent managed to regain order.

"Sergeant Duncan, what is the meaning of this?" he barked

"I ... don't ... know," he stammered, looking genuinely dumbfounded. "I have no idea. I mean ... surely you don't think that I would try to ..."

"I believe I can provide a full explanation," said Holmes suavely, "but first we must restore Mr. Stenson's rightful property to him and put his mind to rest, must we not?" He nodded to Carlyle, who slowly and carefully removed a paper-wrapped object from his inner pocket and handed it over to Stenson.

"I think you will find that this is the real one," the young man said calmly.

After examining it briefly, Stenson said, with obvious relief, "It is indeed; but what on earth is going on?"

"Detective-Lieutenant Carlyle," said Stevenson sternly, "can you explain how you came to be in possession of this necklace."

"I think not, Superintendent," said Holmes, raising his hand, "surely you have not forgotten what we agreed only a few moments ago. In fact, I have it written down here, *verbatim*. It is for Sergeant Duncan to explain how he came to be in possession of this fake with the object of fraudulently obtaining a reward."

Duncan glared at Alleyne who had grown pale and very anxious. "Don't look at me," said the latter testily, "I had nothing to do with it."

"I honestly have no idea how the fake necklace got to be there ..." Duncan stammered out the words.

"Got to be where, precisely?" barked Stevenson.

"In a false drawer in Mr. Alleyne's desk," explained Holmes. "You see, it never left the shop. It is rather unfortunate that it never occurred to the police to search the premises. I believe Sergeant Duncan was the officer on duty that night, and I'm sure he can explain – later perhaps, when he has his lawyer present. Mr. Alleyne will no doubt be able assist him since it is clear they were in conspiracy from the outset. Incidentally, I should lose no time in securing Sergeant Duncan's accomplices in the other two cases, Superintendent, before they decide to go for 'a change of air' as your colleague, Lestrade, calls it. I think you will find there was a confederate in each of the shops which was ostensibly burgled, and perhaps Constable Madden may be able to shed a bit of light on the case too."

"It is really to Mr. Carlyle, then, that the reward is due," said Mr. Crosbie, after Alleyne and Duncan had been taken downstairs. "After all, it is he who produced the stolen goods."

"I do not need, or want, any special reward for carrying out my civic duties," said the young man, waving the idea away. "If you wish to show your gratitude, however, you may consider making a small donation to the Police Widows and Orphans Fund."

"Mr. Holmes, then–"

"Neither Dr. Watson nor I look to be rewarded; to see justice done is its own reward, though you may defray a few small expenses which we have incurred."

"Such as the cost of producing a copy of the Traquair piece," said Stevenson tartly.

"Come now, Superintendent, let us have a truce in that direction; you may have been discountenanced briefly but I see no reason for you to strike this attitude. When this comes into the public realm, you will be lauded for having snuffed out, and punished, corruption in your ranks. And once our friends have departed," here he indicated the rest of the party, "I should be happy to provide a fuller explanation though I should think it hardly necessary; more importantly, perhaps, we may discuss another case entirely. In Lieutenant Carlyle's presence."

The superintendent saw the commercial gentlemen out and returned to sit with us.

"Having already achieved Stoller's respital," said Holmes once we were left in private, "it is now my intention to press on with the—"

"One moment: are you trying to tell me that it is *you* who have brought about Stoller's respital?" Stevenson asked in incredulity.

"Why, yes, of course."

"Friends with the Secretary for Scotland are you?" he asked facetiously.

"Not especially," said Holmes meekly, "only with the Prime Minister and the Secretary for European Affairs, which was why I had to approach the former directly."

"What ... Lord Salisbury?!"

"The third Marquess of Salisbury, to be precise; he has graced our humble diggings in Baker Street on a number of occasions, has he not Watson?"

"Indeed, he has," I replied, picking up Holmes's drift. "In fact, his most recent visit was during the affair of the ... but then, we can hardly disclose that even to you, Superintendent. I recall the occasion very well since it delighted me to hear his lordship's suggestion that my friend's name might appear in this year's honours list."

"To return to our case," said Holmes, "I believe that there has been a huge misunderstanding in the Stoller case, but I believe I am on my way to clearing the matter up, though I should be indefensibly hogging the limelight somewhat if I did not ask Lieutenant Carlyle to take up the story."

"Well, sir," began the young man cautiously, directly addressing his superior, "after the second burglary I detected that there was something of a pattern in both events: the same policemen, the same time of night, the same clean escape for the supposed thieves; also, the swiftness with which the loot was identified, recovered, and returned to the insurers for a reward."

"Come, come, we have cleared up the jewel robbery, there is no more to be said, as Mr. Holmes suggested," said the senior man impatiently. "Let us move on to the Stoller case."

"This *is* pertinent to the murder case, sir, they are very closely connected. You see, it was quite obvious to me what was going on and that Constables Duncan and Madden were behind it."

"Why didn't you report it?"

"I had no evidence, sir. But I was sure that I would get the proof I needed if I watched and waited. I spoke to no one, but somehow Sergeant Duncan divined my intentions – his guilty conscience perhaps. On the night that we went together to take the witness statements in the Stoller case, he asked me some odd questions about who I thought was behind the robberies. I replied noncommittally at the time and terminated our discussion on the subject as swiftly as I could. That leads me to," he paused guardedly, "… I regret to say that I must now raise the painful issue of the missing evidence."

Stevenson nodded for him to continue.

"There is no point in my regurgitating the entire story, for it is well known by now, but I can swear to you that Miss Margaret Healy told me, in the presence of Duncan, that Agnes, or Nancy, Morgan had arrived at her house in a state of fear and alarm to tell her that her aunt had been murdered by one of her nephews, and that the nephew was the man who walked through the hall. I must say that Miss Healy was in a similarly fraught state too. Some time later, the rumour emerged that Lennox Findlater was that nephew – which I do not and cannot believe – no name was mentioned by either of the women to me at the time. Amongst other things, the description given by Butler – in my view the only reliable witness – does not tally in any way with that of Dr. Findlater.

"On the evening of the murder, in fact, more accurately about two o'clock the following morning I completed the report, obtained Duncan's signature, and posted it as per the regulations. Afterwards, as you know, Duncan denied that any of these events ever took place. In fact, I now believe that he took this line in order to discredit me personally as he knew I was suspicious about his involvement the Argyle Arcade robberies."

"You would have done better to confide in me without necessarily committing yourself to a formal complaint against a fellow officer; however, that is past and gone, though please remember it in future. I am concerned as to how your report was abstracted without it being noticed."

"As it happens, I think that can easily be explained by the fact that the station was very busy and the clerk on duty, who would normally see everyone going in and out of the anteroom where the box is located, would have been overwhelmed. Due to the nature of the murder, a large number of constables and sergeants were 'lying on' after their allotted hours had expired. It is likely that if the clerk saw Sergeant Duncan going into the anteroom in order to retrieve the papers, he would not have taken any particular notice, nor would he have known that Duncan and I were working on the same case. I thought no more of the incident until I read of the Stoller verdict and realised that I had evidence that might save him. I went straight to his defence lawyer."

"That seems to clear that matter up, Carlyle. I think I may see my way to permitting you to resume the duties of your post, but you will be more or less constantly supervised until the outcome of the deliberations of the disciplinary committee. There still remains a case for you to answer with regard to your disclosures to McIntosh, although in the light of what we have just heard perhaps a more lenient view can be taken. If I have any criticism of your performance as a policeman, it does not concern your honesty or your diligence, but concerns the occasional triumph of zealousness over discretion on your part. It is something you should bear in mind with regard to your future career."

"Thank you, sir."

"I think I am justified in telling you that it was Sergeant Duncan who confided to me that you had gone to see Crawford McIntosh. The reason for his disclosure is now quite apparent."

Carlyle stood up to leave at this point, but the superintendent motioned him to stay.

"Now, Mr. Holmes, you wished to say something about the Stoller case, I believe."

"Firstly, as with the jewellery cases, I believe that the police started off on the wrong foot. It may have been a burglary, but it was not a jewel robbery although it was made to look like one. The purpose of the burglary was to extract some private papers of Miss Gilbert's."

"Do you know what these were?"

"I am unable to say exactly."

"Unable or unwilling?"

"Well, I will give you a couple of hints as to where I believe the solution may be found. Firstly, there is one flaw in Carlyle's story. No, I do not mean to question his honesty. But, whilst we can understand why Duncan may have set out to incriminate Lieutenant Carlyle over the contested evidence, what possible motive could these two women possibly have for retracting their story? Duress from Sergeant Duncan who wanted to spite a fellow

269

officer? Hardly. It is suggestive that there were far stronger reasons than that for them to play fast and loose with evidence in a murder case."

"That's right, sir," said Carlyle interrupting, "there is one other point I should like to make, something which I don't believe has been noticed by anyone else, and Mr. Holmes's question has prompted my memory. It may or may not be material evidence, and it may even just be a coincidence, but one of the witnesses who gave evidence about Stoller arriving on a train at Stobcross on the night of the murder was a Miss Mary Duncan. You may recall that she said she particularly noticed that the man was anxious and excited – I discovered that the woman is Constable Gavin Duncan's sister! She lives with him and also acts as his housekeeper."

"One moment," said Holmes, "Miss Duncan did not positively identify Stoller?"

"No, she did not," replied Carlyle, "she merely confirmed that an agitated gentleman alighted from the train which bore out the story but did not identify Stoller."

"Of course! Well, that finally settles the question for me," said Holmes animatedly.

"See what? Would you care to enlighten us, Mr. Holmes?" asked Stevenson.

"I can do better than that. If you give me two, perhaps, three days I believe I can produce all the evidence that you need to arrest the killer. And his accomplices."

"Why can't you give it to me now?"

"Because one hesitates to throw suspicions until there are absolute proofs. The suspect I have in mind did not go the house to steal any jewellery, nor did he break in; nor, in fact, did he go there with any intention of committing murder or violence, and I believe I can prove all of that. But I should be incriminating an innocent person if I were to mention any name at present: This case has seen rather enough of that already."

Stevenson coloured somewhat at this barb, "Three days is a long time, what if the culprit escapes?"

"Then I shall bear the responsibility for that."

"And I shall bear the brunt if I lose the man for good."

"I can say no more and shall have to ask you to trust me."

"Senior policemen do not get to be where they are by trusting people, Mr. Holmes, it is a singularly useless trait in my line of work. And I have yet to be shown hard evidence that there *has* been any injustice."

Holmes shrugged meaningfully.

"I see; I have no choice. I am inclined to give you the benefit of the doubt. You have until Thursday then. No longer."

"If I am not able to produce the culprit by then, I give you my word that I shall hand over to you every scrap of evidence and withdraw from the case entirely."

Chapter 11

A singular shock lay in store for us at our hotel. Feeling somewhat rheumatic due to the harsh weather, I had gone by subway to the Turkish Baths in the west end, and when I returned, one glance at my friend's expression convinced me that something grave was amiss.

"You are beginning to look somewhat overworked and strained again, Holmes," I said in alarm.

"Not quite in that black despair that Congreve says succeeds a brown study, but I confess that I somewhat discountenanced by this," he replied, indicating a telegram.

"Not bad news from Callander, I hope?" I asked with a premonition of dread, remembering recent events.

"No one hurt," he replied with a rueful smile, "only my professional pride. I'm afraid the bad news is from Auckland."

"Why, what has happened?"

He tossed me the wire from Spragg, who reported having found no record of any Winton Healy on the ships' passenger lists which Holmes had requested him to check. In fact, he had finally traced Winton Healy to Christchurch where he had been living with a native woman for some years. He was running a drysalters' store there and was serving in the store when Spragg visited the place. The news did not seem to have made any strong impression on the nephew, according to Spragg, nor did the man show any suspicion as to why Spragg had gone to such trouble to find him, ostensibly to inform him of his aunt's death. Moreover, Healy, it appears, had no connection with the James Johnston Trust whatever.

"That rather blows our beautiful theory apart," he said dejectedly. "Not to mention the small fortune I have spent in telegrams. I am only glad that I did not disclose the name of my

272

suspect to Stevenson, who will have his fun with us now to be sure. Such was the disappointment and chagrin etched on his face, that I felt earnestly sorry for him. He began pacing up and down the room, muttering and shaking his head.

"Surely my whole chain of reasoning cannot have been wrong. This is the only solution that fits the data. It is impossible! When one makes a discovery which appears to be opposed to one's theory, it invariably requires either some modification in that theory or one of your so-called facts is no fact at all."

"It must be the latter, surely."

"But we have tested every link in the chain."

"Perhaps there is a skeleton in the cupboard after all; someone whose identity is unknown to us. Which means another trawl through the records," I groaned.

Holmes nodded. "And we should hardly know where to start: Glasgow, Callander, some other place?"

"Then again," I said, "ought we not check again the alibi of the other nephew, Birrell, in London?"

"Your logic is impeccable, Watson, though I fear we are grasping at straws. Lestrade assured me the other day that the fellow who was sent to check on Austin Birrell's alibi is none other than the same Inspector Bradstreet with whom we worked on the Neville St. Clair affair and on the strange case of young Victor Hatherley. You will recall him as a thoroughly reliable and conscientious character; and, moreover, I understand that the fellow Hescott who vouched for Birrell's presence at the gasworks on the night in question is an ex-military man with a plethora of campaign honours and an exemplary record."

Nevertheless, we returned to London on what no doubt seemed to Holmes at the time a dreary, pointless trudge for he was at his most taciturn on the journey and in his blackest mood by the time we got to Baker Street. I must confess I was coming round to

273

agreeing with him that our journey amounted to no more than a counsel of despair against either doing absolutely nothing or setting ourselves a Sisyphean toil in the tangled genealogy of the Gilberts.

The following morning after breakfast we took the train down to Poplar station, whence we walked across to the Greenwich peninsula by the new tunnel. My friend's mood had lightened somewhat, and after some fussing around at the front gate, we managed to obtain an interview with the managing director of the South Metropolitan Gas Company, a Mr. Hescott, who was named in the police report as having provided Austin Birrell's alibi. He was a dapper gentleman with a rather brusque manner of speaking. He seemed the epitome of efficiency, rectitude, and order, and any notion that he may have been mistaken or had acted dishonestly over Birrell's alibi evaporated at my first sight of the man.

Holmes explained the reason for our visit.

"Let us be quite clear then," said Hescott in a brisk manner, "you have come here to confirm the alibi of a suspect in a murder case in which the accused has already been convicted, an alibi which the Metropolitan Police have previously confirmed with me personally and which has been presented and accepted as formal evidence in a court of law?"

"That is correct, Mr. Hescott."

The man shook his head in frank disbelief. "In the first instance I should say that you have left it rather late in the day; and in the second, I should say you exhibit a degree of insolence which I can only assume derives from an exaggerated opinion of your own reputation. To the best of my knowledge the resources and abilities of the Metropolitan Police are sufficient to match the depredations of the criminal fraternity, and I cannot see what you might possibly intend to achieve that they could not. Do you really expect me to renounce a sworn statement which I have made to the police? Or do you think that the police were so incompetent that they–"

"In fact, Mr. Hescott," said Holmes, interrupting, "Inspector Lestrade of Scotland Yard will confirm that my express intention is the avoidance of any damage to the reputation of the force. I can fetch the inspector along if you require."

"That will not be necessary. However, if you accept that the police have not erred, then your questioning of Birrell's alibi can only be based on the inference that I have lied to them."

"Not at all," said Holmes in his most soothing voice, "you see I believe that there may have been a simple oversight which was caused neither by the inspector's failings nor by anything that you may have said to the police."

"Would you care to explain that to me?"

"I believe I can do rather better than give you a long, complicated explanation: What I should like to do, with your permission, is to put one question – one *solitary* question – to Austin Birrell in your presence. That is all. A man's freedom is at stake, a man whom we believe to be innocent."

"Very well then. Please wait outside for the present, and I shall have Birrell sent up from the works."

"If I may beg one further favour from you – please do not mention the nature of our discussion to Birrell; it is of immense importance."

Hescott nodded and indicated the door and we stood outside in silence. Some twenty minutes later he returned and waved us back into his office where a fair-haired young man with a puzzled air, whom I assumed to be Birrell, was standing apprehensively by the desk.

"These gentlemen wish to ask you a question, Birrell; please answer truthfully then you may go straight back to your section," he said curtly.

"Certainly, sir," replied the man. I noticed a subtle change in Holmes's manner, a mere gleam in the eye, like a bloodhound picking up a scent. Hescott nodded to my friend to begin.

"We should like to ask you a question about the murder of your aunt," said Holmes evenly.

Birrell looked startled. "The murder of my aunt?" he repeated, almost absentmindedly.

"Your aunt, Miss Maureen Gilbert, who was brutally murdered in Glasgow in October of this year."

Birrell looked from one to the other of us anxiously, then shot a desperate glance at Hescott. He looked like a boxer who had caught a flurry of punches and might take a fall at any moment. Finally, recovering himself, and looking as though he were making the best of a very difficult predicament, he stammered, with an uneasy clasping and unclasping of his hands, "Mr. Hescott, I am sorry about this, but it will all have to come out now. I am afraid that I have a rather shameful admission to make."

There was a long tense pause as we stared gravely at the man, the room might have been empty so acute was the hush; I anticipated the truly terrible confession that was about to come. Finally, he broke the silence.

"I am not Austin Birrell," he said. Hescott and I were thoroughly taken aback; my friend stood beaming triumphantly.

"Please explain how you managed to substitute yourself for Austin Birrell," said Homes calmly, "I have a presentiment that you are about to tell us something very interesting."

"Austin Birrell sold me a testimonial in a public house in Millwall, 'The Robert Burns' in Ferry Road on the Isle of Dogs. I bumped into this Scotchman – the place is full of them most of the time, and Irish too. You see, I lost my job when the canning factory closed down, and this man Birrell offered me his testimonial, written by a lawyer friend, supposedly, for a fiver and said I could use his name. I must sincerely apologise, Mr. Hescott, for misleading you, but I am sure you all agree you have no complaints about my work or timekeeping."

"None at all ... er, whatever your name is–"

"It's Mandrell, sir, James Mandrell."

"We shall discuss the matter of your minor deception at some later juncture, Mandrell. Now, Mr. Holmes, I observe that this seems to have been the answer you were expecting. Does it clear the matter up?"

"It does indeed. It is one of the final pieces of evidence that I needed."

"Since we have Mandrell here," said Hescott, who had mellowed somewhat, "if there is anything else you to wish ask ..."

"There are two points I should like to clear up," said Holmes, "firstly, can you describe this fellow."

"Hm. Sort of medium height, medium build, twenty-five to thirty, nothing very special about him."

"Facially?"

"Sharp-featured, and dark haired, slightly foreign looking, that's about all. I'd recognise him again though; I've seen him a few times in the pubs down the Glengall Road."

"Recently?"

"No. About four months ago."

"Surely you were asked by the police at the time as to your whereabouts on the night of the murder?"

"Yes, of course. I was called up to the office here and the inspector asked me where I was on a certain day in October this year – I can't remember the exact date; I told the honest truth, but the police did not inform me why they were asking the question. They certainly did not mention anything about a murder. I thought their visit was something to do with pilfering in the docks or from one of the goods depots, hereabouts. Then they asked whether I had any witnesses, checked my story with the governor here, and that was the end of it was far as I was concerned."

Hescott gestured to the man that he could now leave.

"Mr. Holmes, I believe I owe you an apology," Hescott said frankly, "at least, your journey was not a wasted one."

"Well, Watson, we had no face cards in our hand until this moment," said my friend as we made our way back to town, "but I believe we have just picked up a trump."

"You did not seem surprised."

"I turned the case over and over again on my way down, so that I had already begun to suspect that some sort of substitution might have taken place."

"Pardon me, Holmes, but what if that really *was* Austin Birrell, and he has simply told us a cock-and-bull story in order to give us the slip!"

"Excellent, Watson! You are certainly developing the cunning of the serpent. However, he confirmed it the moment he spoke, for he has the proper London accent, and it is not an affected one. Nevertheless, I took no chances and having anticipated this outcome, I wired earlier to Lestrade to have one of his men shadow this fellow as soon as he leaves the gasworks. I recognised one of his plainclothes men as the crossing-sweeper outside the depot gates."

"Do you think you have got your man this time?"

"Absolutely. But simply demolishing Birrell's alibi or piling high a mountain of circumstantial evidence will not be sufficient in itself to bring the murder home to him; for all we know he will have a wife or mistress in London who will swear her life away for him. No, we shall have to do rather more than that."

"But he may still be in Glasgow, or he may have come back to London after his contretemps with us in Callander. How on earth shall we find him?"

"You will recall that Findlater told us he writes a column for *The Globe* when he is sober. Now, as you are yourself a writer–"

"A writer must have an editor and his editor must know where to contact him when he wants a story!"

"Exactly at the very least we should be able to extract a forwarding address."

We hailed a cab to take us to the newspaper office in Fleet Street.

"Mr. Birrell's address?" said the sub-editor looking up sharply. "Not bailiff's men are ye?"

"Not at all," replied Holmes pleasantly, "it is a family matter. The death of his aunt, I am very sorry to say."

"No, ye don't look like bailiff's men, I can see yer both quite respectable gennelmen."

"Why," said Holmes innocently, "is Mr. Birrell accustomed to being haunted by bailiffs?"

The man burst out with a hearty laugh, "I can see ye don't know Austin Birrell very well. Not the first time he's ended up in the street; in the gutter to be precise. Still, ye'd best find out for yerselves. Here's the address then, write it down – 14, Pierhead Cottages, Millwall. By the locks at Fenner's Wharf, you can't miss it."

"Thank you. When did you last see him? We want to be sure he is there and not be going off on a wild goose chase, you see."

"Can't recall that, but he never mentioned anything about a change of address, though he did leave a Poste Restante for his money: It was the General Post Office in Glasgow, where he often goes to visit his family."

"Well, Watson, let us wend our weary way to the unlucky Isle of Dogs, as Pepys calls it."

It was somewhat frustrating to have to retrace our steps back to the East End once more. Across the Thames we could see the lights of Rotherhithe and Deptford twinkling in the distance, which reminded me of our adventures a few years ago in that obnoxious neighbourhood which even locals called "the four corners of hell." Yet, whilst the squalor of such places, and even that of Whitechapel and Ratcliffe, may have something of a picturesque quality, Millwall was perhaps the most unremittingly bleak and grim locality I had ever come across. West Ferry Road was choked by traffic with football crowds pouring out from the Athletic Grounds, which reduced our cab's progress to a snail's pace. It was growing dusk by the time we arrived at the gloomy deserted Fenner's Wharf opposite the Seamen's Institute.

The cottage was the last of a row of low, narrow, neglected looking weather-boarded dwellings, huddled together along the side of the lock. Holmes suggested we walk slowly past and try to gauge whether the house was occupied. We strolled up and down the lockside for a few minutes and noticed that there was no lamp lit in number 14. Holmes nodded to towards the cottage, and we stopped in front of the door, which bore the name Birrell, and rapped a few times. There was no answer. The place certainly gave every appearance of being empty, but at that point, the door of the adjacent cottage opened, and a head popped out.

"Who are you and wot you lookin' for?" asked a querulous voice.

"We were looking for Mr. Birrell," said Holmes brightly, "a Mr. Austin Birrell."

"Wot's it abaht?" asked a thin, eagle-eyed, clean-shaven fellow of about thirty, who looked us up and down doubtfully. Evidently, he shared the same suspicions as the man in Fleet Street.

"It is family matter – the death of his aunt. We are from the insurance company," said Holmes, stepping across and whipping out the letter from the Dalriada Insurance Company and flashing the letter heading.

"Bit late for a visit at this time o' day?"

"We were delayed by the football crowds and–"

"Well, 'e's been gone a couple of months now. Comes and goes quite a bit, gen'r'lly."

"Perhaps I may just check that we have the right person," asked Holmes, repeating the details that Mandrell had given him.

"That's 'im. 'E'll be back at some point no doubt; if it ain't urgent, you could just slip a card through 'is door."

"Indeed," said Holmes, "that is exactly what we shall do. Thank you and good evening."

"A Scotch accent! We've found him, Holmes," I said, once we were a few yards off.

"There are plenty of those around this neck of the woods, but I think we can claim some success. At least, we have found his London lair," he said and led me up the side passage We walked around the rear door of the house in order to make sure, and Holmes turned quickly to me.

"I think it may be worth taking the opportunity while we are here," he said, "this will be child's play."

"What? I had no idea that we were ..."

Holmes was through the door in an instant, leaving me to keep watch. Presently he returned in a glow of satisfaction.

"I shall have one of Lestrade's men here within the hour just in case the occupant of number 14 returns – it's an easy place for even one of the Yard's flat-footed blunderers in which to stay concealed."

We managed to pick up a cab at the stand outside the Anchor and Hope by Tobago Street.

"Drive by West India Dock Road, would you, and stop at number 94?" Holmes asked the jarvey as we climbed inside. Some minutes later, my friend disembarked at a brightly lit shop whose sign he pointed out to me: "Harris Cohen and Sons, Hatters".

Before long he was back beside me,

"Mr. Cohen junior remembers selling the hat to a gentleman answering to Birrell's description and is prepared to swear to it on oath."

"You have, I see, what Lestrade calls the complete chain of evidence, but assuming he is in Glasgow, how do we actually lay hands on him?"

"Well, we have his forwarding address do we not, and his description?"

"Then we could waylay him when he came to collect his telegram."

"In theory; but he knows by now that we are on his trail so he may well take steps to make himself unrecognisable, or he may send an agent for his letters and money. Even so, the G.P.O. is a very busy place; he might dodge us or escape in the crowd if we made such an attempt. No, I see another way to bring matters to a head whereby he will walk straight into our arms."

"How?"

"I am in great hopes that Miss Violet Butler will assist us in delivering him into our clutches," was his enigmatic reply.

"Well, I think we have done quite enough for one day, and we have an overnight journey before us," I said. "I shall be glad to get back to Baker Street and see what Mrs. Hudson has on the menu."

"Let us hope it is not sheep's intestines, for I shall never as much as look at them again," he replied with an insouciant laugh. It was a laugh I knew only too well, one that never augured well for any wrongdoer.

Chapter 12

"Austin Birrell?" cried Miss Violet Butler, her voice rising, shaking her head emphatically, "I think not. What possible influence do you believe I might have over him?"

Arthur was following this exchange with astonishment.

"None at all," Holmes replied, "however, the person whom I should really like to assist me – Miss Nancy Morgan – is hardly likely to cooperate. Since you are a very spirited young woman, I should like you to perform this one small feat of bravery. I want you to lure Birrell to an assignation on the terrace of the Belle Vue. Believe me I should not ask this of you if I had any alternative and did not consider you to be quite a remarkable young woman."

"And you are sure Birrell was the murderer?"

"Absolutely certain; we have the motive, which was his own impecunious state, and the prospect of his aunt's inheritance. We know of his collaboration with Morgan, but we are bound to present evidence of that and so need to decoy him here in order to entrap him."

"How will you do that?"

"By writing to him to arrange it."

"Why should he come to you?"

"Because the note which I sent him purports to be from Morgan, with a request to meet urgently and I have no doubt he come."

"But she is illiterate – how could she possibly have sent a note?"

"Very sharp of you, Miss Butler. I had thought of that and have sent it in the form of a brief telegram; in theory, she would have dictated the message to the postmistress when sending it; it happens quite commonly. Holmes showed us his transcription of the wire:

"Meet me Monday midnight. Belle Vue. Danger."

"Were he to turn up and find no one there, he may become suspicious; however, if you would be prepared to impersonate Morgan, that would be different."

"But I don't look anything like her," she replied, adding, "thank the Lord."

"I can assure you, Miss Butler, he shall not come near enough that he will notice any difference. I only need you to sit on the bench at the end of the Belle Vue terrace until he gets there. There is a modicum of danger – I do warn you, for apart from the old woman, he made a further attempt on the life at least one innocent person. He has become desperate, and I believe he now recognises that Morgan has become a liability to him, someone who can put a noose around his neck."

"If he has killed once ..." she said with a shiver.

"Exactly, but Dr. Watson and I will be concealed in the shrubbery, and I guarantee you he shall not pass us."

"Will you have a gun?"

"We will both be armed."

"Do you think he will, too?"

"I cannot say, but I think it is highly unlikely that he would use arms. The area is far too crowded, and the sound of a shot would bring people running and possibly hinder his escape: Besides, there is a police box and a cab stand at the bottom of the steps. It would be utter folly."

"A knife, perhaps?"

"That is very likely, however, as I suggest, he will not be allowed close enough to do you any physical harm. Our case practically depends upon it."

"I will certainly do it, Mr. Holmes. I won't be afraid; well, not *that* much; not as long as you will both be there."

"Excellent! I am rather more concerned about exposing you for too long to midnight temperatures in winter. It will be easily arranged; all you have to do is sit on the bench with your back to the terrace, just as you might do if you had a secret assignation. Do not turn around for any reason. We will be within a yard or two of you."

"I have said all along that Morgan was involved in it," the young woman said with a sharp glance at her brother.

"As for you, Arthur," said Holmes, "I shall need you to tell me truthfully whether or not you can identify him as the man you saw in the hall. We can do nothing until half past ten on Monday night. If we are in position by then, I am sure all will go well."

Miss Butler was as good as her word. Dressed against the weather with a shawl covering her head to disguise herself, she made her way courageously down to the terrace at the appointed hour. My friend placed his hand on her sleeve in a silent gesture, then we settled into our positions to wait. We heard the church bell strike half past eleven then suddenly we were aware of the tramp of footsteps approaching, not furtive as I had anticipated, but quite assured. He had come earlier than we had expected, perhaps with a view to being ready for the foul deed he had in mind.

Closer still the footsteps sounded, and I drew out my revolver as the figure loomed near us in the dark. On he came boldly, and as it seemed to me unsuspectingly, until he drew level with bushes. Holmes was first to act; he drew Birrell's own walking stick, the one he had left behind in our previous encounter and cast it between the man's legs as he went to stride past, and our man went down like a shot rabbit. We were on him in a flash this time before he could let out a moan, far less stagger to his feet. I pinned his arms to the ground expecting him to have an unclasped knife about his person, but we found none. Around one of his hands, though, we found a ligature of wire bound to two strips of hardwood: a garrotte, the weapon of a silent death. We searched our prisoner and found the tear in the lining of his coat and the note that Holmes had sent him.

"It is no use Birrell, this is the stick you left behind in Callander; we can match the missing lining of your coat; we have been to the gasworks and spoken to Mandrell to whom you sold the testimonial; Cohen the hatter has identified you, and you have betrayed yourself by coming here in response to my note – all is known, the game is up."

"Your note! Who the – are you? Where's Nancy?"

"You may rest easy now, Miss Butler," I called. "It is all over."

The girl stood up and came towards us, pale, grave, and shaking. She cast a glance at our prisoner.

"I have seen this man before," she said, her teeth chattering. "It was around the time that Miss Gilbert's dog was poisoned. I saw him on the river path, down by the mill, with Nancy Morgan."

"Would you be so good as to send Arthur down?" said Holmes quietly. "Dr. Watson will see you home."

I saw the young woman home to number 6 and returned a few minutes later with Arthur Butler who identified Birrell immediately.

"Yes, that was the man I saw in the hall," he said, "I have no doubt of it. He is still wearing the same coat and shoes."

Our prisoner seemed to have lost all heart; he neither struggled, nor did he attempt to escape but remained silent. We went down the Sixty Steps for the last time and handed him over to two astonished constables by the police box at the bridge.

"We found this man prowling about in the dark with a weapon in his pocket," said Holmes. "Please present him to

Superintendent Stevenson personally with my compliments, along with this letter. And you may tell the superintendent I shall call round first thing tomorrow morning."

When we arrived at the police office the following morning, the superintendent's demeanour had changed dramatically since our last interview. Though he looked pale and tired, there was a warmth in his welcome for a change, and he had young Carlyle seated with him at the table.

"Mr. Holmes, Dr. Watson, the case, as far as you are concerned, is complete, although there are a few formalities to conclude. But first I must thank you both sincerely. Despite what you may think of me, my conscience would have been sorely troubled had the wrong man been executed. You will understand that I cannot simply open the prison gates and let Stoller go, but I have communicated with Rabbi Jacobs who will have brought the prisoner the good news by now. Pending the official release papers, which should be issued within a few days, the Prison Governor will see to it that Stoller is treated sympathetically until his release, which will be as soon as is legally possible.

"Birrell has made a complete confession, he saw the strength of the case against him and made a clean breast of everything, though he refuses to incriminate anyone else. Having said that, the notes which you sent to me contained sufficient evidence to justify the arrest of Nancy Morgan and Margaret Healy. Duncan is, of course, already in police custody and, as is to be expected, denies tampering with the evidence; we have had his house searched and it turned up nothing. At least nothing to do with the murder, but the house was a veritable Aladdin's cave of stolen property. The sister who lives with him and acts as his housekeeper has also been charged as she is clearly implicated in providing false information and in the stolen goods. I am glad to have them under lock and key, but if I might point out, though, you seem to have reneged somewhat on your promise to step out of the case for it was you, and not ourselves, who actually arrested the murderer."

"Arrested the murderer? Not at all, Superintendent. We said nothing to your two constables about any murder. What happened was that two public-spirited citizens – who wish to remain anonymous – were returning home late at night from some revelry, spotted some person behaving suspiciously and acted according to their civic duty. The public will discover that from the moment you had him in custody and searched his pockets, you realised exactly who he was. Sherlock Holmes need not appear in the case at all. I believe your colleague, Inspector Lestrade, acting on the suspicions you conveyed to him of the man you had in custody, has now rechecked the alibi and discovered it was false. Lestrade also informs me that Birrell's funds were at a very low ebb and his cottage was about to be re-possessed so you have the motive. No doubt the Glasgow and Metropolitan police forces will be heartily congratulated on their clever cooperation in detecting and redressing their earlier mistakes. Incidentally, you missed the deadline which we agreed on: Birrell was not brought to the station until twenty minutes past twelve – technically that was Friday morning, not Thursday!"

Holmes smiled indulgently.

"Here is the vital document which Birrell was looking for," my friend said, "part letter part invoice from Dr. McDonald, which clearly shows Miss Gilbert's treatment for mental instability. Look at the date: 21st August. This was the period when Mrs. Sutherland went back to stay with her – inference, Miss Gilbert was not entirely of sound mind and body when she made the second will; further inference, that the legatee took advantage of her former employer's temporary insanity to put her under duress

288

with respect to the contents of the will. Solid grounds there for a legal challenge in probate."

"I think I quite see the fall of the cards now, but what was the significance of Duncan's sister being one of the witnesses? After all, she did not identify Stoller."

"That is one of the key points. Even now, do you not see that?"

My friend often made people feel obtuse and this occasion was no different to many others.

"I am afraid not," Stevenson replied.

"If the burglar were unknown to Miss Gilbert all that he had to do was subdue the old woman, gag and bind her, then make an escape. We know she was murdered because she *recognised* the burglar. It seems likely that when Duncan arrived at Margaret Healy's house on the night of the murder, and observed Morgan's erratic behaviour, his experience told him that there was something gravely amiss. You recall Lennox Findlater's words on the subject. Duncan's criminal instincts told him that there was an opportunity to turn the situation to his advantage. I believe that he returned some time later and put it to the two women what he, correctly, deduced had happened: that it was the old woman's nephew – Austin Birrell – who had killed her and that they were shielding him; Morgan because she was his paramour, and Margaret Healy because, should Birrell's plan come off, she would be entitled to a third share. As it stood, they would be incriminated if he were unmasked and captured. In return for a share of the spoils, Duncan would destroy the evidence and they would deny the conversation had ever taken place. That would have the double advantage of placing Carlyle in a difficult position also. Duncan would arrange for his sister, who as you have discovered, is as crooked as he, to give some bland statement about an agitated man dashing off the train and so on, adding a completely vague description. Morgan would give a similar story and add an equally nebulous description."

"Why all these different descriptions – the fools ..."

"Not at all! No, the plan was to completely confound the police by deliberately giving false descriptions, it would simply confuse them and lead them down a blind alley."

"But surely Morgan was set up to identify Stoller to divert attention from Birrell?

"Nothing of the sort! Quite the contrary: the descriptions were purposely vague in order to *avoid* identification. It was pure blind chance that you picked Stoller up, because of the story, which I now believe to be pure invention by Morgan, about this brooch which no one seems ever to have seen. I believe the girl to be an impulsive uncontrollable liar. Emboldened by her little triumph in having the story of the brooch accepted she later changed her description of the stranger in the hall to fit Stoller – that was a colossal error, for in doing so she put not only her own neck in a noose but also that of her accomplices! Either she was egged on by some of your underlings who were sure they had their man, but more likely, she thought she was being very clever."

"Very probable, Mr. Holmes. Sergeant Duncan would have known enough about police procedures to understand that with a pile of useless descriptions and no positive corroborative identification, the hunt for the assassin would simply peter out after a while, then the case would die a natural death after the old woman's funeral and be consigned to the list of unsolved murders."

"Then Birrell would put in train the claim based on the old woman's mental state at the time Kate Sutherland went to stay there, the time when she altered her final will. I should imagine that the story of the murder had not been off the front pages of the newspapers for weeks, and the very last thing Birrell would have intended was to try to hang a completely innocent man, even one as disreputable as Stoller, for his accomplice. Duncan, would have foreseen the hue and cry that would result in a petition of twenty thousand signatures."

"All very clever in its way, the man is no fool."

"Birrell was a writer of third-rate detective stories, Superintendent – the mark of a low, scheming, and venal mind – he knew well how to weave a plot and trail a red herring. I suspect that it was he who also set the rumour going about Lennox Findlater, simply to divert attention from Birrell and confuse the matter even further."

"Yes, I can see how he might approach a fellow newspaperman in the press syndicate with just a hint of *privileged* information. No pressman in his right mind would actually publish it, of course, not with a brother like Archibald in the family, but on the other hand the gossip would be around the city like wildfire."

"But Birrell was consumed with fury when he realised the lethal stupidity of what Morgan had done, and in fact I was able use that against him. As I saw it, Morgan was the one person who might yet betray him. She is impulsive and fickle. I have no doubt that he had promised her marriage or a share of the riches afterwards, or both, as a reward for her complicity."

"How did you manage to capture him?"

"As I have told you, two citizens saw him acting suspiciously and assisted in his arrest. That is all you need for your present purpose is it not? After all, you have had your confession out of him."

"Well, if there is any difficulty, I may be forced to ask you for further evidence. Now, you have explained everything but for one point which has been troubling me. Why did Birrell choose now? Why not earlier or later?"

"The question of the timing of the murder puzzled me at the outset. I believe that Morgan had discovered a letter from Dr. McDonald diagnosing Miss Gilbert's kidney complaint. It turned out to be a minor condition related to ageing, as Archibald Findlater told us, though it was couched in medical jargon. Morgan being largely illiterate, but recognising the doctor's letter heading, no doubt passed the information on to Birrell who misconstrued the seriousness of the ailment and decided to act before it was too late."

"I cannot say what will happen to Birrell. I accept that he did not enter the house with murder aforethought, nor, from what you have told me, did he attempt to incriminate Stoller in any way – rather the contrary. Nevertheless, he has destroyed the lives of three women, not to mention the damage done to Lennox Findlater. I do not believe he can expect much mercy from the court. But one thing I can say, Mr. Holmes," said the superintendent, shaking his head, "is that I am only glad you are not on the other side of the law."

As has often been my fate as Holmes's chronicler, I have found some difficulty in completing this narrative to the extent of providing every detail which might satisfy the most curious reader. I must record, though, that Holmes had come to a judgment, one with which I concurred, that no good would come of revealing the secret history of Miss Gilbert's marriage or of Kate Sutherland's suspected real parentage – it was not certain how the authorities would view this. He had, he told me, retained the copies of the extracts of Miss Gilbert's marriage and James Johnson's death which he had taken from Birrell's cottage. His intention was to keep them until the probate case had run its course, then pass them to Mrs. Sutherland. As my friend said at the time, "it is without question that the legacy now goes to its rightful owner." He had also kept Miss Violet Butler's name out of the case, and since the official police had now extracted a confession from the culprit, they took no further interest in the identity of the man or men who had watched the house from the street.

Invariably with Holmes, one case is hardly ended when another begins, and so it was with the tragic affair of the Sixty Steps. No sooner had we returned to Baker Street, Holmes having completely abandoned his Fulworth retreat and I my sojourn in Southsea, than we were prevailed upon by Holmes's friend in the Belgian police, Monsieur Lissogne, to look into an affair which occupied the attention of the European press for a number of weeks.

To conclude my reminiscence, I can also record that Detective-Lieutenant Carlyle was honourably reinstated to his post but left the force very soon after the retrial of the Gilbert case – and the subsequent conviction of Birrell and his accomplices – and enlisted with one of the Highland regiments, the Queen's Own Cameron Highlanders, which later served under Roberts in the Transvaal. I applaud his bravery and thirst for adventure, but I am saddened to tell that this honest and patriotic young man fell in the field a year later at the fatal siege of Paardeberg Drift during Cronjé's assault.

I must also put on record that Holmes did not claim any financial reward for his work in Glasgow, at least not directly. He reached an agreement with Archibald Findlater for his fees to be paid over to Miss Violet Butler, who had been of such inestimable help to us in cornering the murderer, by not only providing us with such important information at the beginning of the case, but also in putting up such a brave show on that midwinter night on the terrace of the Belle Vue, an episode which neither she – nor, I am sure, any one of her acquaintances – is ever likely to forget. I am pleased to note that, as a result of my friend's kindness, she was able to set herself up in a private musical school which later produced a stream of gifted and able pupils who went on to play in the Scottish Orchestra alongside our famous Mr. Gustav Holst.

As for the funds which Rabbi Jacobs, had accumulated, Holmes intimated that our two informants, Nolan and McHale, deserved to be rewarded for providing some of the evidence which led, eventually, to Birrell's arrest. It was Holmes's suggestion also that, after my lawyer friend's fees were paid, the residue of the money be given to the chastened Osip Stoller in order to provide him with a fresh starting point as far away as possible from the criminous *purlieus* of Glasgow; he would at last be able to join his associates in New York, where there would be an opportunity for him to live a life free of crime. The old rabbi's eye was blurred with a tear when we came to take our leave of him for the last time. He thanked us profusely for bringing justice to his countryman and saving the man's life, and as we left, I thought I heard him use the word "lamedvavnik" when referring to Holmes, or at least, so it sounded – an idiom which made little sense to me. On our way back to London, just as the train was pulling out of the station and crossing the river, I broached the subject.

"Holmes, what was that strange phrase the Rabbi used as were leaving?" I asked.

"*Lamedvavnik?*"

"I think that was it. What does it mean?"

"Translated from Hebrew, Lamed Vav means thirty-six."

"Thirty-six! Is that some sort of code?"

"Not exactly, though it is related to the *gematriyah* where the sum of the numerical value of the two Hebrew letters, *lamed* and *vav,* is thirty-six. There is an old Talmudic legend of the *Lamed Vav w*hich holds that there are always thirty-six righteous but humble individuals, ordinary mortals of flesh and blood, in the world in each generation, and it is only because of their virtue and righteousness that humanity does not descend to the black door of *Dis*, as Virgil calls it. They do their good by stealth and have no acquaintance with one another. When one *lamedvavnik* dies, another is born. A fascinating religion, Watson: clever, subtle, and sensuously symbolic."

"Rather crude and far-fetched, I should say!"

"Quite the contrary," he replied, "it is the soul of pragmatism enfolded in fable, Watson. You see, the *Lamed Vav* do not know who they are, nor does anyone else, nor are they necessarily Jewish, or male. Therefore, any person in any age could be a *lamedvavnik,* so there is an obligation for everyone to behave as if they were one, and to treat others as though they were too, for they keep the world from self-annihilation. Rather more sophisticated and humane than the threat of hellfire and eternal damnation you might get from the Lord Guthries of the world."

"A somewhat heretical departure from Scripture," I replied, astonished at my friend's rather casual apostasy, "I fear it will take rather more than a few dozen righteous people to redress the wrongs of England – far less the world. Thirty-six virtuous souls against the Father of Evil and all his agents? Pshaw! The eternal struggle must be more equal than that."

"I am afraid the heterodoxy is all on your side, Watson," he smiled sardonically as he puffed away merrily at his cherrywood pipe, "for in saying that, you are uttering a species of the Albigensian heresy for which you would certainly have been burnt at the stake in the Middle Ages."

END

The Problem of The Coptic Patriarchs

I note from my records of this case that it was in the second to last year of the old century when, in the early spring, a long, deep frost had set in over the southern part of the country freezing the ground and, on one bitter night, our Baker Street water pipes. The cold weather front persisted for some weeks on end, and I recall that I had gone out one afternoon with Sherlock Holmes for a stroll in Hyde Park, where the paths underfoot were iron hard, and the frozen Serpentine seemed as crowded with skaters as Piccadilly Circus on a Saturday afternoon. Holmes and I circled the park on our silent ramble in the still, chilly air, passing the site of the old Tyburn tree – awakening a reminiscence of our adventures some years previously in the grisly affair which I have chronicled under the title of "The Mystery of the Thirteen Bells." It was an aimless meander in a comfortable companionable silence; indeed, I was conscious only of the distant clatter of the traffic and the musty odour of horse manure when, as we approached the Arch, I was stirred out of my reverie and my attention engaged by the newsboy yelling out the headlines of the afternoon editions.

"The usual drivel no doubt," began Holmes, following my gaze, "trivialities concerning the private lives of some famous–"

"Wait, though," I said, interrupting my friend's justified diatribe, for the word "Athanasian" had leapt out at me from the lower corner of the front page of the newspaper. I looked again more closely.

"Holmes," I said, "you cannot have forgotten the business of the Athanasian Scroll."

"Hardly, Watson. Why do you ask?"

"Well, here is a story in the newspaper concerning the very same!" I replied, fishing in my pocket for some coins to pay the boy.

My notes for the previous year recorded Holmes's retention by His Holiness Pope Kyrillos V of the Coptic Patriarchate in Alexandria, over the theft of the 9th-century Athanasian scroll. The affair had necessitated intercession with a cabal of international thieves, and the bargaining for the return of this rare document entailed translations in three separate languages whilst at the same time striving to maintain complete secrecy of the affair.

When we had returned to Baker Street with the newspaper, I was astonished to discover that the article purported to show that the scroll, which Holmes had gone to so much trouble for over its return, had now been exposed as a forgery.

"A forgery!" cried Holmes.

"So, it would appear," I replied.

"Well, of all that it is wonderful ..."

"You see, the real one has turned up."

"The *real* one?" he stared at me in confusion, over his tea cup. "Watson, you have resorted to your usual mode of telling a tale by beginning in the middle, going on the end and finishing at the beginning."

"Very well then, it is headed: 'Athanasian Scroll is Forgery, Claims Home Counties Don.' I shall read the entire thing.

The celebrated Professor C.N. Beasley, of the School of Orientalism, has claimed that the 10th century Athanasian Scroll, a sacred relic of the Coptic Church currently exhibited at St. Mark's Church, Alexandria, in the Khedivate of Egypt is a cleverly fabricated forgery. Cedric Norbert Beasley, an authority on the history and linguistics of the Holy Land, claims to have had the authentic scroll recently given into his possession but declines, however, to disclose the source. Beasley's predecessor and mentor, Professor Ignatius Coram, of Yoxley, Kent, provoked a storm of controversy last year with his three-volume treatise 'Athanasius of Alexandria' which cast doubt on some of the long-standing assumptions and cherished beliefs of established religions in the western world. The book claimed, *inter alia*, that the monastic tradition and the techniques of illuminated manuscripts associated with the early Celtic church in Britain were developed from Coptic Christians who had visited Glastonbury and Ireland in the fourth or fifth century. The scroll appears to substantiate this containing, as it does, apparent allusions to the Book of Kells. There is, claims Professor Coram, evidence of Alexandrian theology intertwined with that of the Celts, demonstrating an early connection to the Coptic Church, which has a claim to be considered the oldest Christian church in existence. The scroll recently discovered by Professor Beasley does not differ greatly in content from the one presently retained in Alexandria; however, a number of minor discrepancies etc., etc., ...' the article then goes on to say that the present Patriarch of the Coptic Church in England, the Reverend Father Philoxenus, is to meet with Professor Beasley to determine the scroll's authenticity and that the latter is resolved to return the document, which is as priceless as it is unique, to its rightful place in St. Mark's in Alexandria."

"Quite remarkable, Watson. You recall, of course, that several thousand piastres were paid for that alleged forgery. Presumably, someone substituted the forged article for the real one at the time, and one can only wonder at the chain of events which led to the latter coming into the professor's hands. I assumed at the time, of course, that His Holiness would have recognised the genuine article when he saw it. Not only do we find that it is a fake but also that this eccentric academic proposes to simply give the real one away!"

"I suppose it is always gratifying in these days of rampant materialism and self-interest to see an example of the altruistic spirit," I replied.

He smiled ruefully, and our conversation strayed back to more secular topics. And there the matter lay until a few weeks later, on the second day after Easter – April the twelfth to be precise – when we received an unexpected visit from Inspector Lestrade of Scotland Yard.

Holmes waved our visitor to a chair, rang the bell, and gave Billy the order for coffee. Lestrade's occasional visits had the dual purpose of enabling my friend to discover the latest official developments, and of allowing the inspector to hear from Holmes the titbits of gossip he had picked up from his numerous acquaintances in the criminal underworld and even, occasionally, to pick my friend's brain without necessarily invoking his intervention. On this occasion, it was clear that the visit was not a social one.

"It's a strange case, Mr. Holmes," said Lestrade by way of introduction, "two definite crimes were committed last night: a robbery and a kidnapping, but in the very oddest of circumstances. Have you seen the newspapers this morning?"

"Not yet," Holmes replied.

"I don't suppose either of you gentlemen has ever heard of a religious group known as the Coptics?"

"In that bureau by the window," said Holmes languidly, "you will find a letter of thanks from His Holiness Pope Kyrillos V, the one-hundred and twelfth Pope of Alexandria and Patriarch of the See of St. Mark. He happens to have been the longest-serving pope in the history of the Coptic Orthodox Church, and I had the privilege of undertaking a small commission for him last year."

"And beside it," I added, relishing the spirit of Holmes's rejoinder, "you will also find my copious notes on the case which, unfortunately, cannot yet be published."

Lestrade laughed. "I might have guessed! What was the affair, then?"

"It was a private matter," replied Holmes suavely, "and with the best will in the world, I am afraid that I cannot possibly breach a client's confidence and reveal that, not even to you."

Lestrade looked as though he had been struck.

"All right then, Mr. Holmes," he continued testily, "do you know anything about the, er ..." here Lestrade consulted his notebook, "... the Athanasian Scroll?"

"Only that it is a ninth-century document, dedicated to, rather than written by, St. Athanasias, hence the name; indeed, its precise authorship remains unknown, though as it is a product of aesthetic monasticism it is likely to have been collegiate in origin. One of the lodestones of Syriac Christianity, it was spirited away to Europe for safety in the centuries following the Arab conquest of Egypt and was then returned again after the Crusades. It narrowly escaped the fate of burning at the Battle of the Pyramids one hundred years ago for, despite their enmity, both Napoleon and the Mamelukes were united in their scant regard for, one might say in detestation of, the persecuted Copts. There was a rumour that it had been concealed in one of the ancient churches in Abyssinia, believed to be the Zion church at Aksum alongside the Book of Miracles, until the Treaty of Addis Ababa, when it resurfaced. I am aware of the recently publicised allegations – allegations which appear to have substantial justification and carry profound academic authority – that the Scroll which is presently residing in Alexandria is a clever forgery. I am afraid that is all I am able to tell you."

"All!" said Lestrade, laughing. "One of the subjects on which you have written a small monograph then?" he continued, with a slight inflection of sarcasm.

"Ah, no; you are perhaps confusing that with my study of the Syriac Palimpsest, which is fourth-century Aramaic; or possibly with my trifling thesis on the Chaldean Neo-Aramaic origins of the Brythonic languages. Incidentally," my friend continued, "the allegations of forgery came about through an English academic who is a protégé of a certain Russian gentleman with whom your colleague, Inspector Hopkins, had a professional acquaintance some time ago."

"Ah, Coram, of Yoxley Old Place. That old devil! We could never prove anything, of course, since the principal witness, his wife, committed suicide."

"My understanding is that Professor Beasley now claims to have the original scroll in his possession and, once authenticated by the Patriarchate in England, it is to be returned to the Coptic Church in Egypt, after he has made a copy for the University faculty."

"You are correct, that was his intention."

" *'Was'*. What exactly do you mean?"

"Only that the scroll has been stolen."

"Dear me, it is a most priceless relic; it is worth thousands of pounds. How did this happen?"

"I have a few notes here from the local man, Inspector Horsburgh of the Buckinghamshire Constabulary, concerning the two crimes that were committed during the night. Yesterday evening Father Philoxenus of the London Patriarchate went to visit the professor at his cottage in Bourne End, Buckinghamshire, in order to examine the aforesaid scroll. The Patriarch not unnaturally had had a few doubts about whether the scroll was genuine, but having pored over it for some time, he agreed that all was in order. The professor then locked the document away in its usual place, then he and the Patriarch had a conversation during which, the professor recalled, his visitor seemed very excited, as was only to be expected. The visitor, who was quite elderly, said he was tired from the long journey and the excitement – he had come up from Somersetshire which necessitated three changes of train – and he went off to bed very early without taking any supper, saying he wasn't hungry. He had intended to spend the next few days day going over the document with the professor, explaining a few points about the Coptic language to the professor. The visitor then went to bed, and that was the last Beasley saw of him. The following morning the professor awoke to find the house had been entered during the night and that, not only had the Scroll had been stolen, but the Patriarch had disappeared – he had been kidnapped and a ransom note left demanding ten thousand pounds for the return, alive and safe, of the reverend gentleman."

"Dear me," said Holmes, "that is quite a small fortune. It's more than the Scroll itself would fetch."

"Of the Scroll, there was no mention."

"The implication being that the thieves–"

"Singular!" interrupted Lestrade. "One thief, and I think I can also show that the kidnapping was well-planned in advance too, but let me come back to those points in a moment or two."

"Then if the Scroll has not been offered as part of the bargain, the thief most likely intends to keep it and, most probably, sell it privately."

"That's my guess too. He did a proper job whoever he was; a clean sweep."

"It is likely, then, that he already has a purchaser. There is a thriving international market in such antiquities, but it is very largely a *niche* market, and there cannot be many people who would handle something so specialised or so valuable. And yet, taking a hostage for ransom surely complicates matters for him considerably. It would have been difficult enough to escape with the booty, but to compound matters by subduing and force-marching an unwilling party along with him seems absurd. As for asking ten thousand pounds as ransom, it is utter madness."

"Criminals can be completely blinded by greed, Mr. Holmes, and it is never difficult to find instances where sheer avarice outweighs common sense, and often that is how we are able to lay our hands on them."

"That is true."

"At about half past seven this morning, the professor had knocked on his visitor's bedroom door to tell him that breakfast would be ready in an hour as the housekeeper usually comes in about eight o'clock. Receiving no reply to a second knock, he opened the door, and looked in. He was a bit surprised to find the room empty and imagined that the old fellow had gone down before him. The professor is a heavy sleeper and possibly wouldn't have heard his visitor stirring; but there was no one downstairs and it was only when the professor went back upstairs again that he noticed a slip of paper on the dresser beside the bed – the ransom note."

"One moment – had the bed been slept in?" asked Holmes.

"Yes, it appeared to have been."

"And what of the Patriarch's luggage?"

"It was left behind, and apparently still contained a few articles; a clean shirt and some undergarments."

"And the bedroom window?"

"Closed and locked on the inside."

"Was there a skylight?"

"Let me see … ah, yes; and there was no lock on the skylight, according to the local man, Horsburgh."

"*Ah.* Pray continue."

"At first the professor was incredulous but there was the empty bed, the abandoned luggage, and no sign of the Patriarch. It was such a shock that his first thought was to make some strong black coffee to pull himself together. Suddenly he remembered the Scroll and dashed to his study to check, and it was then that he found it missing. It had been in his bureau which was locked, although the key had been left under a small potted plant nearby. The key to the bureau was missing so the professor had to use his spare key to open the bureau. Apart from the note there was not a single clue as to what had happened; he had heard nothing during the night. As you can see, there was an unseasonal fall of snow in the city last night, but it had been much heavier out in rural Buckinghamshire – a few inches. But you haven't heard the best part yet, Mr. Holmes, not by a long chalk!

"As Beasley stood gazing out of the study window which looks out to the front of the building, his wits slowly began to return after the shock he had received, he noticed with a start that there were no footprints in the snow outside leading away from the front door, as he would have expected, for the snow had stopped before the professor had gone to bed; he was sure, in any case, that no-one could have left the house by the front door for it was locked from the inside. He therefore assumed that the thief must have made his getaway by the rear door, but that was also locked from the inside. A thought struck him and so he returned to the Patriarch's bedroom which is at the back of the house and looked out of the window. He could see a clear set of footprints leading from the rear garden fence which backs on to a riverside path, all the way across the garden to the roan pipe adjacent to the window; at that point, the prints were muddled a bit. Furthermore, the snow which had fallen on the windowsill of the bedroom had been greatly disturbed too, so that it seems pretty obvious how the intruder got in – through the fence, across the garden, up the roan pipe, and in through the window. But nothing to suggest how he got away with the Scroll and the Patriarch. It is a complete mystery!"

"And yet if the escape were not made above ground ... well, perhaps it is too early to theorise. I assume you have given strict instructions for nothing to be touched until my arrival."

"Of course. The place is being watched and Inspector Horsburgh, the local man who called me in, is in charge along with Sergeant Canterville."

"I suppose a run out to Bourne End would be in order, Watson?"

"I should be delighted to do so," I replied

"Then ask Billy to call us a four-wheeler for Paddington, would you."

"Unfortunately," I answered, looking at the wet grey slushy pavements outside, "I detect a substantial thaw which may obliterate the footprints."

"Well, we shall still be able to examine the rest," Holmes shrugged.

"Incidentally," said Lestrade, "the ransom note was composed of words cut out from a newspaper, which indicates to me that the kidnapping was aforethought."

"Excellent," replied Holmes, "that may turn out to be a bit of a *faux pas* on the thief's part, for there are very few common typefaces which I should be unable to identify at a glance. I should be quite surprised if we do not glean something from the note."

The journey down to Bourne End was a pleasant one, especially the final leg from Maidenhead where we changed to a short three carriage train. One of our popular writers calls it the pleasantest stretch on the entire river, and as we steamed slowly up through Cookham with the sun at our backs, the Thames glinted and shone in the cool clear air. The top of Winter Hill was still

305

contoured by its light dusting of snow and, although a thaw had begun to set in, there was scarce a breath of wind, the plumes of smoke from the houses and cottages in the sleepy riverside villages rising up in straight lines out of the chimney pots.

A young, uniformed policeman, introduced to us by Lestrade as Sergeant Canterville of the Bucks. Constabulary, hailed us as we alighted to the platform. He had been in conversation with a genial-looking old white-haired railway porter as the train drew in.

"This is Mr. Merryweather," said the sergeant, "he was on dooty yesterday when Father Philoxenus arrived."

"I saw the ole fellow getting off the tray-in," the porter said in that drawling manner characteristic of the small Thames-side hamlets. "Now I hee-aar as he's been kidnapped. Ha! We haven't had so much excitement hee-aar since the Marlow Donkey went off the ray-ils one foggy night at Spade Oak and nee-aar ended up in the river. Gave me a turn, though, when I heard what had happened to old Nobby!"

"Do you know the professor, then?" asked Holmes.

"Oh aye. Went to school together, we did, hee-ar in the village. Nobby were always a bit of an odd bod, right enough. While us normal lads would be kickin' a ball arou-and or mindin' a wicket, ten-to-one he'd have his nose in a book. A bit touched we used to think. But he's travelled all over the Holy Land, and they do say as he can jabber away to a Bedoow-in or an Ottoman, or a Heebroo like a native. Same with these Copticks. Well, the-aar he is now, Principal of whatever-it-is and hee-aar's me trudgin' arou-and in all weathers luggin' suitcases about, and sweepin' draughty waitin' rooms, so who's the daft one now I say."

"Mr. Merryweather was telling me he remembers a queer lookin' fellow loiterin' about the station yesterday," said the sergeant.

"Aye. He hung about the waitin' room most of the day."

"Can you describe him?" asked Lestrade.

"He were a tall, thin, swarthy fellow; he had a broad brimmed hat pulled dow-en almost over his eyes. Even though there were a coo-al fire burnin' in the waitin' room, he had his collar turned up. Lairy lookin' sort of customer, but he weren't breakin' any bye-law, so I leave him be."

"You could not see his face?"

"That's right. He seemed to be waitin' for someone arrivin' on a tray-in, for he had no luggage of any sort himself. He stood well back from the window, too, except when a tray-in come in."

"Did you examine his ticket?"

"He never come off no tray-in and didn't buy no ticket hee-aar to the best of my knowledge, and he never spoke to anyone. From the little I could see of him, I didn't recognise him as bein' anyone from the village."

"But he was here before Father Philoxenus arrived, and remained here afterwards?"

"That's right, he loafed arou-and until after the last tray-in from Maidenhead, then he left."

"One moment," interrupted Holmes, "were there still trains to arrive from other points after he left?"

"There was the last one off Marlow for the bay that terminates hee-aar, and one off High Wycombe that runs rou-and and goes back up empty stock."

"Thank you," said Lestrade, "you have been very helpful."

"This is the address, sir," the young sergeant said briskly to the inspector, handing him a card.

Professor C. N. Beasley,
1, Lime Kiln Lane,
Bourne End,
Bucks.

"I don't know the place," said Lestrade, "so you'd better take us."

We circled the station and crossed the single track railway by the level crossing, then over a narrow stream, and at the end of the road turned into Lime Kiln Lane which was a cul-de-sac. A low picket fence separated the rear of the houses on one side from the river path which was bustling with people.

"There's a fair goin' at Falconer's," said the sergeant by way of explanation. I had already observed, tacked-up notices at various points near the railway station, advertising Bartram's Circus.

"Where exactly?" asked Holmes.

"Just there, that's Falconer's Field under Harvest Ridge," the young man replied, pointing out a steep slope not far off. "In full swing, too, by the sound of it."

"How long has it been here?" asked Lestrade.

"Came on Maundy Thursday – five days now."

Four houses stood in the cul-de-sac some way back from the street, each with its own front garden: two older cottages at the end, and two newer villas nearest the street crossing. The professor's cottage was at the side of the lane which backed on to the river.

"The footprints," said Holmes tetchily, "have been lost in the thaw."

"If you please, sir," said the young sergeant touching his cap to my friend, "the professor took a photograph of them – we have sent it out to be developed."

"Excellent," remarked Holmes, "the professor seems a model client."

"Ah, here is Inspector Horsburgh now," said Lestrade, as an alert-looking man of late middle age strode towards us from the direction of the professor's house.

"Perhaps it would be better to remain and speak out here in the meantime," said the local man briskly, "we have not eliminated the professor as a suspect, yet."

"What motive do you think he might possibly have for stealing his own possession?" asked Holmes.

"None, to be truthful. It's a mere formality, but I want to be sure of my ground. The fact that he appears to have been quick-witted enough to take a photograph of the footprints before the thaw set in could cut both ways – take nothing for granted is my motto."

"An admirable approach!" replied Holmes. "But, assuming the photographs show what the professor described, what would be your theory as to the manner of escape? Can it have been made through some underground passage or other? The cottage hardly looks old enough.""

"Late eighteenth century," said Horsburgh.

"Not impossible but, I should say, highly unlikely. How long has the professor lived in it?"

"Since he was a boy."

"Then that appears to take care of the only other conceivable explanation – any place of concealment would be likely to be known to someone who had lived there all his life, so the thief and the patriarch can hardly have remained concealed in the house, unless the professor is party to the conspiracy."

"I agree," said Horsburgh, "but I still intend to search it from top to bottom. We have interviewed a number of people: first I spoke to Mrs. McGill, the housekeeper – she corroborated everything the professor told me. A quiet, simple woman, her husband is chronically unwell, and she lives at the other side of the village; she has been with the professor for twenty years, it is extremely doubtful that she has had anything to do with this. The owner of number three – one of the new villas – is a Mr. Selborne, the company accountant; a recent arrival in the village, he commutes to the City each day by the eight-twenty, presently on a walking tour of Switzerland, left last Tuesday. I then interviewed Mr. Joshua Bennett, the former rector at St. Nicholas, who lives in the other old cottage, number two – he is eighty-two and stone deaf; I think he can be eliminated. In number four, the other of the new houses, lives Captain Tierney. A very interesting character, to say the least: formerly of the 7th Bombay, Mountain Battery, Royal Artillery."

"Retired?" asked Lestrade.

"Dishonourably discharged!" replied his rural colleague.

"I see. Why?"

"Drinking and gambling. Chased out of India. Youngish chap, bachelor, wild, and a nasty piece when the 'fluence is on him. Motive certainly – gambling debts; thin as a rake and could easily shin up the roan pipe; he will have had a gun or two in the house too, I am sure, and could have frightened the old man into coming with him."

"You mean you haven't searched his place?" asked Holmes.

"Wouldn't let us. Said he knew nothing about it as he was dead drunk last night – he certainly looked pretty woody this morning. Swears he never left the house yesterday, and what's more, as he put, 'couldn't give a damn about any bloody heathen relics,' and went on about sending 'these devil-worshippers' about their business.'"

"Fine fellow!" I replied.

"I had to threaten to run him in after he challenged the young constable to fisticuffs."

"You might get a warrant, though," said Holmes.

"I have already sent to the magistrate for one. I had a word with the circus people too down at the camp in Falconer's but couldn't get much out of them. They saw nothing and heard nothing. Don't like policemen around the place, but they're not a bad lot; if you ask me, they get blamed for a lot of things the settled folk get up to."

"All the same, I may take a look round there later," said Holmes. "Now, I should like to examine the premises where the crime took place."

With Horsburgh at his side, my friend first inspected the garden and the outhouses – which amounted to a coal bunker and a tool shed. He stopped for a considerable length of time at a spot by the rear fence which led, through some bushes, on to the river path.

"There is no doubt that someone has been through here recently," he said, pointing to some broken twigs and twisted branches. "It is impossible, of course, to follow these footprints on the path as there have been so many over it since last night, but the bushes have certainly been disturbed."

"Yes, I saw that," said Horsburgh.

"What did you make of it?" asked Holmes.

"How do you mean?"

"I am slightly confused: it is difficult to be conclusive about the indications on the bushes, as to which direction this person passed through."

"Surely it is obvious," said Horsburgh, looking at Holmes as though he were simpleminded, "the professor saw the footprints leading from the fence to the house therefore ..."

"I thought your motto was to take *nothing* for granted," replied Holmes.

"Well," said the inspector, somewhat ruffled at my friend's remark, "the photograph should clear up any confusion."

"I am not sure that it will," said my friend mysteriously, as he wandered back to the other end of the garden. He then stopped to stare up at the cottage from the ground.

The local inspector followed the line of his gaze, "It's a pity that he didn't take a shot of the windowsill too."

"In point of fact, it wasn't the windowsill I should have wanted to examine," replied Holmes, to the deepening mystification and annoyance of the two inspectors.

"Shall we go inside now?" I asked, breaking the strained silence.

The professor greeted us warmly and asked the housekeeper to bring us tea. In answer to Holmes's question, Beasley said he had seen no-one loitering in the vicinity of the house about or before the time of the kidnapping. No visitors had called – weeks could go by without one, he said.

"In fact, though," Holmes pointed out, "literally scores of people have been making their way past the bottom of your garden to the fairground. You would scarcely have noticed someone keeping a watch on the house."

"No, I suppose not," replied Beasley.

"Has anything unusual happened? Try to think, even something that may seem trivial," Holmes asked.

"The only thing that could be regarded as in any way unusual," continued Beasley, "was that the Patriarch turned up a week earlier than I had expected."

"Did he give any explanation for this?" Horsburgh asked.

"No, and I sought none."

"He is an old man after all and surely it is easy to get the days muddled up?" I said.

"Perhaps," said the professor, though I could see that Holmes did not seem convinced.

"Do you still have the letter he sent?" inquired my friend.

"I am afraid not."

"Can you describe him?"

"Dark skinned, as you'd expect; a long white beard, shaggy eyebrows and a heavily lined face. He was wearing a dark cassock with a red lining on the inside, a white collarless shirt, and very distinctive Coptic headgear."

"What age is he?"

"Before meeting him, I had thought he was similar to my own, which is sixty-two, but he looked much older."

"Then you hadn't met him prior to last night?"

"No."

"I am curious as to why," said Homes warily. "I should have thought that as the country's leading authority on matters Coptic, you would have known him well."

"I am afraid not. In the first place, many Coptic clergymen lead a monastic life, even in this country."

"Yet you have made a lifetime study of the Coptic Church. Why should you not seek him out?"

"This may seem peculiar to you," replied the professor slowly, though explaining a difficult point to a dim pupil, "but my interest in the subject is scholarly rather than devotional, if you understand; it is that of a secular academic. I am not a member of the congregation, and indeed would regard myself as agnostic – quite a common trait amongst professors of theology, though it may surprise you to know that. So, our paths have never crossed."

"Is there anything else you can tell us about him?"

"Not really, I know little about him."

"Do you have any theory as to how an escape was effected?"

"Absolutely none – the whole thing amazes me yet. One thing about the Patriarch I did notice. I am not quite sure how to put it, though, without seeming to sound prejudiced: shall we say, he rather lacked the courtesy of the average Englishman – for example, I tried to speak to him in the Bohairic dialect, but he was quite scathing about my grasp of the language, he being a native speaker of course. I must confess, I learnt the language as one might learn Latin nowadays, as an ancient liturgical language, and therefore I am conscious that I do not speak it well conversationally. Anyway, he said quite plainly that he preferred to speak in English which I found disheartening and somewhat rude. However, he somewhat assuaged my feelings by promising that, before he left, he would go over some of the finer points of the dialect with me."

There was such a stark contrast between Beasley, with his accomplishment in ancient languages as well as his command of English, and the old railway porter with his broad vowels and slurred consonants, that it was impossible to imagine them rubbing shoulders together in the school quad; there seemed a decade in age difference, yet there could hardly be.

"As a scholar of antiquity, yourself, Mr. Holmes – yes, I read your erudite commentary on the Syriac *Codex Sinaiticus* – you can well understand my loss. Really, this is a unique document which I have lost. No sir, which *the world* has lost! It is quite literally priceless. Written in an almost extinct language directly descended from that which the pharaohs spoke – can you conceive of that! And the Coptic Church established by Mark the Evangelist, perhaps *the* oldest–"

"No doubt that is very interesting," interrupted Holmes as the professor seemed about to embark upon an embellishment of his subject, "but I must ask if you have informed the Patriarchate in London of his disappearance."

"Yes, I sent a telegram immediately. The secretary who comes into the office a few days a week should pick it up today."

"You do not think that there is any part of this house which could be used as a place of concealment?" asked Holmes.

"Absolutely not."

"We had better move the investigation along then," said Horsburgh, "and with your permission, we will make a full search of the place – cellar and attic included. We must eliminate any possibility of a hiding place, you understand."

"Of course, go anywhere, do that which you need to do," replied Beasley, "all of the keys are hanging upon the hook in the hall."

Suffice to say that for the next hour or so, between the five of us we paced and measured every inch of every floor of the house, but in no wise was there any discrepancy which would have allowed for any secret chamber, passage, or hiding place. We then unlocked the door to the cellar and started carefully down the steep, narrow winding stairs. Horsburgh lit his bull's eye and shone it round the cellar – a disappointment! We found nothing there but a few pieces of old junk and four blank walls. No loose flagstone or hidden openings. A mouse could scarcely have been concealed there, and no-one could have escaped this way.

"Before I go down to the fairground," said Holmes when we returned to the upper air, "I should like to inspect the ransom note."

"Here it is."

Holmes turned it over once or twice, his keen eyes raking it for the slightest indication.

"'Patriarch' has a capital letter," he said, "and has been made from two smaller words stuck together: 'Patr' and 'iarch'. Possibly from 'Patrol' and 'matriarch' – a reference, perhaps, to our sovereign. I note also that the words 'ten thousand pounds' form one complete phrase. I have closely examined the typeface, but I am unable to recognise it all as a newspaper type. It is possible that it may be some obscure regional one which I have not seen, though I am familiar with the local paper, the South

Bucks Free Press. Perhaps, though, the other side may be more revealing."

"Aha," said Horsburgh, "look at some of the words or rather the parts of words on the reverse side: 'Batter' and 'Field' with capitals, then '-arriage'. The complete words which suggest themselves to me very strongly are: Battery, Field Marshal, and Gun Carriage. And where would we be likely to find such a vocabulary?"

"The Army and Navy Illustrated!" Canterville and I answered almost in unison.

"And we know where we might find a copy of that," said the local man. "The case against Tierney strengthens by the hour."

"Do not be deceived by appearances," said Holmes to our colleagues.

"Appearances! Looks to me as if it's as plain as the nose on your face," said Horsburgh.

"Nothing so misleading as the obvious," cautioned my friend. "Do you not think, Inspector, that there is something odd about that ransom note? For example, the fact that the kidnapper makes a quite exorbitant demand but gives no information about how the ransom is to be collected."

"Then you think the Patriarch is already dead?" asked Horsburgh.

"It is one of a number of possibilities amongst many. Well, if you fellows will wait here, Watson and I shall take a turn down to the field and speak to the show people. I think we may find them less guarded than you did."

We asked amongst the people in the camp and were directed to see the ringmaster, a plump, white-whiskered fellow in a shiny black suit, reclining in a wicker seat and puffing away at a pipe outside his caravan.

"Not the official police, are you?" he asked. "Well, come in then. Bartram's the name, Patrick Bartram. I heard from the inspector what happened, but the Lord knows none of our folk would get up to such capers. The odd chicken or rabbit here and there mayhap. I'm not saying as everybody's an angel here; there's a few rogues amongst us as I know better than anyone; but a kidnapping! No sir! Last thing we want is the police hounding us. You can search any caravan or tent in this camp, Mister, but I'd soon know if there was anyone hiding out here. Know how I'd know? The behaviour of the dogs! You must ha' heard them yowling when you come in. Make a lot of noise, but they wouldn't hurt a flea."

"Have you noticed anything unusual, any comings or goings with the fair folk?" Holmes asked.

"Not exackly unusual, no. There is one thing though ... Vittoria the exotic dancer has ran off with Vigor the strongman – threw over her other beau, Conrad the Clown; it's been going on for months behind Conrad's back; it was the talk of the camp and now it's come to a head. What else? Well, let me think. One of the Italian acrobats, Dino Eusebi, sprained an ankle rehearsing a new manoeuvre – look that's him there hobbling by on his walking stick," said Bartram, as we glimpsed a tall olive-skinned athletic-looking figure limping past the window and entering a caravan opposite. "His brother, Luigi, has had to get a stand-in; oh, and two of the performing dogs are sick. That's about it."

"When did this elopement actually take place?"

"Only last night there was a big row between Vittoria and Conrad after the second house; this morning she's gone off with Vigor."

"It is a remarkable coincidence is it not?"

"All the same, I can't see as they would have had anything with ..."

"Do you have any photographs of them?"

Bartram passed my friend a copy of the *Showmen's Gazette*.

"Middle page, we're all in here, except the new fellow who come in to work with Luigi," he said, spreading out the broadsheet on a low table. "I wrote the advertisement myself. This is Vittoria, lovely girl, ain't she? If I was young enough, I'd ha' run off with her meself, so I can hardly blame Vigor – that's him there. Left me in the lurch he has, though; very hard to replace a strongman you know, they don't come ten a penny like dancers or clowns. Well, thank goodness we are having tonight off, only the matinee performance tomorrow to get through, and we're off again. That's Conrad, the glum-looking one, and his mate, Tibor; they're Hungarians; there's the two Eusebis, and Kaspar the lion-tamer, and that's the other dancers."

Holmes seemed to take an age in perusing the sheet, as though he were memorising the faces.

"Well?" asked Bartram at last.

"I quite believe you when you say that the missing man is not in this camp," Holmes replied, "and that you personally have had absolutely nothing to do with the crimes which took place last night. I can assure you that I will convey that to my colleagues in the official force."

"Thank you very kindly, Mister, if there's anything I can do ..."

"Yes, there is. I might find a copy of this gazette of yours amusing reading for the train journey back to Paddington."

"You may keep it," he laughed, "not worth much!"

By the time we had returned to the cottage, the photograph which the professor had taken had been delivered to the inspector.

"The thief came in through the window, that's clear enough – just look at those footprints, clear as a bell," said Lestrade.

"You can see where he has come through the bushes, straight from there to the roan pipe, then you can see where he has tried to get a footing, before he shinned up," agreed Horsburgh. I could follow their reasoning, but I noticed Holmes was staring very intently at the photograph.

"Something doesn't quite fit here," he said, shaking his head. Lestrade looked at him warily.

"What is it?" asked the local man, rather querulously.

"It's the alignment of the footsteps," replied Holmes. "Look again, more closely. Watson, you are a man with professional knowledge of the human anatomy, yet I surmise that you cannot see it either."

I shook my head, somewhat annoyed at myself for being so obtuse.

"Start from the fence line and examine the trail of prints, step by step," he said

It sprang out at me. "You are correct, Holmes," I ejaculated, "there *is* something strange about the pattern of the footsteps, they seem to go off at strange angles and there is an irregular distance between each footfall – it is perfectly clear now."

The two policemen nodded in agreement. I felt that Horsburgh's scepticism toward my friend, which had been mounting, was now dispelled.

"He was drunk!" I expostulated. "The irregular footprints show his drunken stagger."

"That is certainly one possibility," Holmes replied.

"I know a man who was drunk last night," said Horsburgh.

"Tierney!" cried Lestrade.

"The very man," said his colleague. "We should waste no time in arresting Captain Tierney, warrant or no warrant," said Lestrade.

"I must thank you sincerely Mr. Holmes," said the local man, "you have certainly lived up to the reputation which my colleague here intimated to me."

"And yet, my good fellows," replied Holmes, "your case is by no means complete, and I should urge caution. First of all, how did your staggering drunkard ascend the roan pipe in the dark and subdue the old man without making a sound? How did he then escape? How did he know the professor had anything worth stealing? Where is the Scroll? Where is the Patriarch?"

"Well, the scroll might well be in Tierney's house, which is why he wouldn't let my colleague search the place," Lestrade replied.

"As for the Patriarch," said Horsburgh, "assuming he is not actually inside Tierney's villa, he could have been spirited away somewhere nearby. We have alerted the local farmers to check their barns and outhouses. You mentioned the South Bucks Free Press, Mr. Holmes, they have agreed to carry a front-page article in the evening edition."

"It is comforting to see that at least in some parts of England there are still pressmen who have respect for the forces of law and order," said Lestrade, whom I presumed was still smarting under a recent lampoon in Punch, titled "Oh Mr. Policeman, What Shall I Do?" which poked fun at Scotland Yard's lamentable lack of progress in a capital case.

"There are old derelict warehouses down at the river wharf at Hedsor," Horsburgh resumed. "And there are a few empty manor houses too, like Dovecote Hall and Nine Elms House that haven't had a tenant for years – we have men out searching those at present. We haven't overlooked the old disused Gunpowder Mill and there are some old lime kilns in the district too. As for Tierney's state last night, it's amazing how much drink some of these sots can swallow and still remain *compos mentis*. He may, in any case, have had an accomplice. If he has had anything to do with this, we'll soon have it out of him."

Holmes looked thoughtful for a few moments, then turned to the local man.

"I cannot say yet what involvement, if any, Captain Tierney may have had in this perplexing affair," he said at last. "And I cannot but admire your presence of mind and your energy, Inspector Horsburgh, for initiating such a thorough search. But my earnest advice to you, is to call off the hunt for the Patriarch – you are wasting your time, for I am afraid your men will never find him."

We gazed at Holmes in astonishment.

"Then he is dead as you suggested before?" cried Lestrade.

"On the contrary, I am certain as I can be of anything that the Patriarch is alive and well."

"Then, where can we find him?" asked Horsburgh.

"I am unable to say precisely, but I do not think he can be very far away–"

"Is there nothing we can do to rescue him?"

"Not at present. If my theory holds, the mere passage of time will bring about his appearance," Holmes said enigmatically.

"When?"

"Again, I am unable to say for certain, at present."

"What about the ransom note?"

"Ignore it."

"And the Scroll?" asked Lestrade.

"If my deductions are correct, the Scroll is not far away either."

"Come Mr. Holmes, you are full of riddles and evasions," cried Horsburgh at the limit of frustration. "Tell us where it is, and we'll get it!"

"Frankly, I am unable to state its exact location, and any premature attempt on your part to obtain it may result in its immediate destruction as it is material evidence to a serious charge of theft. However, if you will meet me on the river path just outside this house once darkness has fallen – but say nothing to the professor, you understand. Eight o'clock, then? We will need four constables, two in plain clothes."

"Very well, then."

"Oh, and bring two pounds of raw beefsteak."

Lestrade had become inured to my friend's eccentric ways and histrionics, but Horsburgh stared at Holmes as though he were a lunatic.

"And if you should weary somewhat between now and then," my friend continued, with a glimmer of amusement in his eye, "I strongly commend you to a few hours' light reading of the *Showmen's Gazette*, Inspector Horsburgh. I must say I have found it quite the most interesting and useful thing I have discovered here. No? Well, I shall keep it then for the journey back to Paddington tonight, once we have the case tied up."

With that, he turned upon his heel and led me off. He sent me to reserve a table at the Old Swan Uppers whilst he stopped off at the village pharmacists, an errand for which he did not advance any explanation. Holmes's judgement in food was as impeccable as ever, and we dined exceptionally well at the inn. Once the plates were cleared, Holmes lit his pipe.

"I must say, Holmes, you have my head spinning. Do you mean to say that you have the case cut and dried already? Or was that a bit of bravado in front of Horsburgh?"

"Nothing of the sort, Watson, though I noticed that the inspector's tone changed somewhat throughout our interview. Firstly, he appeared sceptical, then admiring, then finally he seemed annoyed when I disparaged his pet theory."

"I thought you were rather offhand with him, all the same."

"I genuinely admire his energy in getting the case started on a practical footing. But I have presented him with prime clues – including the one on which the entire case turns – and he refuses to acknowledge it! The problem with the official force is that they have an incorrigible tendency to be seduced by their own arguments; what has never been instilled into them is the discipline of searching for an alternative explanation for *apparent* facts. They are incapable of the mental exercise of falsifying their own theories, which ensures that they never rise above the mediocre; sometimes, they do not achieve even that."

"As we are meeting outside the professor's house without his knowledge, I take it that the Scroll and Patriarch are hidden there – is the professor the guilty one?"

"All in good time, Watson."

The policemen were waiting for us at the riverbank, Horsburgh in a sour mood.

"Got your suspect under lock and key?" Holmes asked.

"I've got Tierney down at the station, not without a struggle," he replied curtly, "searched his house and found nothing but an old service revolver which he may have used, but I'd rather have the Patriarch and the Scroll."

"If you do exactly as I suggest, I promise that you will have both very soon."

"I don't see as I have any alternative."

"Excellent. Your colleague here will attest that I have never yet broken a promise."

Lestrade nodded glumly. Holmes asked if he could speak to the four constables in private, then drew them aside and whispered his instructions to them. Then we crept in darkness and silence down the river path to the back of Falconer's Field, stopping at a line of trees close to caravans. A low fence at the farther end of the trees separated us from the camp itself, and the occasional voice from one of the fairground people floated across to us. Holmes paused at one point then turned to Horsburgh.

"Have you the beefsteak I asked for?" he asked. The bewildered inspector handed him a package, which he laid on the grass and then bent over for a few minutes. I could not see exactly what he was doing, though I could now begin to guess at the reason for his visit to the pharmacist. He stood up, tiptoed towards the fence, and gave a low whistle once or twice. We heard the pattering of feet and the yelps of the dogs, then Holmes threw the pieces of meat over the fence, and retraced his steps.

"Give it a few more minutes, and they should be comatose," he whispered by way of explanation and then called the four constables forward. I could see him pointing out some features of the camp to the constables, then off they went through the trees. Holmes then motioned us forward, as though leading a salient upon an enemy territory, until we were within a few yards of one of the vans which was lit by a flickering oil lamp. We were still concealed, and I assumed the object of our visit was Bartram's caravan, though in the darkness I could scarcely tell which was which. My attention was suddenly arrested by the two plainclothesmen who had walked up to one of the caravans and began to fiddle with the door handle as though attempting to effect an entry. Their actions seemed clumsy in the extreme, and it was no surprise to me when the door flew open with a hoarse cry, and the inhabitant peered out. I had expected to see Bartram, but I recognised the man as Dino, the acrobat. A second later his brother appeared beside him. The startled policemen made off in opposite directions, and the two brothers gave chase with heavy oaths. It occurred to me at that point that Dino was reported to have sprained an ankle; his recovery since the afternoon seemed to have been unusually rapid.

"Your men have blown it now!" I remarked to Lestrade.

"Not at all," replied Holmes. "The plan went exactly as I had intended. One moment, and I shall be back." With a few steps, Holmes was inside the caravan, the tails of his long coat flying behind him; in a matter of moments, he was back at our side.

"I have seen all I need to see," he said, smiling.

"Will you please tell me what on Earth is going on?" asked Horsburgh, evidently still far from convinced.

"Yes. You have witnessed the arrest of the culprits you have been looking for since this morning. Your men should be marching the two acrobats down to the station by now, and all that remains is for us to repair to the professor's house and I shall explain everything to you concerning this interesting little diversion."

But a severe shock awaited us on arrival at the professor's cottage. Sergeant Canterville, who had been left in charge, came rushing out to meet his superior.

"You're not goin' to believe this, sir," he gasped, "but a second person claimin' to be the Patriarch arrived here not half an hour ago!"

"What?" cried Horsburgh. "What have you done with this impostor?"

""I have him under lock and key and securely handcuffed to the professor's kitchen table."

"Good man, Canterville. Well, Mr. Holmes," said Horsburgh with a sarcastic glance at my friend, "how does this fit in to your theory?"

"Confirms it in every respect," Holmes replied with a smile. "Indeed, only a few hours ago I predicted as much. I told you, did I not, that the Patriarch would turn up in the fullness of time?"

"With respect sir," said Canterville, "this is definitely not the same man as arrived last night. The professor confirmed that!"

"Of course it isn't – I never said that it was. It is the real Patriarch, however, and I should lose no time in releasing him if you wish to avoid a charge of wrongful arrest. I suppose I ought to say the same regarding Captain Tierney who is equally innocent, though I am inclined to think that a night or two in the cells will do him no harm whatsoever. Now lead on, Inspector."

It took some time to explain the train of recent events to the newly arrived and astonished Father Philoxenus, who now occupied an armchair in the professor's drawing room, particularly as to the train of events which led to him receiving a telegram informing him of his own kidnapping; but once the entire party had been seated Holmes began his recapitulation.

"I am afraid, Professor Beasley, you were taken in badly – the person who appeared last night, claiming to be the Patriarch was the thief himself," he said. "It is astonishing how stage make up and a false beard, added to some stage props, can take one in. It is highly likely that someone had intercepted your mail and knew of the arrangements between yourself and Father Philoxenus. That person could not possibly have been from the Coptic community; the reason will be clear in a moment. It was obvious to me from the outset that the escape of a thief, under the conditions described to me, was completely impossible. I had wondered at first whether the thief had managed to get out through the skylight – I had seen it done before in the Morstan case – but the idea that he could also take along an unwilling hostage was, frankly, ludicrous. You will recall the photograph of the footprints – the strange pattern? The thief was not drunk but in fact was–"

"Walking backwards!" I ejaculated, as the realisation dawned upon me.

"Indeed Watson. I deduced that what happened was that the thief, who was in all likelihood Dino Eusebi, once he had stolen the document opened the window, climbed *down* the roan pipe and walked *backwards* towards the fence – with the scroll in his possession, of course. You will recall my initial difficulty in establishing the precise direction in which the bushes in the garden had been pushed; it was quite clear that the person had gone *away from*, not towards, the house. Incidentally, as Watson will tell you, the involvement of acrobats in burglaries is by no means uncommon: cases in Hillerød, Denmark, in eighty-four, and one in Kensington in ninety-two spring to mind. In the latter case, the Eusebi brothers were actually amongst the suspects as I recall, but Inspector Lestrade's colleague, Tobias Gregson, lacked the proof to bring the case to court, and as I happened to be in Tibet at the time, I was therefore unable to assist. On Monday afternoon Luigi had been lying in wait expecting our friend here – the real patriarch – at the station, in order to waylay him. You will recall Merryweather's evidence of the man loitering in the Waiting Room. Of course, the real Father Philoxenus never turned up, because he had arranged to come on the day after Coptic Easter – *Pascha* – which, as you know professor, is *next* Monday, not yesterday."

The patriarch nodded, "Yes that is correct, I was intending to come next Monday."

"And I," said the professor, "wondered why you had arrived a week early without any explanation!"

"Hence my deduction concerning the person who intercepted the mail. I have no doubt that it was an accomplice of the Eusebis, probably in the sorting office at Mount Pleasant, for the district is full of Italians. He, or she, would not have understood the difference in dates between the Coptic Easter which is reckoned by the Julian calendar and our western feast day, reckoned by the Gregorian.

"Now, the words which made up the ransom note – which was, of course, entirely spurious and cleverly designed to completely mislead us – were not cut from the 'Army and Navy Illustrated' as we initially thought but from the *Showmen's Gazette*, of which I attempted to make you a present, Inspector. I obtained it from the Ringmaster, a Mr. Bartram who, I should add, is not only entirely innocent in this matter, but has also now lost two acrobats, a strongman, an exotic dancer, and will probably have to close the circus down. The *Showmen's Gazette*, I observed, contained an advertisement by that gentleman, as well as photographs of the Eusebis, whom I recognised immediately as the Clerkenwell Acrobats whom Gregson had apprehended, but was unable to convict, in the Kensington burglary. My case was almost complete. There was also an article on the proposals to develop Battersea Fields as a pleasure garden: had you read it, you would have discovered such words as 'Patrick', 'matriarch', 'carriage drive,' at the cost, *nota bene*, of 'ten thousand pounds' – I need hardly elaborate on their significance. Obviously the Eusebi brothers cut these words out and rearranged them on the bogus ransom note which they left. I may say that the note rang false to me from the outset: ten thousand pounds is a quite preposterous sum of money, and it was pure expedience which caused them to use that number. Of course, it was never intended to be collected, but was used purely as a decoy to distract attention. I reasoned that the real patriarch would come here immediately after he saw the telegram which the professor had sent, and I knew that we should see him soon enough. Thus, my advice to you to call off your search. Incidentally, I suppose you will all have deduced that Dino's sprained ankle was entirely spurious, a mere blind. In fact," my friend continued as he extracted an object from the folds of his long overcoat, "this is his walking stick which I took the liberty of rescuing for you, Inspector, as it will no doubt constitute material evidence at the trial. It is an unusual specimen, quite bespoke, and heavy too, I should not like to receive a blow from this. Would you like to examine it, professor?"

Beasley took hold of the walking stick and looked at it doubtfully; more, it seemed to me, out of politeness than from genuine interest.

"Now, is there any detail which I have missed?" asked my friend finally.

"Where is the scroll?" Beasley and Horsburgh cried almost in unison.

"Oh, the scroll! Well, there is no real mystery about that surely? Why, the professor has it," my friend replied with a mischievous gleam in his eye.

"What?" asked Father Philoxenus who had been following the conversation silently.

"My dear Mr. Holmes," began the professor warmly, "whilst I acknowledge that I am under a great debt you for–"

My friend held up his hand. "Dr. Watson will tell you that I love nothing more than a dramatic denouement to a case. If you will simply grasp the top of the stick and twist it counter-clockwise, that's it!" The professor did so, and a roll of parchment emerged from inside the hollow stem of the cane which he then placed it upon the table. I recognised the queer Coptic characters immediately. A cry of mingled triumph and relief erupted from him at the same time.

"They had to conceal it somewhere," said Holmes, "until they were ready to sell it. An ankle sprain was the ideal feigned injury. It had the ring of truth about it when Luigi actually brought in another acrobat to work with him; it also meant that Dino could go anywhere without letting the precious scroll out of his sight for a second. Of course, he quite forgot himself when your constable feigned a break in."

Father Philoxenus smiled politely at us. "I could not have believed this unless I had seen it with my own eyes," he said.

"Words cannot express my gratitude to you, for bringing this most precious, rare, and sacred relic back to me," said the professor, who looked as though he might burst into tears.

"I must add my sincere thanks too," said Horsburgh frankly, "and to that I must also add an apology for having doubted you in the first place."

"I suppose we had best be off then, for I believe that there is just time enough for us to catch the last train," said Holmes.

"But not, surely, before I present you with some reward for your exertions on my behalf," said the professor, standing up, "my cheque book is in the writing desk. After all, I should have been happy to part with my last penny in order to have the Scroll back."

Holmes held up his hand.

"Not at all. Success is my reward, as both Dr. Watson and Inspector Lestrade will tell you. You are welcome to defray the few minor expenses to which we have been put, but that can wait until another day, for no doubt you gentlemen will have plenty to converse about," he said.

The affair of the Two Coptic Patriarchs, as the newspapers called it, sustained a few months' delay in coming to the Assizes, perhaps due to the complication in framing charges against the culprits: After all, as Holmes had later pointed out to Lestrade, the Eusebis could hardly be charged with kidnapping if no one had been kidnapped, and the brothers had made no attempt to collect any ransom; even the allegation of demanding money with menaces could hardly be sustained since there was no theoretical or actual victim, and so the charge was eventually reduced to theft. The case was finally tried the following year, but was kept off the front pages of newspapers, however, by the sensational disappearance of the chess-playing medic, Dr. Ray Ernest, during the same week that the name of Josiah Amberley, the retired colourman of Lewisham, gained infamy in the national press.

END

Afterword

In his article "Is Heathcliff a Murderer?"[21], John Sutherland explains why he thinks it is important to ask searching literary questions whose answers stand outside the text. For example: how many children Lady Macbeth had; what Hamlet studied at Wittenberg University and whether his grades were any good (it may occur to one to further ask whether academic failure there led to his suicidal tendencies, and worse still, to treating his girlfriend so atrociously); what Heathcliff did in the three years between his leaving and returning to Wuthering Heights; and how exactly Victor Frankenstein constructed his *golem.*

Studying Sutherland's "implied and ambiguous world which lies on the other side of the word on the page" is an activity in which we Holmesians have been happily and irreverently engaged for over a century. Although Sutherland is no deconstructionist (indeed, his use of the "D" word is imbued with the sort of casual disdain that Huck Finn showed for "low-down Ab'litionists"), and although he approaches his Elizabethan and Victorian "literary brain teasers" rather light-heartedly, his focus is nevertheless, relentlessly Freudian with an occasional foray into literary-forensic serology[22]. Sutherland provides us with an interesting, and perhaps previously unnoticed (almost certainly uncommented upon) example of the operation of Watson's subliminal perception.

In "The Adventure of the Speckled Band,"[23] perhaps psychologically the darkest story in the Canon, Watson allows Holmes, the sharpest brain in England, to address Helen Stoner as "Miss Roylott" in an exchange concerning her attempt to conceal her stepfather's physical mistreatment of her. With this most Freudian of slips, Sutherland asks, was Watson hinting, through the fug of Victorian reticence, at something even more sinister than mere physical maltreatment by her stepfather? Moreover, "Miss Roylott" makes no attempt to correct Holmes on his *faux pas*: Does she realise that he has perceived the true relationship between stepfather and stepdaughter?

Likewise, Richard W. Clarke[24], delving even deeper into Watson's subconscious, commented that three of the ships mentioned in the Canon ("The Gloria Scott"[25], "The Sophy Anderson"[26], and "The Norah Creina"[27]) are named after females, possibly, he theorises, from the "tender-hearted doctor's" past. Following the claim by one of our well-known Oxbridge Professors[28], that all "Literary works are pieces of *rhetoric* as well as reports (which) demand a peculiarly vigilant kind of reading," we might go further and theorise that, since the ships all suffer a similar catastrophic fate, it may be equally apposite to take the rationalisation of Watson's parapraxis contrariwise and suggest they were the names of women by whom he was coldly and decisively rejected! In fact, when it came to rhetoric in the proper sense of the word, some of Conan Doyle's favourite hobbyhorses – England's unjust divorce laws, British patriotism, and Anglo-American relations to name just three – were regularly trotted around his literary parade ring.

Similarly, that grand heresiarch and arch-deconstructor, Monsignor Ronald Knox, announced his foray into the field of mock scholarship with the following trumpet blast: "If there is anything pleasant in life, it is doing what we aren't meant to do (which, readers will admit, is an uncommonly bright start for a clergyman) … it is finding out what we aren't meant to find out. It is the method by which we treat as significant what the author *did not mean* to be significant, by which we single out as essential what the author regarded as incidental." In other words, a "through the looking glass" examination of the Holmes Canon, which brings us back to Holmesian scholarship.

It was in the spirit of the Monsignor that I began to explore the implied world that lies beyond Watson's written word, and undertook the re-assessment of the role and character of Dr. Mortimer in "The Hound of the Baskervilles,"[29] the full results of which were published in "'A Humble M.R.C.S.' The Man behind the Mask."[30] I very soon discovered a plethora of statements and actions attributed to Mortimer that, as Holmes puts it, "sat at odds with his status not only as a medical man and a man of science, but also as a friend to the Baskervilles." It wasn't merely the odd inconsistency here or there: everything about Mortimer seemed absolutely riddled with discrepancies, improbabilities, and *non sequiturs* that no one discerned—not Holmes, not Watson, not even the outsider, Sir Henry, who is looking at his new acquaintance through unprejudiced eyes (and with his life in the balance). We never see Mortimer's wife, for example, and no one ever mentions her ("his [Mortimer's] wife, of whom we know nothing"). Assuming she ever existed, given Mortimer's tendencies she may well have suspected something untoward and been done away with. After all, being a doctor's wife in Victorian times was a surprisingly hazardous occupation.[31] The original story is, to quote Holmes's rejoinder to Watson at the beginning of the case, "full of obvious things which nobody by any chance ever observes," including, it would appear, the great detective himself, as Watson archly points out almost a year later.

With Sutherland's point in mind about asking questions whose answers stand outside the text, it became apparent that in the denouement of *The Hound of the Baskervilles*, Conan Doyle may have intentionally left certain questions unanswered in a way that seemed to demand a sequel to the vastly popular legend he had created, and to facilitate a later literary return. The result was "The Tragedy of Langhorne Wyke".

Perhaps due to the residual effects of his early Jesuitical training (albeit he renounced the Roman Catholic faith as enthusiastically as his populariser and critic, Knox, had embraced it), Conan Doyle rarely lets the bad guys off Scot free: there's usually a nemesis – that wingèd messenger and daughter of justice of Mesomedes at the end of the *Thirteen Bells* is merely a continuation of a pattern already established, a variation on a retributive theme. Except, of course, on those few occasions either where Watson is placed by Holmes in the hypothetical jury box and delivers one of his famous "Not Guilty" verdicts, or where Holmes himself decides to act as judge, jury, and executioner thus saving both Watson and the Newgate hangman any trouble.

It will be obvious to anyone vaguely familiar with the criminal history of Glasgow that "The Adventure of the Sixty Steps" was loosely based on a real-life murder (a genuine miscarriage of justice with which Conan Doyle was intimately involved), which took place slightly later than the apocryphal date in the novel. The background of police corruption and malpractice, and stark racial prejudice of the judiciary[32] has by no means been exaggerated for effect in the story, nor was the direct connection between the characters involved in the murder inquiry and the jewel robberies *cum* insurance fraud a matter of invention. The denouement of the story demonstrates how fragile the alibis of some of the family suspects were at the time, and how relaxed, in pre-digital times, was the process of registering of births, deaths, and marriages. The complications of that real life case resounded for decades, and whilst it would be fair to say that the reputations of the two unjustly accused – the alleged culprit, and the young detective who had an attack of conscience which (with Conan Doyle's assistance) eventually brought down the Crown's house of cards – have since been rescued, there still endured much speculation as to the identity of the killer, and the casual slandering of the innocent nephew persisted until his death in the 1960s, and continued thereafter. There were therefore, in reality, *three* miscarriages of justice, and the "who killed the old woman/who was the stranger in the hall?" conundrum continued to feed a thriving cottage industry for more than a century, even if it did not quite rival the Ripperology trade.

As regards other unfinished business, friend Porlock (who is never actually seen alive) was guilty of not one but two acts of disloyalty to the Moriarty/Moran organisation (in *The Valley of Fear*, and in the *Nebrodi Sapphire*[33] case), and paid the inevitable price. Like Macavity the Cat, Moriarty's "not there" when the scene of the crime is investigated, and though we know it *must* have been Moriarty[34]—he's "always a mile away." Philosophically, of course, the quasi-allegorical figure of Moriarty/Moran can never be completely eliminated: it must remain forever in the shadows, its Luciferian presence always suspected, occasionally detected, but never defeated – otherwise, what would be the point of the continued existence of the greatest detective the world has ever seen? Surely, as Watson implies at the end of the "Sixty Steps," the forces of good and evil must be in approximate constant equilibrium or one would have vanquished the other by now; though he was, perhaps, motivated more by Newton's "Third Law" than by the calculated heterodoxy that Holmes imputes to him.

It is almost *de rigeur* for any self-respecting *pasticheur* to tackle one of those unpublished cases with which Watson tantalises us from time to time – I think the "Giant Rat of Sumatra"[35] holds the current unofficial pastiche record, and it would be a safe each-way bet that "Wilson, the notorious canary-trainer"[36] and "the disappearance of James Phillimore"[37] cannot be far behind. One feels, though, that the most abstruse unrecorded case in the entire canon must be that of the "politician, the lighthouse and the trained cormorant,"[38] for which I have provided a partial explanation in this book. Perhaps the full story of that bizarre episode will one day, as Watson says, "be given to the public" for no one knows what tales lie completed but unpublished in that tin box marked "John H. Watson, M.D., Late Indian Army" which still lies in the vaults of Cox and Co. at Charing Cross or, indeed, amongst the "draft" files on Séamas Duffy's laptop.

Séamas Duffy,
Glasgow,
March 2022.

Endnotes

Foreword

---

[1] "The New Annotated Sherlock Holmes: The Complete Short Stories, Vol 1," November 2007, Leslie S. Klinger.

[2] "Memories and Adventures," Arthur Conan Doyle.

[3] From "The Adventure of Black Peter," Arthur Conan Doyle.

[4] From "The Disappearance of Lady Frances Carfax," Arthur Conan Doyle.

[5] From "The Sign of the Four," Arthur Conan Doyle.

[6] From "The Adventure of the Noble Bachelor," Arthur Conan Doyle.

[7] From "The Importance of Being Earnest," Oscar Wilde.

[8] "The Adventure of the Beryl Coronet," Arthur Conan Doyle.

[9] Dr. Hans Gross, an Austrian professor of criminology, noted such a case in "The Handbook for Criminal Investigators" (translated into English in 1898).

[10] From "The Methods of Ethics", Henry Sidgwick, 1874.

[11] "Tragedy of the Korosko," Arthur Conan Doyle.

[12] Professor of English Literature at Princeton University, Claudia L. Johnson.

[13] Wordsworth scholar and Oxford Professor of Poetry, Heathcote W. Garrod.

[14] From "The Brontë Cabinet: Three Lives in Nine Objects," Deborah Lutz, Department of English, University of Louisville.

[15] One of which the author must admit to having been invited by the Baker Street Irregulars, no less, following one of his contributions to the "Baker Street Journal."

[16] In "The Adventure of the Priory School," Arthur Conan Doyle.

[17] Leslie S. Klinger, "What Do We Really Know About Sherlock Holmes And John H. Watson?" of which an earlier version was presented as "A River Runs By It: Holmes and Doyle in Minnesota," sponsored by the Friends of the Sherlock Holmes Collection and the Elmer Anderson Library of the University of Minnesota in June 2004.

[18] In "The Man with the Twisted Lip," Arthur Conan Doyle.

[19] In "The Adventure of the Three Garridebs," Arthur Conan Doyle. The evidence presumably being the recollection by Watson, who has just been wounded, informing the reader that "my friend's arms were around me ... his eyes ... were dimmed for a moment, the firm lips shaking", to which Watson reciprocates by revealing that to receive such caresses "... was worth many wounds ..."; the scene climaxes with Holmes ripping off Watson's trousers with a knife ("... his hands were possessed of extraordinary delicacy of touch" Watson tells us in "A Study In Scarlet").

The Adventure of the Sixty Steps

[20] The Jameson raid was an (almost farcical) incident in the prelude to the Boer War. Following their repulsing of a thoroughly botched raid by British forces in the Transvaal, the Dutch colonists received a congratulatory telegram from the German Kaiser. Most, but by no means all, of the British press and public failed to see the funny side of this.

Afterword

[21] John Sutherland, "Is Heathcliff a Murderer? Puzzles in Nineteenth-Century Fiction," Oxford University Press, 1996.

[22] In his troll through some of the classics of Victorian literature, Sutherland manages to detect previously unobserved subliminal references to defecation, masturbation, and menstruation, not to mention one of George Eliot's character in *contretemps* with a detumesced boar's pizzle. One begins to wonder if Victorian readers actually noticed *anything*.

[23] "The Adventure of the Speckled Band," Arthur Conan Doyle.

[24] "On The Nomenclature of Watson's Ships," "Baker Street Journal", No.2 , 1946.

[25] From "The Adventure of the Gloria Scott," Arthur Conan Doyle.

[26] From "The Adventure of the Five Orange Pips," Arthur Conan Doyle.

[27] From "The Adventure of the Resident Patient," Arthur Conan Doyle.

[28] From "How to Read Literature," Yale University Press, 2013, Terry Eagleton.

[29] "The Hound of the Baskervilles," Arthur Conan Doyle.

[30] " A Humble M.R.C.S.' The Man behind the Mask," (under "Jim McGrory"), in the "Baker Street Journal," Autumn 2020.

[31] Doctors William Palmer and William Edward Pritchard were publicly hanged in 1856 and 1863 respectively: in Pritchard's case for poisoning his spouse; in Palmer's case for going on a murder spree in which one of the victims was almost certainly his spouse, though this was never proven at law. Pritchard, who included his mother-in-law and possibly a housemaid in the job lot, holds the dubious distinction of being the last person to be publicly executed at Glasgow Green in front of a crowd of several thousands. In a final irony, the doctor's body was given over for dissection. Palmer appears to have taken well over a dozen scalps, mostly family and close friends, and it is only fitting that his final end was witnessed by a commensurately larger crowd than Pritchard's: some thirty thousand revellers turned up at Stafford Prison to see him off.

[32] "Anti-Jewish Prejudice in Edwardian Glasgow," Ben Braber, History, April 2003, Vol. 88, No.2.

[33] "The Adventure of the Nebrodi Sapphire," by Séamas Duffy (from "Sherlock Holmes and the Four Corners of Hell").

[34] Eliot even called Macavity "the Napoleon of Crime" – Holmesians will know exactly where that phrase originated!

[35] From "The Adventure of the Sussex Vampire," Arthur Conan Doyle.

[36] From "The Adventure of Black Peter," Arthur Conan Doyle.

[37] From "The Problem of Thor Bridge," Arthur Conan Doyle.

[38] From "The Adventure of the Veiled Lodger," Arthur Conan Doyle.

www.ingramcontent.com/pod-product-compliance
Lightning Source LLC
Chambersburg PA
CBHW051530250626
47156CB00001B/309